DAISY COOPER: INTERNATIONAL SCHOOLGIRL

Book One

Daisy Cooper and the Sisters of the Black Night

By

Robert Dee

Cover illustration and design by Leo de Wijs © 2012

For Miss Brewster, my art teacher.

"The most difficult thing is the decision to act. The fears are paper tigers. You can do anything you decide to do." - Amelia Earhart

CHAPTER ONE - THE MOSAIC

The bomb in the briefcase was ticking. The timer was at thirty seconds...
Twenty nine...Twenty eight...Daisy Cooper - green eyed, burgundy
haired and barely five foot in plimsolls - burst through the door onto the
roof. She ran across the tiles scattering pigeons into the air. Looking over
her shoulder, she could see the two men in dark suits closing in behind
her. The edge of the roof was only a few feet ahead and there was no
time for second thoughts. Daisy could hear pupils and teachers in the
music wing below singing "If you're happy and you know it, clap your
hands" - blissfully unaware that there was a bomb about to go off above
their heads and make them very unhappy. As a bullet whizzed past her
ear Daisy leapt from the rooftop, hung in the air for a giddying moment
and then landed with a roll on top of the school gym. She heard a cry
behind her and with a quick glance saw that one of the men in dark suits
hadn't been quite so lucky. Unfortunately, the other one had. He landed
a few feet behind Daisy, a twisted smile on his face. Even more
unfortunately the black helicopter had appeared behind him and was
fixing the sights of its machine guns on her. It was not a good way to end
your last year of junior school.

Daisy got to her feet. A bullet tore through her cardigan as she ran
along the metal frame down the centre of the skylights, trying to ignore
the gasps from the girls in gymnastics below. With a deafening whirring

sound the glass around her erupted as bullets from the helicopter machine guns tore through it. The gym girls ran for cover screaming. Daisy jumped to one side and ducked behind an air vent, clutching the suitcase bomb to her chest. Over the roar of the helicopter blades and the whizzing bullets she could hear the approaching feet of the man in the dark suit. Daisy swung the suitcase out low, catching him in the shins. With a surprised gasp he fell forwards and toppled over the roof into the school swimming pool. Daisy looked at the briefcase. Ten seconds… Nine…Eight… A shower of tarmac exploded next to the vent.

"Perilous," muttered Daisy.

Closing her eyes she took a couple of deep breaths, jumped out from behind the vent and threw the suitcase bomb with all she could up towards helicopter.

"DAISY COOPER!"

Daisy snapped out of her daydream. Mrs Drooper was staring at her over the top of her beaded glasses. So was everyone else in the class.

"Well, Miss Cooper, I'm so glad you're back with us."

There were titters amongst her classmates.

"Sorry, Mrs Drooper," said Daisy.

She felt herself blush.

"Of course, we all know how much you want to be a big reporter," continued Mrs Drooper, "Maybe you'd rather go and interview the pigeons instead of doing science…"

The titters turned into louder laughter.

"No, miss."

"Oh, how lucky for us!" said Mrs Drooper walking down the rows towards Daisy, "Well perhaps you'd like to answer my question and tell the class what the boiling point of water is?"

Daisy looked at the class. The class looked back at Daisy.

"It depends," she replied.

Mrs Drooper opened her mouth wide in mock surprise. The hairs around her lips twitched.

"It depends! IT DEPENDS!"

Mrs Drooper leant on Daisy's desk.

"Tell, Me, Miss Cooper, on what does the boiling point of water depend?"

Daisy stared up into Mrs Drooper's eyes. She had that nagging voice in the back of her head telling her to be quiet again but couldn't help herself.

"It depends what planet you're on," replied Daisy.

Mrs Drooper's face froze for an ugly moment. Then her eyes turned to thin slits.

"OUT!"

Mr Kane turned his pen slowly in his big hands as he looked at Daisy across the desk.

"Daisy, what am I going to do with you?"

"It's not my fault!..."

Mr Kane held up his hand for her to be quiet. He picked up the report note from Mrs Drooper.

"It says here that you were sent out of class for...insubordination and smart talk. Again."

"That's not true!"

"DAISY. Please let me finish."

Mr Kane stood up and looked out of the window.

"I'm the Headmaster of a busy school, Daisy. A London junior school. I have over five hundred pupils to look after every day so why do I seem to spend so much time looking after you?"

Daisy looked down at her feet.

"What is this insubordination and smart talk Mrs Drooper is talking about?"

"I really don't know sir. She...I mean Mrs Drooper... asked me what the boiling temperature of water was and I said that it depends."

Mr Kane frowned.

Uh Oh, thought Daisy, *here I go again.*

"What would it depend on, Daisy? Water boils at 100 degrees."

"Well, on Earth it does. It's different on other planets."

Mr Kane thought about this. Daisy lowered her head.

Here comes the detention, she thought.

Mr Kane started to chuckle.

"Oh, Daisy. Let me give you a piece of advice. You're the smartest girl in your year but you don't know a thing about when to talk and when to keep quiet. If you don't learn that, you'll be getting into trouble long after you leave here, no matter how clever that brain of yours is. Do you understand?"

"Yes, sir."

"I do hope so."

Mr Kane gave Daisy an hour's detention. She had to write 'I MUST NOT SMART TALK' over and over on the blackboard whilst Mrs Drooper scowled at her. The minute the detention was over Mrs Drooper took the board rubber, wiped off all the lines and told her to go. Daisy rubbed her sore wrist all the way home. Still, she told herself, only two more months to go. Then she'd be moving up to Degham Comprehensive. With that thought the clouds above seemed to get a little greyer. Daisy sighed and kicked her feet through the puddles.

Daisy's cat Gibbon greeted her as she walked through the door to the flat and weaved his way between her legs, miaowing. Careful not to step on him Daisy picked up David and Daniel's bags and shoes from the floor and tidied them neatly. She took off her own coat and hung it up.

In the living room Daisy's brothers David (aged thirteen) and Daniel (aged fourteen) were sitting in front of the television eating big bags of crisps.

"Haven't I told you not to eat crisps before dinner?"

David turned to her, smiled, and let out a large burp.

"That's disgusting."

Daniel turned to David and belched even louder, right in his ear.

"Oi! Nutter!" shouted David.

He hit Daniel in the arm.

"Ow. Dead arm!" shouted Daniel.

Within seconds they were wrestling on the floor.

"Brothers," muttered Daisy, rolling her eyes.

In the kitchen Daisy fed Gibbon and put some mini pizzas in the oven for her brothers. She pulled down her mum's old recipe book from the counter and flicked through the pages.

"What shall we cook today, mum?" she said quietly.

Mr Cooper crawled through the door at nine o'clock looking exhausted. Daisy ran to greet him, gave him a hug and hung up his coat.

"Hi Dad!"

"Hi, Daisy. Something smells good."

Daisy took his hand and walked him through to the kitchen. His dinner plate was laid out at the table with a glass for his beer. Daisy's plate was laid out at the other end.

"Oh, Daisy. Please don't tell me you haven't eaten yet?"

"Don't worry. I had too much homework anyway."

Mr Cooper smiled at her. His eyes looked tired and sad. Then he clapped his hands and wandered over to the bubbling pots on the stove.

"So what have we got here, then!"

"No! No!" laughed Daisy pulling him away, "No one can see the cooking except the chef!"

"Ah, and this chef does know how to cook I suppose? I'm not going to get poisoned am I?"

"Of course!" said Daisy putting on a French accent, "She iz from ze best restaurant in all Paris!"

There was a loud crashing sound upstairs. Mr Cooper looked up and shook his head.

"Sacré Bleu! I take it your brothers are in."

"Yep. They're doing their homework."

There was another crash bigger than the last.

"What's their homework? Rugby?"

After dinner Daisy sat as her dad washed the plates. Daniel and David had found a horror film on TV and had settled down at last.

"You know, Daisy, you don't have to cook for me every night."

"I like to do it."

"I just don't want you to feel that because mum's gone, you have to fill her place."

"I know."

Daisy turned away, digging her nails into a mark on the table.

"Those two herberts'll soon learn to look after themselves and I can always grab something on the way home," said Mr Cooper, "You need to look after yourself."

"I enjoy it, dad. I really do."

Mr Cooper dried his hands and put them on Daisy's shoulders.

"Look at me, Daisy."

She looked into her dad's eyes. They looked tired and sad.

"We're okay, Daisy. You've got a bright head on your shoulders and an even brighter future ahead of you. I don't want you to feel that you ever need to hold yourself back just to look after us. Do you understand?"

Daisy nodded.

"Good."

Mr Cooper patted her on the head.

"Now come on, lets see what gory film those boys have got for us to watch after our posh dinner."

Daisy lay in bed and stared at the glow stars on the ceiling. Her mum had bought them for her birthday two years ago. Mum had started to get sick a few months before then but nobody thought it was serious. She'd gone to the doctors after finding a lump in her breast and had been sent to the hospital for tests. Two weeks later they found out it was cancer. At first, the doctors thought they'd cured it but it kept coming back. Eventually Daisy's dad paid for mum to go into a private hospital. He didn't earn much money as a printer but said he'd work the rest of his life if it meant making mum better. When Daisy thought of her mum she always remembered her smiling - her bright green eyes sparkling. Eventually, even the Private doctors couldn't do anything. That had been over a year ago. Dad was working all the overtime he could get to pay off the medical bills. David and Daniel, well, they were boys so obviously they couldn't look after themselves. It was up to Daisy. Daisy put her fingers to her lips and blew a kiss to the glow stars above her head.

"Goodnight mum."

The only exciting thing left for Daisy at St Margaret's School was the final field trip. Every year the leaving students were allowed to choose the place they wanted to visit. At first the choice was completely open but after the sixth year of the teachers being dragged along to roller coaster theme parks, they put their foot down and decided that they would draw up a list of more appropriate places. On a hot Wednesday morning Mrs Drooper walked up and down the classroom putting the sheets in front of eager hands.

"OK, children. Remember, you can only tick ONE place. We will check for cheaters who try to fill in more than one form - I'm looking at you, Ryan - also, you are not allowed to add alternative choices at the bottom. Last year one clever joker thought it would be funny to suggest that we went to Afghanistan. Well he didn't get to go anywhere in the end except DETENTION."

Mrs Drooper slapped the sheet down on Daisy's desk. Daisy picked it up and read the list. There was the brewery - *yuk, no thanks*, the old power station - *yuk again*, a dog biscuit factory - *what on earth?*, the local swimming pool - *oh come on, they're not even trying now* - and a Roman villa. Now THAT was more like it. Daisy put a large tick in the box for the villa.

"OKAY, SETTLE DOWN. The winning choice will be compiled from the results across ALL final year classes and posted on the message board near the lockers on Friday. You will need to get your parents to fill in consent forms over the weekend. NOW..."

Mrs Drooper turned to the board and started writing on it in her squeaky, scratchy handwriting,

" Names and dates...of...battles...in...world...war...two. Who can give me an answer?"

Daisy bit her lip and sat on her hands.

The week went by slowly. Everyone thought they knew where they'd be going and would say so in a very mature voice. The boys all thought it would be either the brewery or the dog biscuit factory. The girls wanted the villa. On the Friday there was a huge gathering of pupils around the noticeboard talking loudly. Daisy met up with two of her friends, Darren and Koola, and the three of them fought their way through to the announcement. Koola read it out loud.

"Final year students have voted to visit a Roman Villa. All pupils are reminded to get their consent forms signed over the weekend for blah, blah, blah..."

"Yes!" said Darren punching the air.

Daisy was relieved.

"Well, that's it then," said Koola.

"I guess so," said Daisy.

"Aren't you pleased?"

Daisy shrugged.

"I'm just surprised that with this bunch of muppets voting, we aren't going to a dog biscuit factory."

The coach journey took over an hour and was filled with screaming, fighting, sing-alongs and travel sickness. Daisy and Koola sat, faces pressed to the window, watching the graffiti riddled walls of London disappear and give way to the wide expanses of the Sussex countryside. Grey streets full of miserable commuters were replaced by green fields filled with contented cows enjoying the lazy summer. With it the mood of the coach party lifted. Even the teachers at the front relaxed, stretching their legs out and sighing. Darren was the only one not paying attention to the world outside. He had his head buried in a book about Roman Gods. Occasionally he would find a particularly interesting quote and poke his head between the seats to tell Daisy and Koola.

"Did you know the Romans had twelve gods just like the greeks. It's where we get the names for a lot of the months of the year!"

Any other time the girls might have been interested but it was too lovely outside. They nodded and then turned back to wave at the holiday travellers who drove past.

The coach pulled into the pothole filled car park of the Villa carefully. The children bounced around as the driver made his way between the other vehicles to pull up as close to the entrance as he could. Daisy looked at the other coaches. Some of them were from abroad and seemed very exotic. As they climbed down from the bus Daisy noticed the most exotic coach of all. Well, it wasn't even a coach. It was a dark green double-decker bus. It looked like it had just driven out of an old photograph. Standing beside it were a group of older girls dressed in smart school uniforms with blazers the same dark green colour as the bus. A couple of them looked over at Daisy as she stared. They had ties on with green and yellow stripes. Daisy had never seen a girl wearing a tie before. A fierce looking woman in a tweed suit with her hair tied up in an enormous bun stood with a clipboard in her hand talking to them. She moved her arms as she talked, waving her pen at the different girls who assembled themselves into groups. Her movements, her dress and her immaculately formed hair made her look like the strictest person Daisy had ever seen. She made Mrs Drooper seem friendly by comparison. Darren grabbed Daisy's arm and pulled her away.

"Come on daydreamer, we're going to miss it."

Mrs Drooper - dressed disturbingly in a purple velvet tracksuit - assembled the children in the entrance hall. One of the volunteer parents tried counting them but everyone was moving about with excitement.

"I make it 75 pupils," he said, scratching his head.

"Well, that's impossible," barked Mrs Drooper, "there were only forty two on the coach."

"Maybe we gained some. There are a lot of schools here."

"Nonsense! I've got an idea."

Mrs Drooper reached into her bag and pulled out some coloured dots that she used to mark report cards. She peeled them off and started dotting the children one by one on the forehead, counting them off as she did so.

"...one...two...three..."

There was a titter of laughter. Daisy turned and saw three of the girls from the posh school bus standing at the entrance to the souvenir shop. They were a couple of years older than Daisy and much taller. They were laughing at Daisy and her classmates. The one who was laughing the most stood in the middle. She had long jet black hair tied in a braided ponytail and milky white skin that looked like it had never seen any London dust. The two girls either side - one blonde, one redhead - had their hair tied in the same long ponytails. Daisy thought that they looked like some kind of strange hair traffic light - blonde, black and red. She giggled and the dark haired girl frowned at her. Mrs Drooper grabbed Daisy's hand and put a sticker on her forehead.

"...thirty two..."

There wasn't much left of the villa to look at. The walls had crumbled away and plant life had crawled over the remaining pillars and stones, pulling a blanket of dirt with it. A lot of the children were complaining and asking to go back to the coach. Daisy loved it, though. Followed by Darren and Koola, she explored behind trees and around ditches, following the numbered sections on the guide and stumbled across hidden treasures. There were great urns and broken pillars, submerged servant quarters with tiny pots and bowls, little cobbled courts and stables for long gone horses. Daisy stepped around a high leafy bush and stopped suddenly, quite shocked. A little way ahead and a few feet down was a great floor mosaic marked off with red rope. It showed a picture of a flame haired goddess with bright green eyes stood proudly in golden armour. The goddess had one hand raised above her head holding a dove. In her other hand was a shield decorated with a snake curled around a spear. The picture was made up of thousands of tiny coloured tiles.

"That's incredible," said Daisy, "Imagine how long that must have taken."

She walked up to the edge of the excavation and put her hands on the guard rope. The goddess seemed to be looking out of the picture directly at her.

"It says here that her name is Minerva," said Daisy reading an information plaque, "Goddess of wisdom, intelligence, the arts and music. What do you think, Darren?"

"Oh, I think it's such as shame that oiks like you should be allowed out of your little rat holes."

Daisy turned around. Leaning against a tree were the three girls from the souvenir shop. The dark haired girl stepped forward, a sneer on her lips.

"I think you'll find your friends are back at the servant quarters. Clearly that's where you should be…"

Daisy stepped back. The blond and red-haired girls walked over and put a hand either side of Daisy, grabbing the guard rope and trapping her.

"…The thing is, oik - may I call you oik? - The thing is, oik, our parents pay a lot of money to send us to a good school so that we don't have to mix with UNDESIRABLES like you. I mean, it's nice hearing you talking about wisdom, the arts, intelligence, but what could you possibly know about those things?"

The girl with the black hair narrowed her eyes and stared at Daisy. There was something scary in her eyes, like a far off madness.

"Well, Oik? You felt good enough to laugh at us earlier, why don't you show us that you can speak? "

Daisy swallowed hard. There was the nagging voice in the back of her head telling her to keep quiet but she couldn't help herself.

"I know one thing," she said, "I know that no matter how much money your parents spent, they didn't buy you any manners."

The dark haired girl's lip quivered. Daisy waited for the worst. Then the girl laughed. She reached out and stroked Daisy's hair.

"Oh, how beautiful! We've got a little fighter here. What's you name?"

"Daisy."

"Daisy? How sweet. Daisy, this is Olga…"

The blonde haired girl smirked at Daisy.

"…and this is Dorothy."

The redheaded girl did the same.

"My name is Eleanore, nice to meet you."

Eleanore offered her hand. She was smiling but her eyes still had the madness in them. Reluctantly, Daisy held her hand out. Eleanore grabbed it and pulled Daisy in close.

"Seeing as you like it here so much, Daisy, why don't you stay here!" Eleanore thumped Daisy hard in the chest. Daisy toppled back and slipped over the side of the excavation. She tried to grab the rope but it was too late. The last thing she saw before she hit the floor was the three girls laughing at her.

Then everything went black.

For a long time.

Daisy could hear a voice in the darkness. It was very faint and it was saying "help me...help me..." over and over. Then the darkness started to fade and she could see the tiles of the mosaic. There were spots of blood on them. That was a bit worrying. There was something else, though. Something more comforting. Daisy realised someone had put a warm arm around her shoulders and was rubbing her face gently.

"...help me...help me..."

The voice was Daisy's. She stopped and looked up. Her eyes were blurry. There was a sharp throbbing pain on the back of her head.

"...try not to talk, sweetie, you've had a fall."

Gradually her vision cleared and Daisy saw an older girl smiling back at her.

"...hey, can you see me now?" asked the girl.

She had a soft, strong voice.

" Who are you?" asked Daisy.

" I'm Roni. What's your name?"

" Daisy Cooper."

" Well, hello Daisy Cooper! A pleasure to meet you, though it could have been in better circumstances."

Daisy laughed.

"Good. Nice to see you didn't land on your sense of humour and break that, because that would be awful. Do you think you can stand?"

"I'll try."

Carefully Daisy got to her feet. Her legs were a bit wobbly and there were grazes on her shins. She realised she was standing in the middle of the mosaic of Minerva.

"How's your head?" asked Roni.

"It hurts."

Roni was wearing the same school uniform as Eleanore and the other two girls. Her dark hair hung loose and crowned a beautiful face with dark, expressive eyes. Roni was much older than the other girls, maybe even eighteen. There was a difference about the uniform too. The tie. Unlike the other girls' ties, Roni's was plain green. In the middle of it, holding it in place, was an expensive looking tie pin made up of a large letter 'I' with an 'S' curled around it.

"Oh, do you like this?" asked Roni.

She held her fingers to it.

"Well, I could tell you a few stories about it. If I was allowed. Here, hold this to your head."

Roni handed Daisy a soft handkerchief. Daisy put it gently to the bump on her head and looked around. It would be a struggle to get out of the excavated hole. The mosaic sat a good six feet below the wooded surface and the walls were finely packed mud.

"You'd fallen just to the bottom of the wall of dirt which was why no one spotted you. I heard you calling. How are you feeling?"

"A bit better."

"Okay, Daisy. Well you hang on. I'll get to the top and pull you up, okay?"

Daisy nodded. Roni walked over to the wall of mud where part of the protective red rope was hanging down. She gripped it firmly and gave a heavy tug. It held fast. Then, to Daisy's surprise, she dug her expensive looking leather shoes into the wall and climbed to the top as if it was the easiest thing in the world. Her head popped back over.

"Okay, Daisy. Take hold of the loose end, wrap it round your waist and keep it tight. I'll have you out of there in no time."

Daisy grabbed hold of the rope. Then she stopped.

"Hang on one second."

Roni watched Daisy from above as she crouched down on the mosaic and mopped up the little spots of blood. She ran back to the rope and tied it around her waist as instructed.

"OK!" she said and with a surprisingly strong tug from Roni, climbed up out of the pit.

Ten minutes later Daisy was sat on the wash counter in the ladies toilets at the entrance to the villa. She was shocked to look in the mirror when they arrived. There were dark crusts in her hair from where she'd hit the ground. Roni was washing the dirt out of Daisy's grazed knees.

"What happened, sweetie?"

Daisy shrugged.

"I fell."

She didn't want to mention the other girls. She'd dealt with bullies before. When you told on them they had a nasty habit of beating you up for it.

"Are you sure you don't want to visit the hospital?" asked Roni.

Daisy nodded. She didn't like hospitals. Not after what happened to mum.

"Well, we'll have to get you back to your classmates. Once I clean you up."

Roni fished inside her satchel and pulled out a green bag which she unzipped and emptied onto the side next to Daisy. The bag didn't contain normal girly things. There was a passport, a roll of money that looked foreign, a couple of candles, a lighter, a ball of string, a penknife, a small pair of binoculars and a penlight.

"Now, sweetie, first things first," said Roni picking up the torch, "I want you to look up while I shine this light in your eyes. Try not to blink."

Daisy did as she said. Roni then did some weird things - clicking her fingers quickly next to each ear and asking Daisy where she heard it, getting her to push back and pull against her hands. It was like a game. Then Roni stood back and stared at Daisy with her hand on her chin and an eyebrow raised. Daisy felt like a bag of potatoes in a supermarket being looked at by a shopper.

"What are you doing?" she asked suspiciously.

Roni smiled.

"You're fine. I was worried you had concussion and those were some tests to see. Apart from cuts, bruises and a jolly old headache, you'll survive. Now lets clean up your appearance."

Roni took out an emergency first aid kit. With the skill of someone trained for battle she ripped the top off a bottle and dabbed some ethanol onto a cotton ball. Moving Daisy's hair aside carefully, she dabbed the cotton onto the skin. It stung like nettles.

"OW."

"I know, sweetie, but we've go to keep those nasty germs out."

Gently, Roni dabbed around the wounds.

"So, do you know where your classmates are? Have you got some kind of assembly point?"

"I don't even know what time it is."

"It's three o'clock."

This shocked Daisy. They'd been looking at the mosaics just after lunch.

"I need to find my school!"

They ran through the turnstile to the car park but the coach was gone. Daisy stood in the muddy tracks wondering how on earth she was going to get back. The old green double-decker from the posh school was still there, some of its pupils getting back on board.

"I guess we must have missed them," said Roni.

She put a hand on her hip and rubbed her chin thoughtfully with the other. Then she snapped her fingers.

"Wait here, Daisy."

Roni walked over to her school bus and started talking to the stern lady with the enormous bun. The girls on the bus seemed strange, so different from her own classmates. Daisy wondered if they'd give her a lift back to London. She wondered if she wanted a lift with them back to London. Roni was lovely, but the other three? Roni came running back over.

"Good news, sweetie. I'm going to put you on a train back to London. The station's about a ten minute walk if your legs are up for it."

The old green school bus started up its engines.

"But aren't you going to miss your ride?"

Roni smiled.

"Don't you worry about that. I've been stranded in a lot worse places than this, I can tell you."

The walk cleared Daisy's head. The path along the road to the station was shaded by overhanging trees and a breeze made the leaves rustle gently. Though Daisy was miles from anywhere she recognised, Roni made her feel comfortable. She was like an older sister. They started talking, mostly with Roni asking Daisy questions. She seemed delighted that Daisy was interested in subjects like science and literature and maths and, well, everything that was to do with learning. She even clapped with delight when Daisy told her she hoped to be a news reporter when she grew up. It was like Daisy was talking to someone who understood her for the first time. She told Roni that most of the time people just told her to be quiet or to stop trying to be clever. Roni looked cross at this.

"Daisy, you appear to me to be a very smart young girl," she said, " and to carry on being smart and interested in the world when you have people telling you not to be, it shows that you have a lot of strength in here."

Roni tapped daisy's chest.

"Let me tell you something, Sweetie, when you have that strength, it doesn't matter what other people throw at you - you'll always get where you're going in the end."

They walked in silence for a few minutes. Eventually they reached a high street and Daisy could see the familiar British Rail sign of the station at the other end.

"Now, don't you worry about the ticket because Darlington's going to pay for that," said Roni as they crossed the bridge over the rail tracks.

"Who's Darlington?" asked Daisy.

"That's where I'm from. Where the bus is from. Darlington School for Girls. You haven't heard of it?"

Daisy shook her head.

"Oh," said Roni, surprised, " It's quite famous. If you know where to look for it, I suppose. You'd make an excellent Darlington Girl, I reckon."

That surprised Daisy. She tried to imagine herself in the school uniform and not in her usual jeans and tee shirt. It was difficult to picture.

"You think so?"

"Oh, absolutely. How old are you?"

"I'm coming up to twelve."

"Then you should take the test."

"What test?"

"The online test. Darlington gets so many girls applying every year that you have to pass it before they'll let you take an entrance exam. Ah. Here we go."

Roni turned into the ticket office and went up to the counter.

"One First Class ticket to Waterloo, please!"

The train was at the platform so they had to run. Daisy wanted to ask more about Darlington School. Could she really go somewhere like that? They got to the platform out of breath and Roni waved the signal man to stop. She helped Daisy up onto the carriage.

"Thank you so much!" said Daisy.

"Don't mention it. You get back safely, okay?"

"I will. Oh."

Daisy reached into her pocket and pulled out the handkerchief Roni had given her for the bump on her head.

"This is yours."

Roni waved her hand away.

"You keep it, sweetie. You might need it again. Besides, you can give it to me next time we meet."

Roni winked at her and walked away with a wave.

"Daisy!" she shouted as the train started to pull away, "Remember… Do…The…Test."

Daisy was exhausted when she got home. There was no point trying to get back to St Margarets. She'd have to deal with that tomorrow. She dropped her satchel down and kicked off her shoes. In the bathroom she dampened a flannel and dabbed it against the bump on her head, hissing through her teeth at the pain. Then she ran a bath and filled it with bubble bath for a good long soak. Pulling keys and change out of her pocket, she found the handkerchief again. She unfolded it in her hands. Stitched into the corner in yellow thread against the deep green was a word.

"Darlington," said Daisy, reading the word out loud.

She hung the handkerchief carefully on the edge of the mirror in front of her and sank beneath the bubbles.

CHAPTER TWO - TESTING TIMES

Daisy kept a cork-board above her bed that she pinned important things to. There were postcards from pen pals around the world, pictures of her mum, post-it notes with interesting facts she had learnt at school and pictures of people she admired printed out from the internet. She cleared a space in the middle and pinned the Darlington handkerchief in the centre. Feeling much better after her bath she put a couple of mini kievs and some curly fries in the oven for her brothers and pulled down the recipe book, turning to a fresh page. Grilled salmon with a lemon sauce and new potatoes.

Perfect.

Daisy wrote the ingredients down, took a ten pound note from the kitty jar and went to the shops.

By the time David and Daniel arrived home, their dinner was on the table. They threw down their bags and started scoffing, barely saying hello. Daisy left them to it and went through to the study. Though the Coopers called it the study it was actually little more than a cupboard. The computer in it was old and clunky and made a lot of noise. Mr Cooper had bought it home from work and despite its tattiness it worked fine. As it booted up Daisy thought back over the day. She thought of the Darlington school bus and the girls that had climbed out of it. They seemed so different to what she was used to. She tried to imagine herself stepping down out of the bus with them but her imagination kept playing tricks on her. In her mind, her uniform was dishevelled and as she climbed down the steps she fell face first into a puddle.

"Stop it, brain," Daisy muttered and clicked onto the internet.

Daisy found the site for Darlington School for Girls. She was disappointed that there wasn't a photograph of the actual school on the front page. The school had been founded in 1837 on the coronation of Queen Victoria at a time when there weren't much expectations for women. Its founder, Professor Thomas Darlington, had established the school and been its first and only headmaster. According to the website it was a Darlington tradition that there had been no other Headmaster since then, only a Deputy Head. There wasn't even any mention of him retiring. Thomas Darlington was a bit of a recluse and though a great painting of him hung in the main assembly hall of the school no one had seen him in the flesh.

That's a bit odd, thought Daisy.

There was a single quote from Professor Darlington on the website where he explained that the school was:

For the education of the young woman with the object of encouraging her to fulfil the blossoming of her natural character. To assist in this venture Darlington promotes eight core virtues: Charity, Bravery, Reason, Culture, Grace, Agility, Fellowship and Honour.

Daisy heard the front door shutting. She switched off the computer and walked out to greet her dad.

The next day at school Daisy found herself back in Mr Kane's office. His face looked tired.

"Do you know what this is, Daisy?"

The Headmaster was holding up a folder. Daisy shook her head.

"This is your conduct report. Every grade you make, every achievement since you started is written down in this document. So is every complaint about you, report of bad behaviour, every detention. When you move onto your next school we have to make a recommendation on the stream you will be joining: top, middle or bottom. That recommendation is based not just on your grades - which we both know are always good - but on your behaviour."

Mr Kane dropped the folder on his desk with a heavy sigh.

"Daisy, you failed to come home on the school coach with the other pupils yesterday. Do you understand how much trouble that can put the school into?"

"BUT Sir, I told you! I was pushed into one of the excavations by some other girls!"

"So why didn't you cry for help."

"I did, eventually. It's hard to call for help when you're knocked out!"

Mr Kane looked at her long and hard.

"Daisy, whether you were knocked out or whether you decided to join the circus for the day it's just one thing too many on your report. I'm going to have to recommend that Degham drops you down to middle stream."

Daisy felt as though she'd been knocked unconscious all over again. She sat, speechless. Mr Kane took off his glasses and rubbed his eyes.

"Daisy, if there was anything I could do I would keep things as they were, but I can't. We have very strict guidelines we have to meet. If you pulled another of your stunts at Degham, they'd come straight back to us."

Tears welled up in Daisy's eyes. She thought of another three years of boring lessons that she already knew all the answers to. She felt like a prisoner who'd walked out of one cell only to find herself in another.

Daisy ran to her room when she got home and pulled the curtains shut . It was so unfair. What made it worse was that she'd no longer be in the same classes as Koola and Darren, the only friends she had. She sobbed until she was too tired to sob any more and lay back, quietly looking up at the glow stars. Outside, behind the dark curtains, there was laughter and talking and people enjoying the summer. Daisy looked over at the window and spotted her wicker chair. Her mum used to sit in it when Daisy was upset, smiling and saying everything would be okay. Now all that stared back was a pile of stuffed toys. Daisy sighed and closed her eyes.

She opened them again when she felt something soft and warm landed on her head. Everything had gone green. It was the Darlington handkerchief. It had fallen down from the cork-board. Daisy's mum smiled back at her from a photograph above the blank space where it had been pinned.

* * *

The mouse pointer hovered over the button that read "TAKE ONLINE ENTRANCE EXAM" for several minutes. Daisy - one hand on the mouse, the other holding the handkerchief - tried to summon up the courage. Her mind raced through several thoughts - she could try later, she needed to feed Gibbon and get dinner ready, she didn't have time, she was too tired, but they were all excuses and she knew it. What she was really afraid of was that she might fail.

"Come on, Daisy," she said to herself, "what have you got to lose."

She clicked the mouse and stared at the first question.

The next few weeks moved slowly whilst Daisy waited to hear how she had done in the exam. School finished and Daisy started the long summer of babysitting her older brothers. She tried to fill her time by cleaning the house, burying her head in books and writing in her journal. Darren and Koola - who were both really sorry they had left Daisy in the villa - had both gone away on holiday with their parents. There was no holiday in store for the Cooper family. Mr Cooper would come home after the long shifts at work and fall exhausted into his chair, barely able to speak. Daisy waited patiently for the exam letter to arrive. With Gibbon winding around her legs miaowing every morning, she would flick through the mail, hands trembling. It was always the same. Bills, bills, bills.

It had been a hot Sunday night. Daisy had found it difficult to sleep and crawled out of bed late the next morning. She stretched with a yawn and made her way downstairs to see Gibbon laying on his back on the kitchen lino. He looked up accusingly at Daisy.

"It's not my fault, Gibbon. Blame the sun."

Gibbon narrowed his eyes and hissed. Daisy filled his food dish and sat at the table with a bowl of cereal. The flip-flap sound of the letter box echoed from the hallway. Daisy frowned at her cereal. She padded down the hallway and picked the letters up from the matt. Bill...Bill...Junk Mail....Miss D. Cooper...Bill....

Hang on.

Daisy turned back to the letter with her name on and dropped the rest. She held it out in front of her and walked slowly back to the kitchen. The envelope was a dark green colour and her name and address were typed on the front in a fancy script. She turned it over. Sure enough, there on the back was the school crest with the words "Darlington School for Girls".

"Blimey, Gibbon."

Daisy ran to her room and climbed on her bed. She put the letter down carefully in front of her. All she had to do was open it and she would know if she had got through. Then again, all she had to do was open it and find out she had failed.

"Come on, Daisy," she said to herself.

With eyes closed she picked up the envelope and tore it open.

Dear Miss Daisy Cooper,

We are pleased to announce that you have made it through to the next round of our application process and are invited to attend a written exam on Saturday August 5th in Hamley village. Please find directions and instructions for confirmation at the bottom of this letter.

Yours sincerely,

Mistress Aiken,

Deputy Head, Darlington School for Girls.

"COME ON!"

Daisy leapt in the air with a shout, nearly falling off the bed. Downstairs, Gibbon panicked and ran out the cat flap.

Butterflies in her stomach, ticket clutched in her hand, Daisy took a seat by the window on the train. The exam was at nine o'clock and it was barely past seven now. She'd left a note at home saying that she had to go out and do something for school (which was kind of true). She just hoped she didn't get back too late. On the carriage there were a few students, a party of Japanese tourists talking about their trip to Stonehenge and a couple of businessmen drinking hot coffee over enormous bundles of newspapers. The train journey was over an hour. Daisy pulled out a book on the moon landings from her satchel and read it to ease her nerves.

When Daisy climbed down from the train at Hamley village, she was shocked. Along the whole length of the platform were girls the same age as her. Unlike Daisy, who was wearing jeans and a tee shirt, the other girls were dressed in immaculate school uniforms.

A hand landed on Daisy's shoulder, causing her to jump.

"HI!"

Daisy turned round to find a girl with hair cut in a sharp, dark bob and a wide, cheeky grin.

"You on your own for this one too?"

The girl was American.

"Yes," said Daisy. "you're American."

The girl laughed.

"Thanks for telling me. The name's Brodie."

The girl held out her hand. Daisy shook it.

"Hi, I'm Daisy."

"Daisy? Cute name. Okay, Daisy, so this is Hamley village. Apparently Darlington is near here. Which way do we go? I reckon some right jolly old tea with the queen and such."

It was a terrible attempt at an English accent and Brodie knew it. She laughed and nudged Daisy gently with her shoulder.

"Come on," she said pointing to the other girls leaving the station with their parents, "lets follow that bunch of geese."

Outside the station a coach was waiting. Daisy, pulled along by Brodie, climbed in and sat near the back. They watched the countryside go by as the coach moved down narrow, winding roads. Brodie seemed excited by every tree and bush. Everything was "really cute" and whenever there was more than one thing - like a herd of cows - she would call it a 'bunch'.

"Hey, look at that bunch of cows over there."

"Which ones?"

"The really cute ones behind that bunch of trees."

Daisy wasn't sure that anything other than flowers came in bunches. Apart from her quirks it was obvious to Daisy that Brodie was as intelligent as she was friendly. In between her excitement for the rolling hills of Southern England she talked about where she was from and asked questions.

"So, my mom and dad live in LA but they're so not LA if you know what I mean…"

Daisy didn't.

"...My mom is Scotch descended and my Dad's family is from Russia so they aren't that great with the sun. You can't move in our house for sun cream bottles. Dad's a computer geek - runs a software company. Mom's a yoga teacher. She could bore you to death about yoga. They sent me here because I love English lessons and they're pretty literal."

"That's interesting," Daisy replied, her head reeling with information. "So what's up with your folks?"

"Well, we live in South London. Dad, well Dad's a printer," replied Daisy.

She felt slightly embarrassed talking about her dad. All the parents on the bus looked so important, not to mention how intimidating Brodie's parents sounded. She felt herself blush. Brodie didn't seem to care.

"Printing? That's awesome!" she said, "I'm into printing and writing and stuff- I used to look after the school magazine back in LA. Your dad sounds cool."

Daisy smiled. Her dad was pretty cool.

"What does your mom do?" asked Brodie.

Daisy changed the conversation and pointed to a river outside the window.

"What a cute bunch of water!"

Hamley was an old market town and the town hall, its great old stones leading up to a high clock tower, sat in the middle. There was a sign fixed to the door reading 'DARLINGTON ENTRANCE EXAM'.

"Wow," said Brodie examining the crumbling brickwork of the town hall entrance, "you Brits really do some serious history."

The other girls hugged their parents and began to pour in through the wooden doors. Daisy felt her nerves coming back but before she could have second thoughts Brodie pulled her into the building.

"What's your name, dear?" said a rugged looking woman dressed in khaki trousers and shirt.

The woman had a small name badge pinned to her lapel that read 'Dr Penrose'.

"Daisy Cooper."

"Daisy Cooper...? Ah, here we are."

Dr Penrose ticked Daisy's name off on the list.

"You can tell your parents that they can pick you up in a couple of hours if you like."

"My parents are not here."

"You came on your own?"

Daisy nodded.

"That's awfully brave of you. Don't you think so, Miss Weaver?" said Dr Penrose to the colleague sat next to her.

Miss Weaver was a tall, wiry looking woman with the maddest, unkempt hair Daisy had ever seen. Daisy was pleased to see there was a paintbrush tucked behind her ear. Daisy had been told off so many times at school for tucking pens behind her ear it was great to see that someone else realised it was a very sensible place to put things. Miss Weaver had very kind eyes that twinkled as she smiled.

"Very brave," said Miss Weaver, "good luck, Daisy."

Daisy walked through to the hall with Brodie. Individual desks were laid out in rows pointing towards a wall with a huge clock on it. It was two minutes to nine. Daisy and Brodie sat at a couple of empty desks and looked around at the other girls. A side door opened and the woman Daisy had seen at the villa with the enormous bun walked into the hall with a tall, blond haired lady. Daisy heard the two teachers talking as they walked past her desk.

"We should only be taking applications from girls from the right schools. Why do I have to put up with this nonsense?" said the lady with the bun who's name tag read 'Mistress Aiken'. Daisy realised that meant she was the Deputy Head.

The woman next to her shrugged. Her name badge read 'Madame Didier'.

"Well, we have more important things to do," said Madame Didier.

She had a strong French accent.

"Even so, we should be keeping standards," said Mistress Aiken, "who knows what troublemakers we might have in here."

The Deputy Head reached the front of the hall and coughed loudly. She looked around with a scowl, making eye contact with every girl. Everyone fell silent.

"Right. The exam will last an hour and a half, finishing at half past ten so if you'd turn over your question sheets...NOW."

The hall filled with the sound of a hundred papers being turned.

* * *

On the train on the way back Daisy was tired but satisfied. She sat in a carriage with Brodie who was talking a mile a minute. She smiled and nodded at her new friend's conversation but her mind was thinking back on the exam. The questions had been on many different things. Some to do with normal subjects like maths and English but there were other kinds of questions too. Not the sort of questions you could learn the answers to. They were all to do with the Darlington virtues. There were questions like "What do you understand by the word 'charity' and give an example of an act of charity you have made" and "Describe what the word 'honourable' means to you and write about a well known figure you consider to have honour, explaining why." It was a bit baffling. For the Charity question Daisy wrote about giving her pocket money to Outside Dave, the homeless guy near her local shops. She wrote about the smile he always gave her when she handed him her coins. It wasn't the money Dave really wanted. What he wanted was to be treated like a human being. She thought of Honour and tried to remember people from the news but none of them seemed particularly honourable - her dad was always shouting at them for a start. Then she remembered the mother fox outside her estate and how she had stolen food to feed her young. She thought about how she refused to leave her babies when the council men came to capture them. She was ready to die to protect the ones she loved. That sounded pretty honourable. There were another six questions like that, all on similar ideas. It made her brain hurt but it was enormous fun at the same time.

Daisy was exhausted when she finally arrived back at the house and it was barely three o'clock in the afternoon. She could hear the banging and crashing of her brothers upstairs. They probably hadn't even noticed she'd gone. She poured some milk for Gibbon and filled the sink to do the washing up. The exam seemed like a dream now. Daisy took the train ticket from her pocket and stared at it again. It could go on the corkboard next to the handkerchief and the exam letter. She told herself to not get excited. There were lots of girls in the room. Many of them very clever. She would just have to wait. Again.

CHAPTER THREE - A MATTER OF HONOUR

Daisy didn't have to wait long to find out her results. A letter in the same green coloured envelope arrived a couple of days later. This time she didn't even wait to go to her room. Fingers shaking, she tore it open. The first thing she saw was the word 'CONGRATULATIONS!' written at the top of the page. She was through to the interviews.

The following Friday morning Daisy waved her Dad and brothers off in the car. It was seven thirty and David and Daniel were asleep in the back, puffy faces pressed against the window. Mr Cooper didn't look happy. He'd arranged a couple of days in Brighton for them and taken time off work. Daisy had told him she wasn't feeling well. It was kind of true because today was the day of the interview and her nerves were making her feel sick. Her dad had argued with her and it was obvious he was disappointed. In the end he relented.

"Well, if you must stay, wrap up warm and get some sleep," he said.

Once the car was out of sight Daisy ran inside and changed into the smart black dress her dad had bought her for xmas. It was the first time she'd worn it and it was itchy. She looked around for shoes to go with it but all she had were battered trainers. In desperation, she pulled her black plimsolls out of her gym kit and slipped them on. At least they were the right colour.

As the train to Hamley snaked through the countryside, Daisy kept thinking about her dad. She had lied to him. There was no getting around that fact. What was worse was that she knew that HE KNEW she had lied, even if he didn't understand why. At some point she was going to have to tell him.

"DAISY!"

Daisy looked up. Brodie was standing in the doorway of the carriage, a big smile on her face.

"BRODIE!"

Daisy got up and hugged her friend, her worries momentarily forgotten.

"So you got through!"

"So did you!"

"So what's the deal with this interview thing then?" said Brodie sitting. Daisy shrugged.

"I'm clueless too," said Brodie, "I'm staying over here with an aunt in Glou-cester-shire - for the summer anyways. My mum's off in India looking for gurus and my dad's got his head stuck in some computer thing so I'm going nuts with a crazy aunt I don't know who does nothing but watch gardening programmes all day. So when I got the letter it was like awesome sauce."

"What questions do you think they'll ask?" asked Daisy.

Brodie rolled her eyes, thinking.

"I had a cousin in the States who went to some posh girl's school in Alabama and she had to go to an interview. They asked her stuff like if she loved the president and stuff like that. I guess they just want to see if you're an honest person, I suppose."

Daisy remembered the lie and bit her lip.

"But this is England," continued Brodie,"you Brit's have got your own rules. They'll probably ask me if I know how to make a cup of tea."

They both laughed.

Daisy and Brodie stepped off the train onto the platform at Hamley station and looked around. There were a few of the uniformed girls Daisy had seen last time climbing out of the first class carriages further up. They followed them out to the car park.

"Where do we go now?" said Brodie looking around.

"I know," said Daisy with a smile.

In the corner of the car park stood the big green Darlington double-decker bus. Mistress Aiken was stood by its door with a clipboard in her hand. They walked over and joined the line of girls waiting to board.

"Where are your parents?" barked Mistress Aiken when Daisy got to the front of the queue.

"They're not here."

The Deputy Head raised a heavily penciled eyebrow and looked at her list.

"Name?"

"Daisy Cooper."

"It's 'Daisy Cooper, *Mistress Aiken*'," said the Deputy Head.

With a short sharp flick of the wrist she ticked Daisy's name off her list.

"On you get, then."

There was a faint smell of lavender inside the bus. The floors were wooden and the seats were made of creaky red leather. It really was like stepping into a old photograph. Daisy and Brodie sat at the back on the top floor. The bus was only about half full. Most of the other girls sat between their parents like prized possessions. Daisy thought about her dad and brothers and wondered if they were in Brighton yet.

"LADIES AND GUESTS, LISTEN UP!" bellowed Mistress Aiken, standing at the top of the stairs.

"We will be traveling to Gateley junior school shortly who have kindly let us borrow their hall for your interviews. These interviews will be an assessment of your character, your intellect and your passion for studying at Darlington school for girls. Be advised that your behaviour will be closely watched from now on and will form part of the assessment. Do not move around whilst the bus is in motion and do not make excessive noise."

Daisy was disappointed. She was hoping to get a look at Darlington School. The bus's engine shuddered into life and they began to move. Brodie turned to Daisy.

"I hope she's not doing the interview," she whispered.

Gateley Junior School was an old building that looked a bit like a church. As the girls climbed off the bus they were handed one of eight pieces of coloured card and asked to queue up next to a pole of their colour. The poles were laid out in a line at the edge of the playground. Daisy was handed a green card. Brodie's was purple.

"Come along, girls, line up!" said Dr Penrose walking out onto the tarmac.

Dr Penrose separated Daisy and Brodie and pushing them towards their different poles. Brodie crossed her fingers and waved them at Daisy. Daisy did the same back. Once all the girls had lined up properly Mistress Aiken took a whistle out her pocket and blew it quickly three times. All the giggling and excited talking amongst the girls stopped.

"Thank you, girls. Shortly each group will be escorted to a classroom by a senior from Darlington where you will wait until you are called for your interview. During this time you are expected to remain quiet. There is to be no talking and no use of mobile phones or music devices. You are permitted to read a book. Under no circumstances should you disturb the senior in charge unless you need to visit the ladies room or have an emergency. Your senior will be reporting back to me. Any misconduct will be taken into consideration on your application."

Mistress Aiken gave another three shrill blasts on her whistle. The main doors to the school opened and out walked the seniors. They crossed the playground, walking in line, each immaculately dressed in the Darlington School uniform and all looking tall and confident. Daisy looked down at her plimsolls and felt embarrassed.

The seniors walked along the row of coloured poles, one of them stopping at each line of hopeful girls. As they approached the green pole, Daisy caught one of them glaring at her. It was Eleanore. The girl from the Roman villa. Eleanore stopped in front of the line next to Daisy's and another Senior - a stocky girl with a kind smile - stood in front of the green pole. Daisy gave a sigh of relief.

That was close, she thought.

She looked over at Eleanore who was still glaring at her and, not being able to help herself, gave a cheeky smile. Eleanore smiled back, her eyes narrowing. She leant over and whispered something to the stocky senior. A discussion went on between them in whispers too low for Daisy to hear. There was another whistle sound. Daisy turned to see the first of the lines walking through the school entrance. When she looked back she saw with horror that Eleanore had swapped places and was now standing next to the green pole. She winked at Daisy.

The clock ticked slowly on the wall above the blackboard. Underneath it, perched on the desk, sat Eleanore. The eight girls who were up for the interview in Daisy's group sat at small desks. Most of them had brought books to read. Daisy had been so busy pretending to be ill to her family that she'd forgotten. Her rucksack had nothing in it but her journal and pens (which she never forgot), some sandwiches and an apple. She wondered whether she was allowed to do any writing but didn't want to say anything to Eleanore. After three quarters of an hour Dr Penrose knocked on the door and entered noisily, flicking through the pile of notes on her clipboard.

"Rita Sharma?"

The girl who had been at the front of Daiy's queue put up her hand.

"Come with me please."

Rita left the classroom with Dr Penrose. There were seven of them left.

What seemed like hours passed. After the first four girls had gone through Eleanore escorted the remaining four to the ladies bathroom and then back to the classroom to eat their packed lunches. They were still not officially allowed to talk. As Daisy was unwrapping her sandwiches Eleanore walked over and sat on the edge of her desk. She picked up one of the sandwiches and looked inside wrinkling her nose.

"Eww. How frightful."

She threw the sandwich down. Daisy picked it up and took a bite. The other girls were busy with their own lunches.

"Well, I must say I was surprised to see you here, oik. I never forget a face, though," said Eleanore quietly.

Daisy took another bite of her sandwich, trying to ignore her. She knew that Eleanore was trying to provoke her into saying something sarcastic so she could report her.

"I imagine people from your background are good at cheating. I assume that's how you got here. Maybe you thought you'd come along to see if you could steal a few purses or wallets from the parents. "

Daisy took a bite. A big one.

"...Tell me, oik," whispered Eleanore, leaning in, "did your parents teach you to cheat and steal or did you pick it up on the streets?"

Another bite. Daisy tapped her feet hard against the floor. She could feel her cheeks burning.

"...was it your oik friends or was it your oik parents? Your oik dad, if you have one, or maybe it was your oik mum?..."

Daisy slammed the sandwich down on the desk and stood up, her chair squeaking noisily. Eleanore jumped back and smiled.

"Go on…" she hissed.

Daisy opened her mouth ready to burst, ready to let Eleanore know exactly what she thought of her. She was too angry to care whether she got into the school or not.

"Daisy Cooper?...Daisy Cooper?"

Daisy and Eleanore turned round. Dr Penrose was at the door.

"I'm here!" said Daisy.

She gave Eleanore a scowl, picked up her bag and left the room.

The interview committee were lined up behind a wide desk in the school auditorium. There was a single small chair in the middle of the empty hall facing them. Daisy walked over to it and sat down as the adults read through her exam answers and scribbled notes. In the middle of the table sat Mistress Aiken. On her left side sat the French teacher, Madame Didier. On the other side was a middle aged lady with a shark like face - small eyes and a wide, thin mouth beneath slicked back jet black hair. The name plaque on the table in front of her read "Mrs Lydia Lyles, Chair of the Darlington Board". Whilst Mrs Lyles looked at Daisy's report she played with a string of expensive pearls round her neck. Beside her sat one of the Darlington schoolgirls. She was a little older than the seniors and wore a shiny metal pin on her blazer that was the same as the one Roni had worn on her tie. Her name was Anita Walker. On the other end of the table sat Miss Weaver, the kind teacher with the mad hair with paint spots in it. Miss Weaver was the only one not looking through her notes. She gave Daisy a friendly wink. Eventually the scribbling finished. They all put down their pens and looked over at Daisy.

"Good afternoon, Miss Cooper," said Mistress Aiken, "there are sixty four girls being interviewed today for eight remaining places in the coming academic year. The purpose of this interview is to give you a chance to tell us why you should be one of the successful ones."

Anita Walker, the head girl at the end of the table took over.

"Darlington School for Girls is one of the top five all girls schools in the world," she said, "with a reputation that comes not just from its high academic results but also from the character of its pupils. Being a Darlington Girl is not merely a measure of where you spend your education but how you live the rest of your life. There is a code that each girl must live up to - a way of behaving and a way of approaching the world."

"So the first thing we must ask, Miss Cooper," continued the Deputy Head, "is what is your knowledge of the Darlington Code?"

The hall fell silent. Daisy could feel all the eyes in the room on her.

"Well...I guess..."

Daisy thought hurriedly. She'd read the information on the internet a hundred times. It had mentioned the code but hadn't explained what it was. Mrs Lyles coughed. The Deputy head's eyes narrowed. Daisy could feel a cold sweat on the back of her neck.

It must be a test, she thought hurriedly. *Test, test, test.... That was it, the exam!*

Daisy remembered the questions on the Virtues. They had to be the parts of the Darlington Code.

"Charity, Bravery, Reason, Culture, Grace, Agility, Fellowship and Honour!" Daisy blurted out.

Mistress Aiken and Mrs Lyles looked at each other and raised their eyebrows. Miss Weaver was nodding at Daisy. It gave her courage to continue.

"I mean," said Daisy lowering her voice, "the Code is based on the eight virtues of the school and is represented in the names of your Houses. They are the things that you expect a girl to have...and to work on...at Darlington...to make her...a Darlington Girl?"

Daisy raised an eyebrow hopefully. The faces stared back blankly. Daisy looked at Miss Weaver but she was busy writing something down.

"And in what way do you think that you, Miss Cooper, embody these qualities? With examples please," asked the Deputy Head sternly.

"Well, with Duty. I suppose I have a duty to my family. Since my mum died and my dad's at work long hours I have to sort out my brothers, make the tea, wash up. Feed Gibbon..."

"Who's Gibbon?" asked Mistress Aiken, looking confused.

"My cat," said Daisy.

"You have a cat called Gibbon?"

"Yes. He's always swinging from the curtains like a monkey so we called him Gibbon."

There was a titter of laughter between the adults. Daisy pressed on.

"....Bravery? I don't know how brave I am but I taught myself to ride a horse in our local urban farm. She was a bit of a crazy horse - she had been mistreated so was really nervous. No one else would dare ride her but I managed to calm her. Eventually we were doing jumps in the paddock. Reason? The teachers at my old school tell me I try their patience because I'm always questioning them but I think it's important to make sure you get something right, which is reason, I think... Culture?"

Daisy stumbled. Culture? When she'd read about it in magazines it was always about classical music and Shakespeare and she'd had none of that. Not at school or at home, really. She looked over at Miss Weaver again who gave her an encouraging nod.

"Culture..." she said with a sigh, "I've never been to the ballet or an opera but I've read about them. I've read about a lot of things like that and I'd love to see them for myself but I haven't had the chance. Not yet. That's why I want to get into Darlington so much because I want to know all about this stuff, I really do. Grace? Probably not a lot of that. My Nan used to say I was about as graceful as a frog on roller-skates..."

There were a couple of laughs. Even the Deputy Head let out a slight smirk. Daisy wasn't sure why but that was probably a good thing.

"I know I have a few rough edges but I'm a fast learner so maybe I can learn to be more graceful. Agility? I'd say the Horse riding again. I also did swimming and gymnastics and taught myself to play the piano - I didn't have a real piano, though, I had to draw a keyboard on a piece of cardboard and then practice on it. When they let me at school, I'd stay late and try out what I'd learnt on the music room piano...I can bang out a tune if I've heard it a few times. Fellowship..."

Daisy paused again. She thought about the word. She supposed it meant the same thing as friendship. Daisy didn't have many friends.

"I don't know if I'm strong on that one, either. I'm always doing things with my family. Not that I wouldn't love to have lots of friends."

Daisy went quiet. The interview was turning out to be pretty difficult. The Darlington Code was making her think about her life. Now she thought about it, she really didn't have many friends in the world at all.

"And what about Honour, Daisy?" asked Mistress Aiken.

"Honour?"

"Answer the question, Miss Cooper. Would you say you were an honourable person?" snapped Lydia Lyles, her cold shark eyes boring into Daisy.

Daisy thought about her Dad and brothers in Brighton and how she'd lied not to go with them. A memory popped into her head. It was from when mum was sick. Daisy had gone to the hospital after school one day to visit and spotted her dad through the glass window of the private room. He was sat by the side of mum's bed holding her hand whilst she slept and crying. Daisy couldn't bring herself to go into the room. It was the first time she'd ever seen her dad cry. Daisy had promised herself at that moment that she would always look after her dad and her brothers, whatever happened. Yet here she was sitting an interview for a place in a boarding school miles away from them.

"Daisy?"

Daisy looked up. Mistress Aiken had removed her glasses and was looking at her with a frown. Daisy sighed.

"No," she said, "I don't think I am an honourable person."

Daisy got up and picked up her bag.

"I'm really very sorry for wasting your time. Your school seems very beautiful."

"Daisy!" called out Miss Weaver.

Feeling like she was going to cry, Daisy walked quickly out of the hall without turning back.

Daisy switched trains at Clapham Junction to get to Brighton. She'd phoned her dad to tell him she was feeling better and was on her way to meet them. Finding an empty carriage to sit in she thought about the interview. Part of her wanted to go back and say she'd made a terrible mistake but deep down she knew that she'd given the honest answer to the question. What could be more dishonourable than lying to your family and leaving them? Daisy felt bad that she hadn't said goodbye to Brodie and felt even worse when she realised she'd probably never see her again. If Brodie was successful at getting into Darlington (and why wouldn't she?) maybe Daisy could send a letter to the school and they could be pen pals. It gave her little hope.

As the train made its way to Brighton Daisy couldn't stop thinking about what life would have been like at Darlington. Sure there were scary things like Eleanore and Mistress Aiken but there were bullies and scary teachers in every school. There were also people like Brodie and Roni and Miss Weaver. So much of it seemed so good. It was one of the top five schools in the world! Daisy thought of the future, of the last few weeks of summer before going to Degham.

I'm going to be a Degger, she thought.

The window shuddered as a train thundered past.

* * *

Brighton was fun. Daisy was pleased to see her dad and brothers enjoying themselves. She ran to greet them at Brighton pier where David told her they'd been on the roller-coaster all morning. He boasted that he'd managed to be sick four times already. Daniel then said he'd been sick five times and won the "roller-coaster being sick contest". They started fighting again. If nothing else it made it clear to Daisy that they needed her.

Daisy spent the next few weeks at the urban farm. She hadn't been there in ages after getting obsessed with Darlington and she wanted to say hello to Pickle. Pickle was a grey eleven year old Welsh pony - the horse that she had told the interview committee about. She got there early every morning to muck out the stables and spent the afternoon riding Pickle around the paddock practicing jumps. It helped take her mind off what had happened.

One Friday morning, a couple of weeks before she was due to start at Degham, Daisy returned home from the farm exhausted and a little bruised. Pickle had refused one of the bigger jumps and thrown her off. Daisy kicked off her wellies and padded through to the kitchen to run her bruised elbows under the tap.

"Hello Daisy."

Daisy's mouth fell open. Sitting at the kitchen table was Miss Weaver. Dad was sat next to her with a pile of forms in front of him. Daisy recognised her exam papers amongst them.

"You've been a tricky girl to track down," said Miss Weaver.

"I think you have some explaining to do," added her Dad, raising his eyebrow.

Daisy sat down and told her dad everything. The words poured out almost faster than she could speak them, like they'd been bottled up inside for weeks. She told him about the Roman villa, the mosaic and how she'd met Roni. She told him about the double-decker bus and Mistress Aiken with her enormous bun. She told him about finding the school online and taking the online exam. Saying sorry between every sentence she explained how she'd let him and the boys go off to Brighton without her so she could go to the interview and finally she told him how she'd given it all up because she felt so guilty about being selfish. She collapsed back in the chair, exhausted. Miss Weaver poured her a cup of tea. No one said anything for several minutes. For once Daisy wished

David and Daniel were around with all their crashing and banging. Eventually her Dad picked up one of the letters in front of him.

"Do you know what this is, Daisy?"

Daisy shook her head. Her dad turned the letter round and held it out in front of him. The word "ACCEPTANCE" was written in big bold letters under the Darlington School crest. Daisy bit her lip. Acceptance? She'd been accepted? She couldn't believe it.

"Daisy, your answers in the exam were a little, let's say unconventional, but they were the best pieces of writing we had. You have a real honesty in your writing and that's rare," said Miss Weaver, "you shocked us all when you ran out of the interview and ruffled a few feathers, I can say. I've spent the last few weeks arguing that we should contact you and give you a place. I got your number from your address and called your father a while ago. He explained how important it was to you to look after your family. He also told me how smart you are. After careful discussion the committee decided that your reasons for running out on us demonstrated a thoughtful and considerate character - characteristics that are perfect for a Darlington Girl."

"You knew about it all this time, dad?"

Mr Cooper shrugged.

"I thought it best to wait until they offered you a place, Daisy."

"So, are you going to be joining us at Darlington, Daisy?" asked Miss Weaver.

Could I? thought Daisy.

"Can I speak to my Dad?"

"Of course, but I will need an answer today. As it is, it's not going to be possible to get everything worked out for you to be there for the first week of term. I'll leave you to have a chat."

Miss Weaver quietly left the room. Daisy's dad put the letter down and slid it across the kitchen table towards her. She picked it up and ran her fingers under the word ACCEPTANCE.

"I'm sorry, Dad. I thought it was just another silly project. I didn't mean to hurt you."

"Hurt me? Daisy, how could you ever hurt me?"

He reached across the table and squeezed her hand.

"I'm proud of you. You're a right handful at times but once you get your teeth into something you never let go. That's what makes you 'you' and it's what makes me the luckiest dad in the world."

"Aw, come on, Dad," said Daisy, feeling embarrassed.

"Does this school mean a lot to you or is it really just another one of your projects?"

Daisy wanted nothing more in the world than to go to Darlington.

"It's probably very expensive," she said.

"Miss Weaver says because I'm a single parent there's a scholarship place waiting for you."

"But I promised to look after you and the boys," said Daisy.

"Well, you didn't make that promise to me, because if you had, I never would have accepted! I've told you, we're big enough to look after yourselves!"

Mr Cooper stood up.

"MISS WEAVER?"

Miss Weaver appeared in the kitchen doorway.

"Yes?"

Dad turned to Daisy and gave her a big smile.

"Tell me where I need to sign. My daughter is coming to your school."

CHAPTER FOUR - THE 88ERS

It was the biggest map Daisy had ever seen. She had to move her head from side to side to take it all in. It hung above the great oak doors to the assembly hall and stretched from one end of the school entrance foyer to the other. Made of dark wood, it was very old and showed the whole world with the boundaries of countries etched in wiggling black lines. Daisy mouthed their names: Portugal, Spain, Italy, Turkey, Russia, Mongolia....

When she reached The Netherlands Daisy noticed something. Next to each country name was a bright green and yellow symbol made up of a letter 'I' with a letter 'S' curled around it like a snake. The same symbol she had seen in the tie pin Roni had worn at the Roman villa. Daisy stepped back from her family to read the large words written above the map.

"Orbis...Terrarum...Est...Nostrum...Schola"

"It's Latin. It means 'The World is Our School'"

Daisy turned to see Miss Weaver smiling down at her.

"Well, Miss Daisy Cooper, I'm very pleased to welcome you to Darlington."

Miss Weaver held out her hand. There were specks of paint on it. Daisy put her hand in the teacher's hand and shook.

I might have to get used to this handshaking thing, she thought.

There was a piercing ring and suddenly the hall began to fill from all directions with schoolgirls. They bustled past, laughing and talking. Every one of them looked older and bigger than Daisy. She looked around for Dad and the boys and spotted them huddled together looking slightly terrified at the sudden commotion. She giggled.

"Come on," said Miss Weaver, "lets rescue your family."

Miss Weaver's office was in the Teacher's Wing at the end of a long series of corridors hung with old pictures and cabinets full of awards and trophies. The office was full of piles of art books, canvases, sculptures and paint speckled plants. Apologising for the mess, Miss Weaver cleared away some paint pots revealing a sofa which Daisy and her family squeezed into. She then disappeared into a small room off to one side behind a paper maché sculpture and appeared moments later with a tray of tea and biscuits.

"The term is already a week in so the other new pupils have filled out all their details, dressed their bunks, decorated their work books and generally started to get into the swing of things," said Miss Weaver, "I'm sure once we get the paperwork out of the way, you and I can leave Daisy to catch up and get acquainted with the girls in her new dorm."

"Oh, absolutely!" said Mr Cooper.

"Is this where you live?" asked David, looking around the room.

"HA!" barked Miss Weaver, "good heavens, no! This is where I work. I teach art at the school, if that isn't obvious. We teachers live in different places around the grounds. It's a bit higgledy-piggledy but that's part of the charm. You could get lost in the grounds for hours if you wanted to."

"Why would you want to get lost?" said Daniel.

"Getting lost can be a wonderful thing," said Miss Weaver, "how on earth do you find new places if you don't get lost once in a while?"

Daisy had indeed noticed the higgledy-piggledy nature of the school and it did look very, very easy to get lost in.

"Now, as well as the art teacher here, I'm also the house mistress for Honour House which is the dormitory building Daisy will be staying in. If you ever have any questions or concerns, Daisy, please come and find me."

"Yes, Miss Weaver," said Daisy.

"Good girl," said Miss Weaver, "Now, Mr Cooper, I've got a couple more forms to fill in, I'm afraid."

* * *

Daisy hugged her family goodbye and waved them off in the car. Once they had gone she looked around. She was stood in the large courtyard of the school which sat in the middle of the dorm houses. There were eight of them in total, each named after one of the virtues of the Darlington Code and each with eight floors. They were very tall and made of fancy stonework. At the top of every dorm was a balcony with ornate gargoyles and a large sloping roof that led up to a bell tower. Daisy picked up her suitcase. It was filled with all her possessions and seemed very small. Daisy felt strangely fragile, like she could blow away in the breeze at any moment. She shivered and pulled the collar of her new blazer around her neck.

"The whole world is your school," she said to herself.

Daisy crunched through the gravel towards Honour House, her new home.

Miss Weaver was inside waiting for Daisy. She led her up a large staircase that spiralled all the way to the top of the building. Hanging right down the middle of the staircase was a large thick rope that was used to ring the bell in the tower. Half way up Miss Weaver stopped to catch her breath.

"I keep asking them to get lifts installed but they don't like the idea. They think it goes against tradition," she said, puffing, "but between you and me, Daisy, tradition's a lovely thing but only when it doesn't involve stairs. Oh, before I forget, you'd better take this."

She handed Daisy the school rule book. It was as thick as a doorstep and just as heavy. Tucked inside the front cover was the timetable for Daisy's lessons. There was a number 88 scribbled in the corner.

"What does the '88' mean, miss?" asked Daisy as they started walking again.

"Every dorm and every House has a number, a bit like a class number at your old school. Honour House is the eighth dorm building and your dorm is on the eighth floor, so you're an 88er."

"An 88er?" said Daisy.

She'd never been a number before.

When they reached the top Miss Weaver pushed open a pair of ornate glass doors and led Daisy through to a wide balcony which looked out across the school grounds.

"It's quite a view, isn't it?" said Miss Weaver.

It was breathtaking. Far below schoolgirls moved in long lines like ants between classes. As well as the main school there were lots of other buildings of different shapes and sizes dotted around the grounds. Paths wound between trees and ponds, through wooded tunnels and over delightful bridges linking them all. There were tennis courts, an outdoor swimming pool and even a school maze. Flags with the school's emblem on them fluttered in the wind on the top of every tower. It made the school look a bit like a ship with the towers as the masts.

"I'll never take it all in," whispered Daisy.

Miss Weaver chuckled. She took Daisy back through into the dorm itself which was empty. None of the other dorm girls had arrived back from class. Pictures showing smiling faces of family and friends decorated the wardrobes and the bedside cabinets were littered with notebooks, novels, alarm clocks, radios and hairbrushes. Laid out against the walls were beds, four on each side. All of them were covered in colourful duvets. Pyjama cases, heart shaped cushions and teddy bears sat on the pillows. The only bed that was bare was the one in the corner, Daisy's new bed. Miss Weaver led Daisy to it and helped her lift her suitcase onto the mattress.

"I don't have a duvet cover!" Daisy realised out loud.

"Don't you worry. See me after evening meal and I'll have one ready for you," said Miss Weaver, "After school hours you can find me in my boarding rooms on the ground floor of this house. I'll leave you alone to get your bits and pieces sorted. I'm sure the other girls will be back soon to introduce themselves."

It didn't take Daisy long to make her little area a bit more homely. After putting her clothes away and her toothbrush and mug out on her cabinet she took out the photographs from her cork-board at home. There was one of her dad in his work overalls, one of her brothers on the pier at Brighton and an old one of mum that was taken on a picnic a couple of years ago. She pinned them to her wardrobe. When she was done she took out the glow stars from her satchel and, standing on tip-toe on the mattress, pinned them to the ceiling above her new bed. Satisfied, she lay down on the mattress and looked up at them.

"Well, I'm here, Mum," she said.

"HELLO!"

Daisy jumped. Standing in the doorway was a thin girl with curly brown hair. She was dressed in a school sports top that had the word 'Honour' written across it in big yellow letters. She also wore a short sports skirt that sat above grass stained and slightly bloodied knees. There was a hockey stick in her hand.

"YOU MUST BE OUR MISSING 88ER!" said the girl marching across the room with her hand held out and a big grin on her face. Daisy sat up and shook the girl's hand which was cold and slightly muddy.

"Hello, I'm Daisy."

"I'm Millie! Sorry about my shocking appearance. I've just been whacking the old hockey balls about."

Millie motioned with the stick a couple of times.

"They have a fantastic hockey pitch here. Have you been shown round yet?" said Millie.

"No. Not really."

"Well we can't have that, Daisy! Let me get cleaned up and give you a tour."

The bathroom was across the hall from the main dorm and Millie insisted that Daisy chat to her whilst she washed. The bathroom had a row of four sinks against a long mirror, four showers and two toilets. There was also a big wicker laundry basket overspilling with dirty towels.

"We really are such a mess!" shouted Millie over the top of her shower cubicle door.

Daisy looked at herself in the mirror. Standing there with Millie's towel in her hand she felt a bit like a bathroom attendant.

"How long was your journey?"

"About an hour and a half from London," said Daisy.

"Are you nervous, Daisy?"

"Erm…"

Millie's head poked out above the shower door.

"Don't worry, we're all new too!" she said, "we have been here a week, mind. Seems like a lifetime already though we haven't actually had any lessons yet! The first week was all about the school code and getting settling in. You'll get into the swing of things."

Millie's head disappeared again.

"YOU ON SCHOLARSHIP?"

"Yes."

The head reappeared. This time it was covered in shampoo and soap.

"Same as the rest of us, then. Apparently 88ers are traditionally 'sponsos' as the snots call us."

Daisy wasn't sure what a 'sponso' or a 'snot' was and wasn't sure she wanted to.

"I'm a sponso," continued Millie happily, "sure I'm a bit plummy, good background as the snots say, all that rubbish but..."

She paused to wipe the soap out of her eyes and leaned closer.

"...damned parents are hippies," she said, "hopeless."

Then she was gone again.

Millie took Daisy on a quick tour to show her some of the school grounds. Millie talked enthusiastically and was funny and friendly. Her granddad had worked in the City of London and left her parents "pockets of cash" in his will. Her parents, the hippies, bought a farm and moved the family out to the country. They intended to grow strawberries but didn't know the first thing about farming and the fields soon became rocky grasslands. Millie didn't mind because she loved nature and animals, though she did get the mickey taken out of her when she went to junior school in her wellies.

Daisy told Millie about her family and life in South London. She explained that she had learnt everything she could at junior school and had dreaded going to Degham. She told Millie the story of how she had met Roni, applied for the entrance exam and passed.

"That's wonderful, Daisy. I'm so glad you're here! I was worried what the last 88er was going to be like but I think you'll do."

Daisy laughed.

Whilst the school had seemed delicately laid out from the Honour House balcony Daisy was surprised at how quickly she became lost on the ground. Millie moved along the paths and through vine strung archways with excitement and ease and Daisy had to struggle to keep up with her.

"...and coming up is the main picnic area where apparently in the summer they have barbecues and teas and even some lessons out on the lawn...," Millie called over her shoulder, stepping across one of the small bridges over a stream.

They came to a large green area decorated with pools and finely trimmed trees. Even though it was turning into autumn Daisy was amazed that she couldn't see a single leaf on the lawn. In fact, ever blade of grass looked like it had been cut by hand and she felt guilty walking on it. Around the green, small groups of girls lay with their heads in books or sharing gossip. They seemed less scary than earlier. A couple of them even turned to smile. Next to the green was the restaurant and through its large glass windows Daisy could see cooks and dinner ladies clattering about preparing food.

"And over on the left is the school maze!" said Millie walking off again.

"I think I'm having trouble taking it all in," said Daisy.

Millie stopped and turned with a smile.

"Well, I guess it is a lot. It's only your first day. Shall we go back to the dorm?"

Daisy nodded.

By the time they got to the top of the eighth floor of Honour House again Daisy was exhausted. She'd been laughing with Millie all the way back. Climbing the stairs they pretended they were old women, staggered out onto the balcony and collapsed onto the stone.

"Oh dearie me!" said Millie,clutching her chest, "I think my old heart's about to give out!"

"Fetch the doctor!" said Daisy, giggling and rolling onto her back.

A frowning face popped into Daisy's view.

"'Who are you?"

The girl's hair - which was as black as the thick mascara around her eyes - hung in pigtails that swung like curtain tassels above Daisy's face.

"This, Layla, is the last of the 88ers," said Millie sitting up, "but she likes to be called Daisy."

Daisy brushed herself down. She held out her hand to shake. Layla looked at it, still frowning.

"What's that for?"

"It's...it's nothing," said Daisy pulling her hand away.

"Just ignore Layla, Daisy, she likes to be difficult," said a dark skinned girl dressed in shorts and a tee shirt who had just walked out onto the balcony.

"You better watch what you say," Layla muttered, "I know where you live!"

"Of course you do! Unfortunately it's in the bed opposite yours!" said the other girl.

She turned to Daisy.

"Hi, Daisy, I'm Marsha."

Marsha smiled, took a seat in one of the chairs and opened a book on crime mysteries. Layla tutted and walked over to the railings of the balcony. Daisy wasn't sure about Layla. She wondered what it would be like spending the next year in the same room as her.

"Well, this is all very nice," said Millie, "and now that you've met Layla and Marsha, let's see who else is around."

The Dorm was full of activity. Three girls were charging about, emptying exercise journals and books out of their satchels and pulling clothes out of drawers and wardrobes. They were all singing along loudly to the tinny screech of a pop song on someone's phone. They had even dumped books and clothes on Daisy's bed. Millie turned off the phone, put her hands on Daisy's shoulders and held her out in the middle of the room.

"Everyone...EVERYONE!!!"

The blathering and movement stopped and the three girls in the room turned to look at Daisy.

"Everyone, the 88ers are complete!" said Millie, "Let me introduce you to our final Dormie, Miss Daisy....Daisy...er..."

"Cooper," Daisy finished.

"Hello Daisy Cooper!" the three girls called back.

The dorm door slammed as Layla came in and jumped on her bed. Unlike the family pictures the others had, Layla's wardrobe was decorated with pictures of wolves. There was a picture of her on the bedside table howling up at the moon. Millie turned Daisy around and pointed her at Layla.

"There, you can see the one and only Layla who you've already met."

Layla smiled and then, remembering herself, quickly turned it into a frown.

"The empty bed next to hers is Marsha's who you met outside, of course."

Millie spun Daisy around to face the other three girls. On the first bed knelt a well built girl with short blonde hair who, to Daisy's horror, seemed to be pulling apart an oily bicycle chain on her duvet.

"Introductions!" said Millie.

"I'm Tina," said the girl with the bike chain, holding her hand out.

There was oil on her fingers. Not wanting to make a bad first impression, Daisy shook it and smiled.

"Next!"

Laying on the bed next to Tina, sucking her thumb and twirling her ponytail was a girl even smaller than Daisy. The girl popped her thumb out and sat up.

"You a Londoner?"

Daisy nodded.

"What's your manor?"

"What's my..."

"Where's your 'hood?"

"My..."

"Bleedin' 'ell, girl. Where you from?"

"Oh, South London."

The girl raised her face and looked at Daisy carefully. Then with a slow nod of approval, she put her thumb back in her mouth and carried on twirling her hair.

"Don't mind Tracy. She thinks because she's on a sports scholarship that she can pretend not to be a lady."

The girl who had just spoken was standing with her back to Daisy, combing her long brown hair in the mirror. She held a hand out over her shoulder. Daisy reached up and the girl took the tips of Daisy's fingers, shaking them gently.

"Penelope, darling but you can call me Penny. Nice to meet. What are those on your feet?"

Daisy looked down.

"Plimsolls."

"Are you a gymnast too?" asked Penny.

Daisy shook her head.

"I can do a forward roll," she said.

"Oh, OK." said Penny.

"And then there's just our last member," said Millie turning Daisy to face the empty bed opposite hers.

On cue, the door to the dorm opened behind them.

"NO FREAKING WAY!"

Daisy recognised the voice before she even turned round.

"Brodie!"

"DAISY!"

Brodie ran across the room and gave Daisy a hug.

"I KNEW you'd do it, D.C.!" said Brodie.

"Same here! I mean, with you. Getting in, that is!" said Daisy.

"And we're both 88ers! How awesome is that???" said Brodie.

"A bunch of awesome!" said Daisy.

They jumped up and down excitedly.

"Well, I guess they know each other already," said Millie.

CHAPTER FIVE - HIDE & SEEK

After washing and changing clothes Daisy made her way down the stairs with the rest of the 88ers to go to dinner. The courtyard was full of girls walking towards the restaurant. They seemed to have come from all over England and places further still. There were girls in casual clothes like Daisy's, some in formal skirts and blouses with their hair tied back neatly and girls in expensive looking designer clothes. Penelope seemed to be looking at these the most.

"There's so many of them," said Daisy.

"There's so many of *us*," said Brodie, correcting her.

The dining hall was laid out in eight rows of eight tables, one table per dorm. The 88er's table was made of dark oak and laid out beautifully. There were two vases of lilies at either end, large baskets of fresh bread all the way along and a big bowl of fruit in the centre. Daisy sat opposite Brodie. There was a delicately folded napkin with the word "Honour" embroidered on it between her knife and fork. Following Penny's example, she flapped the napkin open and lay it across her lap. Millie reached over and pulled out a slice of sesame bread.

"Come on, Daisy, dig in. We're at the end of the dining rota so it'll be a good ten minutes before we get soup."

As they sat munching on bread and waited their turn Millie explained how the dining rota worked. The restaurant, under the watchful eye of the Head Cook, Mrs Lynch, used a finely tuned system that enabled them to feed the 600 plus pupils three times a day without a single mouth going hungry. A long line of cooks in starched white tunics washed and peeled and cooked and baked throughout the day preparing food. The pupils themselves did the serving and each house took it in turns on a weekly basis. This week it was Bravery House's turn and they were required to wear their uniforms whilst serving. Daisy watched as they lined up along the great food counter picking up the plates from the cooks and carrying them over to the tables. It was all very well organised. Eventually it was Honour's turn to get their food. A dark haired first year girl put down a bowl of hot bean soup in front of Daisy.

"I see you girls are up to full numbers now," said the girl.

Millie nodded and waved at Daisy, quickly trying to swallow her bread.

"This is the wonderful Daisy Cooper from London," she said, " Daisy, this is…"

"Annabel Speck," said the girl.

Daisy smiled at her. Annabel didn't smile back.

"Are you another sponso?" asked Annabel.

"I guess so," said Daisy.

"I'll keep my eye on you, then," said Annabel and walked away.

"That was rude!" said Tracy.

Daisy shrugged and picked up her spoon.

"You can't expect everyone in a school to like you," she said.

She watched as Annabel went over to the far side of the restaurant where she spoke with Eleanore, Dorothy and Olga - the girls who had pushed her into the mosaic pit at the Roman Villa. They looked over at her and frowned.

After a dinner of shepherds pie followed by blueberries and chocolate ice cream Daisy was feeling slightly stuffed. She followed the 88ers out to the green and lay down in the soft autumn sun. Millie had run off to Hockey practice which Daisy thought couldn't be a good idea on a full stomach. Layla was listening to loud music through her headphones while the others sat in a circle talking about classes and other girls. Daisy closed her eyes, listening to them. She was beginning to feel more comfortable. After all, the others had only been at Darlington a week and they fit in perfectly fine.

"So what's your story then, Daisy?"

Daisy opened an eye. Marsha was looking at her. The other girls stopped chatting and looked at her too.

"In what way?" said Daisy.

Marsha shrugged.

"What did they give you the scholarship for?"

"Well, I..."

Daisy paused. Of course, Daisy wanted to be a reporter - like the people who wrote for the newspapers her dad helped print - but she was too embarrassed to say. Marsha laughed.

"It's okay, Daisy. I'm here on a science scholarship. Criminology is my real interest - forensics - you know those guys who wear white suits and work out what happened at crime scenes? That's what I want to do. My Dad's a scientist, a marine biologist. Sometimes he takes me diving. You see the most amazing things underwater. Have you ever been diving?"

Daisy remembered swimming in the local pool. She'd never seen anything more amazing underwater than a mouldy plaster.

"No," she said.

"Well, you should come."

"Really?"

"Sure. Why not? I'm sure Dad won't mind. Millie's already insisted on coming."

"I'd love to!"

Marsha nudged Tina.

"Come on then, Tina. Your turn."

"Engineering scholarship - building stuff. Engines, cars, anything big and dangerous. The more explosions the better."

"You're such a tomboy, Tina," muttered Penelope, "one day I'm going to pin you down and give you a makeover."

Tracy, sucking her thumb, giggled loudly.

"That's a laugh, Penny," she said, "you'd never pin her down. You might break a fingernail."

"Tracy, please don't speak to me with your mouth full," said Penny.

Brodie's head snapped up from her laptop.

"Come on, gals, play nicely."

Tracy sucked noisily on her thumb. Penelope rolled her eyes.

"That's disgusting Tracy, not to mention childish."

Tracy jumped up from the grass and knocked Penny over, waving her soggy thumb in her face.

"THIS DISGUSTING NOW, PEN?"

"Get off me! Get off, you peasant!"

Brodie stood up.

"HEY!"

The girls stopped wrestling. Layla opened an eye and looked over. Brodie was furious.

"Come on girls! You're supposed to be *English*. You know, good manners and all that?"

Tracy jumped off Penny who quickly pulled a mirror from her pocket to check her hair.

"I gotta go, anyway," said Tracy, "I've got gymnastics practice."

With that, she flipped backwards and disappeared across the lawn in a series of hand springs.

Two hours later they were still relaxing on the grass when Tracy and Millie returned from the sports block. Layla had taken off her headphones and joined the group.

"I don't think I'll ever get used to this school," said Daisy, "It's so huge."

"Nonsense!" said Millie, "You'll be used to it before you know it."

"Only after I've got lost about a million times!"

"Well, why don't you get lost deliberately?" said Millie.

"What do you mean?"

"We could play Hide & Seek. That would be a great way for you to find your way around. Who's up for it!"

The 88ers with the exception of Penny loved the idea. Millie volunteered to go first and started counting to forty while the others ran off to hide. Brodie took Daisy's hand and dragged her to a shed behind the kitchens. They slid between the sticky wall of the shed and the outside of the kitchen block.

"Are you sure this is a good idea?" Daisy asked, feeling a little trapped.

"It's perfect. They always check the shed, but never behind it."

They stood in silence listening to the sound of Millie's far off laughter as she found the others.

"What's up with Tracy and Penelope?" asked Daisy.

"They've been like that since the first day."

"What do you mean?"

"Penelope's a Prom Queen but she's insecure and Tracy is completely happy who she is. Therefore they don't like each other."

"Are Penny's family posh?"

Brodie shook her head.

"I doubt Penelope is from a posh family or she wouldn't be here on scholarship, unless they're hippies like Millie's parents. She'd be lording it up with the other snots."

Daisy felt uncomfortable talking about the other girls. Brodie sensed it.

"Look, I think we should all get along," whispered Brodie, "It's going to be hard enough without getting into fights with the people in your own dorm. We should stick together."

Suddenly Millie burst around the edge of the hut.

"Found you!!!"

A couple of rounds of Hide & Seek later and it was Daisy's turn to be the Finder. The courtyard was getting dark and a lot of the girls from other dorms had left. After counting to forty Daisy crept across the green looking for movement and listening carefully for whispers. She tried the shed again but no one was there. She tried the large clump of trees to the south of the green. There were a couple of girls sat in the branches swinging their legs but neither of them were 88ers. Edging round the bushes, checking in the obvious places, Daisy made her way further out. Round the back of the dining hall Daisy found Tracy squatting in the bottom of a large packing box by the bins.

"Found you!"

"Nightmare!" said Tracy.

Having caught one of the 88ers Daisy became more confident. In the changing areas of the outdoor pool she found both Marsha and Brodie. They fell on the floor in a fit of giggles as Daisy opened the door. Walking across one of the ornamental bridges Daisy heard tinny music coming from underneath. She stuck her head over the side and saw Layla listening to music through her headphones. Spotting Daisy, Layla rolled her eyes and pretended to choke, falling back against the muddy bank. The next place Daisy tried was the big laundry room behind the kitchens. It was full of piles of dirty washing with lots of cupboards and hidey holes under the long counters. A great place for someone to hide. Apparently Penny had thought so too except she hadn't anticipated the washing room being quite so dirty and smelly. As Daisy checked the second cupboard Penelope couldn't take it anymore and crawled out from behind a tumble dryer. She brushed herself down and sighed.

"Okay. That's me done, Daisy. Who's left?"

The school bells started ringing lights out. The 88ers who had been found made their way back to the dorm. Daisy tried the courtyard. In one corner, behind a few of the teacher's cars was the green school bus. Daisy crept along, peering through its windows when she heard a sudden scrabble underneath. She ducked down and spotted Tina lying wedged between the wheels.

"FOUND YOU!"

That left just Millie.

"Millie!"

There was no answer.

"Don't worry about Millie, she's so enthusiastic she's probably hiding in Scotland," said Tina.

Daisy was worried, though. It was getting quite cold and dark. The prefects were making their rounds between the dorm houses, the beams from their torches bouncing across the courtyard.

"You go back, Tina," said Daisy, "I'll quickly check back on the green and make sure she's not there."

Daisy walked along the path towards the green. She kept seeing shadows in the bushes and thinking it was Millie but it was just her eyes playing tricks on her. When she reached the green it was deserted. Turning back, she noticed the path to the school maze. That's where Millie had to be. It would be the sort of thing she would find exciting - hiding in a maze.

The entrance to the maze was a narrow path of gravel that crept between high bushes and curved out of sight. Next to the entrance was a large wooden board with a map of the maze from above on it. Daisy looked at it and tried to memorise the right path to the centre.

Left, second right, left again...

If only she had some paper with her to write it down.

"Hang on, Daisy, this is crazy," she said to herself.

It would be mad enough to go into the maze during daylight without a map, let alone at night. She turned to walk back to the dorm when she spotted a flicker of light coming from inside the maze.

Well, I can take a quick look, she thought.

Following the flickering light, Daisy walked deeper and deeper into the maze. Ten minutes later she turned a corner and realised she was on a path she'd been down several times already.

It looks like I'm well and truly lost, she thought with a shiver.

Daisy wondered about calling for help but was worried the Prefects might report her. She wondered how cold it got at night in case she had to sleep there and as the light dimmed, it started to get very scary. Panicking, she ran round a corner straight into a statue - a large goddess with a ship in her hands - in one of the dead ends. Daisy stumbled backwards and fell over. She sat in the dark, not sure what to do, her heart pounding. Then she heard the voices. Still worried about Prefects Daisy crept behind the statue and spotted the flickering lights again through the hedge wall of the maze. She pulled down a branch and peered through into the centre of the maze.

The maze centre was a large rectangular courtyard with a stone pool at one end. In the pool stood another tall statue of a woman in a long flowing dress. The statue had a stone jug in one of her enormous hands out of which water poured. The other hand was raised above her head holding an orb. Around her stone feet swam orange and white Koi carp, glistening in the moonlight. Near the pool were two rows of figures wearing long hooded purple gowns and carrying torches. It was the flickering light of the torches that Daisy had spotted. Between the two rows a long black and white checkered rug ran from the base of the fountain to the entrance of the courtyard. Daisy could see a young girl standing at the entrance. It was Annabel Speck, the girl who had served her soup at dinner. Annabel was blindfolded and her arms were held on each side by two robed figures.

"WHO DARES ENTER OUR SANCTUARY?"

Daisy jumped, worried that she had been spotted. The female voice was harsh and raspy.

"WHO DARES ENTER THE SANCTUARY OF THE SISTERS OF THE BLACK NIGHT?"

The voice came from a tall figure standing in front of the pool. Unlike the others, her robe was deep black. She was holding a large silver sword in outstretched hands.

"It is I, Annabel Speck, Great Sister," said Annabel, her voice stumbling over her words with fear.

"THEN STEP FORWARD, ANNABEL SPECK, THAT WE MIGHT JUDGE YOUR WORTHINESS," boomed the Great Sister.

The two people holding Annabel shuffled her forward across the rug.

After a couple of steps a figure from each of the rows either side stepped into Annabel's path and placed their hands on her shoulders.

"We say she should not pass!" they cried in unison, "not until she has told us what brings her to this place!"

"I come seeking truth!" said Annabel.

The figures stepped out of the way and Annabel was moved forward a few feet again before her path was blocked by two more.

"And why should we grant you access to our secrets!" said the second pair.

"My mother's sister and my grandmother were Sisters of the Black Night before me!" said Annabel.

The path cleared and Annabel was moved forward until, once more, they were stopped.

"And what will you grant us in exchange for this knowledge?" the final figures asked.

"I grant you my life and my loyalty!" called out Annabel.

After what seemed like a long pause to Daisy and must have felt like forever for Annabel, the final two figures stepped aside. Annabel was shuffled in front of the Great Sister who pointed the sword at Annabel's chest. Moonlight slithered along the sharp edge of the blade.

"ARE YOU PREPARED FOR YOUR LIFE TO COME SECOND TO OUR GREAT CAUSE?" growled the Great Sister.

"Yes," said Annabel.

"ARE YOU PREPARED TO DO OUR BIDDING WITHOUT QUESTION AND WITHOUT CONCERN FOR YOUR OWN SAFETY?"

"Yes," said Annabel.

"ON PAIN OF DEATH?"

Annabel didn't answer. The sword blade rose from her chest and the tip settled under her chin.

"ON PAIN OF DEATH??" repeated the black figure.

"Yes!" said Annabel, her voice cracking.

The two rows of figures began to hum a long low note that made Daisy shiver. The Great Sister rose her sword slowly, tracing its sharp point over Annabel's lips and the tip of her nose. The humming became louder. A couple of birds fluttered out of the bushes into the night. With a quick flick of her wrists, the Great Sister swung the sword up high towards the full moon. Annabel fell back onto the rug. The humming stopped. Daisy put her hand to her mouth, terrified. Had they just killed Annabel? After a moment though, Annabel got shakily to her feet. The blindfold she had been wearing, now sliced in two by the sword's blade, fell to her feet. One of the figures approached Annabel from behind and wrapped her body in a purple robe. The Great Sister held out her hands to Annabel.

"WELCOME TO THE SISTERS OF THE BLACK NIGHT."

The ceremony now seemed to be over. The group huddled around Annabel and Daisy could no longer hear what was being said. She folded her arms tight around her chest for warmth and leant back against the statue. She knew that eventually they all had to leave the maze so she waited patiently for them to go. After a while they began filing past and Daisy, keeping a safe distance, followed them to the exit.

"WHERE ON EARTH HAVE YOU BEEN?"

The 88ers sat up in bed looking at Daisy with cross, worried expressions on their faces. Daisy wasn't sure what to say. She wasn't even sure what to make of what she'd seen in the maze. She was also very, very tired and decided to wait till morning to tell them. Apologising she stumbled across the dorm. Brodie bounced over and gave her a hug.

"Don't worry, D.C., everyone gets lost on their first day," she said.

"Where were you hiding Millie?" asked Daisy.

"Oh, I came back and hid here. It was getting cold. Next time we stick to Scrabble. No one gets lost with Scrabble. Most of the time."

Everyone giggled and the mood lightened. Daisy changed into her pyjamas and got into bed. She looked up at the glow stars on the ceiling above her head.

"Good night mum," she whispered, like she always did, and drifted off to sleep.

CHAPTER SIX - FIRST LESSONS

The loud sound of the bells ringing woke Daisy. Before she opened her eyes she could hear the other 88ers murmuring and complaining.

"Can you believe it?" muttered Marsha, "Bells at dawn every morning."

Marsha was exaggerating. It wasn't quite dawn but it certainly felt early. Daisy slouched out of bed and pushed her feet into her slippers. Rubbing her eyes she walked out onto the dorm balcony with Marsha, Millie and Brodie. The bells were ringing from the tower of every dorm building.

"We've got this thing in the States called alarm clocks," said Brodie, "they have snooze buttons."

Daisy's mind was elsewhere. She was thinking about what she had seen in the maze the night before. She'd also realised that it was her first proper school day at Darlington School for Girls.

Daisy picked up a plate of scrambled eggs and boiled tomatoes from the canteen and sat down with the 88ers. Rules stated that every girl had to show up for breakfast in full school uniform and it was obvious by the dishevelled ties, the wrongly buttoned blouses and the twisted skirts that quite a few of the girls were just as sleepy as Daisy felt. A few of the sixth form girls - dressed perfectly of course - moved down the breakfast tables tidying uniforms. Daisy felt a pair of hands come around her neck.

"Here, Daisy, let me help you there."

Daisy looked up. It was Roni. Roni gave her a wink.

"I knew I'd see you here, sweetie."

"Hi Roni! I'm sorry, I'm not used to wearing a tie," said Daisy.

"Don't worry, it will be second nature to you before you know it. Have you got your curriculum?"

Daisy reached into her pocket and pulled out the timetable with her lessons on it and handed it over.

"Oh, good for you! You've got Miss Kapoor for Maths first thing," said Roni.

She finished off Daisy's tie with a neat pull and tapped her on the shoulder.

"Miss Kapoor's a riot. You'll get on fine."

Daisy turned to say thank you but Roni had already moved down the line.

"Now, does anyone know why a metre is a metre?"

Miss Kapoor was a young Asian lady with spiky hair and large expressive eyes. She stood in front of the blackboard looking at the class. The maths room was an old study in the main building. Instead of the desks Daisy was used to there were long benches laid out in rows that rose up towards the back. The 88ers were split into two groups for some of their lessons. Daisy, Brodie, Millie and Marsha shared the same timetable and they were sat at a bench half way down.

"Anyone know the answer?" asked Miss Kapoor.

Daisy remembered something her Dad had told her about measurements once. She wanted to answer but was also afraid of making a fool of herself if she got it wrong. The rest of the class was silent.

"Miss Cooper, it looks like if you don't say anything your head will explode," said Miss Kapoor.

"It's just…" said Daisy.

"Raise your hand."

Daisy raised her hand.

"That's better, Miss Cooper. It might seem a bit stuffy but if everyone started blurting answers at me, I'd be deaf in a week. Now, do you think you have the answer?"

Miss Kapoor gave Daisy a warm smile.

"Well," said Daisy, "Isn't there a metre long metal rod locked in a vault somewhere and all the measurements are taken from that, Miss?"

"It's true that the people who decided what a metre should be created a template from which all others would be measured but why did they chose a metre to be the length it is and not any other length?"

Daisy thought about it. She tried to recall what her dad had said.

"Isn't it that if you had a piece of string that went from the South to the North pole and you cut it into a million pieces, each piece would be a metre long? So it's like based on the size of the earth, I guess."

It was a bit of rambled answer.

"Very descriptive, Miss Cooper, but you'd need to cut your string into twenty million pieces if you wanted them to be a metre long each. A metre is roughly one twenty millionth of the distance from pole to pole," said Miss Kapoor.

Daisy blushed with pride. She hoped Miss Kapoor would ask her about the boiling point of water as well.

"Okay, girls. The reason I am asking you this is because I want you to understand that maths is a language. A very accurate one, of course, but still a language. Even our most basic measurements like the metre are invented. We use these measurements to do amazing things like travel to the moon but I want you to try and remember that if even our most basic measurements are not set in stone, you should not just accept everything you are told. That is not the Darlington way. Now, this term we're going to be focusing on statistics and probabilities..."

There were a few groans from girls in the class. Miss Kapoor smiled and pressed a button on her desk. The top flipped around to reveal a roulette wheel.

"...And to do that," continued Miss Kapoor taking out stacks of coins and piling them on the table, "I'm going to teach you how to bet on odds."

Miss Kapoor picked up a stack of cards and shuffled them in her hands expertly.

Wow, thought Daisy.

"How was Maths?" asked Penny.

The girls were sitting on the restaurant green eating lunch and enjoying the autumn sun.

"It was cool. We learn how to play Poker," said Daisy.

"I don't think my dad would approve!" said Millie.

"I think I owe Miss Kapoor a thousand bucks," muttered Brodie.

"Geography was a bit weird too," said Tina, "We had a Japanese tea ceremony."

"What's a Japanese tea ceremony?" asked Daisy.

"Long!" said Penny frowning into her salad, "You'll find out."

The geography wing of the school sat in a block by itself behind the sports ground. It was an unusual circular building made of lots of small rooms joined by a long corridor that ran around the outside. Mrs Briskett, the geography teacher, was a tall woman in a long green dress with equally long white hair. As Mrs Briskett led the girls down the corridor Daisy noticed that the door to each room had a map of a different country fixed to it. Miss Briskett stopped outside a door with the Japanese flag on it.

"Now, before we enter you will need to know a thing or two about tea ceremony etiquette. You will also need to be dressed appropriately," she said.

Suddenly a couple of Japanese ladies dressed in silk robes appeared behind them. With polite bows, they took each girl by the arm and lead them into a small side room. Daisy was made to take off her plimsolls before entering and told to kneel on the matted floor. Once they were all inside, a wide paper door slid open and another group of Japanese ladies entered carrying fine silk robes. There was one for each of the girls. Getting dressed was tricky. First, there was a floppy white shirt which they fitted over Daisy's school shirt.

"This is called your juban, or under-kimono," said Mrs Briskett.

Before Daisy got used to wearing the juban, she was being wrapped in a bright green robe. She rubbed her fingers on it. It felt very expensive.

"…And this is your kimono, a traditional Japanese garment for ladies. The word 'kimono' literally means 'thing to wear'. A kimono is often made up of twelve separate pieces and many elements about the kimono tell other people about the wearer."

Brodie waggled her arms in the long sleeves. They flapped over her fingers.

"What's the deal with the wizard sleeves?" she asked.

"Traditionally, the length of the sleeves of the kimono tell people about the age of the wearer," replied Mrs Briskett, "the shorter the sleeve, the older the wearer."

Once dressed the girls were led to the edge of the matt where they knelt in a line. The silk felt lovely and smooth but the big belt around Daisy's waist - called the date-jime - made it a little hard to breathe. Daisy peeked down the line. The girls were all in various colours so that together they looked like a rainbow. Mrs Briskett, now dressed herself in a bright blue kimono, knelt in front of them.

"Okay girls, before we enter the tea ceremony room you need to understand a few of the rules. You will wait on the bench outside until you are invited in. When you go in, there will be a small stone basin for you to wash your hands and rinse your mouths in. This is to purify you for the tea ceremony ritual."

Daisy scrunched her toes together. They had given her weird socks to wear which had a split between her toes like flip flops. It was itchy. It was lovely to be dressed up but Daisy was having trouble keeping up with the instructions. She didn't realise having a cup of tea could be so complicated. Everything meant something - every arm movement, every sip of tea, even how you held the bowl that the tea was kept in. By the time they were taken from the bench to the tea room there were butterflies in her stomach. Once inside, however, it all seemed much calmer. They were led to a small shrine with flowers on it which they bowed in front of before kneeling at a long table. Daisy thought of the coffee table in her living room at home, the one her dad rested his feet on while watching the football. This table didn't look like anyone had ever rested their feet on it. An old Japanese lady with very short sleeves crept in carrying a tray. Daisy felt the urge to get up and help her but she wasn't supposed to move. The lady set the tray down in front of them and carefully arranged the teapot, bowl and utensils. She then started a small fire in a charcoal burner under the pot and cleaned the utensils with a cloth.

"This better be one great cup of tea," whispered Brodie out of the side of her mouth.

Daisy bit her lip to stop herself giggling.

The bowl of tea was handed to them one at a time. They had to bow to the host and admire the patterns on the bowl before taking a sip and handing it back. After that they were given delicate little cakes made of fruit and sugar. Daisy had to stop herself from wiping her sticky fingers on her kimono out of habit. Finally they were each given an individual bowl of tea to drink from and were shown all the items that were used to make the tea which looked very old and expensive.

Changed back into their blazers and shoes and walking out into the courtyard they let out a sigh of relief.

"Aaah," said Brodie, "that was painful."

"I thought it was more interesting than learning names of places," said Martha.

"When am I ever going to need to know what to do at a Japanese tea ceremony?" wailed Brodie.

"I liked the cakes," said Millie.

"I liked the kimono," replied Daisy.

"You looked like one of the cakes in your kimono," said Brodie, laughing.

The girls hooked arms and wandered over to the restaurant.

"Not more tea!"

Brodie put her head in her hands. It was afternoon tea in the restaurant. They were sat outside at a table on the green.

"I'd give my right arm for a cappuccino!" she mumbled.

The other girls were munching on scones and watching the other girls go by.

"I think the tea ceremony's done something to my brain," said Millie.

"I know what you mean," said Daisy.

Since they'd come out, she'd felt strangely awake and had noticed little details around her more.

"Maybe the point of it is not about tea at all. Maybe it's just about making you slow down and notice things more," said Marsha.

Brodie leant over, picked up the tea pot and gave Marsha a bow before filling her cup, pretending to be the old tea lady. Daisy looked around and spotted Annabel sat in the shade by the entrance to the school library. She was sat talking to Olga and Dorothy. Maybe they were Sisters of the Black Night too. Daisy pulled her journal out of her satchel, turned to a new page and wrote 'S.B.N.' at the top. Underneath she wrote 'Annabel' then beneath that 'Olga and Dorothy'. She felt a little excited. Wanting to tell the others, she turned back to the table where Marsha and Brodie were bowing to each other with hands clasped and laughing. Maybe now wasn't the time to mention things. Maybe she'd do a little more investigating first.

After afternoon tea they had a free period and Daisy went with Millie to the library to look up information on Japan for their private study assignment. The library was huge and made of many tall rooms. There was a map just inside the entrance showing where the room for each subject was.

They like their maps at Darlington, thought Daisy.

"Where's the librarian?" she asked Millie.

"I don't think they have one of those," whispered Millie, balancing her satchel under her chin and pulling out her course reading list.

"So how do we find the books we need?" asked Daisy.

"I guess we have to look for them."

They wandered through a doorway into the History hall. Daisy had never seen so many books in one place, let alone on just one subject. The shelves were stacked so high that there were three separate walkways joined by spiral staircases. The middle of the hall was filled with tables where girls sat in silent study under the orange glow of brass desk lamps.

"Come on, Daisy," said Millie, pulling Daisy through into the Geography hall.

The Geography hall was as big, if not bigger, than the History hall. Daisy spotted Marsha and Brodie up on one of the high walkways and climbed a rickety staircase to join them.

"This stuff is so interesting," whispered Marsha as Daisy approached with Millie.

She was sat cross-legged on the floor with a pile of books open in front of her. Daisy recognised a map of Japan on one of the pages. Another page showed a Japanese woman dressed similar to the old tea lady with the parts of her clothing clearly labelled. Another had bright pictures of sushi.

"Did you know sushi was made to look so pretty because there wasn't much food to go around?" asked Martha.

"Man, I could do with some sushi right now," said Brodie.

She had her laptop open on her knees, fingers clicking away at the keys.

"What are you going to do your assignment on?" asked Martha.

Daisy frowned. She didn't really know.

"I'm not sure. How did you find the books you needed? This place is huge."

"They've got an online guide," said Brodie, "Type the subject you need to find and it'll tell you where the books are."

"Oh, and if you can't look online?" asked Daisy, suddenly realising that not having a laptop might be a problem.

"You can use my laptop if you like," said Brodie, "Or there's the old card system down there."

Daisy looked to where Brodie was pointing. There were a couple of long wooden filing cabinets between the study tables.

"Everything's numbered," said Brodie, "but, I'd really, really suggest you use my laptop."

"Thanks," said Daisy.

She looked down at the cabinets. The laptop would be easier but she couldn't always rely on Brodie being around.

"I think I'll see how I get on with the cabinets," she said.

The cabinets contained lots of square drawers, one for each letter of the alphabet. Daisy reached over to pull out the drawer marked with the letter 'J' for Japan when she saw that someone had left the 'H' drawer open. She started to close it when she noticed the title of one the cards sticking out of the others as if someone had just put it back. The name caught her attention.

HIDDEN HISTORY OF DARLINGTON SCHOOL by S. Darlington

Daisy took the card out. It was very tattered and a lot older than the rest of the cards in the drawer. She knew she was supposed to be looking for information on Japan but it wouldn't hurt to spend a few minutes looking for the Darlington book. It might explain what she saw in the maze. She jotted down the shelf and book number before putting the card back and shutting the drawer quickly. The shelf number indicated that the book was back through in the History hall. Daisy looked up at the 88ers. They were busy studying, heads stuck in books. She walked through to the History room and climbed the staircase, feeling a bit like an adventurer. She counted along the numbers on the book spines until she was in the right place. The book was missing.

"What are you looking for?"

Daisy looked up to see Annabel staring at her. There was an old book sticking out of her satchel. Daisy could just make out the word 'Darlington' written on it. Standing beside Annabel was Olga and

Dorothy.

"Erm, is this where the Japanese books are kept?" asked Daisy

Annabel frowned at her.

"You know it's not," said Annabel, "This is the History hall. What are you doing over here?"

"My mistake," said Daisy.

She smiled and walked away quickly.

After dinner the 88ers were on the balcony looking out over the courtyard. The moon was coming up over the distant hills and it was getting chilly so they'd brought their blankets and sat huddled beneath them in the chairs. While Marsha and Millie swapped stories of their day with Penny and Tracy, Brodie opened a box of homemade brownies sent by her mum and handed them out. Daisy and Tina talked.

"I'm feeling homesick," said Tina, "I miss my brothers."

"I miss my brothers, too," said Daisy, quite surprised that she meant it.

"Do you want to send them an email?" asked Brodie.

Daisy shook her head. She thought it might make her feel even more homesick.

"Come on, girls. I must be the furthest from home and you don't see me pouting. Turn those frowns upside down," said Brodie, giving a cheesy grin.

Daisy laughed.

"Let's make a deal," said Brodie, "Lets promise each other that while we are here, we will be our own family."

"I'm in!" said Millie.

"Aight!" said Tracy.

"Deal!" said Marsha.

Tina and Penelope nodded.

"Daisy?" asked Brodie.

"Of course!" smiled Daisy.

"My only family are the wolves," said Layla, standing at the balcony and staring up at the full moon.

The others looked at her, slightly worried.

"I'm joking," she said and rolled her eyes.

The girls laughed and walked over to look at the moon with her.

"I do like wolves, though," Layla said.

"So lets be a wolf family!" said Millie and howled at the moon,

"Aroooooooo!"

The rest of them joined in, howling and laughing up at the sky. Out of the corner of her eye Daisy caught a glimpse of torch light moving through the pathways of the school maze down below.

CHAPTER SEVEN - THE MAGAZINE

The next morning after breakfast Daisy popped her essay on Japan into Mrs Briskett's cubby hole outside the Teachers' study. It didn't need to be finished for a week but Daisy thought it best to get it done while everything was fresh in her mind. Today was Daisy's first English lesson. Afterwards, in the afternoon she had P.E. At St Margarets, P.E. meant an hour or two of getting shins whacked with hockey sticks, cricket bats and whatever else the bigger kids could find. In Daisy's Darlington timetable, it said that this term her P.E. class would focus on fencing. Fencing! Now, that was something Daisy could look forward to.

As she was passing the school foyer with Brodie on the way to English, Daisy spotted Annabel standing in the doorway talking to Olga and Dorothy.

"Brodie, can I tell you something in secret?" she asked.

"Of course you can, D.C.," said Brodie, "Scouts honour."

"Have you noticed that some of the girls in the school belong to certain groups?"

"Hell yeah, you can't get away from cliques. Back home we have the nerds, the jocks, the emos, the preppies."

" Well, yes," replied Daisy, "But I mean something more than that, like some of them belong to a secret club."

"You're beginning to sound like mad cousin Howard. He wore a tin foil hat to stop the aliens reading his brain."

"What if I told you I saw something very odd on the night we were playing hide & seek?"

Brodie stopped, suddenly interested.

"Intriguing. Tell me more."

Daisy gathered her thoughts. She didn't want to sound like mad cousin Howard, whoever he was.

"How about I show you instead? After dinner tonight?"

"Cool."

Daisy and Brodie followed the signs to the English rooms and soon found themselves on a cobbled road behind the library that took them through an orchard of apple trees. As it was autumn the trees were quite bare but one or two reluctant apples hung shrivelled to the branches. At the end of the cobbled road they came to a courtyard in the middle of a group of large farm cottages. Outside the largest, they spotted Millie and Marsha.

"It's like my home!" chirped Millie giving them a wave.

The 88ers followed the other girls through the door of a cottage into a room with a low ceiling and wide black beams. A couple of fires roared and spat in hearths. There were no desks but lots of comfy armchairs with a small table next to each of them. In one of the biggest chairs, surrounded by a pile of books, sat the only male teacher Daisy had seen at Darlington. He was also one of the biggest. Mr Calloway peered at them over a great bulge of a belly that threatened to burst the buttons on his silk waistcoat. He had a cup of tea in a saucer perched on top of his stomach and his eyes twinkled at them through half moon glasses.

"Take a seat, girls. Don't be shy."

Daisy, Brodie, Millie and Marsha found chairs next to a window and collapsed into their soft cushions. Daisy's legs sprung into the air as she fell back into the seat and Millie had to pull her up with a giggle.

"Oh yes, they can do that," said Mr Calloway, "I'm sure we've still got one or two girls stuck down the sides of the armchairs living off biscuit crumbs."

Once the other girls had taken their places Mr Calloway put his tea down carefully on a pile of books and straightened up.

"Now, as I'm sure you've already noticed we take a slightly different approach to learning at Darlington. Whilst it's all very good to have facts and figures and knowing which king killed another king, we think it's much more valuable not to tell you what to do and what to think but to bring out the best in you. There is no greater teacher in life than life itself."

One or two of the girls in the room raised their eyebrows.

"Some of you may have come here from strict schools with rows of single desks and teachers who barked at you all day. You may even feel that what we do here isn't 'proper' learning. You may worry that your parents are wasting huge amounts of money on a lot of messing about. Well, apart from the fact that you only have to look at any number of old Darlington Girls to see how successful the education here can be, I'd suggest you put any doubts you may have on hold for at least a term and see the result for yourself in your own progress. I think you'll be pleasantly surprised."

Mr Calloway shuffled his body in the chair and stamped his left foot on the floor a couple of times.

"Damn pins and needles! I get it in my feet when I sit still too long."

The 88ers tried not to giggle as he fidgeted in his chair. Eventually he seemed to find peace and got back to his speech.

"So, for English classes, how do we do things differently? After all, English is English, isn't it?"

Daisy opened her mouth to speak. The old urge to jump in when she got excited by questions. She bit her lip but it was too late. Mr Calloway had spotted her.

"Do you have something to say, young…"

"Daisy. Daisy Cooper, sir."

"Oh, please don't call me 'sir', Daisy. I've not been knighted yet. Call me Mr Calloway. What was your question?"

"Well, Mr Calloway, you said English is English but isn't it the case that English is really made up of lots of other languages? There's French, Latin, Greek…."

"American," added Brodie.

"You're quite right, Daisy, but we don't want to get too ahead of ourselves. For now, lets assume that when we talk about English we mean the language most often used in this country. Of course that's difficult to pin down, itself. Some people think English is about strict rules and grammar and exact meanings but English changes all the time. It always has. The only rule is whether it helps you communicate effectively or not."

One of the girls, a bright blonde girl called Helen Marks put her hand up.

"But what about learning the rules? What about knowing how it all works before you, well, start messing about with it."

"True, true," nodded Mr Calloway,"which is why you are going to need to do a lot of reading for this class. I won't be telling you what to read but I expect you to do plenty of it. You may have noticed that we have a rather splendid library. You'll find all the books you can imagine there. The chairs aren't quite as comfy but you are free to visit the English cottages and read here when they are free."

There was a knock at the door behind them. Daisy turned to see Roni standing in the doorway.

"Sorry to interrupt, girls," said Roni giving Daisy a little smile,"Mr Calloway, did you get a chance to ask for volunteers?"

"Oh!" said Mr Calloway fidgeting again, "Do beg my pardon, dear. I forgot."

He cleared his throat.

"Every year we look for a couple of volunteers from each English class to spend their lessons working on the school magazine instead. Is anyone interested?"

Whilst the other girls sank back in their comfy armchairs, Daisy and Brodie gave each other a look of wide-eyed excitement and shot their hands up into the air.

"Perilous!"

It wasn't what Daisy had imagined. After the amazing parts of the school they had seen so far, the school magazine room was a bit of a disappointment. It had certainly seen better days. The room was a large basement under the school entrance foyer. To get there Daisy and Brodie had to walk down a rickety staircase on the edge of the courtyard and through a rusty windowless door. Ugly yellow striplights covered in dust flickered over oily and very noisy machinery. The printing press itself was a huge contraption that looked old and dangerous. Nothing like the printing presses Daisy's dad had shown her at his work. There were a few girls, dressed unflatteringly in rubber aprons and wellies, working on it. A couple were loading large spools of paper into the side while two more stood on a thin walkway above the back of the machine pouring gloopy ink through funnels. Another two girls stood either side of the juddering conveyor belt at the front unloading the printed magazines and putting them into boxes.

"It's not exactly glamorous," said Roni with a shrug, "but it does have character."

Roni led Daisy and Brodie tip-toeing through black splodges of ink spills to the editor's office which was a small glass box room up a short flight of stairs at the back of the basement. As they stepped inside and closed the door behind them Daisy felt relief at being away from the noisy clank-clanking of the machinery. Roni fixed them some tea as she told them about the school magazine.

"I know it may not look so great but the school magazine is important. Very important. You see, we don't write articles on sports days or jumble sales or school plays - unless they're very good, of course - and we don't just write for Darlington Girls. How many readers do you think the school magazine has?" she asked.

Brodie did the maths out loud.

"There's about 800 pupils, 20 teachers...janitors, nurses, cooks, cleaners. About a thousand?"

A thousand seemed like an awful lot of magazines to print to Daisy. Roni smirked and waved her hand a few times in the air, indicating that the number was higher.

"Two thousand?" asked Brodie.

Roni laughed.

"The last edition of the magazine had a circulation of twenty thousand."

"Twenty thousand!" said Daisy spluttering her tea.

"No offence," said Brodie, "but how do you FIND twenty thousand people who want to read a school paper?"

Roni frowned.

"Have neither of you read a copy?"

Daisy felt her cheeks go red with embarrassment. Here she was volunteering to help on a magazine she hadn't even read. Roni flicked through a filing cabinet and pulled out a few copies for them. Despite the way the machinery looked, the magazine was pretty impressive - like a proper newspaper that Daisy's dad might read with his bacon and eggs. It had several black and white photographs on the front page with the title written in proud letters across the top. Daisy read it out loud.

"International Schoolgirl."

"Exactly, Daisy Cooper," said Roni, "International Schoolgirl. The widest read magazine in the world that nobody has actually heard of. At the moment we send it out to over fifty different countries. The twenty thousand readers we have are made up of former pupils from Darlington and other girl schools around the globe and a lot of them hold some of the most important jobs in the world, too. If you see a high powered woman in the news, you can be pretty sure she reads International Schoolgirl."

Daisy looked at the stories, flicking through the pages. Roni was right. There weren't any stories about jumble sales or sports days. The front page was a story about pirates in Thailand. Inside there was an article on shrinking ice bergs in Antarctica and another on protecting gorillas in Africa. Turning the pages, Daisy spotted Roni's picture under an article on a Paris fashion show. The title with the picture read 'Veronica Taylor, International Schoolgirl'.

"Wow," Said Daisy.

"Cool," Said Brodie.

"You wrote this?" asked Daisy.

"Of course!" said Roni, "All the articles are written by schoolgirls."

"Darlington schoolgirls?"

"Well, not just Darlington. It all started here but it's grown over time. There are other schools across the country and several in many other places as well. There are lots of reporters - or International Schoolgirls as we call them - dotted about all over the planet."

"Can we get to write for it?" asked Daisy, her heart pounding.

Writing for a magazine like this would be her dream come true. Roni frowned and sat down.

"I'm sorry, Sweetie. It doesn't quite work like that. Remember, the magazine has been going as long as the school which is nearly two hundred years old. We've got this charter that was written when the school was set up. We only take on new International Schoolgirls once a year to take over from the ones who are leaving. We have a competition which should be happening in a few months time. That gives us enough time for the character of the girls who are applying to be assessed."

"How do you get into the competition?" asked Daisy.

"Well, you have to be put forward by the housemistress. Sweetie, if you want to go for it, work hard and try to live by the school virtues. Remember this, though, it won't be easy. Out of all the girls who compete only eight of them get through. Last year we had nearly 200 girls in the competition."

Daisy felt crushed. Here she was so close to her dream and it seems impossibly out of her reach. She'd felt like the smart one in St. Margaret's but at Darlington she was surrounded by girls just as smart as her. How could she compete with that? Roni sensed how she was feeling and gave her a friendly hug.

"Listen, Daisy. If you want it badly enough, I know you'll do it. You have a spark in you. I wouldn't have recommended you to apply to the school if I didn't."

"What about me?" said Brodie, "Am I wallpaper over here?"

"I'm sure you're lovely too, sweetie," said Roni.

The door opened and a tall blonde haired girl came in. Daisy recognised her as Anita Walker, the girl who had asked her questions at the interview for the school. On her lapel she was wearing the badge with the intertwined letter 'I' and 'S' which Daisy now realised stood for International Schoolgirl. She also realised that all the pins in the map in the foyer had to show where International Schoolgirls were reporting from.

"Sounds like the gears have gone again," Anita said to Roni.

She spotted Daisy and Brodie staring at her.

"Hello? Who have we got here?"

"Daisy Cooper and Brodie Newman meet Anita Walker, the International Schoolgirl Editor."

Daisy and Brodie stood up.

"Nice to meet you!" they both said in unison, a little awestruck after Roni's magazine history lesson.

"Oh, don't be so formal," chuckled Anita, "Now, you're both here to help I assume?"

Daisy waggled her fingers in the oversized rubber gloves and giggled at Brodie who was wafting her apron around her knees.

"This thing weighs a ton."

"And smells funny," added Daisy.

The girls picked up two large pots of sticky black ink and climbed the rickety ladder on the side of the printing press carefully. After an hour of loading buckets of ink into the press while the machine noisily cranked out magazines Daisy and Brodie were exhausted, not to mention ink stained. They slouched over to the lockers and packed up their aprons, rubber gloves and boots and tried their best to scrub away the ink from their faces in an enormous stained sink. Feeling about as far from being a glamorous reporter as it was possible to feel, Daisy frowned across at the great machine. Above the noise she could hear a loud tapping and turned to see Anita beckoning her over from the window of the editorial office.

"I'm glad you girls didn't just run off without letting us thank you," said Anita.

"My pleasure," said Brodie collapsing into a chair.

Anita Walker pointed to her desk where various pieces of paper were laid out on a grid.

"This is the layout for the front page of the next issue. Tell me what you think."

Daisy and Brodie looked at it. There was a large picture of an elephant in the middle of it.

"Do elephants sell newspapers?" asked Brodie.

"It's about the ivory trade. Elephants are being hunted for the ivory in their tusks. Oh dear, is that not clear?" asked Anita.

There was a headline that read DARK TIMES FOR THE AFRICAN ELEPHANT.

"I think it needs to be clearer, if you don't mind me saying so," said Daisy, "It doesn't tell what the story's about really."

Roni walked over and looked over Daisy's shoulder.

"She has a point, Anita," she said.

Anita pulled the headline away.

"How about FRESH RISE IN IVORY TRADE THREATENS AFRICAN ELEPHANT?"

Daisy frowned. It was a bit boring. She cast her mind over what she knew about elephants. They were intelligent. They had knees (was that really useful?). They were pregnant for a long time and lived for ages. Then Daisy remembered something she had seen in a film about elephant graveyards. The story was that elephants when they got old returned to the same place to die.

"How about RETURN TO THE ELEPHANT GRAVEYARD?" she said.

Annabel and Roni exchanged looks.

"I like it," said Anita, "lets go with that."

Daisy's heart leapt. First day on the magazine and she'd managed to get some words into print after all, even if there were only five of them.

"Brodie, do you have anything you'd like to add?"

Brodie was looking out of the window at the clunking machinery. She looked deep in thought.

"Not yet," she said.

Daisy was in high spirits as they walked to the sports hall. Roni had joined them and chatted with Daisy, asking her how she was finding the first few days. Daisy was more interested in International Schoolgirl.

"So the magazine sent you to Paris?" she asked.

"Yes. I've been there several times now, in fact."

"For the magazine?"

"Yes. My first job was in Paris."

"It must have been amazing!" said Daisy.

"It was," replied Roni, "if slightly terrifying. I was barely older than you are now."

They crossed a bridge leading to the back of the school and dodged a group of girls who bustled past them towards another class.

"Anita must have been impressed with you today to take your suggestion on board," Roni said, "she's not really supposed to. We don't have much of a choice in who gets to work for the paper, unfortunately."

Roni looked unhappy. Daisy got the feeling there was something she wasn't telling her.

"So who's decision is it?" she asked.

"Aah! Here we are!" said Roni.

In front of them were the large sports halls.

"I'll say goodbye, Sweetie," said Roni, "I'm off to Norway tomorrow. They'll soon enter their winter which means no daylight for weeks. Can you imagine that?"

Roni gave Daisy and Brodie a hug and walked away.

"Blimey, can you imagine how exciting her life is, Brodie?… Brodie?"

"Hmm?" said Brodie.

"Are you okay? You've been awfully quiet," said Daisy.

"Oh, I'm fine. Just thinking about some ideas. Some things that might help make the magazine run a little better."

CHAPTER EIGHT - EN GARDE!

The sport halls were three large brick hangars that sat next to each other with an athletics field to one side and a large running track around them like a big   red moat. The first building contained an olympic sized swimming pool complete with high diving boards. The middle building was a big echoing space with lots of different coloured lines along its polished floor to mark out courts for indoor tennis, badminton, netball and football. The third building housed the changing rooms and a couple of smaller rooms full of gymnastic equipment, trampolines and stranger equipment that Daisy could make head nor tail of. Dorm girls shared sports lessons together so when Daisy and Brodie got to the changing rooms all of the other 88ers were there changed into their gym tops and shorts. There were quite a few others, some that Daisy recognised including Annabel. Daisy hoped she wouldn't have to speak to her. Once changed, they walked out into a large matted room with big wide windows in the roof. Daisy watched as a couple of older girls wheeled out two large racks - one lined with protective clothing and strange head masks and the other lined with dangerous looking swords. All of the girls got quite excited and began chatting loudly, a few miming pretend sword fights.

"Man, this is so cool!" said Brodie, "Proper medieval stuff."

"I think those swords look quite pointy and dangerous," replied Millie, not quite as happy.

There was a loud swooshing sound and the girls went silent. Walking across the mats towards them was a tall woman fully dressed in the clothing and mask. As she walked she swished her thin blade in front of her, switching it between her hands expertly. Halfway across the room she crouched down and made a few quick thrusting movements that showed years of practice and incredible speed. All the girls watched silently, suddenly aware that this was probably a class where it wouldn't be a good idea to misbehave. The woman stopped in front of them and took off her mask, shaking out a long mane of dark golden hair. She had piercing blue eyes that shone against her porcelain white skin. Daisy recognised her as Madame Didier, the French lady from the entrance exams.

"Good afternoon class," she said, her words wrapped in a soft French accent, "I am Madame Didier and I will be your fencing teacher for the next semester. Have any of you any experience with fencing before?"

A few hands went up, one of them Tracy's.

"*Bon*. You girls form a group by the equipment stands and get changed. The rest of you please take a seat on the benches and we will go through rules. I suggest you listen well because I will not be 'appy if I have to explain to your parents why you lost an eye."

"She's quite scary," said Daisy.

"I'm a little worried she might actually murder me with one of those swords," said Millie.

"At least we'll have a story for the school paper," joked Brodie.

The three of them started to giggle but stopped quickly when Madame Didier spun around and glared at them with her intense blue eyes.

The girls were put into pairs. Daisy teamed up with Millie while Marsha worked with Brodie. The masks were hot and smelly and Daisy felt like a bee looking through the thick metal gauze. The tunics covered everything down to their legs but were heavy and stiff and difficult to move in. Madame Didier told them that the swords were actually called foils. The blades were long thin metal rods tipped with a hard rubber ball that still looked like it could hurt pretty badly. Daisy glanced over at Tracy who was fencing in the group of experienced girls. Tracy moved quickly against her opponent, one of the older girls, looking like a pirate in an old film as she knocked the blade out of her way. The end of the foils were hooked up to electronic boxes. Tracy landed the rubber tip of her foil against the heart spot on the other girl's tunic and the box made a loud buzzing sound to indicate a hit.

"Remind me not to make Tracy angry when she's got a knife in her hand at dinner," said Daisy to Millie.

"Come on, you two. Quit chatting and start practising!" said the girl who was tutoring their beginner group, "You Two. Stand up."

Daisy couldn't see the girl's face underneath the mask but the voice was familiar. She got to her feet with Millie and lifted up her foil. Putting her free arm behind her back she squatted down into her knees as they had been told. It felt awkward and a little silly. Millie did the same and tapped Daisy's blade with hers.

"En Garde!" shouted the masked tutor.

Daisy and Millie moved back and forth, not really sure what they were doing.

"Pathetic!" bellowed the tutor, "Attack! Parry! Thrust!"

Daisy felt embarrassed. Tracy had made it seem so easy. It wasn't.

"You're useless!" shouted the tutor, "Neither of you would last five seconds in a proper duel!"

Daisy's embarrassment was turning to anger. She swung her foil sideways and Millie's blade slide down it. Daisy felt a hard prod against her chest quickly followed by a loud buzz.

"I won! I got a point!" cried Millie.

"You're dead, Daisy," said the tutor, "That was a direct hit to your heart."

The group tutor walked over, snatched Millie's blade from her hand and took her place in front of Daisy.

"Now, follow my instructions and we'll see if there's any life left in you. En garde!"

Before Daisy even had time to think there was another prod against her chest, this time much harder, and another loud buzz.

"Another killer blow! Come on Daisy," taunted the tutor, "Prove to me that you deserve to wear the Darlington colours because all I'm seeing is an untalented oik who got lucky!"

Daisy felt a sharp prod in her stomach. Even through the protective tunic it still hurt, pushing her backwards.

"Stop it!" said Daisy.

She looked over to Madame Didier but she was busy with the

experienced group. Daisy lowered her foil and held up her free hand to signal for her tutor to stop.

"Well that's a surprise," said the tutor sarcastically, "Who'd have thought you'd give up so quickly."

The tutor swirled the tip of her blade around Daisy's foil and with a quick flick of her wrist, knocked it out of her hand and onto the floor.

"Just what I'd expect from a loser."

The tutor lunged forwards again and pocked the blade into Daisy's side. Daisy felt a sudden hot pain. The end of the blade had gone between the tunic and her trousers, piercing the skin in her left hip. Daisy let out a cry and fell to the mat, clutching her side. Madame Didier came running over.

"Eleanore!"

The tutor pulled off her mask revealing herself to indeed be Eleanore.

"I'm sorry, Madam Didier," said Eleanore, "I was teaching her how to parry and the blade must have slipped through her clothing. She couldn't have put her tunic on properly."

"You did it deliberately!" gasped Daisy.

She put her hand down to her hip. It felt warm and sticky. Daisy lifted her fingers to her face and was shocked to see blood on them.

"Don't worry, Daisy, it's nasty, but not fatal."

It was Millie. She was knelt at Daisy's side, a first aid box open in front of her, rapidly unravelling a roll of gauze.

"Keep your fingers pressed here."

Millie took Daisy's hand and put it on the gauze.

"I don't care if she bleeds to death!"

Daisy looked up to see the gym doors swing shut with a bang as Eleanore stomped off. Miss Didier came over and knelt down.

"It doesn't look that bad to me. You'll have a bruise and be a bit stiff. A rest will make it fine. Good that your friend is quick with the first aid."

"Salvation Army training!" said Millie, happily.

Daisy woke up in the nurse's room to see Brodie, Millie and the rest of the 88ers sat around her bed. They all cheered as she opened her eyes and sat up. Marsha plonked a bowl of grapes onto the bed table.

"For you, Daisy Cooper, for fighting so perilously in a duel," she said.

"Against the evil Eleanore Lyles," said Millie.

"Queen of the Brat Pack," said Brodie.

"Voted most likely to be pushed off a tall building," added Tracy.

The girls laughed.

"Seriously, though," said Penny, "Why's she got such a big problem with you?"

Daisy shrugged, wincing slightly.

"I don't think she has a reason. I think she's just mental."

"Maybe I should challenge her to a duel," said Tracy, angrily.

"We could always poison her tea," said Layla, scratching at her black nail polish.

"I'm sure the school will deal with her," said Daisy.

She was surprised to see the other girls staring at her with raised eyebrows.

"What?" said Daisy.

The girls explained to Daisy about Eleanore Lyles and her "special" relationship with the school. It turned out Eleanore Lyles was the daughter of Lydia Lyles - the shark faced lady from the school board who had been on Daisy's interview panel. The Lyles family donated large amounts of money to the school each year and because of that the teachers tended to turn a blind eye to the bad behaviour of Eleanore and her friends Olga and Dorothy or as Brodie called them, the Brat Pack.

"You're crazy," said Brodie.

Daisy and her were sitting on the balcony. The other 88ers were having a pillow fight in the dorm and their giggles were drifting through the open door. Daisy was missing home. She'd spoken to dad and her brothers on the phone and told them everything was okay but her confidence was shaken.

"But I'm not like the other girls here," said Daisy, "Maybe Eleanore is right, maybe I am an oik."

"Daisy Cooper, pull yourself together," snapped Brodie, angrily.

Daisy was taken aback.

"Why are you going to let that nasty Brat Pack get to you like this?" said Brodie.

"But it's easy for you to say, Brodie. Your parents are rich," muttered Daisy.

"Have you MET my parents? Having money doesn't make you a better person. Millie's parents have no money but she's ace. Roni probably has money AND posh parents and you couldn't ask for a nicer gal. It's all about who you are as a person. Don't you remember how you got in? You fought for it. You worked hard for everything you've got. They can't take that away from you and that's why Eleanore is crazy. That's why they're out to get you and the rest of us. They're scared because, secretly, they know that without their family sitting on the board of the school or paying for their posh clothes, they're nothing."

Daisy knew that Brodie was right. Still, she couldn't shake the way Eleanore and the others made her feel and knowing that only made her feel angry at herself.

"I wish you could see yourself as others see you, D.C.," said Brodie.

Brodie got up, gave Daisy a hug and walked off to the dorm. Daisy sat looking out at the glorious orange sunset over the roof of the school.

"She's right, you know."

Daisy jumped and looked round. Layla was stood in the shadows at the edge of the balcony.

"How long have you been there?"

"Long enough," said Layla with a shrug, "Pillow fights aren't really my thing. I've been watching you, Daisy Cooper."

Daisy wasn't quite sure how to take that.

"Erm, thanks?" she said.

"Oh, don't worry. I haven't been spying. Well, actually, I suppose I kind of have…"

Daisy wasn't sure she liked the idea of being spied on.

"I say 'spying'," said Layla, "but I suppose 'keeping an eye on' you would be closer to the truth. You remember the night we played Hide & Seek? I followed you. To the maze."

Layla stepped out of the shadows and sat down next to Daisy. She leant forward, narrowing her eyes.

"I saw them too," she whispered.

Daisy's heart jumped in her chest.

"I was beginning to think I'd imagined it," she said, "I was going to show Brodie before I get, well, kind of stabbed."

"When you got lost in the maze I was coming to get you when I saw them," continued Layla, "Do you know who they are?"

"Only Annabel but I think the Brat Pack are involved. Do you know who the others are?" Daisy asked.

Layla rolled her eyes.

"I have my suspicions. Whoever they are, they're up to no good."

"That's what I think, too," whispered Daisy, "Have you told the others?"

Layla shook her head.

"No point telling the others until we know more ourselves, even Brodie."

"But I have to tell Brodie," said Daisy.

"And get her into trouble?"

Daisy was unsure. She didn't want to keep things from Brodie but she also didn't want to get her into trouble. Layla leant in closer.

"How about we find out a little more and then, if you like, you can tell her. Are you feeling well enough for some spy work?"

For the next few days Daisy and Layla became a spy duo. The first thing Layla noticed was that Annabel was following Daisy. Daisy suspected it was because she'd been looking for the book on the Secret History of Darlington in the library. Between lessons, Layla followed Annabel, who was herself spying on Daisy. It was all a bit of a game and Daisy and Layla laughed about it in secret whispers over dinner. Brodie was a little put out about it and Daisy felt bad not saying anything but there really wasn't anything to tell. Not yet.

Daisy got to know Layla quite well. Her mum had a very important job for the government and travelled the world. Layla said that she didn't even know what her dad did as he'd had to sign a special secrets form with the Prime Minister. Layla had spent most of her time growing up in boarding schools because her parents were so busy. Layla could play the violin and the piano and spoke German, French and Spanish.

"I have an ear for language," she said to Daisy sitting on the lawn one afternoon, "It must rub off on me from all my mother's foreign visits."

Layla was also into spying big time. She said she'd got into the habit at her junior school when the other boarders had decided to treat her like a freak for dressing in black and having mysterious parents. She learnt to hide in the shadows to stay out of trouble and soon the other girls just ignored her.

"Did that upset you?" asked Daisy.

"At first," replied Layla with a shrug, "Then I started watching them and realised how silly all the stuff they thought important was."

Layla said that she had begun to spot secrets the girl boarders in her other schools hid from each other. They would be nice to each other's faces and then run each other down behind their backs. All of them were secretly afraid of anyone finding out their own little secrets. By being the outsider, the shadow in the corner, Layla was the only one who really knew what was going on. On the way to Maths one morning Layla pulled Daisy back from the other 88ers.

"There's something going on tonight," she whispered.

"What's happening?" asked Daisy.

Layla shrugged.

"I don't know exactly but I saw Annabel talking in the rose garden with Eleanore, Dorothy and Olga. I can lip read a little bit and I definitely saw Eleanore mention the word 'Maze'. They all looked at their watches so it must be happening tonight."

"Well, lets see what they're up to," said Daisy.

CHAPTER NINE - UNDESIRABLES

After dinner that evening Daisy decided to go to the library on her own to do some homework and write in her journal. She couldn't stop thinking about International Schoolgirl magazine. It was a lot of work keeping the old print press going and certainly not glamorous but part of her felt connected to something. Something she was destined for. Another part of her felt she shouldn't be going spying on the Sisters of the Black Night with Layla but she wanted to be a reporter and reporters investigated things that weren't right. After she had written down her thoughts in her journal she left the library and crossed the courtyard back to Honour House. On the way she noticed the doors to the main school foyer still open. Through them she could see the great map above the assembly hall doors. There was no one around. She stepped inside to take another look at it.

"The world is our school…"

She studied the map carefully, her eyes moving across the countries, counting the International Schoolgirl pins that covered the whole world.

"Quite impressive, really," said a voice.

Daisy jumped and turned to see a very old woman sat beside her in a wheelchair. The woman chuckled quietly to herself. Though she was very frail, almost ghostlike, there was a fiery twinkle of life in her eyes.

"Did I give you a start, dearie? I'm Hattie" said the woman extending her hand.

Daisy gave it a gentle shake. It felt even more boney than Miss Weaver's hand.

"Nice to meet you, Hattie. I'm Daisy Cooper."

Hattie pushed a button on her wheelchair and it rolled closer towards the map.

"It's amazing to think they're out there now, all over the planet, getting into goodness know's what kind of mischief. Are you one of them?" asked Hattie.

"One of who?" asked Daisy.

Hattie rolled her eyes.

"An International Schoolgirl, of course!"

"Oh, no!" said Daisy.

Hattie laughed. She looked Daisy up and down slowly which made Daisy feel quite self-conscious.

"Hmm," she said, "you might be one day. You look like you have the spirit. Hard to tell these days, though, what with my mind going almost as fast as my eyes."

"Are you visiting?" asked Daisy.

Hattie snorted.

"I LIVE here!" she said, "I've got a cottage by the duck lake. I feed them bread every morning."

Daisy hadn't seen a cottage on the school grounds. She was beginning to think that Hattie might be just the slightest bit mad.

"That's nice," she said.

Hattie snorted again, louder.

"NICE, she says! It's not nice, it's terrible! Who wants to spend their life feeding ducks!"

Hattie turned and looked up at the map.

"No, what you want, is to be OUT THERE - traveling, meeting fascinating people, making a difference. Do you want to make a difference, Daisy?"

"Absolutely!"

"Well...Your chance might come," said Hattie with a wink, "now, I've got to get back. There's wrestling on the telly."

Hattie turned her wheelchair round with great difficulty and moved it towards the steps to the courtyard.

"Let me help you," said Daisy running after her and taking hold of the back of the wheelchair.

"I'm not an invalid, dearie. Just because someone's in a wheelchair doesn't mean they need help all the time."

Hattie moved the chair forward to the first step and peered down.

"Well, okay. You can help. Just this once."

Daisy tipped the chair back gently and slowly bounced it down the steps.

"We really need to get a proper ramp. It's disgraceful!" tutted Hattie.

Daisy was quite surprised to see that there actually was a duck lake with a cottage next to it. It was in a clearing hidden behind a clump of trees on the far side of the school grounds. A small path just wide enough for the wheelchair snaked between the trees and led right up to the door. As they arrived the ducks at the edge of the lake started quacking hungrily as Hattie fished inside her jumper for a key on a piece of string. She put it into the lock and opened the door.

"Are you okay now?" asked Daisy, "Or do you need help with anything else?"

Hattie looked at Daisy with a sly grin.

"What are you like at making a pot of tea?"

"Go on, you bleeder!"

Hattie had pulled herself up into a threadbare armchair and was shouting at a couple of wrestlers on the television set in the tiny living room when Daisy came in with a tray of tea and biscuits. Without taking her eyes off the screen Hattie dropped six sugar cubes into her cup, stirred it and took a long, noisy slurp. Daisy sat down in the other tatty armchair. The cottage was small but cosy. The walls were lined with old books and photos of what looked like a younger version of Hattie. The photos showed places from all over the world. There were pictures of the Hattie lookalike shaking hands with important people. Daisy recognised Winston Churchill in one of them and John Lennon in another. Another one showed the young woman smiling from the cockpit of a plane.

"What did you used to do?" asked Daisy.

"I was a dinner lady," said Hattie, shaking her fist at the television.

"A dinner lady?"

"Yes. Does that make me less important to you?"

"Oh no! Not at all!" said Daisy, "It's just that you have all these pictures."

"That's my sister, Irene. Travelled all over, she did. Used to send me a picture wherever she went. Just to bloody rub it in, I reckon."

"She looks a lot like you," said Daisy.

"Not now she doesn't," said Hattie, "she's dead."

That was a bit of a shocking thing to say, thought Daisy. It was obvious Hattie must have still cared for her sister or she wouldn't have decorated her cottage with all the pictures.

"So does the school let you stay here because you worked at the school?" asked Daisy.

"You're full of questions, aren't you dearie? Are you sure you aren't a reporter?"

"I'd like to be," said Daisy, "one day, that is. I'm just interested in people."

Hattie turned away from the television and gave Daisy a big smile. The fierce twinkle was back in her eyes.

"People are brilliant, aren't they Daisy?"

Hattie said it like it was an exciting secret. Daisy nodded.

"The world would be a boring place without them," she said.

"Ha!" barked Hattie spluttering tea, "Too true!"

Eventually Hattie fell asleep. Daisy found a blanket and tucked it over her knees, turned off the television and crept out of the cottage. The ducks quacked at her as she wandered through the twilight back down the path towards the school courtyard.

It was dark as the 88ers sat on the balcony. While the others sat chatting, Layla leant over to Daisy.

"There are lights flickering in the maze," she whispered.

Daisy got up and stretched.

"I think I'm going to go back to the library to do a bit of last minute prep for tomorrow's lessons," she said, slipping on her plimsolls.

"Me too," said Layla.

Daisy tried to ignore Brodie's suspicious looks as they left.

Outside, moving along the edges of the dorm houses, Daisy and Layla made their way to the maze entrance. When they got there, sure enough, a faint glow of torch lights was just visible through the leafy walls of the maze.

"Stay behind me," said Layla, "I know the way."

With a quick check to make sure they weren't being followed the girls ducked inside. They crept quietly, not speaking. After a few turns in the maze Layla held her hand up, stopping Daisy in her tracks. She pointed ahead of them. Daisy looked over her shoulder and could see a couple of the Sisters of the Black Night walking up ahead. They were almost invisible in their dark robes. Daisy would have walked straight into the back of them if Layla hadn't stopped her. They waited as the two hooded figures turned the corner.

"One of them is Annabel," whispered Layla.

"How can you tell?" Daisy whispered back.

"She ties four bows in her shoe laces," said Layla creeping forward again.

She moved up to the corner, crouched low and ducked her head around to look at the path ahead.

"Coast is clear," she said.

Layla had discovered a hiding spot that was closer than the one Daisy had found before. It was in another of the alcoves with one of the scary looking statues. This statue was of a woman in a sea captain's hat looking up at the moon through a marble telescope. Daisy snuck behind it with Layla and peered through the bushes into the centre of the maze. The Sisters were knelt around a stone altar behind which stood the Great Sister in her jet black robe holding the ceremonial sword. With the exception of Annabel's tell-tale laces It was impossible to know who any of the others were but Daisy felt sure that the Brat Pack had to be there too. She also noticed that the Great Sister and a few of the others were a lot taller. They had to be adults. She leant forward, squinting in the darkness, trying to get a glimpse of one of the faces when she felt a hand slap her shoulder.

"Caught you!"

Daisy's heart leapt into her mouth. She turned to see Brodie smiling down at her. Layla grabbed Brodie and pulled her down behind the statue quickly.

"What are you gals doing?" whispered Brodie.

Daisy pointed through the leaves.

"Well, look at that," said Brodie, "Is this some kind of weird British thing?"

"We don't know what they're up to but we're trying to find out," said Daisy.

"And you thought you'd leave me out of it?" said Brodie.

Her voice showed she was obviously hurt.

"I'm really sorry, Brodie. I was going to tell you but I wanted to see them again for myself just to make sure."

Brodie shrugged.

"I'll forgive you," she said, "Just this once. It could make a good story for International Schoolgirl."

"Exactly," said Daisy.

The three girls watched as the Great Sister raised her sword towards the moon.

"OH GREAT MOON, OH WONDROUS EYE OF NIGHT, LOOK DOWN UPON US AND KEEP OUR SECRETS TIGHT!" bellowed the Great Sister.

"If she wants to keep her secrets tight," whispered Brodie, "It would probably be better if she didn't go around shouting about it."

The kneeling figures in front of the stone altar repeated the words back to the Great Sister as she pulled a velvet cloth away from a small stone pedestal in its centre. Something silver flickered on it.

"What's that?" said Brodie.

The Great Sister picked up the object which was hanging from a chain and held it above her head so that the moon light hit it. It was quite small but Daisy could just make out that it was a round pendant with what looked like an eye carved on it.

"SISTERS OF THE BLACK NIGHT, DO YOU SWEAR TO KEEP THE EYE CLEAR FROM IMPERFECTIONS?" rasped the Great Sister.

"WE DO!" intoned the kneeling figures.

"Is this magic?" asked Daisy.

Layla shook her head.

"Looks like nonsense to me," she said, "When my dad was around he used to do this kind of thing with his business partners. Before they all got drunk."

"DO YOU SWEAR TO ROOT OUT UNDESIRABLES LEST THEY STEER US OFF COURSE IN OUR GREAT SEARCH?"

"WE DO!"

Undesirables? thought Daisy. That's what Eleanore had called her back at the Roman villa when they had first met.

"WHAT WILL YOU DO TO ANYONE WHO GETS IN OUR WAY?"

"FEED THEM TO THE SHARKS!"

They certainly liked chanting. It didn't sound good though and Daisy was pretty certain that if Brodie, Layla and her weren't already on the undesirables list, they would be if they were caught. The Sisters got up and grouped together in a huddle. It was impossible to hear what they were saying. After a while they began to leave in pairs. Daisy, Layla and Brodie peeked out at them as they walked past the sea captain statue. When they had all left and the girls were quite sure they were alone, they slipped back out onto the path.

"Well, this has been fun," said Brodie starting to walk back to the entrance with Layla.

After a few steps they realised that Daisy wasn't following them. They turned. Daisy was smiling at them with a mischievous grin on her face.

"Let's take a quick look," she said.

When they entered the middle of the maze the air still smelt of smoke from the torches.

"What if they come back?" said Layla.

"We're not doing anything wrong," said Daisy, "we tell them we just went for a quiet stroll through the school maze."

"At night?"

"Look!"

Daisy walked over to the altar and pointed at the pedestal. Carved into it were the letters N, E, S and W.

"It's a compass," she said.

"Well, what does that mean? Oh, Daisy look!"

Brodie was pointing at Daisy's plimpsolls. There was a bright purple powder over the soles.

"What is all this stuff?"

Daisy tried brushing it off but it was stuck. She looked around. The dust lay in a big circle around the altar.

"They must have put that there to catch out anyone who stepped in it," said Brodie.

"Come on, we'd better leave!" said Layla, suddenly nervous.

Daisy and Brodie didn't argue with her.

CHAPTER TEN - PENGUINS AND ROCKETS

There was an announcement over the loudspeakers at breakfast saying that there was a special assembly. As she had missed the start of term it was the first time Daisy had been into the main hall and she was feeling a little anxious as she shuffled in with the other girls. The hall was lined on each side with large glass windows that revealed hidden gardens filled with an incredible selection of exotic plant life. Heavy, deep green curtains hung on either side of each window tied with gold rope.

Daisy and the rest of the 88ers took their seats with Honour House. Off to one side, separated from the rest of the hall, were two lines of benches. The girls sat on these, including Roni and Anita, were International Schoolgirls. Daisy was surprised to see that they weren't all sixth formers but a mix of ages from different years. One thing was certain, though. They looked like the smartest and coolest girls in the school. Some of them had sun tans and had obviously just got back from warm and exotic places. Daisy looked up at the big stage at the front of the hall. It looked like the stages she had seen on trips to the West End of London. An intricately carved stone arch stretched over a large black curtain in front of which was a long row of chairs and a big wooden lectern. When all the girls had taken their seats Anita Walker got to her feet and clapped her hands quickly three times. Instantly all the chatter in the hall fell silent.

"PLEASE STAND!"

Everyone shuffled to their feet and the teachers walked out onto the stage. Last to walk on was Mistress Aiken who stood in front of the lectern.

"PLEASE SIT!" she bellowed.

There was the sound of a few hundred chairs scraping as the girls sat.

"Good morning girls," said Mistress Aiken.

"Good Morning, Mistress Aiken," said everyone else.

"First of all, may I say I hope all you new girls are settling into Darlington. As I'm sure you are aware from your short time with us, this is a special school for some of the most gifted girls across the globe. It is not a place where you can coast through expecting to get a few good grades on your way to university. All our lessons here, as well as being of the highest educational standard, are designed to nurture each of the eight qualities that make up the Darlington Code. You are expected to be able to show a willingness to learn all these qualities and to demonstrate them in your treatment of the the staff and each other."

That's all well and good, thought Daisy, *but the rules don't seem to apply to some people.*

"Now, while we expect high spirits in the first years during their first few weeks there are certain things that will absolutely not be tolerated and any girl caught involved in these will face immediate expulsion. It is with great dismay that I must inform you that already two first years have been expelled for possessing alcohol and cigarettes on school grounds."

There was a ripple of gasps across the hall. Daisy looked around and spotted two empty chairs in the row of seats belonging to Charity House.

"It has also come to my attention that some girls have been creeping around the school after lights out."

Mistress Aiken glared across the room. Daisy was sure she was looking directly at her. She glanced down at her shoes. The purple dust from the maze was still there. She'd tried to scrub it off but there were still stubborn patches that refused to go away.

"Any girl found outside their dorm after lights out without sufficient reason will be punished. It is a privilege to be here. There are always plenty of other girls waiting to fill your shoes."

Daisy turned and gave Brodie and Layla a quick glance. They looked worried.

"Now that piece of unpleasantness is out of the way I'd like to bring your attention to our programme of school trips," said Mistress Aiken attempting a smile, "As you may know we organise trips once a month to places around the country. These are usually places of historical interest and all girls are welcome to put themselves forward but it is on a strict first come, first served basis..."

After the assembly they had biology for first period. Millie was beside herself with excitement. Daisy, however, couldn't stop thinking about Mistress Aiken's warning about creeping around after lights out. They were following the directions on the school map that pointed the way to the biology wing.

"It must be here somewhere" said Millie as they turned the far corner of the school maze.

"There's a sign!" said Brodie.

An old wooden arrow pointed through a dense thicket of fir trees.

"Menagerie," said Daisy reading the sign, "What's a menagerie?"

"It's a ZOO!" squealed Millie, right in Daisy's ear.

"The school has a zoo?" said Daisy.

The school did have a zoo. Walking through the fir trees the girls came upon a wide garden filled with bronze barred cages, high netted bird enclosures and pool areas filled with marine creatures.

"They must have every animal under the sun here!" said Daisy as they walked down a long stone path that weaved through the enclosures towards a large domed hall in the centre. There were camels, monkeys, horses, polar bears and many other creatures that Daisy couldn't even put a name to.

"So what do we do in biology?" asked Brodie as a zebra sneezed at her, "Put band aids on otters?"

"Pretty much, girls."

The 88ers looked up to see Doctor Penrose. She was wearing a khaki shirt, short trousers and enormous boots that were covered in muck and straw.

"I'm Doctor Penrose, your biology teacher," she said.

Dr Penrose took the girls through into the large hall. Inside there were rows of cages full of animals making various squawks, roars and moans that echoed in a cacophony of noise under the high glass domed ceiling.

"This hall is the animal hospital!" shouted Dr Penrose over the din, "One of main things we focus on here is treating injured animals and nursing them back to health. There's not a better way for a person to understand the diversity of life on this planet than to get stuck in and help it. Here, girl, take this!"

Daisy was shocked to discover that she had just been handed a baby penguin.

"I want a penguin!" said Millie.

Dr Penrose picked up a couple more from a pen and placed them into Millie and Brodie's hands. She led the girls through to the far side of the hall where it was a little quieter. A few rickety wooden seats were set out, each filled with a different schoolgirl, each holding a penguin. Daisy carefully took her seat as the penguin in her hands fidgeted and squeaked.

"First day is penguins!" Dr Penrose called over her shoulder as she walked to the front of the class, "Thanks to global warming their homeland has been melting and there wasn't enough room for these. Fortunately they were picked up by an Icelandic fishing ship. Penguins are hungry blighters. Eat lots of fish. Problem is that these ones are too young to eat on their own so you're going to have to feed them."

Dr Penrose pulled out several buckets that were overbrimming with chopped fish. It stank.

"Eeewwww!" said pretty much every girl in the class except Millie.

"Come on, come on," tutted Dr Penrose, "Don't be afraid to get your hands dirty!"

Millie was the first one up. She took a metal scoop from a pile, shovelled up a pile of fish meat from the bucket and fed it to the snapping penguin in her hands. Reluctantly the other girls got up and wandered over with their penguins.

"Good show girl!" said Dr Penrose, "Name?"

"Millie, Miss!"

"Millie, eh? Like animals, Millie?"

"Love them, Miss!"

"Not afraid to get your hands dirty are you, Millie?"

"No Miss!"

"Good show! We could do with some extra help around here. See me afterwards if you're interested."

"Yes, Miss!"

"Rather you than me," muttered Brodie, wrinkling her nose up as she fed a fish head to her penguin.

While they were feeding their penguins Dr Penrose told them about the history of the zoo. It had started fifty years ago when an injured heron was found in the courtyard by a couple of girls who nursed it back to health again. A few months afterwards, one of the International Schoolgirl reporters discovered a zebra who had been shot by poachers and had arranged for it to be flown back to the school to be taken care of in a makeshift enclosure in the school stables. The next one to join the family was an Orang-utan who had escaped from a travelling zoo. Within a couple of years more animals arrived and it was decided by the school that they needed somewhere fitting for the animals to be taken care of so they had built the menagerie. Dr Penrose was proud that since that time they had looked after almost every species on the planet. The goal was always to return the animals to their natural habitat but with so many International Reporters around the world coming across injured or endangered animals the zoo was pretty much full all of the time. The girls were told that the purpose of the biology classes was not just to teach them hands on about the animals but also to show them how to protect themselves against creatures that could often be quite dangerous.

"What's the most dangerous?" asked Daisy, giving her penguin another scoop of fish mush.

"Well, the big cats. We've only got one at the moment, a lion called Sankofa but he can be particularly troublesome. What makes it worse is he's very unhappy and doesn't understand that what we are doing is trying to help him. Apart from that, hippos, spiders, rhinos, tigers…well, they're all pretty dangerous, actually. Keep away from the school sewers. We lost a couple of freshwater sharks a few years ago. They're probably down there."

Daisy laughed. Dr Penrose didn't.

"Oh, I'm quite serious," said Dr Penrose.

The afternoon's lesson was a combination of physics and chemistry which meant Marsha and Tina were very happy. What made the rest of the 88ers happy was that they all shared it together. The 88ers followed the map to a hanger in a deserted concrete strip behind the sports fields where they were greeted by a white haired lady in a lab coat called Glenda Parsons who insisted that the girls call her by her first name. Inside the hanger it looked like the lair of a mad scientist. There was lots of buzzing equipment with dials and switches and strange electric devices which sent great sparks of purple electricity up to the high ceiling and made their hair stand on end. Glenda told them they were going to learn about the laws of physics.

"Boring," whispered Tracy in Daisy's ear.

"What's that, young girl?" said Glenda raising her plastic goggles, "Boring? It might look boring but without the laws of physics you wouldn't have all those fancy cars your parents drive you around in or those noisy gadgets you insist on talking to each other with."

"I think she means cell phones," said Brodie with a giggle.

Glenda gave a frown and pulled a sheet off of a large worktable. Tina and Martha gasped with delight. On the table were two boxes, one marked 'rockets' and the other 'explosives'.

"Okay, girls. Today's lesson is all about Newton's First Law of Motion, or if that sounds boring - today's lesson is all about firing rockets into the air and trying not to get blown up in the process."

By the end of the lesson Daisy felt wildly exhilarated. The fact that there was danger involved with the explosives made everyone forget everything else and pay extra attention. Glenda started the lesson by firing off a small rocket into the clouds and then told the class that they had to do the same. The girls had to work out calculations on paper to see how much explosive powder and how much fuel they needed to mix together so that their rockets would fire straight up and not at a crazy angle and crash through a classroom window somewhere. After all their calculations were checked, they were allowed to take their rockets outside and launch them. Glenda was eccentric but also had a very sharp mind. The minute a girl looked like she might be about to do something either dangerously stupid or stupidly dangerous, Glenda was beside them in a flash and pulling their hands away from danger. Daisy took pleasure in seeing how well Marsha and Tina worked together. Marsha calculated the amounts whilst Tina expertly poured the explosives and fuel carefully into the rocket's body. Their rocket flew higher than any other group and Glenda was very pleased, asking them if they'd like to help on some of her bigger rockets in their free time.

After dinner, Daisy was scraping her scraps into the bin when she overheard a couple of the dinner ladies talking.

"I haven't got time to take it. I need to prepare tomorrow's breakfast!" said a red faced cook.

"Well, I have a mountain of dishes here, I can't do it!" replied a thin lady wearing an apron dotted with stains.

There was a tray next to her with a dinner on it and a cup of cocoa that was getting cold.

"Can I help?" asked Daisy.

The two cooks looked at each other, a little surprised.

"Well, if you wouldn't mind. Do you know the cottage by the duck lake?"

Daisy smiled.

"Where Hattie lives? No problem. I'll take it."

"Well, thank you very much, Daisy Cooper!" said Hattie, "If you hadn't been so kind I'd probably have had to share stale bread with the ducks."

Daisy laughed. Hattie was sat in her wheelchair by the window in the living room of her cottage with a purple blanket over her knees enjoying her cocoa.

"Tell me about the pictures," said Daisy.

Hattie waved her hand dismissively.

"Pictures aren't worth a thing. Not really. People standing around smiling like twits. Memories are what count."

"What about your memories?" asked Daisy, "What was the school like when you came here?"

Hattie gave her a sly grin.

"It was exciting. So many possibilities. Like most good things though, after a while some people get involved for the wrong reasons and you get trouble. That's why it's good to have the Darlington Code. The Virtues. It helps keep students, teachers and the school on track. Like a compass. That's the idea, anyway."

"Well, I think it's a very good idea," said Daisy.

"It is," agreed Hattie, "when people stick to it."

Daisy thought about The Sisters of the Black Night. She wondered if Hattie knew about them. She wanted to ask but not in an outright way.

"So do you think there are people at the school who don't like the Code, who try and do things by their own rules?" she asked.

Hattie set down her cup of cocoa and wheeled her chair over to where Daisy was sitting.

"Well it sounds to me like you're investigating something."

Daisy blushed.

"My old teachers always said I couldn't keep myself out of trouble. It's not that I look for it. I can't help myself."

Hattie chuckled.

"That's because you're a born reporter, Daisy. If we didn't have good people looking out for trouble, goodness knows what mess we'd be in."

"But how do you know what you are doing is right?" asked Daisy.

"Well the Code will help you but you know what's right in your heart, Daisy. Trust in that. The minute you start playing the same games as wrong 'uns, you've lost."

"But what if the wrong 'uns win anyway?" asked Daisy.

Hattie chuckled.

"Well, that's why you have to have trust!" she said.

They sat in silence listening to the ducks outside.

CHAPTER ELEVEN - TROUBLE ON THE EAST TOWER

History classes took place in the main school building.

"It's this way," said Brodie spotting a brass plaque that pointed off down a corridor.

The number of classrooms and the noise of girls studying in them became less and less as they moved on. Soon they were walking down an empty passageway lined with dusty shelves. The only noise was the sound of their footsteps on the old wooden flooring.

"Are you sure this is the right way?" said Millie, "It seems awfully quiet."

They turned a corner and saw a great black door with iron locks on it. The other 88ers were stood outside. There were also girls from other dorms including Annabel who sneered at them. Daisy ignored her. In the middle of the door, slightly too high to see through, was a small porthole window and beneath it an old plaque that read 'Museum'. Under the plaque was a big metal ring.

"We tried knocking a few times but no one answered," said Marsha.

She lifted the ring and gave it another loud rat-a-tat-tat. There was no response.

"Wait a minute," said Daisy.

She stepped up and took a close look at the door knocker. It was held in place by a brass plate that had small circular scratches around it. Daisy lifted the ring and instead of knocking, gave it a twist. Sure enough the handle turned and from inside the door there was the sound of old gears turning.

"Whoa!"

Daisy turned to see Layla stumbling backwards as the wall she had been leaning against slid away to reveal a gloomy passageway. Daisy helped Layla to her feet.

"Are you hurt?"

"Only my pride!" said Layla, brushing dust off her skirt.

"GOOD MORNING GIRLS."

Daisy peered into the passageway which ended in an archway. Behind the archway there was nothing but dark shadows.

"Don't be afraid. Step forward!" said the unseen voice.

The girls stepped cautiously into the passageway.

"Come! Come! We haven't all day!" said the voice again, sounding irritated.

Daisy shrugged and walked through the archway. Immediately a long line of old hanging lamps flickered on one by one to reveal a large room filled with glass cabinets containing a whole manner of strange items. In front of them stood Mistress Aiken. She held a big wooden cane and was flexing it in her gloved hands like she was itching to use it.

"Come, Come, Girls! We've got a class to start!" said Mistress Aiken, marching off.

The girls had to run to keep up with her as she ducked and weaved between the exhibits.

"My name is Mistress Aiken. Not Mrs Aiken. Not Miss or Madame or any other name you should care to call me. You will address me as Mistress Aiken at all times or you will find yourself with a detention. As well as being the Deputy Head at Darlington and the Head of History, I am also the Curator of the museum you are currently walking through. It is my job to ensure that every girl here has a thorough knowledge of all our exhibits."

Mistress Aiken stopped suddenly and turned, causing the girls to pile into each other behind her.

"For instance," said Mistress Aiken, "Can anyone tell me about this?"

She slapped her cane loudly against the glass case of an exhibit to her left. It contained a stained white tunic with a big red cross on it. None of the girls had a clue. There was an embarrassed silence. Mistress Aiken sighed and rolled her bloodshot eyes.

"I can see I'm going to have to light a fire under you girls if you're to have any hope! This tunic belonged to Joan of Arc - a girl not much older than you who led the French armies against the British and helped them regain control of many cities in France. This tunic is the one she wore at the Battle of Patag. It was donated to the school by her descendants. Like everything else here it is one of a kind. Also like every museum piece it represents the core values of Darlington. Poor Joan was burned at the stake at the age of 19 for her beliefs. It would have been easy for her to get married and have children but in her brief life she put her own needs second to a cause greater than herself, showing grace, bravery and honour."

Daisy raised her hand to speak and as Mistress Aiken's eyes slowly turned to her, instantly regretted it.

"What," she said in a low voice.

"Can I ask a question, Mistress Aiken?" said Daisy.

"That was a question. Do you have another?"

"Erm, yes, Mistress Aiken."

"Spit it out then."

"Well, if Joan of Arc didn't have any children how did you get it from her descendants?"

Mistress Aiken glowered at her. Her fingers flexed the cane in her hands.

"I didn't say they were direct descendants. What's your name?"

"Daisy Cooper, Miss."

"MISS? What did I just tell you? Mistress Aiken is how I am to be addressed. Congratulations, Miss Cooper, you've just earned yourself your first detention from me. I very much doubt it will be your last."

Daisy was feeling hot and flustered for being told off as Mistress Aiken led them off again through the exhibits. The Deputy Head stopped here and there to point out individual items. Even though Mistress Aiken was a battle-axe the museum was fascinating. There was part of a chariot that had been ridden into battle by Queen Boudica nearly two thousand years ago and the mourning dress Queen Victoria had worn after her husband had died. There was Florence Nightingale's famous lamp and many, many other items. All of them were related to great women throughout history. Finally, after moving through several long rooms, they came to a bolted door. Mistress Aiken stopped and turned back to the girls, her beady eyes moving, unblinking, looking for troublemakers.

"As you can see our collection at Darlington is priceless which is why we keep it secret and safe. In your time here you will be expected to know every single piece and its history. It will be a lot of hard work but much more rewarding than reading facts and staring at grubby drawings in books."

Mistress Aiken slid aside a stone tile in the wall next to the old door. Behind it was a keypad into which she entered a four digit number. There was a series of beeps and clicks and finally the sound of a lock sliding away deep within the wall. She grabbed the metal ring in the door and gave it a turn. The door opened with a creak.

"Girls, move into the museum sanctum and take your seats around the outside. Complete silence at all times or I will be throwing out detentions like confetti at a wedding."

The girls filed through the door into a circular room lit by rows of candles stood in tall candlesticks. Daisy and the other 88ers shuffled round a row of old wooden benches and took their seats facing the centre of the room. There was nothing in the room except a large object in the centre of the circle covered with a dark purple velvet cloth.

"That cloth looks familiar," whispered Layla.

Daisy nodded, conscious not to make a sound. It did look familiar. It was the same fabric as the gowns the Sisters of the Black Night wore. Mistress Aiken pulled away the cloth. Every girl in the room let out a sigh of awe. Underneath the cloth was a large egg made of gold and precious stones that shone brightly in the flickering candlelight.

"This is Cleopatra's Egg, named after the last Pharaoh of Egypt. It is made of the finest gold, rubies and emeralds. The craftsmen who made it began work on it on the day of Cleopatra's birth and it was finally completed and presented to her on her twelfth birthday. Throughout her great reign it stood at the side of her throne and was never to be left without light shining on it. She had special servants called lightservers who's job was to keep it in the sun's rays during the day and the glow of candles at night. It is said that on the night before her empire fell to the Romans the lightservers were drugged and fell asleep, allowing the lights to go out and the Egg to fall into darkness. From that moment Cleopatra's reign was over. The Egg was kept secret throughout history until it was smuggled out of Egypt by pirates and finally ended up here. It was the museum's first exhibit so, in a way, everything else you see here started with it."

Daisy was so fascinated by the story she forgot about her detention. Afterwards Mistress Aiken grouped them into pairs and assigned them an exhibit to study. Daisy had teamed up with Marsha and been assigned exhibit number 322. They searched through the cabinets reading off the numbers until they found a large old motorcycle stood on a pedestal. Next to the exhibit there was a photograph of a woman sitting on it.

"It says she is an unknown courier messenger from world war two," said Daisy reading aloud the information plaque, "It says here she raced from Paris to Dunkirk with secret codes whilst being chased by Nazis! Afterwards, they never saw her again."

"Cool!" said Marsha.

Daisy couldn't help but think the woman in the picture looked a lot like the pictures of Hattie's sister.

"This really is not a good look on me," said Brodie.

They were working in the International Schoolgirl basement. Brodie's left forearm was covered in sticky ink. She brushed her hair out of her face and accidentally left a black smear across her forehead.

"Oh, drat!"

Daisy climbed down one of the ladders on the printer's side and dropped the empty ink cans onto the floor with a rattle. She picked up a couple of fresh tins and prized the lids off with a screwdriver. The machine gave a violent judder, let out a coughing sound and spat a cloud of paper across the room.

"Not again!" shouted Anita from her office.

She ran down the stairs and hit a big red button on the side of the machine. With a loud buzzing sound the print drums fell silent and the press let out a long hiss.

"This is really not good. Not good at all," said Anita, pacing back and forth.

"What's the problem?" asked Daisy.

"Well, as you may have noticed, Bertha's getting quite old now."

"You call your printing press Bertha?"

"All of our presses have had names since the magazine started. There was Hambel, Maude, Connie and Bertha. Bertha's the last one left."

"Can't you call an engineer to fix it?" asked Brodie.

"There's only one engineer who knows how and he's retired and lives in Scotland. Even if we could persuade him to come and fix Bertha it would take several days to get him here. We need to get this print run finished before then."

Daisy stared into the press. Now that she thought about it, it did kind of look like a Bertha.

"I might have an idea," she said.

Fifteen minutes later Anita, still worried, was staring down at a small pair of legs sticking out from underneath the press.

"Are you sure she knows what she's doing?" she asked Daisy nervously.

"If anyone knows how to fix it, she does," said Daisy, hoping she was right.

The legs slid out from beneath Bertha and Tina's inky black face smiled back at them. Putting a spanner under her arm, she held up a squashed metal pot.

"Here's your problem," she said, "All fixed now. Give her a go."

With fingers crossed Anita hit the big red button again. There were a couple of low metal grumbles. Bertha made a huge belching noise and spat out a long splutter of ink that caught Daisy right in the chest.

"Ewww!"

"Sorry about that," said Tina, "It's a bit like burping a baby."

She banged Bertha on the side with her wrench. With a sudden jolt the drums began spinning and the machine flew into action.

"Wow. She's much faster!" said Anita, watching the magazines flying off the runners.

"Go team 88!" said Brodie and gave Tina a high five.

Daisy removed the apron, goggles and wellies and saw that some of the the ink had managed to slip inside her gloves, turning her wrists and hands bright red. The sinks in the basement, being themselves clogged with ink, were out of order so she had to go to one of the bathrooms in the main building.

Daisy was scrubbing the ink off her fingers when she heard the the bathroom door being locked. She turned to see Annabel, Dorothy, Olga and Eleanore standing in front of it. There was a look of menace on their faces.

Oh, no.

Daisy looked around for an escape and spotted the window to the courtyard open. She leapt for the window sill but Olga and Dorothy were too fast. They pushed her hard against the sinks.

"Oh look, the oik is all dirty," said Eleanore, "You can take the girl out of the muck but you can't take the muck out of the girl."

"Let me go!" shouted Daisy.

Eleanore laughed.

"What? You think people will hear you? Go ahead. No one will care."

Eleanore looked at Olga and Dorothy.

"Take her shoes off," she said.

Daisy struggled and fought but the older, bigger girls were just too strong for her and easily removed her plimsolls. Eleanore took one and turned it over, studying it carefully.

"Ah, here we are," she said.

She held the shoe up to Daisy's face. Daisy could see the purple dust from the maze still smudged into the rubber.

"And where do you suppose this came from?" said Eleanore.

"I don't know. OW!" said Daisy as Dorothy and Olga twisted her arms painfully.

"Wrong answer!" said Eleanore tapping Daisy's shoe against her forehead, "Annabel spotted this dust on your shoes in History."

Eleanore ran her finger along the edge of the shoe until the tip was covered in the bright purple dust. She then used it to smear an 'X' shape on Daisy's forehead.

"I think you'll have to agree that it is…quite incriminating."

"Let me go!" shouted Daisy, her fear turning to anger.

Eleanore gripped her chin and stared into her eyes.

"You want me to let you go, Daisy Cooper?" she snarled, "No problem."

Eleanore covered Daisy's hand with her mouth as the Brat Pack dragged her out of the bathroom. They marched Daisy across the empty corridor and through a door to the East Tower. Daisy tried to fight back as they pushed her up the steps but only succeeded in banging her ankles against stone. The top of the East Tower held the great East Bell and it was humming in the wind as Eleanore pushed Daisy past it and hung her out over the edge. The wind snatched at her clothes as she stared down in panic at the tiny vehicles in the courtyard a hundred feet below.

"You and I both know where that dust came from which means you've been a sneaky, nosy little oik," Eleanore hissed in Daisy's ear.

Olga and Dorothy let Daisy's arms slip. She felt herself drop forward a couple of inches and started crying. She thought of dad and her brothers and suddenly wanted nothing more than to be safely at home with them.

"If I hear you've told ANYONE about what you've seen or if we catch you sneaking around again, this is what will happen to you!"

Eleanore threw Daisy's plimsolls off the parapet. Daisy watched them spin though the air and hit the ground far below. Suddenly she was pulled back. Olga and Dorothy let go and Daisy fell to her knees, clinging to the big East Bell for support. She sat there, terrified, as the Brat Pack walked away.

"Where have you been?" said Tina, "and what have you done with your shoes?"

Daisy looked at her feet. The bottoms of her socks were black with dust and dirt.

"Have you been crying?" asked Brodie seeing Daisy's swollen eyes.

She ran down the ladder on Bertha's side and put her arm around Daisy.

"What happened?"

"It's nothing," said Daisy, brushing away her tears and picking up a pot of ink, "let's just get on with refilling Bertha."

Brodie badgered Daisy all day but she refused to talk. It got worse when she returned to the dorm after dinner and the other 88ers started to quiz her as well.

"Look, please leave it alone," said Daisy, "It's nothing."

She was sitting on her bed. She'd found her plimsolls in one of the rose bushes at the side of the courtyard and was scrubbing them with a scouring brush from the bathroom.

"I bet it's Annabel," said Tracy who was practising her headstands against the wall, "That girl needs a check up from the neck up."

"Oh, please, Tracy, you're not in a boxing ring right now," said Penny.

"You want to start as well? You're as much a bloody snob as they are," said Tracy pushing herself up into a handstand.

"Just because I show a bit of decorum doesn't mean I'm a snob. I doubt you'd understand, though, as you seem to have enough trouble staying the right way up," said Penny.

"No fighting!" said Millie, "How about we all have a lovely cup of tea on the balcony and watch the sun go down. Hmm?"

"Or we could go exploring," said Layla looking over at Daisy.
Daisy said nothing and went back to scrubbing her shoes.

"Hi Dad."
"Hi Princess! How's school?"
Daisy was alone on the balcony. The other 88ers had gone to bed. She was watching the dark clouds, her mobile phone against her ear.
"It's okay. How are you and the boys?"
"We're fine. Daniel and David are getting into cooking, could you believe it. You should see the mess, though. It's like a war zone. Gibbon was a bit confused for a few days but he sleeps on my bed now. What's going on with you?"
Daisy felt a lump in her throat.
"I'm homesick."
There was a pause on the other end of the line.
"You will get homesick, Princess. That's natural. Have you made many friends?"
"Yeah. The girls in my dorm are all lovely. They're so different and talented."
"That sounds great. Are you studying hard?"
"As hard as I can. It's a lot more work, but great fun."
"Well, that's good, isn't it? You always felt bored at your old school."
"I know. I just miss you all."
"We miss you too but you're in the best place you could possibly be. You know that don't you?"
"I guess."
"Do you have the pictures of us by your bed?"
"They're right near my pillow where I can see them."
"Well, in a way, we're always with you then. You're always in my thoughts - even David and Daniel's though you'd never get them to admit it."
Daisy laughed.
"There's a visiting weekend coming up soon isn't there?" said Dad.
"I think so."
"Well, we'll see you then. Until then I'm only a phone call away."
"I know. Thanks for listening."
"Hey, I'm a dad, it's my job. Love you."
"Love you too."

Daisy hung up and looked up at the clouds. They were slowly breaking to reveal the moon.

"So who grabbed you?"

Daisy jumped. Layla stepped out of the shadows.

"I don't know what you're talking about," said Daisy.

"Daisy, you were scrubbing the dust off your plimsolls like your life depended on it. Someone noticed didn't they? Someone's said something to you."

"I can't talk about it."

Layla sighed and took a seat next to Daisy, pulling a blanket round her shoulders.

"Your dad must be nice," she said, "sorry to listen in like that."

"No problem."

They sat in silence for a moment listening to the night birds in the trees.

"If you can't talk about what happened," said Layla eventually, "how about I try and guess and you give me a nod if I'm right?"

Daisy nodded. In all honesty, she was desperate to talk to someone about it.

"Is it because someone spotted the dust from the maze on your shoes?"

Daisy nodded.

"So, was it a teacher?"

Daisy shook her head.

"A pupil then?"

Daisy nodded. Layla went quiet, staring at the moon.

"Okay. Then I think we both know who were are talking about. Annabel, Eleanore, Olga or Dorothy."

"You can't say anything," said Daisy, "not even to the other girls. If they find out I'd said anything they'll throw me off the East Tower."

Layla's eyes widened.

"THEY? So it was ALL of them???"

Daisy said nothing.

"Aaah," said Layla, "that makes sense. They said they'd throw you off the East Tower?"

"They didn't just say it. They showed me. They dragged me up there and threw my shoes off."

"Oh my god!" said Layla, "What total psychos! You know what this means though?"

"What?" asked Daisy.

"Well, it means we were right. It means all of the Brat Pack are involved."

"Promise you won't tell the others," pleaded Daisy.

"I promise," said Layla, "but that doesn't mean I'm not going to think of a way to get even with them."

CHAPTER TWELVE - VISITING DAY

The weekend of the family visit Daisy was nervous about the behaviour of her brothers and, sure enough, when the car pulled up they virtually fell out onto the courtyard fighting. Still, she was glad to see them.

"Dad!"

Daisy grabbed hold of Mr Cooper, hugging the breath out of him.

"Oof! Pleased to see you too, Daisy!"

"Dad, you've got to meet the girls in my dorm. They are the best! We call ourselves the 88ers because we're on the eighth floor of the eighth school house. When we're done there I can show you the school zoo. There's also tea in the restaurant all day so Daniel and David will be able to have as many biscuits as they like, all home made..."

"Daisy, slow down, we've got all day!"

Daisy led her family up the dorm stairs to the balcony which was crowded with people. Daniel and David ran over to the railings and looked down at the courtyard far below.

"Wow, this is so high up!" said David.

"They look like ants!" said Daniel, spitting over the side.

Daisy's dad whacked him on the side of the head with his newspaper.

"Ow! Abuse!" cried Daniel.

"Shut up, wuss," said David.

"Boys!" said Daisy sternly, pushing a tray of biscuits into their hands.

It seemed to distract them.

"So you must be Daisy?" said someone behind her in an American accent.

Daisy turned to see a tall man dressed in denim with short grey hair and a dazzling white smile.

"It's so nice to meet you, Daisy. I've heard a lot about you."

"Would you like a brownie?" said a tanned, shiny woman dressed in a silk wrap stood next to him, "I make them myself."

She held out the tin of chocolate brownies. They looked really good.

"Thanks" said Daisy, taking one.

"We're Brodie's parents."

"I guessed that - what with your accent," said Daisy.

"Oh, honey, don't talk about accents. We gotta talk to everyone here just so we can hear you guys speak. So adorable."

"Please, mom. Don't embarrass me," said Brodie coming over to join them.

"Well, the thanks I get for traveling all the way over here, missy. You know your dad's allergic to the air on planes - he put himself through it so we could see our little cutie."

Brodie's mum grabbed Brodie's cheek in her fingers and gave it a playful squeeze. Brodie was not enjoying it.

"Thanks, mom. Now if you'll excuse me I think I'll go jump off the balcony," she said.

Daisy giggled. She looked around at the other visitors. Mr Cooper was talking to a very tall red faced man in a green striped shirt. There were two stocky boys next to him dressed the same and eating cupcakes that looked silly in their enormous hands. It was obviously Tina's family. Next to them were Marsha's parents who had given her some chemistry books and a new encyclopaedia of crime which she looked way too happy with. Tracy's parents, who were dressed quite cool, were pointing to the tattoos on their arms and describing them to Millie's posh country parents.

"'Allo, sweetheart. 'Oo might you be then?"

Daisy turned to see a scrawny woman in a tattered fur coat and too much make up. She had her arm around an oily looking man in a sports jacket with slicked back thinning hair. The man held a hand out. Every finger had a gold ring on it. Daisy took his hand and the man shook it roughly.

"We're the Wilkies, Penny's parents. You are?"

"Daisy," said Daisy, taken aback.

She looked at Penny who was sat in a chair with her head buried in a magazine, trying to ignore them. Daisy looked back at the Wilkies.

"She don't give a stuff about us being here. She thinks she's too good for us, the little madam. She don't forget us when she needs more money for magazines and lip gloss, though. DON'T YOU SWEETHEART?" said Mrs Wilkie, yelling over at her daughter.

Penny flicked through the magazine pages noisily.

Daisy smiled and stepped away from them politely. It was odd seeing the 88ers' parents. They were all as different as the girls were. As she watched them chatting, Daisy realised someone was missing.

Daisy knocked gently on the dorm door. Layla looked up. She was alone, lying on her bed.

"You okay?" asked Daisy, " Where are your parents?"

Layla shrugged.

"I think mum's in Gibraltar and Dad's in Iraq. I don't know what they're doing except that it's Very. Important. Stuff. More important stuff than visiting their daughter, of course."

Daisy sat on the edge of the bed.

"I'm sure they care about you."

Layla snorted. Daisy could see that Layla - normally so cool and aloof - was upset.

"It's always this way. Every school I've been to - they never show up on visiting days. I'll get a lovely card from one of their secretaries saying 'sorry' and that's it. I've been expelled three times. They barely noticed."

Daisy opened her mouth to comfort her when Mr Cooper ran into the dorm.

"Daisy! Your brothers! They've gone missing!"

Daisy and Layla sprinted across the courtyard and into the main building. The assembly hall, decorated with bunting and welcome signs, was full of pupils and parents.

"Aah, Daisy and Layla! When can I expect to meet your parents?"

It was Miss Weaver. She looked for once like she'd managed to avoid getting covered in paint.

"Erm, later this afternoon Miss!" said Daisy hurrying past.

"I wouldn't wait up for mine!" Layla called over her shoulder.

Miss Weaver raised an eyebrow and scratched her head.

Pushing past hundreds of bodies (and saying sorry, of course) Daisy and Layla explored every room and corridor in the main building. The boys were in none of them.

"Won't they come back when they're bored?" said Layla, puffing to keep up with Daisy.

"You don't know my brothers. If they're not in sight, they're in trouble. My mum used to say they'd bring the devil to tears."

Daisy wondered if you could get expelled for your family's behaviour.

"Hello, Oik."

It was Annabel. She stepped out of the trees into their path as they ran past the school maze.

"Oh, not now, Annabel!" said Daisy, brushing past her.

She had more important things to worry about.

"Where are we going?" asked Layla.

"I made the mistake of mentioning the zoo," said Daisy.

Sure enough, they found David and Daniel in the zoo. They were leaning over the edge of an enclosure waving a chicken drumstick at Sankofa the lion.

"Oi!" shouted Daisy.

Her brothers turned round.

"Oi yourself!" said David.

Daniel took a bite out of the drumstick. Daisy walked up and pulled it out of his hand.

"Are you trying to get me thrown out of here?"

"We were trying to feed the lion," said David, "who's the vampire?"

"Her name's Layla and she's not a vampire," said Daisy.

"She looks like a vampire," said Daniel.

"Be quiet or I'll bite you," said Layla.

The boys went quiet.

"So this is what you call family?"

Daisy turned to see the Brat Pack walking towards them. They were carrying hockey sticks.

"Come on, boys, let's go," said Daisy.

Her brothers didn't move. They seemed much more interested in the older girls. Daisy looked around. There were a lot of parents and children about which was a good thing. It was too public for them to cause any trouble.

"Stay for a bit, boys," said Eleanore, "Daisy hasn't told me about her two brothers. I'd love to hear about your fascinating lives."

The boys started giggling. Eleanore stepped forward and hooked the toe of her hockey stick round Daniel's neck.

"How would you like an older girl to show you around the place? I can make you feel at home."

Olga hooked David round the neck. With a quick sneer at Daisy, the two girls walked away, leading the boys with them. Dorothy and Annabel stepped in Daisy's path, blocking her way with their sticks. Dorothy laughed.

"Relax, oik. They're just taking your brothers to have a look at the sea life section. Maybe let them have a little swim."

That was it. Feeling her blood boil, Daisy gripped Annabel's hockey stick and twisted it out of her hands.

"Ow!"

Daisy hooked the stick around Dorothy's ankle and gave her a shove, knocking her to the floor. She grabbed Layla and ran through to the sea life section just in time to see David and Daniel fall into the water of the seal enclosure.

It was the first time Daisy had been back to the Staff House since she had been in Miss Weaver's office on her first day and she was making a mental note not to go back in a hurry. Near the museum, the Staff House was made up of dark panelled hallways with scary looking doors and old paintings of stern looking former teachers. Daisy, Layla, Daisy's dad and a dripping wet Daniel and David were sat on a bench outside Mistress Aiken's office. Eleanore, Dorothy, Olga and Annabel sat scowling on a bench opposite. Eleanore didn't take her eyes off Daisy. Daisy wasn't afraid. She was angry. Eventually the door opened and Doctor Penrose stepped into the hall. They all stood up, even David and Daniel.

"Come in," said Doctor Penrose.

The Deputy Head's office reminded Daisy of the school museum. Everything looked ancient. The walls were lined with leather books and there was a large old wooden globe in one corner. Behind the oak desk at which Mistress Aiken sat was a large portrait of a fierce looking blonde haired lady. The lady was stood on the helm of a ship. She was dressed in a crimson leather suit and holding a sharp cutlass menacingly. The portrait must have been a couple of hundred years old.

"Sit down!" barked Mistress Aiken.

Everyone squeezed into two uncomfortable sofas.

"Now. Who's are these?" said Mistress Aiken, pointing at David and Daniel.

"They're mine miss, erm, missus..." said Mr Cooper a bit confused.

"Mistress. Mistress Aiken. Why were they swimming with the seals in my zoo?"

"We weren't swimming!" said Daniel.

"We was pushed!" said David.

The deputy head held up her hand for silence.

"Doctor Penrose, what do you know about this?" she asked.

"I was washing the elephant when I heard shouts and an enormous splash coming from the sea life area. I ran over and these two boys were splashing about in the water."

"We was pushed!" said Daniel.

Mr Cooper shushed him angrily.

"And these girls?" asked Mistress Aiken, pointing at Eleanore and the rest of the Brat Pack.

"When I got there they were reaching into the water with their hockey sticks, trying to pull the boys out."

"We were on our way to the sports field. We saw these boys with Daisy and, to be honest, we were a little suspicious. They were making quite a bit of noise by the lion enclosure," said Eleanore.

Eleanore was completely twisting the truth. Daisy was fuming but she tried to stay calm. Mistress Aiken got up from her desk and wandered over to the wooden globe. She pushed a button in the rim and the top slid back revealing a decanter of rum with a few glasses. Next to the glasses was an old leather-bound book. It looked like a very old copy of one of Daisy's journals. There was a hand drawn compass on the cover in faded ink.

"So were you boys causing mischief at the lion enclosure?" asked Mistress Aiken, pouring herself a glass.

"We wanted to feed him. He looked sad," said David.

"Boys will be boys, eh?" said Mr Cooper, laughing nervously.

Mistress Aiken narrowed her eyes at him with distaste.

"Indeed they will," she muttered quietly.

She closed the top of the globe and sat back at her desk taking a long, slow sip of rum.

"So when the lion wasn't interested in your japes you decided to go and play with the sea lions instead?" said Mistress Aiken.

"They were pushed!" shouted Daisy, unable to hold back any longer.

"I BEG your pardon?"

"They were pushed, Mistress Aiken," said Daisy, gritting her teeth.

"Did you see them being pushed?"

Daisy hadn't seen it.

"Well, not actually. I got there just afterwards."

She could see Eleanore and the rest of the Brat Pack smirking out of the corner of her eye.

"It seems there's no one else to back up your story," said Mistress Aiken to Daniel and David, "and you've already admitted interfering with the lion."

"But if they admitted to trying to feed Sankofa, why would they lie about the seals?" said Daisy.

"Daisy Cooper! If I have to remind you to address me properly one more time you will be spending a week in detention, do you understand?"

"Yes, Mistress Aiken. Sorry," said Daisy.

"Now, it appears - despite Daisy's protestations - that you boys were clearly causing trouble in the zoo. I'm going to have to ask you to leave the school premises immediately."

Daisy was embarrassed and heartbroken. There was a big feast for the parents planned in the evening and now, like Layla, she would be alone.

"And Daisy?" added Mistress Aiken.

"Yes, Mistress Aiken?"

"That will be an hour's detention for addressing me inappropriately. Now, if you'll excuse me I have other, better behaved families to meet."

Daisy could tell her dad was very angry. She gave him a quick hug and told him not to blame himself or her brothers. They were naughty but not crazy enough to go swimming with sea lions. Daisy waved goodbye as the car drove away.

"I can't believe those girls," said Daisy as she trudged with Layla back to the dorm.

"Remember what the Sisters of the Black Night said about Undesirables? I guess that's us," said Layla, " Do you remember the two girls who were expelled? The ones mentioned in the assembly?"

"Yes, they had cigarettes and alcohol on them," said Daisy. "I was doing a bit of asking around and it turns out that one of them, Sandy, is asthmatic. She couldn't even be in the same room as a cigarette."

"Even if they were undesirables, it seems pretty extreme to expel them. Maybe they found out something the Sisters didn't like," said Daisy.

"That's exactly what I was thinking."

The dorm was empty. Layla, Brodie and Daisy sat on Daisy's bed. Daisy opened her journal and read out her notes on the Sisters of the Black Night. They knew the Brat Pack were involved. Not much more than that. Daisy thought back to what she had seen in the maze and tried to remember how many other figures were there. As well as the four girls they knew about, there was the Great Sister and another eight.

"Number thirteen. Spooky!" said Layla.

"Some of them are too tall to be pupils," said Daisy, "What if some of the teachers are involved too?"

"We should look up Sisters of the Black Night online," said Brodie.

She pulled out her laptop and entered the phrase into a search engine. There seemed to be a lot of angry guitar bands with the words 'black night' in their song titles but not much more.

"What about that?" said Daisy as Brodie was about to close the laptop down.

"Pirate ship?" said Layla reading the details under the link, "What would that have to do with it?"

"That lady in the portrait in Mistress Aiken's office looked like a pirate," said Daisy, "maybe there's a connection."

Brodie clicked on the link.

"It says here that the Black Night was the name of a pirate ship from two hundred years ago owned by a couple of pirates called Rotten Mario and Cut Throat Jack who were the scourge of the seas. I don't see how that can be connected."

"Well, it was worth a go," said Daisy disappointed.

The girls wrote a list in Daisy's journal about what they DID know about The Sisters of the Black Night. They liked the night, obviously, but it didn't look like there was anything witchcrafty going on. It seemed to be more about secrets. There was the pendant that the Great Sister had held up. The one with the eye on it. Daisy made a note about that - maybe she might see one of the teachers wearing it. Then there was their mission of clearing what they called "the undesirables" out of Darlington.

"I don't think it's going to make a difference how careful we are," said Layla.

"She's right," said Brodie, "They know we've been up to something. I think they're going to try and get us expelled too. Or worse. We have to find out what they are up to and get some evidence against them."

"But what about their threat to throw me off the bell tower?" said Daisy.

Brodie shrugged.

"Well, I guess we'd better make sure that none of us are ever alone with them. What were the names of those two girls who got expelled?"

"Karen Bickford and Sandy Pedlow."

Brodie tapped away at her keyboard.

"Bingo!"

On the screen were two windows, one for each of the girl's Facebook profiles.

"Wow, that was fast," said Daisy.

"It helps when your dad's a computer geek."

"Do you mind if I contact them?" asked Daisy.

Brodie shrugged. Daisy logged into her Facebook profile and wrote a message:

Dear Karen/Sandy,

My name is Daisy Cooper and I am a first year at Darlington. I was very sorry to hear about you getting expelled. I understand you say you are innocent and I believe you. Some of us first years have had similar things happen to us. It would be great to meet up with you and have a chat to see if we can work out what's going on.

All the best,

Daisy.

Daisy hit send.

Layla, Brodie and Daisy decided to sneak out the next time they saw torches in the maze and take photographs of the Sisters of the Black Night. That would at least give them some evidence they could show to some of the teachers they trusted like Miss Weaver. It was a long shot but it was better than nothing.

Later on Daisy practiced her fencing moves with Tracy whilst the others did homework on the balcony. Brodie told the rest of the 88ers to be careful of the Brat Pack. Tracy parried Daisy's lunge and countered with a quick flick of her wrist, the tip of the blade quivering inches from Daisy's chest.

"Shouldn't you be wearing your fencing gear?" asked Penny.

"Danger keeps the brain sharp," said Tracy.

Daisy knocked Tracy's blade aside and poked her in the belly with the rubber end of the foil.

"Ow!" said Tracy.

"Do you really think they'd try to get us into trouble? Aren't they just after Daisy?" asked Millie.

"If they're after Daisy, they're after all of us," said Layla.

"Exactly," said Marsha, "We said we'd be our own family and family members protect each other."

Daisy turned as Tracy made another lunge and with a quick twirl, knocked the blade out of her hand.

CHAPTER THIRTEEN - TUNNEL TROUBLE

When Daisy, Brodie and Layla spotted the flicker of lights in the maze a couple of nights later they were ready. They got changed into black trousers and long sleeved sweaters. Layla packed her rucksack with her camera, a torch, a coil of rope and at Millie's insistence a first aid kit.

The school grounds were quiet. Daisy and Brodie followed Layla as she made her way along the dorm houses and into the maze. As they turned corners Daisy was surprised that the path to the centre seemed obvious to her now. After a few minutes they could see the tell tale glow of the torches. They found the statue with the telescope and crept behind it. It looked like the ceremony had been going on for a while.

"Step forward, candidate!" bellowed the Great Sister.

Annabel, recognisable by her shoelaces, stepped forwards.

"Are you ready to step deeper into the mysteries of the Sisters of the Black Night?"

Annabel nodded.

"She looks nervous," said Daisy.

"Maybe they're going to eat her," said Layla.

"Well, that would be one less goon to worry about," said Brodie.

It was all Daisy could do to stop herself from laughing.

What they saw next they couldn't quite believe. One of the hooded figures stepped onto the wall of the fountain and, reaching up, pulled the statue's arm that held the orb. There were a couple of low thudding sounds like trapdoors being opened and the water from the fountain drained away. The hooded figure pulled the arm again and there was the sound of heavy stone moving. The Great Sister stepped over the wall of the fountain and seemed to disappear into the ground. She was followed by each of the Sisters, one by one, until they had all gone. Daisy, Brodie and Layla looked at each other, their mouths hanging open. After a moment the silence was broken by the rumble of stone again followed by the sound of rushing water.

"What. Was. That?" said Brodie.

"I don't know," said Daisy, "but we should have a look."

Before they entered the centre of the maze Daisy pulled some cotton shoe covers from her pockets and handed them to Brodie and Layla.

"What are these for?" asked Brodie.

"I picked them up from the zoo. The assistance use them to keep their shoes clean when mucking out the cages. They'll stop us from getting any of that purple dust on our shoes."

"Good thinking," said Brodie.

"That reminds me," said Layla, "I bought these for us to wear. They'll stop us being recognised."

She reached into her bag and pulled out three balaclavas.

"Now I don't want to sound like Penny but this is not a good look. Seriously," said Brodie looking at the balaclava in her hands.

After covering their shoes and putting on the balaclavas the girls crept into the centre of the maze, keeping the torchlight low and looking for any hooded figures that might be hiding in the bushes. Up close the fountain didn't look odd at all. Daisy stepped up onto its low stone wall. There were Koi carp still in the water, swimming around just beneath her feet. She leant over to the statue and grabbed hold of the crook in its arm. The orb was a good two feet higher than she could reach.

"Here!" said Layla tossing Daisy the coil of rope from her rucksack.

Daisy made a lasso and threw it up high, catching it onto the hand with the orb in it.

"You go, cowgirl!" whispered Brodie.

"Just like throwing hoops over fishbowls at the fair," said Daisy.

Daisy gave a tug on the rope. There was a loud gurgling sound as the water disappeared through a vent taking the bewildered fish with it. Daisy gave another tug and the stone floor of the fountain slipped away, revealing a set of steps going down.

"O.M.G.," said Brodie peering down.

The stairway was narrow and dark. Daisy stepped into it, putting her hand against the wall for support. The stone felt slimy to the touch. Slowly, she made her way down followed by the other two. At the bottom of the stairs they stepped into a tunnel that disappeared into shadows. They stood in silence, listening. Far off, they could her the footsteps of the Sisters.

"Come on," whispered Daisy.

Keeping close enough to be able to hear the footsteps but far enough away to not be seen Daisy and the others crept through the tunnel. A couple of times they thought they had lost the trail only to discover a secret doorway or another tunnel hidden in the shadows. Every time they turned a corner Layla drew a small 'X' into the brickwork with a stick of chalk so they would be able to find their way back. The tunnels made the hedge maze look like a children's puzzle by comparison. They could easily get lost down there and never get out again.

They reached a drainage tunnel with water flowing through it. On either side of the water there was a narrow thin ledge about a foot wide. The sound of the Sisters was fading. Daisy and the other two edged their way along the ledge until they came to an archway that led into a small passageway. At the end of the passageway was an old door with a heavy wooden latch. There were voices echoing on the other side. Quietly they lifted the latch and opened it very, very carefully.

The door opened onto a balcony that overlooked a massive underground hall. The balcony went all the way around with doorways and staircases leading off from it at different points. It was held in place by giant marble pillars a good twenty feet above the black and white checkered floor of the hall. In the middle of the floor were two large semicircular metal grates locked together with a heavy padlock. The hall was at least as big as the school hockey pitch and there were eight large statues, like those in the maze, lined up around the edge of the hall. Daisy recognised some of them as Greek Goddesses from Darren's books at St Margarets. A great, old chandelier filled with half melted candles hung from the roof above. With her heart thumping in her ears Daisy crept over to the railings and peered down into the hall. The Sisters of the Black Night were gathered below. There seemed to be an awful lot more than they had seen at the maze.

"Where did they all come from?" whispered Brodie coming up beside Daisy.

"They must have come through the other doorways," said Layla.

There was a loud bang that made the three of them jump. One of the Sisters had hit a large silver gong standing in the corner of the hall. As if on cue the figures split up into small circles, each around one of the goddess statues. The Great Sister - recognisable by her purple robe - stood at the lectern by the locked grates in the floor. Around her neck she was wearing the pendant with the eye on it.

"SISTERS, NEW AND OLD!" she bellowed, "WELCOME TO THE GREAT HALL!"

The others nodded in unison. The Great Sister held aloft the pendant.

"Some of you have travelled far to make it here this evening but we have received important news that is only safe to share in person," she said, "As you know we have spent many, many years collecting certain items from museums at home and abroad. As great as the items are, our hope has been that one of them might lead us to something more valuable. The legacy of one of our great ancestors, Jacqueline Lyle."

"Jacqueline Lyle?" whispered Daisy, "That's Eleanore and her mum's surname. They must be related to her."

The Great Sister continued.

"A week ago during a storm on the Devonshire coast, at a place called Serpent's Tooth, part of a cliff collapsed and fell into the sea. When the storm cleared some local fishermen found the remains of an old ship washed up on the shore. The name written on the side of the ship was The Black Night."

There were large gasps amongst the Sisters. The Great Sister held up her hands for silence.

"As I'm sure you are aware this is a dramatic development for us. Our hope, of course, is that on board is what we are looking for. At the moment they are restoring The Black Night and moving it to a small museum on the cliff tops. In a few weeks they will be finished and we will organise a trip to the museum and make an offer to buy it."

No one was listening. The Sisters were talking excitedly.

"Very well! It is exciting news. I'll let you take a few minutes to discuss this amongst yourselves," said the Great Sister.

The groups of figures huddled into groups, their voices lowering.

"So The Black Night is a ship? Like the one we saw online?" said

Daisy.

"That is a cool name for a ship," said Brodie.

"We can't hear them anymore. Lets get closer," said Layla.

Before Daisy knew it Layla was pulling her and Brodie across to the nearest staircase. As they got to the bottom, the voices of the Sisters became clearer and Daisy could hear what was unmistakably Eleanore's voice talking to another girl.

"…We're trying to get rid of a few of the nosy ones. We can't have anyone we don't trust snooping around now. We can't trust all of the teachers, either."

Daisy peeked out from the stairwell. The figures were about ten feet away. In front of them was a statue of the Goddess Hecate, half hidden in shadows. The statue had three heads looking different directions and held aloft a metal torch in one hand.

"If we get closer we may be able to see who she's talking to," said Layla.

"I think we're close enough," said Daisy, "let's just take some pictures and go."

She turned to Layla but she was no longer there. She was running out into the hall towards the statue.

"Layla!" whispered Daisy.

She watched helplessly as Layla took the camera out of her satchel and climbed up the back of the statue.

"That girl has a death wish," said Brodie.

Layla climbed to the top of the statue and, hiding behind one of the great stone heads, looked down on the huddle of figures beneath her. Careful not to fall she lifted the camera and started taking pictures.

"Do you think she can see who they are?" Daisy asked Brodie.

The Great Sister tapped her sword a few times on the floor and the figures began to walk back into the centre of the room. Daisy waived her hands at Layla, beckoning her back. Layla took one last photo, swung her legs off Hecate's shoulder and slid down the left arm. As she did so she knocked the metal torch in the statue's hand. It fell to the ground with a bang. Daisy and Brodie ducked back into the shadows. Layla hit the ground and froze. It was too late. Everyone in the room had spotted her.

"INTRUDERS!"

There was a loud crashing sound as the gong was sounded.

"QUICK!" shouted Daisy.

Layla sprinted across the hall to the stairwell.

"INTRUDERS! INTRUDERS!"

The whole room seemed to be running towards them. Daisy and Brodie ran up the stairs, closely followed by Layla.

"Go! Go! Go!"

The staircase was tight and narrow and much more difficult to go up than come down. After a couple of shin-grazing slips, Daisy used her hands to pull herself up as fast as she could.

"Intruders!"

The voices were barely a few feet behind them as they ran out onto the balcony. Daisy ran towards the door to the tunnels but stopped sharply as a couple of hooded sisters charged through it. She looked around, eyes wide with panic. There seemed to be hooded figures coming out of every staircase and doorway.

Think, Daisy. Think, think, think.

She looked up across the great hall and spotted the chandelier hanging high in the ceiling with its candles lit. Guide ropes were attached to each balcony, holding it in place.

"This way!"

Daisy climbed up onto the wooden railing of the balcony and grabbed hold of the rope. Without looking down she swung her legs around it and pulled herself, hand over hand, out across the hall and up towards the chandelier. After a moments hesitation, Brodie and Layla did the same.

"They're not following!" said Layla.

That's good, thought, Daisy, *now all I have to do is not fall.*

Arms aching, ignoring the shouts from below, Daisy made her way across to the chandelier. She grabbed the wide wooden base and, carefully avoiding the hot candles, pulled herself up onto it. Brodie and Layla climbed up after her. There were hooded figures all the way around the balcony and even more below.

"We're trapped!" said Brodie.

Daisy looked over her shoulder to see a couple of the Sisters clambering along the ropes towards the chandelier. Layla was still snapping away with her camera. Daisy looked around. No way forward. No way back. Certainly no way down. Daisy looked up. The rope that held the chandelier in place went through a large metal ring that was fixed to the ceiling by four large metal bolts. Next to these was a small square maintenance door with a latch on it. It was just big enough for them to fit through.

"This way," said Daisy as she reached for the central rope.

"Are you crazy?" said Brodie.

"Probably," said Daisy.

There was a sudden jolt as the chandelier dropped a couple of feet. Daisy looked down, instantly wishing she hadn't. The figures below looked tiny. Off to one side of the hall a couple of the Sisters were turning the winch that lowered the chandelier. With a shudder it dropped another foot. Daisy scurried up the rope towards the ceiling. She was glad they were wearing the balaclavas. If they did manage to get away at least they wouldn't be recognised. She reached the top of the rope and grabbed hold of the latch on the door. It was stuck. The rope dropped a couple of feet again.

"Hurry, Daisy! I can't hold on much longer," said Brodie.

Daisy climbed up to the latch again and gave a hard tug. The hinge snapped and the door popped open nearly knocking Daisy off the rope. She grabbed hold of the hatch and pulled herself through. Feeling the safety of the floor beneath her she rolled onto her back, out of breath. The other two crawled through after her. After a couple of seconds they sat up and looked around.

"Where are we?" asked Brodie.

There were no lights. All they could see were big shadowy things in the dark. Gradually, as her eyes became accustomed to the dark, Daisy spotted the familiar shape of Bodicea's chariot.

"We're in the school museum."

The girls got to their feet and just as they did so the strip lights across the ceiling flickered into life.

"Quick!" shouted Daisy.

They ran into the shadows.

"My rucksack!" said Layla.

Daisy looked back at the hatch. Layla's satchel was sitting next to it.

"I have to go back! The camera is in it!" said Layla.

She sprinted past the exhibits and slid across the floor, grabbing hold of the bag. She turned quickly and ran back towards Daisy and Brodie, smiling.

"That was…" she started to say.

"CLOSE?" said a figure stepping out into her path.

It was Mistress Aiken. Next to her, out of their robes, were Eleanore, Dorothy and Olga. Eleanore grabbed the rucksack as Mistress Aiken pulled Layla towards her.

"Snooping around the school dressed like a ninja spells trouble to me," said the Deputy Head.

She pulled Layla's balaclava off, taking some of Layla's hair with it.

"OW!" cried Layla.

"That's 'OW, Mistress Aiken'," corrected the Deputy Head.

She shook her head slowly, tutting.

"Young Layla, troublesome Layla. It's such a shame you had to be a disappointment to your well bred parents. I'd expected better from you. No doubt it's the company you've been keeping. Hand me her bag."

Eleanore stepped out of the shadows and handed over the rucksack. Mistress Aiken pulled out the camera.

"There are people in the school who are up to no good, Mistress Aiken! These idiots are involved!" said Layla, pointing at the Brat Pack.

"Nonsense, girl. These are three of the best students Darlington has."

"It's true, Mistress Aiken! Check the photos on the camera."

Mistress Aiken went quiet. She flicked through the images on the camera.

"You see!" said Layla, "I wasn't lying!"

Mistress Aiken let out a long sigh.

"Maybe," she said.

Her eyes narrowed to slits and she put her face close to Layla's.

"But who's going to believe you?" she said.

The Deputy Head handed the camera to Eleanore and clicked her finger at Olga who stepped forward holding Cleopatra's Egg, the most prized possession in the museum.

"On the other hand, a troublesome girl found running round the school at night gets caught stealing…"

Mistress Aiken dropped the Egg into Layla's rucksack and thrust it back in her hands.

"…Now that's something we can all believe in."

"SAY 'CHEESE'!" said Eleanore pointing the camera at Layla.

There was a flash.

"Oh, you're not smiling," said Eleanore, "never mind, I'm sure it will look fine on the cover of International Schoolgirl."

"Make sure you delete the other pictures before you give the camera to

Anita," said Mistress Aiken.

Watching from the shadows Daisy felt hot with anger. She tried to run out and grab Layla but Brodie pulled her back.

"There's nothing you can do, Daisy," Brodie whispered.

"But she's lying! They're setting Layla up!"

"And we'll get set up too if we run out there. I'm sorry."

Mistress Aiken grabbed the bag back out of Layla's hands and carefully handed Cleopatra's Egg back to Olga.

"Now, you'll be expelled of course. We can't have dirty thieves in the school. If, on the other hand, you tell us the names of the other girls involved with you, I might be able to arrange it so that we don't get the police involved. You don't want to end up in a juvenile prison. Those places are not very nice at all."

Layla's mascara ran down her cheeks as her eyes filled with tears but she stared back defiantly at the Deputy Head.

"I will never tell you," she said.

Mistress Aiken sighed.

"We'll that's very stupid of you. I have a pretty good idea who else is involved anyway. They'll be out of here almost as quick as you. Trust me."

Dorothy and Olga grabbed hold of Layla's arms and marched her off towards the museum entrance.

Daisy and Brodie waited in the shadows until the museum was empty and then crept back to the dorm in shock. The other 88ers were in their pyjamas doing homework on their beds.

"Where's Layla?" asked Millie looking up from a book on lion training.

Daisy threw her balaclava on her bed and collapsed into the pillows. Brodie picked up her laptop and stared at the screen blankly.

"Where's Layla?" said Penny coming in from the bathroom with a toothbrush in her mouth.

"Something's very wrong," said Tracy.

"What happened, Daisy?" asked Martha.

Daisy rolled over and stared up at the glow stars on the ceiling, unable to answer. Everything had been fine one minute and then the next...

"She's gone," said Brodie quietly.

"Gone!" said Millie, "Gone where?"

"Expelled."

The 88ers froze, mouths hanging open.

"I don't believe it," said Tracy eventually.

"Neither do I," said Brodie, "but it's true."

"What happened?"

Suddenly the 88ers were all talking at once, crowding around Daisy and Brodie's beds, wanting to know the details. Brodie told them what happened. She explained how Daisy had discovered the Sisters of the Black Night in the maze and about the underground hall. She told them how the Sisters were looking for something amongst the museum pieces the school was collecting. Finally she told them how Mistress Aiken had planted Cleopatra's Egg in Layla's rucksack and framed her as a thief.

"But it's a total fib!" exclaimed Millie.

"It's Layla's word against the Deputy Head. Who's going to believe her?"

"But what about the pictures she took? Can't we show them to someone?" said Marsha.

Brodie shrugged.

"They were on Layla's camera they've probably deleted them already."

"So where is Layla now? They can't send her home this late, surely? Where is her home? Her parents work abroad," said Tina.

Daisy looked over at Layla's empty bed. On the bedside table there was a photograph of her standing under the moon, howling up at it.

Daisy didn't sleep that night. None of the 88ers did. Every now and then she looked back over at Layla's bed to see if somehow she had snuck back in. No matter how much she hoped, the bed stayed empty.

The next morning there was a knock on the dorm door and Miss Weaver entered with a couple of Prefects.

"I've got some sad news," said Miss Weaver, "quite unbelievable news, really."

Tracy opened her mouth to speak. Martha coughed loudly, hinting at her to keep quiet.

"It *appears*," said Miss Weaver, "that Layla was caught last night in the museum trying to steal a valuable item from the school. I don't know the full story yet but she was held in the detention room overnight and has been expelled from the school this morning. I know this is going to be sad for you but we need to take her possessions so we can forward them to her home."

"Can we see her?" asked Daisy.

Miss Weaver smiled. Her eyes were kind but sad. "I'm sorry, Daisy. Layla left two hours ago."

CHAPTER FOURTEEN - SOME QUICK DETECTIVE WORK

"I heard about that girl who got expelled," said Hattie.

Daisy and Hattie were sitting by the lake throwing bread to the ducks. Daisy felt like she needed to talk to someone older that she could trust. Mistress Aiken had held another assembly that morning and announced Layla's expulsion. The unfairness of it all had made it hard for Daisy to concentrate on her lessons.

"It's not fair," said Daisy, "she didn't do anything wrong."

"She was a friend of yours, I can see. I heard she stole from the museum," said Hattie.

"She didn't. She was set up," said Daisy, quickly adding, "at least, that's what I heard."

Hattie gave her a sly look.

"Daisy, I'm going to give you a very important piece of advice. Knowing something is wrong is not enough."

"But you said it was important to do what's right," said Daisy.

"Oh, it is! But before you tell anyone else what's wrong, you have to have proof or nobody will believe you! You'll only get yourself in trouble otherwise. I suppose it was Gertrude who expelled your friend, eh?"

"Who's Gertrude?" asked Daisy.

Hattie laughed loudly.

"That snake, Gertie Aiken! The Deputy Head!"

Daisy was shocked.

"You don't like her?" she asked.

Hattie snorted loudly.

"She wormed her way into that job. She used to be a pupil - her family always sent their daughters here - she was never trustworthy enough to be accepted as an International Schoolgirl. Boy, I can't tell you how much that bothered her. Anyway, a few years after finishing her studies she managed to become the History teacher. Seemed more interested in collecting treasures than history though, if you ask me. She kept trying to get promoted to Deputy Head but none of the other teachers liked her and we had a brilliant Deputy Head anyway called Doctor Wendy Bishop. Wendy knew more languages than anyone else alive and could run a hundred meters in eleven seconds at the age of fifty. About ten years ago Gertie organised a school trip. She invited Doctor Bishop along and on the trip Wendy accidentally fell off the boat and got eaten by a killer whale. By that time Gertie had a lot of friends on the school board and they all voted to make her the new Deputy Head so here we are now. In some ways I fear the school has lost its way since that time. I'm sorry about your friend."

"I'm sorry too," said Daisy.

Hattie yawned loudly.

"I need my sleep now, Daisy. Thank you for dinner. It would be good if you brought it along for me again sometime. I like our little chats."

Daisy smiled.

"I look forward to them too, Hattie," she said but Hattie was already asleep.

"We should write a story about it for International Schoolgirl," said Daisy.

Brodie and her were washing the print drums with the large jet hoses they used to clean Bertha.

"Nice way to get yourself expelled, Daisy," said Brodie.

"But we have to do something!"

Anita looked over at them from her office. Daisy realised she was talking a bit too loud.

"We have to do something," she whispered.

"I agree." said Brodie, "but there's not much we can do about it without proper proof."

Daisy ducked for cover as a huge explosion sent a shower of flaming metal across the concourse.

"Oops!" said Marsha, climbing out from underneath a workbench.

Daisy coughed, waving the smoke out of her face as she wandered over.

"Is that supposed to happen?"

"Not quite," replied Marsha picking up a nasty looking shard of metal and inspecting it, "though it does seem to happen every time, so maybe it is supposed to happen."

They were outside the engineering labs where the science teacher Glenda, Marsha, Tina and a few other girls were trying, unsuccessfully, to launch large rockets without them blowing up.

"Aah! Daisy Cooper!" said Glenda spotting her, "Care to sign up to be our first test pilot?"

"For what?" asked Daisy.

"Our jet rocket, of course!"

Daisy looked at the scattered bits of debris that littered the courtyard.

"Not on your nelly," she said.

"Oh well, if you ever change your mind…" said Miss Gaynor, cheerily picking up a bag of chemicals with the word 'DANGER' written on it.

"I need your help with something," Daisy whispered to Marsha, "something secret."

Daisy told Marsha about the old journal she had seen in the wooden globe in Mistress Aiken's office when David and Daniel had been thrown out of the school. If the journal was being kept in such a special place it was obviously important. Marsha was Daisy's study partner in History and they were still doing their assignment on the World War Two courier motorcycle. The plan was to use that as an excuse for an appointment with Mistress Aiken and get into her office. Brodie would then call the office and create a distraction so that they could examine the book.

"What are you doing here?" sneered Eleanore as Daisy and Marsha walked up to the Deputy Head's office.

It was no surprise that Eleanore was working for Mistress Aiken in her free time.

"We've got a question about out private study assignment," said Marsha.

"Mistress Aiken only sees girls who have appointments," said Eleanore.
"I have an appointment. My name is Marsha. Marsha Laine."
Eleanore snorted and flicked through the appointment book on her desk. Sure enough, Marsha's name was there.
"It doesn't mention *that,*" said Eleanore, pointing at Daisy.
"Daisy is my project partner," said Marsha.
"What are you two doing here?"
Mistress Aiken was standing in the doorway.
"They say they have an appointment. Well, one of them does…"
"Very well, very well, let's get it over with," said Mistress Aiken, marching back into her office.

Mistress Aiken sat forward in her leather chair and knitting her fingers together over her desk.
"You're Honour girls in my history class."
Daisy and Marsha nodded.
"You're from the dorm that Layla Lynch stayed in, aren't you?"
"Yes, Mistress Aiken," said Marsha
"Bad egg, that girl. Experience tells me once one egg goes bad the rest quickly turn. I have my eye on you."
Daisy smiled as sweetly as she could.
"Well, spit it out. What are you here for? I don't have all day."
"It's the courier motorcycle," said Daisy, "we're having difficulty finding any information on who used it."
Mistress Aiken put her head in her hands.
"Dear God, girl, WHY can't you learn to address me properly? When you speak to me, it's Mistress Aiken. Detention! Now what are you babbling about?"
"We wondered if you could tell us more about what the motorcycle was used for, Mistress Aiken," said Daisy.
"Of course not!" said Mistress Aiken.
Daisy glanced at the phone on the desk, willing it to ring.
Com on, Brodie, where's your distraction?
"Every year there's at least one pair of jokers who are stupid enough to think they can persuade me to do their study work for them. Do you have a proper question or do I have to give you another a detention for wasting my time?" barked the Deputy Head.
Daisy thought hard but Mistress Aiken's eyes were boring into her and

it was making it difficult to think. .

"Erm…" said Daisy.

The phone rang. Mistress Aiken let it ring a couple of times before breaking eye contact with Daisy and picking up the receiver.

"Yes? Who is this?… What??…Where??…WHO IS THIS?"

Daisy heard the line go dead on the phone. The Deputy Head's face went ghostly white.

"What's the problem, Mistress Aiken?" asked Marsha.

Mistress Aiken put the receiver down and looked around blinking. She stood up confused and, without saying a word, stormed out of the office. Daisy and Marsha looked at each other.

"Quick!" said Daisy.

Marsha took out her phone and turned on its camera. As Daisy watched through the gap in the door for Mistress Aiken's return Marsha took photos of the room from every angle. She took a photo of the large portrait of the scary pirate looking woman on the wall. She looked behind it.

"What are you doing? We need to photograph the book in the globe!" said Daisy.

"I was seeing if there was a safe there! There's always safes behind old paintings!"

Marsha ran over to the globe and felt under the rim until she found the switch. The top slid back. Inside was the old journal. Marsha took a photo of the cover and then opened it.

"It's all handwritten," she said, "it looks ancient."

"Photograph the pages!" said Daisy.

There were footsteps coming down the hall. Marsha flicked through the pages one by one, taking a picture of each. There was the sound of shouting outside.

"She's coming back!" said Daisy.

"Just a few more…" said Marsha.

Daisy could see the deputy head turning the corner towards her office. She looked very, very angry.

"THERE'S NO TIME!" said Daisy.

"One more.." said Marsha.

Daisy ran over and pulled her away, slamming the lid shut. They just got back to their seats when Mistress Aiken crashed through the door.

"DAMN IDIOTS AND FOOLS WASTING MY TIME WITH

NONSENSE!" she bellowed.

She walked over to the globe, opened it and poured a glass of rum. She took a long swig.

"What are you two still doing here?" she said spotting Daisy and Marsha.

Mistress Aiken crossed to her desk and stopped. She looked up at the portrait on the wall and frowned. The picture was hanging at an angle. Slowly, she put a finger under the low hanging corner and gave it a push until it was level.

"I think it nearly fell off the wall when you slammed the door, Mistress Aiken," said Daisy, swallowing hard.

"Thank you for your time, Mistress Aiken," said Marsha, pulling gently at Daisy's cardigan and edging her towards the door.

Back at the dorm Daisy and Marsha met up with Brodie.

"What did you SAY on the phone to her?" Daisy asked Brodie as Marsha printed the pictures from her phone.

"I said 'excuse me governor, I'm one of the farmers who's land backs onto your school and I fink your lion has escaped from the zoo. 'es eatin' me bleedin' chickens'," said Brodie.

"Well, as terrible as that accent is, it worked!" said Marsha.

She handed the printed pictures to Daisy.

"Are they readable?" asked Brodie

"Just about," said Daisy.

She lay back on her bed and read out the first few words.

"I was born Jacqueline Lyle in Portsmouth in the year 1776..."

"Jacqueline Lyle?" said Brodie, "That's the name of the woman the Sisters were talking about. Eleanore's family name."

Daisy read on...

CHAPTER FIFTEEN - CUTTHROAT JACKY

Jacqueline Lyle was born in 1776 to a poor family in Portsmouth, England. At the age of eleven her parents could no longer afford to feed her so she stowed away on a merchant ship bound for China. For the first few weeks of the journey she managed to hide below deck and help herself to the crew's rations at night whilst they slept. As time went on she became bored and would spend most of the night above deck watching the moon over the bow. One evening, when the water was so still it looked like a large black mirror holding a perfect moon, someone spotted her.

"Who are you?"

Jacqueline turned to see Mary, the Captain's twelve year old daughter, standing behind her.

"I'm Jacqueline, please don't tell, miss!" she begged.

Stowaways were often forced overboard when discovered. It didn't matter whether they were male or female, adult or child. Fortunately for Jacqueline, Mary had become rather bored on her own so she agreed not to tell and the two girls struck up a friendship. Each night whilst the Captain and his crew slept they would climb up to the crows nest to watch dolphins leap through the waves. Mary told Jacqueline how her mother had been a schoolteacher who had died giving birth to her. As a result she had spent most of her time growing up in boarding schools

while her father was away at sea. Now that she was twelve her father had
decided she was old enough to have a husband and she was being taken
to Hong Kong to be married to a wealthy businessman. It did not make
Mary happy. At all. Mary's dream had always been to be a schoolteacher
like her mother. Now here she was being taken to a strange man in a
strange land, her dreams dashed. Jacqueline told Mary how her own
mother was a drunkard who would beat her with sticks and that if she
hadn't ran away she feared she would have died.

The journey to the East was a long one so the two girls found new
things to do. Jacqueline could neither read nor write so Mary gave her
some of her notebooks and a fancy pen and taught her. It made Mary
feel like the schoolteacher she always wanted to be. Using an
encyclopaedia of great treasures and worldly achievements Mary would
teach Jacqueline how to read words. Jacqueline was a fast learner and
soon knew enough to start writing entries in a small diary. In exchange
for her education Jacqueline taught Mary what she had learnt on the
tough streets of Portsmouth such as how to sword fight and pick pockets.

One seasick afternoon when the waves were as tall as mountains and
the clouds black with rain Jacqueline was woken by the sounds of
shouting and clashing swords. She crept out from behind the salt barrels
and peeked through the boards at the deck above. The ship had been
overrun by pirates and by the look of it they were not taking prisoners.
Jacqueline watched, terrified, as the crew were cut down one by one and
thrown overboard until the only people left standing were Mary and her
father, the Captain. They were held to the main mast by a couple of
pirates as a figure in a black oily coat walked across the deck towards
them. He was was one of the most frightening looking men Jacqueline
had ever seen. A thick mane of matted yellow hair ran down to a straggly
beard which was tied in black bows. The man's face was so wrinkled and
knotted it was hard to call it a face at all. The most disturbing thing was
that he only had one eye. Unlike the stories Jacqueline had heard about
one-eyed pirates this man made no effort to cover the socket with an eye
patch. In its place was a black hole as deep and cold as the darkest well.

"Do you know who I am?" asked the one-eyed pirate, quietly.

The Captain nodded.

The pirate turned to Mary.

"And do you know who I am, little lady?"

Mary shook her head. The pirate let out a low chuckle. It was a horrible sound, like a shark clearing its throat.

"So why don't you ask your father who I am. He knows it," said the one-eyed pirate.

Mary looked at her father. She had never seen him scared before.

"He's Blackheart Bob."

Blackheart Bob nodded.

"And do you know why they call me Blackheart Bob?" he said, pulling a great sword from his belt.

He took Mary's hands, placed them around the handle of the sword and pointed the tip at her father's chest.

"It's because I make people do things like this."

Blackheart Bob pushed Mary's hands forward, plunging the blade of the sword into her father's heart. Down below Jacqueline held her hands to her mouth to stop herself from crying out.

The pirates broke into the hold and began to empty it. Jacqueline tried to hide as best she could but there was nowhere left once they had taken the last of the barrels.

"What have we here?" said Blackheart Bob as a scrawny tattooed pirate dragged her kicking and screaming up from the hold.

"I'm a pirate too!" shouted Jacqueline.

Blackheart Bob laughed. He picked Jacqueline up and put his face close to hers. She could smell the sour stench of old rum on his breath.

"Well you'd be the smallest pirate I've ever seen!"

Blackheart Bob dragged Jacqueline over to the side of the ship and dangled her by her hair over the black waves.

"We've got enough pirates on this ship, Missy."

Blackheart Bob let go. As she fell Jacqueline grabbed hold of his beard and he toppled forward against the rail.

"Well, this one's got a little fight in her!"

He grabbed her arm, trying to pull her free.

"Could be a good watch to see her boxing the sharks!"

"AND IT COULD BE A GOOD WATCH SEEING YOU SAIL A SHIP WITHOUT YOUR HEAD!" shouted Jacqueline.

Blackheart Bob stopped laughing. Jacqueline had taken the dagger from his waistcoat and was holding it against his throat. Bob leant in slowly, his one bloodshot eye burning into hers.

"If you drop me, I swear it will be the last thing you do," hissed Jacqueline, her heart pumping with fear.

Bob raised an eyebrow and broke into a grin.

"Okay, Missy. I like your spirit. You give me back my blade and I'll make you a pirate."

"And her!" said Jacqueline, nodding at Mary.

Blackheart Bob shrugged.

"If she shows spirit, I'll gladly have her on my crew. If she causes trouble, she's shark-bait. Deal?"

Jacqueline nodded.

"Deal."

Jacqueline and Mary were packed into rowing boats with the stolen barrels and sailed across the choppy waters to Blackheart Bob's pirate ship, the Salty Dog. Mary was quiet. She didn't even look back as her father's ship which, having been set alight by the pirates, was slipping beneath the water. Jacqueline knew that even if Mary's father had been planning to give her away, it was unforgivable what Blackheart Bob had made her do. She wanted to tell Mary it wasn't her fault but the look in Mary's eyes scared her. It was like something had broken inside her.

On board the Salty Dog there was no time to think and for Jacqueline and Mary it meant working from sunrise to sunset. They had to do all the horrible jobs that the other pirates wouldn't do. Washing down the deck, scrubbing the sails and picking maggots out of the meat. They never complained and Blackheart Bob, as cruel as he was, was fair to them. One of the other pirates said that having girls on board was bad luck and threatened mutiny. The next morning Jacqueline saw his body tied to the top mast being pecked by seagulls. She asked Bob what had happened.

"He thought you were bad luck. Turns out, he was right."

Soon the months turned into years and Jacqueline became Jacky the Pirate. Her and Mary, working twice as hard to prove themselves, became twice as good as any man on board. Mary had the idea that she and Jacky should act as decoys in a rowing boat, flagging down passing ships for help. Once brought on board they would quickly disarm the Captain so the Salty Dog could pull up alongside. One thing Jacky quickly noticed about being a pirate was that you didn't tend to live very long. By the time Mary and her reached the age of eighteen most of the original crew had died and been replaced. Barely a week went by without one of them being killed in a raid or falling overboard drunk on rum. Even though many years had passed Jacky could see that Mary still hated

Bob for what he made her do to her father and Bob knew it. Despite his respect for her he never allowed her to carry a sword or pistol near him and always asked her to taste the meals she prepared for him before he ate.

After sunset, like when they were children, Jacky and Mary would watch the dolphins jumping through the waves and it was on one of these quiet evenings that Mary started a conversation with Jacky that would change the course of their lives.

"He's getting old," she said.

Jacky turned to look at Mary who's eyes were fixed on the full moon.

"Be careful, sister. That talk's mutinous."

"You know it, Jacky. The crew know it. On the last raid we lost three men," said Mary, "It's only a matter of time until he kills us all. Unless we kill him."

Mary looked at Jacky.

"We're the quickest and the smartest on board and capable of running our own ship."

"Even if that were true and we did manage to get rid of him," said Jacky, "we'd never get the crew to follow us."

Mary laughed. It was a low, mean laugh like Blackheart Bob's.

"They don't have to."

Mary put her hand on Jacky's shoulder.

"You're the only family I have now, sister. If anyone caused you harm I'd gladly feed them to the sharks."

So it was settled. There was an ambush planned on a tobacco ship leaving for Australia. It was heavily protected by the British Navy but Blackheart Bob was determined to attack. It was a suicide mission. They had to act fast.

"You're very quiet tonight, missy," said Blackheart Bob.

He was sat at the table in his cabin eating chicken.

"I'm tired, Captain," said Jacky, carving pineapple for his dessert.

"A tired pirate is a dead pirate," Bob muttered back.

He glanced across the cabin at Mary who was stood in the corner holding his rum pitcher.

"And how's Mary?" he asked.

Mary shrugged.

"She's a real talker, that one," he said, taking a swig of rum.

As he lowered his arm Mary ran across the room and hit him in the side of the head with the pitcher. It shattered, sending glass across the table. Bob roared and staggered to his feet.

"I always knew you were rotten, Mary!" he snarled, stepping back and reaching for the sword in his belt.

It wasn't there. He looked around with his one good eye, dumbfounded. Jacqueline stepped in front of him and pointed his sword at his chest.

"Mutiny!" he roared, "MUTINY!"

"The others won't come," said Jacky, "you may have us taste your food for poison, but you don't get us to taste theirs. We've put so much sleeping tonic in their meat the screams of hell couldn't wake them."

Jacky tossed the sword to Mary who put the tip of the blade at Bob's throat.

"So you plan to kill me then?" he muttered.

"No," said Mary, "you'll die at your own hands."

The sky was full of a thousand stars. They shone down on Mary and Jacky as they marched Blackheart Bob out onto the deck. With a thick rope Jacky bound the Captain's waist to the mast. Mary placed the tip of the sword against his heart and bound his hands to the hilt tightly. She then tied a rope to each of his wrists and threw the ends over his shoulders where Jacky attached the ends to a barrel of gold that stood on a small stool.

"Now, Captain, I suggest you keep your arms out straight if you don't want to be run through by your own blade. If you're lucky the seagulls might rescue you," said Mary.

She kicked the stool away and the barrel dropped, pulling the ropes which in turn pulled on Blackheart Bob's wrists. The tip of the sword pierced his shirt as he struggled to keep his arms straight. His muscles trembled with the effort. They were not going to hold out for long.

"You swarthy dogs!" he cursed, "You harpies! What black night is this?"

"Scream all you want," said Jacky as she lowered a rowing boat filled with barrels of gold over the side of the Salty Dog.

Mary kicked over a barrel of oil onto the deck and lit it with a torch. As the flames leapt across the deck towards the captains boots she jumped over the side of the ship into the rowing boat.

They were halfway towards the coast when the Captain's cursing and screams finally stopped. Jacky watched the ship as it sank beneath the water. Mary, rowing towards the shore, didn't look back once.

Mary and Jacky knew the best inns to go to in the port of Tasmania to find a good pirate crew. They were surprised to learn that their reputation had spread quickly. Everyone knew that Blackheart Bob had been outsmarted by Rotten Mary and Cutthroat Jacky. There were pirates lining up to join them. They bought a new vessel off a ship merchant and ordered it to be painted black so it would be better hidden in the dark and named it The Black Night. With their new crew preparing The Black Night for sail Jacky and Mary bought fine clothes and new swords. Soon they were ready to set sail on the long trip back to England....

"Where's the rest?" said Brodie, "Is that it?"

Daisy nodded. She put the pages down.

"Was there any more in the book?" asked Daisy.

Marsha shook her head.

"No. Those were the only pages that had anything written on them."

"Well, I think it tells us a lot," said Daisy, "It tells us that the Sisters of the Black Night are the descendants of pirates. What we don't know is what they are looking for. We have to find out more."

CHAPTER SIXTEEN - A BATTLE OF HONOUR

"If the Sisters of the Black Night are pirates, it doesn't surprise me. Pirates like drinking rum all the time and so does Mistress Aiken," said Marsha.

All the 88ers were on the balcony except Tracy who was off at hockey practice. The talk of pirates had got Daisy in the mood for a bit of fencing so she was hoping Tracy would be up for a quick duel when she got back.

"So the Lyle family have a pirate in their past. I bet no one's family history is totally clean," said Penny, "It still doesn't explain what it's got to do with Mistress Aiken. As far as I know they're not related."

"Penny's right," said Daisy, "even though we know Mistress Aiken is the Great Sister, we can't prove it. We need to expose them all somehow."

"I might be able to help you with that!" said Brodie, running out onto the balcony.

She reached into her satchel and pulled out Layla's camera.

"Ta-daaa!" she said triumphantly.

The 88ers ran into the dorm and Tina dragged her wardrobe in front of the door to stop anyone getting in. Brodie plugged the camera into a wall socket and connected it to her laptop.

"Bingo!" said Brodie clapping her hands together, "Just as I was hoping - they put the photos in the trash but didn't empty it."

"Meaning?" asked Penny.

"Meaning I can save the pictures that Layla took."

While the pictures were copying across to Brodie's laptop she explained what happened. She had been in Anita's office trying to persuade her to upgrade the print room equipment with some computer parts Tina had found in the engineering labs. Anita was not interested. Annoyed, Brodie had turned to leave when she saw a camera sitting on the editor's desk. Spotting a sticker of a wolf on the side she knew it had to be Layla's. Mistress Aiken had given it to the editor so she could print the picture of Layla stealing Cleopatra's Egg for International Schoolgirl. Anita hadn't been able to turn the camera on so it was still sitting there.

"The battery had gone flat and she didn't realise. I said I'd get it fixed for her," said Brodie.

"Well, why are we barricading the room?" asked Penny.

"The Brat Pack saw me running across the courtyard with the camera. I'm sure they'll be here any minute," said Brodie.

As if on cue, there was a loud knock on the door.

"Oh dear," said Millie.

The knocking got louder and the whole door started shuddering. Tina jumped off the bed and pressed herself against the wardrobe but the force from the other side was too strong. The door slipped open a crack and Dorothy and Olga pushed their faces through.

"Open the door!" Dorothy shouted.

"Find your own door, this one's ours!" Daisy shouted back.

"Nearly there!" said Brodie, staring at her laptop.

Marsha ran over to help Tina but didn't get there in time. With a big push Annabel, Olga, Dorothy and Eleanore broke into the dorm waving hockey sticks above their heads. Annabel pushed Brodie off her bed and yanked the camera away from the laptop. Eleanore ran straight for Daisy. She grabbed her by the neck and pinned her against the wall.

"WHAT DID I TELL YOU ABOUT KEEPING YOUR NOSE OUT OF THINGS, OIK?" she shouted.

"Let go of her!" shouted Millie.

She jumped off her bed and landed a punch on the back of Eleanore's head.

"OW!" said Eleanore, more surprised than anything else.

Olga knocked Millie to the floor with her hockey stick. Daisy was struggling to breath. She kicked her legs out wildly, hoping to knock herself free from Eleanore's grip.

"Keep the rest of them here," Eleanore shouted at the Brat Pack, "I'm going to fix this problem right now."

Whilst the 88ers wrestled with the Brat Pack, Eleanore dragged Daisy out onto the balcony. Annabel followed her and jammed her hockey stick through the handle on the dorm door, locking it in place.

"What a lovely view," hissed Eleanore as she pushed Daisy up against the railings.

She let go of Daisy's neck and spun her round. As Daisy gasped for air Eleanore tipped her forward until she was dangling over the railings. Daisy stared down with panic at the courtyard. A couple of girls were walking into the doors of Honour House far below. She tried to call for help but her throat was sore from Eleanore's grip.

"I told you what would happen if you didn't keep your nose out of things," said Eleanore in Daisy's ear.

Daisy looked around desperately for help. Annabel was standing in the doorway.

"Annabel…" Daisy whispered.

"Annabel, throw the camera off the balcony when I push her. We'll say she stole it and fell trying to run away," said Eleanore.

"I don't think this is a good idea, Eleanore," said Annabel.

"SHUT UP AND DO WHAT I SAY!" snarled Eleanore, her eyes wild and crazy.

Annabel, still unsure, walked over and dangled the camera over the railings.

"Help!" Daisy cried.

"There's no help for you here," hissed Eleanore.

She grabbed Daisy's feet and tipped her over the balcony.

For a moment it felt like the whole world had turned upside down. Daisy threw her hands out wildly, desperate to grab hold of something, anything. Her fingers caught something sharp and clung to it. With a painful jolt that shook down her body from her arms to her feet, Daisy stopped her fall.

"Damn you, oik!" screamed Eleanore.

Daisy looked around, stunned. She was hanging from the wing of one of the old gargoyles sticking out from the wall of the dorm building. Down below, Layla's camera hit the courtyard and shatter into pieces.

Daisy hooked her hands around the gargoyle and tried to swing her legs up only to find Eleanore jabbing at her fingers with a hockey stick.

"Just like poking crabs in a bucket!" laughed Eleanore.

Annabel was glancing between the two of them, not quite sure what to do.

"This little piggy went to market…"

The toe of Eleanore's hockey stick cracked against Daisy's right hand little finger.

"This little piggy stayed at home…"

Eleanore jabbed at Daisy's ring finger, knocking it from the gargoyle.

"HELP!" cried Daisy.

"This little piggy had roast beef…"

Eleanore cracked her stick against Daisy's thumb and she lost the grip with her right hand. Daisy swung out into the darkness, the trembling fingers of her left hand the only thing keeping her from falling.

"Annabel, please…" said Daisy.

Annabel turned to Eleanore and opened her mouth to speak. There was a sudden flash of movement behind her and she dropped out of sight. Eleanore hadn't noticed. Her eyes were crazy as she jabbed away at Daisy's left hand.

"…And this little piggy…"

"OI! WHO ARE YOU CALLING A PIG, YOU MENTAL SNOT-NOSED BITCH!"

Eleanore spun round. Tracy was standing a few feet behind her twirling a hockey stick in her hands. Eleanore screamed wildly and ran towards Tracy. Keeping calm, Tracy ducked into a crouch and shot her arm out low, hooking the toe of her stick around Eleanore's left ankle. With a quick jerk, she pulled her off her feet. Eleanore landed flat on her back with a painful thud. Tracy ran to the wall and spotted Daisy clinging desperately to the gargoyle.

"Here!" said Tracy, holding out her hockey stick.

Daisy grabbed hold and, with a grunt, Tracy pulled her back up onto the balcony.

"How are ya?" asked Tracy.

"A little bruised," said Daisy.

"Good job I came back early from practice or you'd be pavement pizza," said Tracy.

"That's nice," said Daisy.

Relieved to be back on safe ground, Daisy looked around. Annabel was laying against the wall with a nasty bump on her head where Tracy had whacked her. Eleanore was back on her feet and looking like a wild dog. Hearing the commotion, Olga and Dorothy ran out to join her. They raised their hockey sticks and walked towards Daisy and Tracy.

"Here! I always carry a spare."

Tracy pulled a second hockey stick from her backpack and tossed it to Daisy. Daisy extended it like a fencing foil as Eleanore lunged forward, swinging her stick wildly. Daisy blocked it easily. There was no technique to Eleanore's approach. She was too mad and angry. As the blows came, Daisy managed to dodge or defect them. Out of the corner of her eye she caught a quick glimpse of Tracy who was fighting off Olga and Dorothy simultaneously. There was a smile on Tracy's face. She was way too quick for either of them.

Catching Daisy off guard, Eleanore grabbed hold of Daisy's stick and twisted it out of her hands. She tossed it over her shoulder where it landed at Annabel's feet. With a manic laugh she charged forwards, swinging at Daisy's chest. Daisy jumped out of the way and her back hit the railings.

"Hang on, Daisy!" shouted Tracy, trying to fight her way past Olga and Dorothy.

There wasn't enough time. Eleanore came forward and Daisy, seeing nowhere else to go, jumped up onto the railings. A stone outcrop jutted out from the roof a few feet away. She could make it in a couple of steps. From there it would be a quick climb down into the dorm window where the others were.

"Tracy, follow me!" shouted Daisy.

Daisy ran along the wall to the outcrop and pulled herself onto the roof. The wind rippled through her clothing as she stood up carefully on the tiles and looked round. The roof was so high up it looked like it was level with the moon. Wobbling slightly, Daisy edged backwards across the tiles, trying to get level with the dorm window. She had to be quick. Eleanore was climbing up onto the outcrop to reach her.

"Catch, Daisy!"

Daisy looked down to see Brodie swinging a fencing foil up to her from the window, tied to the end of school tie. It clattered onto the roof ledge a few feet away. As Eleanore came towards her, Daisy grabbed the foil and held it out.

"EN GARDE!" shouted Daisy.

Eleanore jabbed with her hockey stick but Daisy batted it away. Eleanore swung again and caught Daisy's shoulder. The force behind it was strong enough to cause her to lurch dangerously in the wind. Daisy stepped away, feeling cautiously along the tiles with her right foot. Eleanore lunged and the toe of the hockey stick slid down the blade and into Daisy's stomach, knocking her backwards. Daisy's foot slipped over the edge of the roof and she fell to her knees, dropping the foil. It bounced off the guttering and spun away into the darkness. There was nowhere else to go. Daisy could hear the 88ers calling to her from the dorm window but there was no way she would make it past Eleanore. She looked up and spotted the bell tower at the top of the roof. That was it. Daisy kicked Eleanore as hard as she could in the shins and clambered up the roof tiles to the tower. She didn't look back until she had jumped over its short stone wall.

"I'm not finished with you!" bellowed Eleanore, climbing up onto the wall behind her.

As Eleanore swung her stick at Daisy's head, she ducked. The stick hit the bell with a deafening clang. It was the loudest sound Daisy had ever heard. In an instant she understood why people said their ears were ringing when they heard loud noises. Even Eleanore looked shocked. It gave Daisy a couple of seconds. She spotted the bell rope hanging through a hole in the wooden floor. Quickly, she pulled off her jumper and wrapped it around her hands.

"Perilous," muttered Daisy.

She grabbed the rope and jumped through the hole.

Daisy slid down the rope all the way to the entrance hall. She hit the stone floor and ducked into a roll. The rope jumped away from her and bounced up and down wildly, clanging the bell above and sending rumbles through the building. Daisy got to her feet and put her jumper back on. There was a big hole in the middle from the rope burn. She looked up. There was no sign of Eleanore but the whole of Honour House was now out on the stairs looking down at her. There wasn't much chance of making it past them to the dorm. Daisy ran out into the courtyard where the sound of the bell was alerting everyone in the school. The courtyard was filling with people.

"Look!" cried a Prefect, pointing to the roof of Honour House.

Daisy looked up. In the light of the moon she could see Tracy on her own battling Olga, Dorothy and Eleanore on the roof. Daisy felt helpless staring up at the battle. She tried to push her way through the crowd to get back and help when a hand landed on her shoulder. Daisy turned to see Miss Weaver.

"Stay here, Daisy," she said firmly.

Miss Weaver, along with Madame Didier and Mrs Brisket, stormed into Honour House. After a few minutes, Madame Didier appeared on the balcony and climbed up onto the roof. The crowd let out a sigh of disappointment. The Prefects started ordering everybody back to their dorms. Finding herself alone in the courtyard Daisy realised there were going to be a lot of awkward questions.

For the second time in as many weeks Daisy was sat outside Mistress Aiken's office. All the 88ers were with her this time. So were the Brat Pack. Tracy was certain she was going to get expelled.

"Oh well, back to join the oiks in London," she joked.

"Good riddance," said Eleanore.

"Ignore them, Tracy," said Brodie, "They're pathetic. Pathetic and scared."

Eleanore smiled. Dorothy and Olga laughed.

"You're the one who should be scared, cowgirl," said Eleanore, "we've got plans for all of you."

The office opened and Miss Weaver appeared.

"OK, girls, lets see if we can sort this mess out."

Mistress Aiken's face was purple with anger. She glared at the girls one at a time. When she finally spoke, her voice was quiet. Somehow that was worse than if she'd started shouting.

"I hear you've been playing hockey on the roof of Honour House."

"It wasn't our fault! They attacked us!" shouted Tracy.

"BE QUIET," said Mistress Aiken, standing.

The girls all took a step back.

"When I speak, you LISTEN. You don't so much as squeak unless I give you permission. Do I make myself clear?"

"Yes, Mistress Aiken," the girls said in unison.

"Good. YOU!" said the Deputy Head pointing at Daisy, "Why are you in my office again? What is your involvement in all this?"

Daisy didn't know what to say.

"Daisy rang the bell and alerted us," said Miss Weaver.

Eleanore opened her mouth to protest but Mistress Aiken shot her a frosty stare and she snapped it shut.

"Is this true?" she asked.

Daisy looked across at Miss Weaver who nodded at her.

"Yes, Mistress Aiken. It's true," she said, "I rang the bell which, erm, alerted Miss Weaver and the other teachers."

"Well, why didn't you just come to the teachers quarters rather than alert the whole damn school?"

Daisy thought quickly.

"It would have taken too long, Mistress Aiken."

Daisy could feel the Brat Pack glaring at her but ignored it.

"What about you?" said Mistress Aiken, now looking at Tracy.

Tracy said nothing.

"Oh, so NOW you can't speak? From what I'm told, you decided to have a fencing match with the older girls and Madame Didier when she tried to intervene."

"I didn't fight Madame Didier. She'd murder me!" said Tracy.

"That's not what Madame Didier says," said Mistress Aiken.

Tracy hung her head.

"Tell her what you girls told me," said Madame Didier, turning to the Brat Pack.

"We heard these girls stole property from the school magazine so we went to get it back," said Eleanore.

"That's not true, you liar!" shouted Tracy.

"Tracy, if you don't keep quiet I will expel you on the spot right now," said Mistress Aiken, "What had they stolen?"

"A camera."

Mistress Aiken looked nervous.

"And where is this camera?"

"I have it. What's left of it," said Madame Didier, "It fell from the roof."

"Well…good," said Mistress Aiken, "So how did the fight start?"

"When we took the camera, this one went crazy so we had to fight back," said Eleanore, pointing at Tracy.

"And was anyone else involved in the fighting?"

Eleanore looked at Daisy. Daisy could tell she was thinking, probably about how she had tried to throw Daisy off the roof. She wouldn't want that coming out. She shook her head.

"I see," said Mistress Aiken.

She sat back down.

"Well, from what I can tell, you girls are all guilty of stealing property," she said pointing at the 88ers.

"We didn't steal the camera, Mistress Aiken. I work for International Schoolgirl. I took it to the dorm to get some pictures off it for Anita Walker, you can ask her," said Brodie.

"What images?" asked Mistress Aiken looking worried again.

"I don't know," said Brodie, "these chuckleheads threw it off the roof before I got a chance to do it."

Mistress Aiken laughed. She was obviously relieved.

"Well. I guess that clears it up. It sounds to me like these girls acted with good intentions."

She waved her hand at the Brat Pack.

"You can go but in future I suggest you speak to one of us before you do anything stupid."

The Brat Pack left. Mistress Aiken looked at the 88ers.

"You may have been right about taking the camera - I will check with Anita Walker. Quite frankly, I'm annoyed she let it out of her sight. That said, this is the second incident with your dorm in a very short time. I'm putting you all on probation. Any more mischief and you can wave goodbye to Darlington. Do I make myself clear?"

"Yes, Mistress Aiken."

"You can go."

Daisy sighed with relief. They turned to leave.

"Not you, Tracy. You stay here."

Tracy stopped in her tracks. She looked at Daisy and Brodie helplessly.

"Go, you two! Back to lessons!" barked Mistress Aiken.

Daisy could see tears start to roll down Tracy's face as Mistress Didier closed the door behind them.

CHAPTER SEVENTEEN - EMAILS, PHOTOS AND

CONVERSATIONS

Tracy had been expelled.

Daisy and the other 88ers threw themselves into their studies. Now they were on probation they had to be on their best behaviour. They learnt about Russian culture in geography whilst painting eggs and listening to folk tales from Miss Brisket's Babushka (the Russian word for grandmother). It was during this lesson that Daisy finally understood how the geography lessons worked. She was looking at the pretty embroidery on the dress she was wearing when she noticed it was made up of the Russian words Miss Brisket's grandmother had been singing to them. Daisy looked around the room and saw that hidden everywhere were facts, figures and phrases. They were written in the patterns of the carpets and the wallpaper. Even the lampshades. After the class she was discussing it with Brodie and they realised they remembered everything. It was a bit like hypnosis.

Things were changing at the magazine office. Brodie had persuaded Anita to hook up a couple of computers and with Tina's help had managed to get Bertha to print out a couple of sentences. It wasn't quite a full magazine and Bertha had complained and belched smoke all the way through but it was a start.

The more interesting the lessons became though, the sadder Daisy felt. She spent all her spare time in the library doing private study. The teachers were very impressed with her work but she found it hard to feel good about it. All she really wanted was Layla and Tracy back. One evening after dinner Daisy borrowed Brodie's laptop to check her emails. There was a message from dad.

Hi Daisycakes,
Missing you lots. Hope everything is going well. The weather here is fine. The boys are OK though they are arguing as they think one of them should have your room while you are away. I told them to get stuffed. I wouldn't worry - they'll never agree which of them should get it anyway. Be good to see you at xmas. Missing you loads but very, very proud of you.
Love and hugs
Dad
X

The email brought a lump to Daisy's throat. It also made her feel guilty. The message was over a week old. She'd been so busy throwing herself into her studies she hadn't thought to check her old email account. She tapped back a reply.

Hi Dad,
Thanks for your message. Weather here has been lovely but the evenings are getting shorter really quickly now. Sorry I haven't written back sooner but it has been mad busy. I know that sounds like an excuse but you'd be amazed at all the stuff here. Every week I'm finding out something new about the place.
Love and hugs
Daisy
X

P.S. If the boys go in my room, I'll break their legs!

Daisy clicked send. She looked through the other messages. They were mostly spam. Weird medicines and offers for bank loans. She flicked through them quickly until she saw one that said "Hello Daisy!". She opened it up.

* * *

Dear Daisy,

Thanks for contacting us. We'd love to meet up and tell you what happened. We've both been heartbroken since getting expelled. We did nothing wrong.

Karen (and Sandy)

On Saturday, clinging onto their umbrellas and battling their way through the bad weather, Daisy and Brodie walked into Hamley, the nearby village. There were no other girls from the school in the Hamley Tea Room when they arrived which was quite a relief as they didn't want to be spotted. They ordered cream teas and took a seat by the fire at the back to warm themselves up. Sandy and Karen showed up a few minutes later and Daisy poured tea for the three of them (Brodie, as always, preferred a coffee).

"We didn't do anything," said Sandy.

Sandy was a small girl with short mousy hair and lots of nervous energy. Karen on the other hand was tall, blonde and quiet.

"So what happened?" asked Daisy, taking out her journal to make notes.

Sandy let out a heavy sigh and told their story.

It was the first day of term and Sandy and Karen had moved into their new dorm in Charity House. They both came from the North of England so quickly formed a friendship. The other girls in the dorm were nice to them but already knew each other from junior school. One of them - Annabel - did talk to them, though it was mostly boasting. She told Sandy and Karen that her cousin Eleanore and her friends were in one of the upper years. She said knowing them meant that she was special, that she couldn't get into trouble.

"Annabel is Eleanore's cousin?" said Daisy, "Well that makes sense."

"Annabel was telling us how her family had been involved with the school for a long time and we thought that sounded interesting for a history project so we went to the library to do some research and found an old book called The Secret History of Darlington," said Sandy.

"I tried to find that book!" said Daisy, "I found Annabel in the library with it just after I started!"

"Well, she wouldn't have wanted you to read it," said Karen, "That's what got us into trouble."

Karen told them that the book said no woman was allowed to start a school when Darlington was established so a mysterious Professor Darlington was invented as the Head Master. Professor Darlington never actually existed. The man in the portrait that hung in the assembly hall was a local farmer who had been dressed up by the painter to look important.

"That's amazing!" said Daisy.

"It gets more interesting," said Sandy, "This S. Darlington, the author of the book, explained that the oldest pieces in the museum were donated by pirates."

Sandy leant in closer.

"It even hinted that the school itself was set up by pirates."

Daisy and Brodie looked at each other.

Karen told them that they had mentioned the book to Annabel but she appeared not to care. After that, however, she didn't speak to them again. A few days later they came back from dinner to find Madame Didier, the house mistress for Charity House, standing over their suitcases with a bottle of rum and a packet of cigarettes.

"And then we were expelled," said Sandy.

"So what you're saying is my parents are spending a fortune to send me to a pirate school?" said Penny.

The girls were sat at a table in the far corner of the empty dining hall. It was late. They were the last ones left.

"No," said Brodie, "all the book said is that the school was set up with pirate money. Maybe the money was stolen from the original Sisters of the Black Night. Maybe they want it back."

"Well, how do you steal back a school?" said Tina.

"I don't think it's the school they want," said Daisy, "I think they're using it to find something else - some more treasure or gold that's out there. That's why they've been spending all the school's money on buying the exhibits for the museum. That's why they keep going on these trips. They're looking for something."

"And they don't want anyone around who might find out what they're up to," said Marsha.

"Like us," said Millie.

"So they're going to get us expelled whatever we do," said Penny.

Daisy nodded.

"What about the photographs Layla took?" asked Marsha.

Brodie shrugged.

"I've looked through the ones we managed to copy across before the Brat Pack burst in and although there's a lot of hooded people in them, none of them show anybody's face."

"So what do we do?" said Millie.

Daisy looked at Brodie who sipped her espresso and gave a shrug.

"Don't look at me, D.C. You found out about this. That makes you team leader."

Daisy blushed. She'd never really been a leader of anything but the 88ers faces were tired and scared and it made her feel determined to do something about it.

"We fight back," she said.

"And how are we going to do that?" said Millie.

Daisy pointed to the noticeboard behind them. There was a picture of a scary looking lighthouse perched on some cliffs. Underneath it were the words SERPENT'S TOOTH SCHOOL TRIP.

Walking back to the library after dinner Daisy spotted Roni leaning against a tree on the path.

"Daisy Cooper, as I live and breathe. How's it going, sweetie?"

"Fine, thanks," said Daisy.

Roni gave her a frown.

"Hmm. I'm not quite sure I believe you. I think we need a little chat. Come with me."

Roni led Daisy through a path past the sports fields where girls were practicing hurdles and past the art block, inside which Daisy could see Miss Weaver sculpting a giant fish out of clay. The path led into a wooded area where they had to push aside branches and ferns to keep going. Eventually they reached a large and very old crumbling tower hidden from the rest of the school. Roni reached into her blouse and pulled out a key on a ragged piece of string. She stuck it into the lock of a door covered in vines and turned. The door creaked open. Daisy hesitated. She wasn't sure she was ready to step inside any more mystery school buildings.

"Come on, Daisy Cooper. Chop, chop!" said Roni.

The inside couldn't have been more different than the outside. The room they entered was a large white space with plush looking sofas. One of the International Schoolgirls sat behind a wide desk staring at Daisy suspiciously. On the wall behind her was a big bank of computer screens that were covered in satellite maps of different countries of the world. Every map had blinking markers to show the position of International Schoolgirls and scrolling texts and diagrams. Some of them had little windows in the corner showing faces of girls talking on web cams. It was all very high tech.

"What's she doing in here?" asked the girl behind the desk.

"Don't worry, it's Daisy Cooper," said Roni.

"Ordinary girls are not allowed in here! " said another girl approaching from a dark room with yet more computers.

The girl was tapping away at a tablet in her hands.

"Daisy's very discreet, aren't you Daisy?" said Roni, walking straight past the girl.

Daisy followed Roni, trying not to make eye contact with anyone else. Roni led her through into the dark room. The computer screens were touch sensitive and every one of them had an International Schoolgirl in front of it, tapping away and talking over a headset. A large metal cast of the International Schoolgirl logo hung on the wall at the far end.

"Come on, slow coach," said Roni pulling on Daisy's sleeve, "No need to make the girls any more antsy."

They walked down a corridor to a lift entrance. A keypad with glowing numbers stuck out of the wall next to the polished metal doors. Roni pressed several buttons in sequence.

"How many floors are we going to?" asked Daisy.

Roni laughed.

"It doesn't work like a normal lift. Every floor has a special code, like a pin number on your bank card."

Daisy didn't have a bank card. She had a piggy bank and if she wanted to open that she didn't need a special number code, she needed a hammer. The lift doors opened and Roni and Daisy stepped in.

When the lift stopped, the doors opened again to reveal another hallway. The walls were brilliant white and a soft black carpet ran along the floor. There were doors every few feet, each with a tall plotted plant outside in an ornate vase. It looked like a corridor in a very posh hotel.

"Here we are," said Roni stopping outside a door marked with the number twenty three.

Roni inserted a black card into the metal lock on the door. The lock made a beeping sound and the small red light above the handle turned green.

"Welcome to my dorm room," said Roni.

The room was as posh as the hallway. At the far end a large circular window as big as the wall looked through vines into a forest of trees. In one corner was a small but comfortable looking bed and next to that a big oak desk with a mirror on it and a small laptop. On the other side was a wardrobe with mirrored doors and an enormous bookshelf filled with books.

"Wow," said Daisy, "nice place."

Daisy walked over to the bookcase and looked at the titles. There were phrase books for different languages, books on art, history and fashion. Then, as Daisy got to the higher shelves, the subjects got weirder. Books on medicine and anatomy, hypnosis, self defence and wilderness survival manuals.

"I might have known a budding reporter like yourself would head straight for the bookcase," said Roni, pouring a pot of tea.

"My mum loved books," said Daisy, "she used to read three or four at once."

"She sounds lovely and smart," said Roni.

"She was," said Daisy, "she said you could always tell a lot about a person from their book collection."

"And what do my books tell you about me, sweetie?"

Daisy paused. In front of her was a book titled 'History of Female Spies'.

"It tells me that you have a lot of, erm, interesting interests."

Roni laughed and set down the teacups on a table between two sofa chairs.

"I'm sure you'll get to know plenty about my interests in time. Now, lets have some delicious tea."

The tea *was* delicious. Roni opened a tin of shortcake biscuits and Daisy ate one while they talked about the school and its teachers. Daisy wanted to ask about the Sisters of the Black Night but remembered that Hattie had told her not to tell stories until she had proof.

"One of the problems with being an International Schoolgirl and getting sent all over the place is that it's easy to lose track of what's happening at home," said Roni, " You've obviously realised that Darlington is not a normal school. In a way, it's more of a training camp. Everyone here will leave well educated and strong. There are a few special ones who go a lot further though."

"Are you talking about the International Schoolgirls?" asked Daisy.

Roni nodded.

"And it's not just reporting for the school magazine. We get much more *involved* than that. It's about making the world a better place. The problem is that there are some people who think the world should only be a better place for them. You've met a few of them. From what I hear, you've ran across the rooftops with a couple."

Daisy opened her mouth to speak. Roni put a finger to her lips before a single word escaped.

"Whatever it is you are doing, Daisy, it's your story. If you want to be an International Schoolgirl you'll have to show that you can finish it on your own. Just be careful. Here, I want you to have this."

Roni open a drawer in her desk and took out a green bag. Daisy recognised it. It was the one that Roni had used to fix Daisy at the Roman villa all those months ago. She handed it to Daisy.

"Why are you giving this to me?" asked Daisy.

"Because it's useful for emergencies and you're the kind of girl who gets herself into emergencies often," said Roni.

"Thanks!" said Daisy.

She started to pull on the zip to look inside but Roni stopped her.

"Uh-uh, sweetie. Emergencies only."

Daisy walked back to the dorm with a whirlwind of thoughts in her head. Roni made her promise to keep quiet about what she had seen in the International Schoolgirl dorm. It was obviously quite a privilege being allowed in there. Roni was leaving that evening on a new assignment and said she would explain a lot more when she got back. It made Daisy want to be an International Schoolgirl more than ever.

"I don't think that you girls are quite ready to be reporters just yet," said Anita.

The office was its usual mad bustle as they struggled to place headlines for the next edition of the magazine. Daisy and Brodie were trying to persuade Anita to let them represent the school magazine on the trip to the Serpent's Tooth.

"You don't have to use anything we write," said Daisy, "we just want to get some experience. Brodie takes wicked pictures."

"Yeah, I'm awesome," said Brodie.

Anita shrugged.

"OK, I'll approve you going but I can't guarantee using anything. You better hurry, though. The deadline is this afternoon."

CHAPTER EIGHTEEN - THE SERPENT'S TOOTH

A seagull hit the window of the bus waking Daisy with a start. Bleary eyed she looked out at the landscape. The bus was driving over the moors. Barren brush land extended as far as the eye could see. The clouds hung low, pregnant with rain. It was cold on the bus. Draughty. Daisy kicked her plimsolls off, pulled her feet up under her skirt and tucked her arms deep in her jumper, trying to keep warm. She was missing Brodie.

Ten hours earlier, at four o' clock in the morning, Daisy had woken to see the bathroom light shining across the hallway into the dorm. She climbed out of bed and tiptoed through the dorm.

"Bleurgh," mumbled Brodie as Daisy entered the bathroom.

Brodie's head was over the toilet bowl. Her face looked grey.

"I do not feel good," she croaked.

"I can see that," said Daisy, brushing the hair away from Brodie's face.

"I feel like my stomach has been turned inside out."

"Have you eaten anything funny?" asked Daisy.

"I ate the same as you guys. Oh, and the brownie my mom sent over."

The Brownie.

Daisy had thought it odd at the time. Usually Brodie's mum sent a whole box of brownies but this time, there was only one. It had been

163

delivered in the morning mail in a plain postage box and Brodie had eaten it after dinner.

"I think you should go and see the nurse," said Daisy, worried.

"We're going on the Serpent's Tooth School Trip. I'll be fine," said Brodie.

"I don't think so."

Despite Brodie's protests Daisy got her to the Infirmary where the nurse answered the door sleepily in her dressing gown and slippers. Once she saw Brodie's sick face she insisted on putting her in one of the beds.

Without Brodie the plan was going to be difficult. Daisy could still get what they needed to catch the Sisters up to no good but she would have to do it on her own. There was no time to swap Brodie's name for one of the other 88ers. Just before breakfast Marsha attached the tiny camera she had picked up from engineering to the knot in Daisy's tie.

"Keep still!" said Marsha.

"The wire's itchy," replied Daisy, scratching.

"Say something so I can check the sound," said Marsha.

"Scrambled eggs. Beans. Hash browns…"

"What's up with all the food?"

"I'm hungry," said Daisy.

Marsha pressed the play button on Brodie's tablet computer and listened through the headphones.

"SOUND'S GOOD," said Marsha, "Turn and look around the room."

Daisy turned. On the tablet screen Marsha could see the room as the camera in Daisy's tie picked it up.

"It's picking up the video too. The camera is wireless but the range isn't good so you'll need to keep the tablet close to you or you'll lose the signal. I'd suggest keeping it in your satchel. It will be recording all the time. You need to get the Brat Pack or Mistress Aiken to say something incriminating on camera while standing in front of them. Remember not to block your tie. When you've got what you need, turn off the tablet or it will record over it. Are you nervous?"

Daisy nodded.

"Good," said Marsha, "people who aren't nervous make mistakes."

The bus went over a pot hole jolting Daisy awake again. She looked around. Apart from the Brat Pack there were about fifteen other girls on the bus, all sat on the top deck. There were two teachers, Madame Didier and Mistress Aiken, who were sat downstairs with the driver. Daisy scratched at the wire taped to her chest. It was still itchy.

The Serpent's Tooth was a small outcrop of dark rock just off the coast of Devon upon which stood a tall lighthouse. The only connection between The Serpent's Tooth and the mainland was a rickety wooden rope bridge. The lighthouse was still working and had been warning ships away from the jagged cliffs for over three hundred years. Recently part of the cliffs had fallen into the sea and revealed an old smuggler's cave full of barrels of whiskey and boxes of cigars as well as The Black Night pirate ship. There were excited whispers amongst the girls on the bus that there were many more caves yet to be discovered and that some of them contained treasure.

The sea wind lifted Daisy off her feet as she stepped from the bus. The Brat Pack were out in front with Mistress Aiken making their way towards the lighthouse. Daisy stepped up to the edge of the cliff where the bridge started and looked down. Seagulls floated over the crashing waves a hundred feet below. She looked ahead to the rocky island of the Serpent's Tooth where the light of the red and white striped lighthouse blinked silently in the mist. Beyond it was nothing but deep grey water.

"Come on, Daisy, *toute suite!*" said Madame Didier.

Daisy took hold of the guide rope and stepped onto the first wooden plank. The bridge swayed under her feet. She could feel the wind rushing up beneath the slats as she crossed.

Don't look down, Daisy, she thought to herself.

She focused on the other schoolgirls who were now huddled under a wooden canopy at the bottom of the lighthouse.

"What kind of crazy school sends their pupils here?" she said to herself.

Carefully, one foot at a time, she made her way across.

The base of the lighthouse was made up of two small buildings. One building was a cottage for the lighthouse keeper who was an old, bent backed man with a wispy beard called Bert Doble. The other was a rusty barn that had been converted into the museum. Bert led the girls through the museum pointing at the exhibits.

"This 'ere is Craggy Pete," said Bert pointing to a large shark's head fixed to the wall, "a great white that used to hunt these parts. Ate a few little 'uns too till 'e were caught. Blew him up with dynamite they did. Found 'im on the roof of the barn."

Bert shuffled round the museum slowly, the girls following.

"These 'ere is barrels of contraband found in the caves. Serpent's Tooth used to be a big place for smuggling, what with it being so remote. Pirates used to store stuff here - whiskey and cigars and what not - to sell on the mainland. Went on fer years and years. Rumour has it there's a lot more caves around but the King's army sealed them up with dynamite long ago."

"What happened to the smugglers?" asked Daisy.

"Killed 'em all!" said Bert, running a shaking finger across his throat.

That's nice, thought Daisy.

"An 'ere's the thing you lot are supposed to be interested in," said Bert.

He stopped in front of a bow of a ship that sat in the middle of the museum.

"The Black Night. This were the ship that were used by the pirates. She'd been all over till the British Navy finally caught up with her. We found this floating in the cove when the rocks came down. Must have been trapped all this time."

Mistress Aiken was staring at the ship with wonder in her eyes. Daisy got chills herself. This was the Black Night she had read about in Jacqueline Lyle's book. All that was left of the ship was the front half. Daisy climbed the steps up to the deck. The old wood, stained black with pitch, still smelt of salty water. She stood in front of the great wheel that had been used to steer the ship. For a second, it felt like she was back in time with the pirates.

"Rotten Mary's the pirate what sailed her," said Bert, " At least, that's what legend says. Most fearsome pirate of her time."

"What about Cutthroat Jacky? I read she was the true captain of The Black Night," said Mistress Aiken.

"Well, folks been arguing about which of those two was the real captain for years now."

"I've never heard of them," said one of the girls.

"You never 'eard of them," said Bert stepping up close, "because the British Navy didn't want people to know that their most dreaded foe was women. Rumour has it that Rotten Mary fought with a sword in each hand and fireworks tied in 'er hair."

"What happened to them?" asked Daisy.

"Cutthroat Jacky went on to pirate with other ships," said Bert, "no one knows what happened to Mary but some folks say that she's still buried down in the caves somewhere. We ain't found 'er yet, though."

After Bert's tour the girls broke for lunch. Daisy wasn't hungry. She was busy watching the Brat Pack and Mistress Aiken. Eleanore, Dorothy and Olga were ignoring Daisy which was unusual. They weren't even playing their usual staring game. She was beginning to wonder if they would do anything that she could video.

"Right, girls!" said Mistress Aiken when they had finished eating, "You have an hour to look around the lighthouse whilst I make arrangements for the school to pick up the ship for the school museum with Mr Doble."

Bert opened a small door in the stone wall of the museum. Daisy followed the other girls through it into the tall dark column of the lighthouse. There was nothing inside the lighthouse except a long steep staircase that wound its way up to the light above.

"Keep inside at all times, girls!" said Madame Didier as the girls brushed past her and began to climbed the stairs excitedly.

The stairs seemed to go on for ever. Daisy gave up counting them after the first hundred. By the time she got to the top she was exhausted.

The top of the lighthouse was a small round steel room with one large opening through which a giant spotlight shone its light outwards. Looking around at the other girls chatting, Daisy realised the Brat Pack were missing. Apart from the large light the only other noticeable thing in the room was a rusty door that was slightly ajar. Daisy crept along the wall and peeked through the gap. Standing on a rickety metal gangway, half hidden in the mist, were Dorothy and Olga. There was a tiny flicker of orange light in the gloom. They were smoking.

This is it, thought Daisy.

This was what she needed to catch on film. As she opened the door a little wider Dorothy and Olga walked round the gangway out of sight. She would have to go outside to film them.

"Perilous," muttered Daisy.

She waited until Madame Didier turned her back to talk to a couple of girls before stepping out into the cold fog.

The door slammed shut behind her.

"Hello, Oik. What did I tell you about being noisy?"

Eleanore had been hiding behind the door waiting.

I might get beaten up, thought Daisy, *but at least I'm recording it.*
"I'm not doing anything. What are you doing?" she said.
"We're out here catching birds," said Eleanore.
"Looks like we've caught one," said Dorothy.
Dorothy and Olga walked over and put a hand against the railing either side of Daisy, blocking her. Daisy got a sense of deja vu. It was just like it had been back at the mosaic at the Roman villa.
"It's a bit of a scrawny looking bird," said Eleanore, "shall we see if it can fly?"
Eleanore grabbed Daisy and pushed her against the railings. Daisy felt the wind whip through her hair.
"YOU CAN'T THREATEN ME ANYMORE!" shouted Daisy, hoping someone would hear her.
Fortunately someone did. The gangplank door opened and Madame Didier stepped out.
"KEEP THE NOISE DOWN," she said.
"Help, Madame Didier!" said Daisy.
"Let go of her," said Madame Didier quietly, closing the door behind her.

The 88ers were sat around Brodie's bed in the infirmary. Though she hadn't eaten anything, Brodie was feeling much better. They'd been talking about The Sisters of the Black Night and pestering Brodie to see the photographs.
"Sure, but there's really nothing to see. All their faces are covered."
Brodie opened her laptop and clicked open the folder with the pictures from the camera.
"Oh, wow!" said Millie.
The first photo showed the underground hall with the hooded Sisters of the Black Night standing in a large circle in the centre. Brodie clicked onto the next image which showed a closer image of the hooded figures. The Great Sister, her face not visible, was holding up the silver pendant with the eye on it.
"I didn't realise there were so many of them," said Tina.
"I think there are some pupils from different schools. Other adults. Who knows?" said Brodie.
"Isn't it enough to show someone these? It's clear something funny is going on," said Marsha.

"Yeah, but who do you show them to? If Mistress Aiken's involved we can't trust anyone," said Brodie.

Brodie clicked through some more. There were a few from above that Layla had taken from the top of the Hecate statue. Whilst it was clear something very mysterious was going on, no one was recognisable. After that, the photos became blurry and looked like Layla had taken them whilst running away.

"See, we got nothing," said Brodie, flicking through the last of them.

"Hang on, go back a couple of pictures," said Penny.

Brodie clicked back. There was a photo of two hooded figures climbing along one of the ropes to the chandelier.

"We still can't see their faces," said Tina.

"Go back one more," Penny insisted.

Brodie clicked back. There was an almost identical photo of the same two figures.

"There," said Penny.

"I don't see anything," said Brodie.

"THERE!" said Penny pointing at the boots one of the Sisters was wearing, "I'd recognise those boots anywhere. Vintage French lace-ups."

"Who's are they?" asked Millie.

"I mean they're really expensive," said Penny, "you shouldn't go climbing ropes in them."

"WHO'S BOOTS ARE THEY, PENNY?"

"Who else would have expensive boots that were only available in Paris? Madame Didier, of course."

"She's on the trip with Daisy," said Brodie, "We have to call her and let her know!"

Daisy could feel her mobile phone vibrating in her pocket. Eleanore was still holding her against the railings.

"I said, 'let her go'," said Madame Didier.

Eleanore frowned and let go of Daisy. Daisy fell onto the gangplank, relieved. The fencing teacher sighed and rolled her eyes.

"Not like *that*, Eleanore, you stupid girl. I meant LET HER GO. Over the side!"

She marched over, grabbed Daisy's shoulders and lifted her up over the railings.

"Madame Didier..." Daisy started to say but it was too late.

* * *

It was too late.

It took Daisy a couple of seconds to realise she was actually falling. By that point the lighthouse had disappeared out of sight and the sharp walls of the cliffs were whizzing past.

"Mum…" cried Daisy as she tumbled into the angry, black sea.

CHAPTER NINETEEN - THE PIRATE SKELETON

Blackness.

Then, the sound of sloshing water.

For a moment it all seemed like a bad dream and Daisy went back to sleep. Soon though the sloshing water returned, this time closer. With it came a cold dampness and the sound of chattering - like a mouse tap dancing somewhere very close to her head. Daisy slowly realised that the chattering was the sound of her own teeth. She opened her eyes. Nothing. She blinked a couple of times just to make sure she had done it properly. Nothing but blackness.

"Okay, Daisy, where am I?" she asked herself.

Her voice echoed.

Hmm. That was interesting.

Daisy thought about sitting up. She was pretty sure she was lying down. Gently she tensed the muscles in her body one by one. Legs. Arms. Back. Neck. Head. They all seemed to be working properly. They also seemed to be very wet and very cold.

LET HER GO!...

Daisy sat bolt upright. She remembered Madame Didier pushing her off the railings and falling into the sea. She remembered hitting the water and getting sucked under in the current. She remembered losing her satchel and phone before trying to swim to the surface but the sea dragged her down and down. After that, there was only the blackness.

So was she dead? She imagined death might be pretty dark but she never imagined it being quite so wet. Daisy reached around with her fingers trying to make sense of things.

"OUCH!"

Okay. That was a sharp rock. She'd have to be careful. Daisy reached out again and her hand landed in icy water. It stung the fresh cuts on her fingers which meant it was salt water. It rushed up over her wrist before sliding away again. It must be a wave. That explained the sloshing noise.

"Hello?" said Daisy.

Hello, hello, hello said the darkness.

"Daisy, I think you've found a cave," she said to herself.

Daisy stood up carefully. At the back of her mind she was aware that perhaps she should be feeling a little more upset about being pushed off a lighthouse. Then again, she'd never been pushed off a lighthouse before so how did she know how she was supposed to react? Maybe it was shock. Yes, that was probably it.

Daisy turned slowly, hoping to get a glimpse of light. There wasn't one. There had to be a way out though, or she'd never have been able to get in. Daisy looked over to where the sloshing was coming from and could just about see tiny glimmers of light on the tops of the waves. She looked up.

Aaah.

High above Daisy's head was a small crack and through it she could just about see the white glow of the full moon.

"Well, if it's night, that tells me I've been here for some time," said Daisy.

Daisy squeezed the water out of her jumper. She had to keep busy. If she started panicking it would only make things worse. Seeing the moon was a good thing. It meant that at some point there would be daylight and she'd be able to see even better. It was probably a good idea to find a wall as she may well have to climb up it. Stretching her hands out Daisy stepped forward carefully. The ground was rocky and quite slippery. Probably seaweed. She tried to feel the contours of the rock through the soles of her plimsolls. Her foot kicked something. It moved. There was something familiar about the sound. Daisy's heart skipped a beat.

Could it be?

Daisy bent down and put her hand out, patting the object. Yep. There it was. There was her satchel. She picked it up and felt around inside. It was very wet. Daisy took Brodie's tablet out and pressed a button but the tablet did nothing. She fumbled around inside the bag some more and found her pack lunch. That was useful. She was pretty hungry. Daisy felt some more. Her journal. Some pens. Then her fingers fell on the bag that Roni had given her. Roni had said it was for emergencies and this was definitely one of those. Daisy took it out. The material was wax coated which meant it was waterproof. Daisy unzipped it.

"Oh, Roni, you beauty!" said Daisy as her hands fell on the penlight.

Daisy twisted the penlight and the darkness disappeared.

It took a few moments for her eyes to adjust. Daisy shone the torch around to get a good look at the place. The cave (for that's what it was) was pretty narrow. By her feet there was a small pool of water that undoubtedly led back to the sea. She must have been washed through it. It looked dark and dangerous. Daisy had been lucky enough to make it through there once. She wouldn't stand a chance if she tried to get out that way. Next to the pool, sticking out of the wall, was a cluster of sharp looking rocks. Behind the rocks was a large flat boulder covered in a light dusting of sand. Daisy swung her satchel over her shoulder and climbed up onto it. She shone the torch up to the crack in the ceiling. It had to be a hundred feet above her head. The lower half of the wall of the cave was very uneven with lots of pockets of smaller caves and jutting out stones. Above that, the wall was very smooth and impossible to climb. This was going to take some thought.

Daisy emptied Roni's emergency bag. First aid kit, a lighter, a couple of candles, a roll of tape, a ball of nylon rope, needle and thread, aluminium foil, a small pair of binoculars and a Swiss army knife.

Cool.

She took out one of the candles, stood it on the rock and lit it. Sitting down on the boulder Daisy ate her sandwich from lunch and wondered what to do next.

When she had finished eating Daisy blew out the candle and fixed the penlight behind her ear. She put the contents of the emergency bag back in her satchel and walked over to the wall. There was a hole about three foot wide halfway up. The seaweed hanging over its mouth was blowing back and forth so there had to be a wind coming from somewhere. Daisy grabbed a crack in the stone and pulled herself up. It was just like being on the climbing wall at the sport centre back home. It was slow but steady work. By the time she got to the hole her fingers and ankles were aching. She shone the torch inside. It was long and seemed to get narrower as it went on.

"Perilous."

Daisy hoisted herself up and crawled on her hands and knees into the tunnel. After a while the walls got so tight she had to lie flat and wriggle along. Eventually she reached the end and squeezed through, rolling down a slip of rock and coming to a stop on a stone ledge. The torch fell from her ear and bounced a few times before landing in a pool of water. Daisy got to her feet, brushed grit off her knees and stretched. She had the odd sensation that she was being watched. She picked up the torch and shone it into the gloom.

"O.M.G."

It was more than a cave she was standing in, it was a cavern. The floor was a shallow pool full of green algae that glowed. In the middle of the pool was an island of stones and on top of it, surrounded by dusty, old barrels and wooden chests, sat a skeleton in a mouldy red dress staring back at Daisy.

"You must be Mary," said Daisy, "No offence, but you do look pretty rotten right now."

Daisy stepped into the pool and waded over to the island. Mary's skeleton was sat with its back against a couple of barrels, legs outstretched. In Mary's right hand was an old pistol still gripped in her bony fingers. The left hand was shut tight.

"What have you got there, Mary?"

Daisy took the Swiss army knife out of her satchel and used it to carefully prise open the skeleton's fingers. They were gripped firmly, almost fossilised, and she could only manage to open a couple of them. It was enough. A pendant slipped out and swung back and forth on a silver chain. It had an eye on it, the same as the one Mistress Aiken had worn when dressed as the Great Sister.

"Well that's interesting, Mary," said Daisy.

There was a scrabbling noise behind her followed by the sound of tiny feet hitting the water. And squeaking. Lots of squeaking. Daisy turned to see a swarm of rats swimming across the water towards her.

"Ugh!"

Daisy held the blade of the army knife out in front of her. The rats took no notice. She looked around. By the barrels there were a couple of old burnt out wooden torches. Daisy grabbed one.

"Sorry, Mary!" said Daisy and pulled one of the sleeves off the pirate's red dress.

She wrapped it around the end of the torch and lit it with her lighter. It was so dry and dusty that it caught fire immediately. The rats started nipping at her plimsolls. Daisy jabbed at them with the burning torch and they fled back into the water. She waved the torch in wide arcs, scareing them away until they scrabbled up onto the far rocks and disappeared.

Daisy sat down and let out a sigh of relief.

"Well that was quite horrible."

Eak!

Daisy looked down. Next to her feet was a rat sat staring up at her. Daisy grabbed for the torch but then stopped herself. The rat was tiny, obviously a baby. It stood up on its hind legs and cocked its head to one side.

"If only you could talk, maybe you could show me a way out of here," said Daisy.

Eak!

Daisy laughed. She reached into her satchel and pulled out a bit of crust from her lunch bag. She held it out to the rat who took it in its tiny hands and started nibbling away.

"Want a bite?" said Daisy to Rotten Mary.

Mary stared back blankly out of her eye sockets. Daisy smiled at her. The truth was Mary's skeleton scared her. In fact, the whole thing was starting to scare Daisy now that the shock was wearing off. If Rotten Mary, one of the greatest female pirates, had not been able to find a way out what hope did a silly little schoolgirl have?

"How can I get out of here?" Daisy asked the rat.

The rat blinked and sniffed her plimsolls.

Daisy looked at Mary, at her red dress, and a memory popped into her head. In the shadows of the cavern it seemed very real, like it was happening all over again. It was a memory of the last time she had seen her mum. Mum had been pale and as frail as a bird in her red nightie in the hospital bed. Daisy remembered how thin her fingers had been as she held Daisy's hand. Suddenly Daisy found herself crying. Not just weeping, but real sobbing. It felt like she'd been holding back the memory for years and now it was coming out as she sat alone and helpless in the darkness.

The hospital room was bright, white and clean and filled with flowers and cards but it wasn't home.
"Daisy Cooper, my beautiful daughter," said Mrs Cooper.
Her voice was frail, like a whisper at the end of a long corridor, but her eyes shone with a bright, fierce light that clung to life.
"I'm here, Mum," said Daisy.
She had a lump in her throat but was determined not to cry.
"What did the doctor say?" asked Daisy.
"Perilous. He said my situation is perilous. What an unusual word to use," said Mrs Cooper.
She laughed slowly. Daisy didn't find it funny.
"You look fine, mum."
"Daisy, I didn't bring you up to lie. You know better than that."
Daisy blushed.
"Now I know you will look after my boys for me when I'm gone…"
"Mum, don't say that."
"Daisy, shush. It's a terrible thing and I'm going to miss you so much. I need you to listen to me, though. I need you to promise me one thing."
"Anything, mum."
"Live your life, Daisy. Live it like every day is your last and love every minute of it. There's a lot of bad things in this world but no matter how dark it gets, there's always light around the corner."

Eak!
Daisy looked up through blurry eyes. The baby rat jumped into the water and swam to the far shore. He scrambled up onto the rocks and turned back to look at her.

"It's alright for you," she said, "you can probably come and go as you please."

Daisy sat upright.

Of course! she thought, *if anyone knew the way out of somewhere, a rat would.*

Daisy got to her feet, wiped away the tears on her sleeve and splashed through the water after the rat.

The rat turned a few corners and Daisy struggled to keep up with it.

Ducking - and sometimes crawling - through tunnels she followed it. Eventually, amazingly, she saw a tiny chink of light coming through a gap in the stone. As the baby rat ran through it, Daisy put her eye to the gap and looked out. Her heart jumped into her throat. She could not only see the sea but also the bottom of the rope bridge a few feet above. Daisy stepped back and gave the stone a couple of hard kicks. It didn't budge. She reached into her satchel, pulled out the army knife and began scratching away at the rock.

Daisy must have scratched away at the rock for hours. Eventually she sat back against the wall, exhausted. The gap in the rock looked no bigger. Frustrated she threw her knife against down. She was so close! She thought about Mary sat in the middle of her rock island. All the gold and barrels in the world had been no use to her.

The barrels. There's something about the barrels.

Unwinding the ball of rope so she could find her way back Daisy returned to the cavern and splashed across to the stone island. She rubbed her hand across the middle of one of the barrels, clearing away the dust. The letters written on the side became visible. G…U…N…

YES!

Daisy rubbed some more until she could see all the letters.

"Gunpowder. Thanks Mary!" said Daisy, with a chuckle.

She turned the barrel over, ready to roll it through the water to the other side but then stopped.

"So, why didn't you use the gunpowder, Mary?"

Daisy spotted the pendant in Mary's hand. She picked it up carefully and examined it. The eye on the front had writing round the edge of it.

"Devil's Eye," said Daisy, reading aloud.

She turned the pedant over. On the reverse side, etched into the silver, was a map. There were lines showing what looked like different parts of countries but none of them were complete. Daisy tried to make out which countries they were but it was impossible. Without names, they were little more than squiggly lines. It was like someone had deliberately left out enough details for it to be of any use.

Why would someone engrave a map that wasn't complete? thought Daisy.

Suddenly she realised why. Whoever had made the pendants had made sure that the map would only be seen clearly by someone who had both pendants. The pendant the Great Sisters had must show the rest of the details. Daisy looked at Mary. Mary could have left if she had wanted

177

but had decided not to. She had decided to keep the pendant buried with her.

"Did Jacky betray you? Is that what happened?" said Daisy.

Daisy spotted a small, old book tucked into Mary's belt. It was about the same size as Daisy's journal. She picked it up and flicked through the pages. It was a handwritten diary, like the one from Jacky.

"I tell you what, Mary, for keeping me company I'll tell the world about you."

Daisy put the diary in her bag and tugged at the pendant. The chain was stuck, gripped tightly in Mary's bony fingers. Even after all those lonely decades she wasn't ready to let go. Daisy gave it a sharp pull and the pendant snapped free, leaving the chain dangling.

"Sorry, Mary, but if I do get out of here I'm sure they will find you and you won't want them having this. I promise I'll make everything right."

Daisy slipped the pendant into her pocket and gave the barrel of gunpowder a push. It was tough getting it across the pool and even tougher squeezing it through the tunnels but eventually Daisy had it resting against the gap in the rock. She cut a small length of the rope cord and stuck it through the cork hole of the barrel.

"I'm not sure if this is right but I've seen them do it in lots of films," she said to herself.

Daisy lit the cord with the flame from the old torch, made sure it was going and then ran as fast as she could back down the tunnel. Before she even had time to wonder if it would work there was an almighty bang that shook the floor and knocked her off her feet.

Coughing and waving away the smoke Daisy turned back round the corner and found herself looking out of a wide hole at the sea. She stepped over the rubble and peered through it. The rope bridge was a couple of feet above, looking a little ragged from the explosion but still in place. Daisy tied the wooden torch pole to the cord rope and threw it up and over the rope bridge a few times until it jammed between a couple of wooden slats. She tugged to make sure the rope was firm, swung out of the caves and climbed up to the rope bridge.

Bert Doble dropped his egg sandwich when he saw Daisy Cooper walk through the door of his cottage.

"Where in blazes 'ave you been?" he squeaked.

"I've been keeping Rotten Mary company," said Daisy.

She laughed to herself, took a couple of steps into the room and collapsed on the rug.

CHAPTER TWENTY - DAISY THE DEGGER

Daisy sneezed herself awake, which was a first. Her head felt like an angry bear had taken up living in it. She opened her eyes and the room wobbled into view. There was a beeping sound and the smell of disinfectant.

"How are you feeling, Princess?"

Daisy sat up groggily. She seemed to be laying in a strange bed. Her Dad was perched on the end, looking at her with concern in his eyes.

"Ugh," said Daisy.

Dad patted her on the knee.

"Well, I'll get some onion soup and some posh bread if you're hungry."

Daisy was terribly hungry. She tried to remember when she had last eaten but her memories were all a bit jumbled. She remembered the cave. She remembered the explosion and climbing up onto the rope bridge from the cliffs. After that it all got a bit wonky. She remembered being annoyed at lots of voices that kept asking her questions when all she wanted to do was sleep. Then there were the painful bright light that a man in a white mask kept shining in her eyes.

Daisy looked around.

Opposite her were a couple of beds. A small boy with his arm in plaster sat upright in one. Next to him there was a frail looking girl with tubes going into her arm from a beeping machine. Daisy looked at her own arm. There was a bandage on the inside of her elbow and a tube feeding into it from a bag of fluid hung on a hook next to the bed.

"Where am I?" asked Daisy.

"You're in a hospital, Daisy," said Mr Cooper, "We were very worried about you. The doctors said if you'd have been stuck underground for another night, you might not have made it."

Daisy didn't know quite what to make of that.

"The teachers said you fell off a lighthouse into the sea," said Mr Cooper.

He didn't seem angry, just confused and a little scared. Daisy shook her head. She wanted to tell him the truth but was too exhausted to speak. Mr Cooper saw her struggling and lay her back on the pillow.

"Don't worry, Daisy. It's not important now. You rest up and get better."

Daisy fell back into a silent sleep.

When Daisy woke again her father was sat in the chair next to the bed. There was a steaming bowl of onion soup on a tray in front of her with a chunk of tasty looking farmhouse bread. Mr Cooper broke off a piece, dipped it into the soup and handed it to her. It tasted so good. Warm, salty and savoury like a mouthful of roast dinner. It made Daisy feel better immediately. She sat up, broke off another piece of bread and dipped it into the soup hungrily.

The next couple of days Daisy did little else but sleep and eat. Her dad continued to sneak meals in for her so she didn't have to eat the groggy hospital food. Her strength returned slowly and as it did, so did her excitement. She wanted to tell Brodie and the others about finding Mary. She wanted to show them the pendant and read the journal with them. She tried to tell her dad but he stopped her every time. As far as he was concerned it was an accident and that was that. After three days in the hospital Daisy was bored and worried about getting behind with schoolwork.

"Can you pick me up some of my coursework from school, Dad?"

Dad looked at the floor and shifted his feet nervously.

"Your brothers send their love," he said, " they care about you in their own way. You should see them. They've decided to have a moustache growing competition. I've seen more hair on a pair of peaches."

Daisy kept asking for study work but every time Dad would change the conversation. At the end of the week Daisy woke to see him sitting on the end of the bed with a smile on his face. In his hands he had a present wrapped in pirate wrapping paper.

"What's that?" she asked.

"Early xmas present. You kept mumbling about pirates in your sleep so the paper seemed appropriate," said Mr Cooper handing it over.

Daisy opened it slowly.

"A laptop! I won't have to keep borrowing Brodie's now! How did you afford it?"

"I've been putting some money aside."

Daisy leant over and hugged him.

"Thanks Dad! Now you HAVE to get me my study work!"

Mr Cooper sighed.

"Daisy, we need to talk about something," he said, nervously.

"WHAT!??"

Mr Cooper put his arm around Daisy and tried to calm her down.

"LET GO OF ME, DAD!"

"But, dear girl, we all thought you were *dead*," said Mistress Aiken trying to look sympathetic.

Daisy, her father, Mistress Aiken, Madame Didier and Miss Weaver were in the Deputy Head's office.

"You EXPELLED me because you thought I was DEAD??" shouted Daisy, "What do you do if someone loses a leg, give them detention???"

"Well, we didn't expel you, as such. We simply took you off our records until the matter is dealt with."

"Well, put me back ON the records then!" shouted Daisy.

"Put me back on the records then, *Mistress Aiken*," said Mr Cooper, correcting her.

Daisy was too angry to care. She looked over at Miss Weaver.

"This is crazy! Can't you see what she's doing? She doesn't want me sticking my nose into all her pirate business…" said Daisy.

"PIRATE BUSINESS!" laughed Mistress Aiken, nervously, "Goodness, it seems like you're still not quite well, dear girl!"

"I'm sure Daisy's still suffering from a lot of stress," said Miss Weaver, "perhaps the best thing would be to put her back in Honour House and reinstate her in lessons."

"Oh, I don't think so," said Mistress Aiken, "I think you're forgetting about what caused this whole mess in the first place."

"I'M not forgetting. SHE pushed me in the sea!" said Daisy pointing at Madame Didier.

"DAISY COOPER!" said Mistress Aiken.

Her voice was so loud everyone in the room jumped.

"You're clearly confused," continued the Deputy Head, 'we went to the Serpent's Tooth to look at a pirate ship and you've obviously got it all muddled in your head. Madame Didier told me everything that happened."

"Eleanore and the other girls saw you go out on the lighthouse gangway after being expressly forbidden to do so and I came to get you back in. You ran from me and the winds blew you off," said Madame Didier.

"YOU'RE LYING!" said Daisy.

She turned to Miss Weaver who looked back at her with sadness in her eyes.

"Daisy, whatever you think happened, I don't think accusing people is going to help you. Unless you have anything to back up what you are saying," she said.

Daisy went quiet. She had no proof. The tablet that had recorded everything had been ruined by sea water.

"I suggest you take your daughter home, Mr Cooper," said Mistress Aiken, "I'll overlook her appalling manners today and put it down to the stress of her ordeal. Until we get to the bottom of this, however, she must stay away from Darlington."

Daisy bit her lip. She wasn't going to cry. She wouldn't give Mistress Aiken the satisfaction.

Daisy pulled the glow stars off the ceiling above her bed one by one. The 88ers were sat on their beds, watching.

"I'll try and fix this," said Tina waving the broken tablet Daisy had given her.

"I'm going to miss our little adventurer," said Penny.

"We'll find out what they're up to! We'll film them again!" said Millie.

Daisy smiled.

"Don't get yourselves in trouble."

She turned to Brodie and gave her a hug.

"You'll be back, D.C., I promise," said Brodie.

"Don't make promises you can't keep," said Daisy.

Outside, Mr Cooper sounded the horn of his Volvo, signalling that it was time to go.

"DAISY COOPER!"

Daisy jumped and turned back from the window. Mr Barlow and the rest of the class were staring at her.

"Sorry, sir?" said Daisy.

It was difficult getting used to being at Degham. She kept daydreaming about Darlington.

"Perhaps you'd like to answer the question, or maybe you think you're too good for us and would rather join the pigeons outside?" said Mr Barlow sarcastically.

The class laughed. Daisy looked at the whiteboard at the front of the class. The names and dates of the Tudor kings and queens were written on it, facts that Daisy had known since she was eight.

"I'm sorry, sir. I didn't hear the question," said Daisy.

Mr Barlow lifted his bushy eyebrows and groaned.

"Greg, you're nearer. Ask Cooper the question for me. She has something wrong with her ears."

Greg, a pink faced boy with piggy eyes, turned and smiled, showing teeth stained with liquorice.

"What he said was 'What stuff did Sir Walter Raleigh introduce to Engerland,'" said Greg, very impressed with himself for being smart enough to repeat a question.

Daisy shrugged.

"Well, people think he brought potatoes and tobacco back to England but it isn't true," she said.

Mr Barlow opened his mouth in surprise.

"Oh it isn't true, Miss Cooper? Well, please tell us why you disagree with our history books?"

"Potatoes were already here before Sir Raleigh was born and tobacco was brought over by the Spanish fifty years before he got back from his travels," said Daisy.

She knew that she was causing herself trouble but, frankly, didn't care anymore.

"What nonsense," said Mr Barlow, "of course it's true."

"No it's not, Sir," said Daisy.

"And why not?" said Mr Barlow, starting to look angry.

"Well, for one thing, if the Queen was expecting a present from you after you'd been traveling round the world and you handed her a potato, she'd chop your head off."

The class erupted in laughter.

Daisy felt she was becoming quite the expert on Head Master's offices. Mr Thomas didn't have nearly as many books in his as Mistress Aiken. In fact, it didn't look much like a school office at all. It looked more like an accountant's office. The room was filled with filing cabinets with drawers that didn't shut properly. An old beige computer sat on the desk next to a photograph of Mr Thomas standing by a river with a big fish in his hands. In the photo he looked like the happiest man in the world. He didn't look happy now.

"I see you were expelled from your last school," he said looking at Daisy's report.

"That's not true, Sir," said Daisy.

"Oh really? It says here that despite excellent grades, you have a habit of getting into trouble," said Mr Thomas, "something about sword fighting on rooftops and diving off cliffs into the sea?"

"It wasn't a sword fight. It was mostly hockey sticks and it wasn't a cliff, Sir, it was a lighthouse and I was pushed," said Daisy.

Mr Thomas frowned at her.

"So none if this was your fault? You just happened to be around when these things happen?"

"I guess so, Sir."

Mr Thomas let out a long sigh that whistled through his nostrils.

"You might think that because you've come from a posh school that you are better than us, Cooper."

"That's not true, Sir."

"Your history teacher Mr Barlow seems to think so."

Mr Thomas took a battered tin out of his desk drawer and opened it. Inside were sheets filled with coloured sticky dots.

"I have a system for troublemakers, Cooper."

Mr Thomas peeled off a red sticker and fixed it next to Daisy's name on the front of her folder. He crossed to the filing cabinet and pulled out a drawer that had the word TROUBLE written on it in red letters.

"I'll be keeping my eye on you, Cooper."

He dropped the folder into the drawer.

Join the club, thought Daisy.

Daisy drained the potatoes and mashed them for dinner. She took the mini kievs out of the oven and popped them onto the plates.

"No pizza?" moaned David, plonking himself down at the table.

"Quit moaning and be thankful," said Daisy.

"Thanks, Princess," said Mr Cooper, cutting into his kiev.

He hadn't been able to look at Daisy properly since she'd been home. She wanted to tell him it wasn't his fault but felt too upset to talk about it.

"Daniel, stop flicking peas at your brother," said Daisy

Daniel was firing peas off his fork and David was trying to catch them in his mouth. He wasn't very successful and the peas went bouncing off the table and across the lino where Gibbon chased them under the skirting.

"School was good," said Daisy, looking at Dad.

"I heard you got sent to Mr Thomas's office," said David.

"Yeah," said Daniel, "Is he your boyfriend or what?"

"Stop annoying your sister, boys," said Mr Cooper.

"I'm thinking of talking to my year tutor to see if I can start up some after school clubs. Language club, science club, maths…"

"You are such a nerd," said Daniel.

"A nerdette. I think that's what girl nerds are called," laughed David.

Daisy slammed down her fork and stood up.

"WHY ARE YOU SO NASTY TO ME ALL THE TIME!", she shouted, "YOU'RE SUPPOSE TO BE MY BROTHERS. YOU'RE SUPPOSED TO BE ON MY SIDE!"

David and Daniel looked at her, shocked. Daisy burst into tears and ran to her room.

Daisy lay on her bed stroking Gibbon. She heard dad shouting at her brothers downstairs. It didn't make her feel any better. After a while, there was a knock on her door.

"Come in."

Mr Cooper stuck his head round the door.

"Come in, Dad."

Mr Cooper sat down on the end of the bed, moving a couple of books out of the way. He picked up one of them.

"Customs and Costumes of Russia? Are you studying this? Looks interesting."

Daisy shook her head.

"No. We're doing Spain in Geography and I kind of know what they're teaching us already."

"So what's with the Russia stuff? Is it from Darlington?"

Daisy nodded, feeling slightly guilty. Mr Cooper put the book down and smiled at her.

"Daisy, I can't lie to you. I'm glad to see you home, especially after what happened with the lighthouse. Most of all, though, I want you to be happy."

"I know, Dad."

"If I can do anything to help you get back to Darlington, let me know what it is."

Mr Cooper leant over and kissed his daughter on the forehead.

"I love you, Princess."

"Love you too, Dad."

After speaking to Dad, Daisy started to feel a bit better. She picked up her new laptop which had hardly been used since getting back and opened it up. One of the little icons on the desktop was bouncing up and down and making beeping sounds. She didn't recognise what it was. She clicked on it and a webcam window popped up.

"About time, D.C.!"

Daisy's heart jumped. There, in the little window on the screen, she could see Brodie and the other 88ers staring back at her.

"Brodie!"

"Daisy!" shouted Millie, grinning over Brodie's shoulder.

"D-girl!" said Tina.

"Miss Cooper!" said Penny.

Daisy started laughing.

"How's it going?" asked Brodie once the giggling and excitement had died down.

"It's OK," said Daisy, hoping to change the subject, "how did you get hold of me? I never set a webcam up?"

"Your brothers sent an email to me and told me they'd set it up for you. They said you'd want to talk to us."

Daisy smiled.

So they do care after all, she thought.

"So why haven't you had your laptop on?" said Brodie, "We've been waiting like forever to get in touch with you!"

Daisy shrugged.

"You know. Settling in to a new school and all that."

"New School? Rubbish!" bellowed Penny, "You are a Darlington Girl? Isn't that right, girls?"

The 88ers nodded.

"Well, thanks, but I'm not sure if that's true anymore."

"Of course it's true!" said Brodie, "Did that bun-haired witch Aiken TELL you you were expelled?"

"Well, not exactly…"

"Hell, no!" said Brodie, "There's a lot of people here fighting for you, Daisy. Miss Weaver and Roni, especially. You should see Miss Weaver, she can be a shark when she wants to. A shark!"

Brodie put a hand on her head, miming a shark fin and snapped her teeth.

"You know, the nurse says Brodie was poisoned?" said Marsha.

"NO?!" said Daisy.

"Yep," said Brodie, "the muffin I ate that made me ill wasn't sent by my mom. Must have been the Brat Pack. They are still up to their old tricks, too. Tried to blow up Marsha and Tina in engineering."

"WHAT?"

"Yeah," said Marsha, "they swapped round some of the chemicals we were using for the rocket experiments but fortunately I know what chemicals I'm looking at - I don't need to read a tin. Good thing, too, or we'd be in hospital."

"Or several hospitals," said Tina making an explosion shape with her hands.

"We need you, Daisy!" shouted Millie.

"Well, thanks, but I don't think that's going to happen," said Daisy.

The 88ers went quiet.

"We haven't given up on you, D.C.," said Brodie, "Don't give up on us."

After that the mood lightened. Millie told Daisy how she was making progress in the zoo. Penny had persuaded the school to start a fashion day where girls could wear their own clothes once a month, "but only if they are tasteful". Brodie told Daisy how they had finally managed to get

Bertha to work properly with computers.

"I think Anita is worried I'm trying to steal her job as the International Schoolgirl Editor, which of course I am," joked Brodie.

The girls talked for over an hour until they were told it was lights out in the dorm. Daisy got into bed at the same time, trying to believe she was still there. If only in spirit.

"Night, night," said Daisy.

"Don't let the bedbugs bite," replied Brodie.

The webcam image froze on a still of the 88ers blowing kisses. Daisy left her laptop open on her bedside table and looked at the image until her eyelids got heavy and she fell asleep.

It was Sunday. No school. David and Daniel had gone out to the cinema with Dad so Daisy was alone. She fed Gibbon and made a sandwich for herself. Not quite sure what to do she watched some TV for an hour and then decided to finally unpack her suitcase. She'd been putting it off all week. It felt like she was admitting defeat.

Daisy unzipped the suitcase. She took out her Darlington uniform and hung it in the wardrobe. At least she'd always have it as a memory. She emptied out the rest of the clothes and put them away, throwing a ball of socks across the bed for Gibbon to chase. When Daisy got to the bottom of the suitcase she stopped. There was her satchel. It was still battered and scratched from the caves. Daisy lifted it out and opened it up. Inside was the journal of Rotten Mary. The cover was battered red leather and smelt of the sea. Daisy opened it up. She couldn't help but feel excited seeing Rotten Mary's handwriting inside. It was surprisingly neat for a pirate. Opening her wardrobe again Daisy reached into the jacket pocket of her Darlington blazer. There it was. The pendant.

"Devil's Eye," she read, tracing her finger around the letters etched into the silver.

Daisy say back on the bed and opened Mary's journal as Gibbon curled up in a ball at her feet.

Within three years of sailing The Black Night, Cutthroat Jacky and I, Rotten Mary Sweeney, had become the scourge of the Royal Navy…

CHAPTE TWENTY ONE - THE JOURNAL OF ROTTEN MARY

PART ONE

After three years of being at sea The Black Night had become the scourge of the British Navy. Mary and Jacky discovered that as well as taking chests of treasure there was plenty of money to be made from any barrels of spices, tobacco and whisky too. Once The Black Night's hold was full they would sail to the west coast of England and unload their cargo into caves where they would exchange it for silver and gold with criminal gangs. Stories about The Black Night and her dreaded crew spread through the inns across the ports of Europe. The stories never mentioned that the crew was run by women - that would have been a tale too hard for the male sailors to swallow - and it was this that allowed Mary and Jacky to sail right up to their victim's ships without being suspected.

As time went on Mary began to notice changes in Jacky. It was inevitable for some pirates that the sea madness would get to them. With Jacky it was helped by the daily diet of rum she was drinking. Her eyes began to take on the haunted look that Blackheart Bob had shown in his one good eye. One morning whilst cleaning the deck a crew member slipped and fell overboard. Jacky just stood and watched him scream for help as the sharks approached.

Soon the Black Night's hold was so full of coins and treasure that the ship sat dangerously low in the water. High waves washed over the deck. One night after another successful raid Jacky came out of her cabin, swigging a bottle of rum, to find Mary looking out at the stars.

"That's another ten chests of silver, Captain," said Jacky, "it's getting mighty crowded down there. We must have more gold than the King of England, I reckon."

Mary handed Jacky a newspaper. There was a picture drawn on the front of a navy officer with a mean face and bulging eyes. The headline under the picture said 'PIRATE HUNTER CAPTAIN WILLIAM AIKEN VOWS TO CLEAR HIS MAJESTY'S WATERS OF THE DREADED PIRATE SCOURGE.' The article said the King had commissioned a fleet of warships to hunt down every pirate ship in the British Seas.

"Most notorious of these pirate ships is The Black Night. Tales describe the most fearful crew of hardy men, giants with flaming beards who fight with two swords in each hand," read Jacky.

"Poppycock!" growled Mary, "Not one of those dogs is man enough to admit they've been bested by a woman."

"No mind, Sister," said Jacky, "we've got their money - who cares what they say we are?"

"I care," said Mary quietly.

Jacky took a long swig of her rum. Mary stared down at the black waves beneath the ship.

Pirate Hunter Captain William Aiken was going to be a big problem for The Black Night. Just off the coast of Spain on a moonless August night the ship pulled up to a merchant vessel. When they were less than twenty feet away the supposedly quiet ship erupted with cannon fire.

"About ship! About ship!" shouted Mary, swinging down from the mainsail.

Parts of the deck exploded in puffs of splintered wood. Mary dodged past the flying debris and ran down to the fire deck. A cannon ball ripped through the hull knocking crew members over like human skittles and buried itself in a chest of silver, throwing the coins into the air.

"Return fire!" Mary bellowed, "RETURN FIRE!"

Another iron ball tore through the side of the ship as the half dazed crew fought to turn their cannons on the enemy. Water rushed in through the holes, sweeping away the gold and silver. A few crew members grabbed rags and barrel lids to try and block the flow. Mary ran back up to the main deck and grabbed the ship's wheel from Jacky's hands, turning it hard right to steer the ship away. Fortunately the wind was on their side and, with all sails up, they finally managed to get out of reach of the cannon fire. The galleon chased them long through the night until just after dawn when The Black Night managed to hide in an unseen lagoon off the coast of Ibiza.

"We were ambushed!" said Mary.

Her eyes were narrow and wild and her fingers danced dangerously on the handle of her cutlass. She was pacing up and down the Captain's cabin in front of Jacky. Jacky lifted a bottle of rum to her lips. Mary grabbed it out of her hands and threw it in the corner.

"You were steering us drunk straight at the enemy!" she shouted.

Jacky jumped to her feet.

"They were disguised and waiting for us!" said Jacky, "If you knew otherwise you said nothing!"

The two captains stared at each other long and hard. Finally Mary walked away and stared out through the cabin window.

"We have too much weight aboard, Sister. We could barely turn around," she said, "we have to offload our treasure."

"What are you saying, Sister?" asked Jacky.

"We bury it," said Mary.

"And then what?" asked Jacky.

Mary pulled a book from her desk. It was the same book she had used to teach Jacky how to read all those years ago. An encyclopaedia of great treasures and worldly achievements. She opened it. Here and there, entries had been circled in red ink with notes scribbled in the margins. Amongst the entries that had been circled there was one for Bodicea's chariot, another for statues of greek goddesses.

"We've been taking silver from men for years now," said Mary, " yet still they give us no attention. They think of us as no more than common pirates."

"But, Sister, we are common pirates," Jacky replied.

Mary shook her head.

"We are not common pirates. We are women pirates and they refuse to say it. We need to let them know by stealing back the treasures they've taken from us for centuries, starting with this."

Mary pointed a finger at a sketch in the book of a round jewelled object. It had a heading above it that read CLEOPATRA'S EGG.

"Sister, these things have no value. You'll not sell them," said Jacky.

"They have a different kind of value," said Mary.

"The only value I know of is measured in silver," replied Jacky.

After a few days of fixing the ship and burying the dead Jacky sailed The Black Night into the port of Bologna in Spain. Mary dismissed the crew for a couple of day's rest whilst she and Jacky scoured the port for a mapmaker. They found one in a narrow street down by the harbour.

"My sea legs aren't good," said the old man, squinting at Jacky and Mary through thick glasses.

The mapmaker's shop was small and dark with hundreds of rolls of maps tucked into shelves. In the middle of the shop was a wide desk filled with half finished charts and elaborate measuring equipment.

"We hear you are the best mapmaker in Spain," replied Mary putting a boot up the desk, "whoever heard of a cartographer who couldn't stomach the sea?"

The old man said nothing. He avoided Mary's gaze, playing nervously with his brass instruments.

"Grandpa!"

A young girl came running in from the back of the shop with rolls of parchment under her arms.

"Grandpa, I've worked out how to measure distance in sea leagues!"

The girl spotted the two pirate women glaring at her and stopped abruptly.

"And who might you be, young girlie?" said Jacky.

"Sally," said the young girl.

"Be quiet, child. Let the grown ups speak," said her grandfather.

"Oh, come now," said Jacky, "Mary and I were both little girls once. Tell me, Sally, we hear your grandfather is the best map maker in the Southern shores. Is this true?"

"Oh, yes!" said Sally, "There's no one better."

"Let's leave them," said Mary, getting to her feet.

She smiled at Sally. It was a sad, distant smile. Jacky, however, was not interested in leaving.

"So, Sally, if we were to seek an island - one so secret no one knew about it - would you say your grandfather was the man to make us a map so that we might find it again?"

"Oh, absolutely, Miss," said Sally.

"Jacky, let's leave these people be," said Mary.

Jacky ignored her. She took one of the rolled parchments from under Sally's arm.

"You like maps too, young Sally?"

"I love maps," replied Sally, uncertain.

She could smell the rum on Jacky's breath and with it, the danger of the sea.

"Then you wouldn't mind coming with your grandpa and us in our search of an island, would you?"

Jacky put her hand to the dagger in her belt, making sure that the old man could see. She put her other hand around Sally, stroking her hair away from her neck.

"Jacky…" said Mary.

Jacky slowly pulled the dagger from her belt.

"Fine!" said the old man, "I'll help you find your island, just leave my granddaughter alone."

Jacky shook her head slowly.

"I think Sally should come with us. You might be difficult to persuade once we get out to sea if we don't have a little insurance."

In a couple of days The Black Night set sail again and not before time. An innkeeper told one of the crew that Pirate Hunter Captain William Aiken had been asking about them. With Sally and her Grandfather, Thomas, onboard they headed East towards the South Pacific. The hull was stocked with enough fresh supplies to keep them going for weeks without having to touch land again. Occasionally, the crow's nest would spot the Pirate Hunter's ship as a tiny but unmistakeable dot on the horizon behind them, patiently following.

One morning Sally spotted a school of unusual looking creatures chasing alongside the boat. They were like dolphins except they had long horns protruding from the ends of their noses.

"They look like unicorns, Grandpa, what are they?"

"Those are narwhals," said Mary stepping alongside them, "and legend has it when a good pirate dies at sea, they becomes a narwhal. That's why they always chase alongside boats."

Sally watched the magnificent creatures as they dived in and out of the water.

"Is that true, Grandfather?" she asked.

Her grandfather shrugged.

"Anything is true if you believe it hard enough," he said.

"So where are we headed?" asked Mary.

The Black Night had been at sea for two weeks and the cramped conditions were starting to affect everyone's mood. Thomas, Sally and the two Sisters were stood around the captain's table. Thomas adjusted his glasses and pointed with a shaking finger at a blank area on on map just below China.

"This area is mostly unrecorded yet we have good information from sailors that there are several small islands here. One of those would be the kind you are looking for," he said.

"And how much longer till we get there?" asked Jacky.

The old man shrugged.

"Hard to tell with uncharted waters but I would imagine three or four weeks from now."

"What are you going to call it?" asked Sally.

Mary and Jacky looked at each other confused.

"What are you going to call the island? You have to name any island you find," asked Sally, "even if it's just to bury treasure."

Jacky stood up, her hand reaching for the dagger. Quick as a flash, Mary drew her cutlass.

"Be careful now, Sister," she warned.

"She's being too nosy, talking about treasure," said Jacky, "and nosy people get their noses chopped off."

"I'd call it 'Devil's Eye'," said Sally.

Mary turned to her. Sally smiled, trying not to look scared.

"If I found an island and I didn't want people going there I'd pick a frightful name to keep them away," said Sally.

There was a long silence filled only by the slow creaking of the ship. Then Jacky burst out laughing. She put her dagger away.

"Now, that's a fine idea," she said taking a swig of rum, "Devil's Eye it is."

Four weeks later, as thunderstorms shook The Black Night, they still hadn't found the island. The waves were as tall as cliffs and the ship rocked back and forth like a tiny cork. Mary, Jacky, Thomas and Sally stayed in the cabin and tempers were at breaking point.

"He's lying to us!" screamed Jacky, "He's taking us round in circles till we drown or get caught and hanged!"

"I'm not, Captain! I promise you!"

"Then where's our island!" boomed Mary, throwing the maps off the table.

"We should be almost upon it! It's not easy trying to find an island that isn't on any maps!"

"What I want right now is for you to stop your lying tongue!" shouted Jacky.

She staggered across the cabin as the ship tilted and grabbed Sally by her hair. She held her dagger to the girl's throat.

"Now, I'll ask you one more time, where's our island!"

There was an enormous crashing sound as the ship rocked backwards, sending everything sprawling across the cabin. Sally fell to the floor as Jacky dropped the dagger. Everyone lay in silence, wondering if they had been hit by cannon fire. It took a few moments to realise the ship had stopped moving.

"Captain! Come quick!"

It was the crow's nest. Mary staggered out of the cabin. The wind whipped at her clothes as she climbed the ladder to the wheel deck. Squinting through the stinging rain she saw the outline of a small forest of trees barely a hundred feet in front of her.

"We've beached!" said Jacky coming up behind her.

Mary nodded. She looked over the bow to see that The Black Night was now half buried in the sand.

They had found their island.

While Thomas stayed onboard putting the finishing details to the map with Sally, Mary and Jacky ordered the crew to unload the chests of treasure and bring them ashore. They marched deep into the forest through the rain until they found a clearing. Fifteen crew members dug with spades and shovels long into the night until they had a hole as deep and wide as a house. Under Jacky and Mary's watchful eyes they lowered every chest of treasure and silver into the hole and buried it.

"So our deal is done," said Thomas.

He handed the finished map to Mary and Jacky who unrolled it

carefully on the cabin table. There it was. A clear path from the shores of
Spain to Devil's Eye island with distances and degrees marked clearly for
them to find their way there again. Mary folded it up and put it in the
safe.

"Now," said Thomas, his voice cracking with fear, "I hope you will
honour your side of the bargain and return my granddaughter and I
safely home."

Mary looked at Sally and nodded slowly.

"Would be a shame, of course, as this one would make a fine pirate
but a deal is a deal."

"How do we know he won't go back and get the treasure for himself?"
said Jacky.

Thomas laughed.

"Captain, I am an old man. There is not much use in my life for gold
and silver now, nor was there ever much. The only treasure I care about,
I already have."

Thomas put his arms around Sally and kissed her head.

"I don't trust him," said Jacky, "everyone wants gold and silver."

"A deal is a deal," said Mary, "we take them home, pay them, and
leave them be."

In the days that followed The Black Night and her crew made their
way back to Spain. Since burying the treasure, though, things were
turning sour between the two Captains. The first incident occurred early
one morning when Mary was writing her journal entry. Hearing a loud
scream she ran out onto the deck to see Sally hanging by her fingers
fifteen feet up from the main sail. Quick as lightning Mary climbed up
the rigging and pulled the young girl to safety. When they were safely
back on the deck Mary pushed the girl hard through the door of her
cabin and sat her down.

"What in blazes were you doing, girl?" she growled.

Sally was sobbing uncontrollably. Mary slammed her fist down hard
on the table causing Sally to jump. It also made her stop crying.

"Jacky said we were near home and that if I climbed up the mainsail I
would be able to see the dock."

"Are you mad? We're days from land. Any land!"

"I got excited and I thought…"

"Think nothing, girl! Stay on deck and stay safe. I've kept you alive long enough and I'll be damned if I'll let you break your own neck!"

Sally nodded, starting to cry again. Mary reached into her jacket and pulled out a green handkerchief. She handed it to the girl.

"Clean yourself up."

Mary sat down in her chair with a long sigh.

"Is Jacky your real sister?" asked Sally.

"As good as," said Mary, "every woman on this boat is a sister to me, the way I see it. Even you. Until we get you back to land."

She smiled at Sally.

"I don't trust that little witch," said Jacky.

It was after sundown and she was sitting with Mary in the cabin.

"She's just a girl, Jacky," said Mary.

"So were we. That's no excuse."

"What are you afraid of a little girl for?"

"I'm afraid of her babbling her mouth off in port about us. They know what we look like. They know where the treasure is."

Mary chewed on a chicken leg and watched Jacky drink rum from a bottle. Mary couldn't remember the last time she'd seen Jacky without a bottle of rum in her hands. She was worried it was making her brain soggy. A soggy brain made people dangerous.

"So you want to kill them then?" she asked slowly.

Jacky shrugged.

"If they had an accident it wouldn't be so bad is all I'm saying."

"We've never killed children and we've never killed old men. I don't fancy starting now," said Mary.

Jacky took another long swig.

"Where's the map?" she asked.

"It's in the safe, same as it was yesterday. Same as it was the day before and the day before that."

Jacky laughed.

"Do you not trust me anymore, Sister?" asked Jacky.

Mary put her chicken bone down and wiped her greasy fingers along the brim of her hat.

"Treasure does strange things to people. It makes them hungry for things they can't even eat. I trust you no more than I trust myself."

With that, the conversation was dropped and they finished their supper in silence.

* * *

"Sally, come here girl," said Mary the next morning as she stepped out onto the deck.

Sally ran over and Mary crouched down, bringing her eyes level with the girl. Behind her she could see Jacky looking over at them both as she steered the ship.

"Sally, you're grandfather has been instructing you knowledge of maps, yes?"

"Oh yes, but I don't know where your island is. I can't read stars or anything."

Mary waved her hand to silence her. Jacky grabbed a midshipman, stood him at the wheel and walked towards them.

"Come with me, Sally," said Mary.

She ushered Sally into her cabin and locked it shut behind them. Inside she pulled a pile of charts off a stool and offered it to Sally. Taking off her hat and long coat Mary rubbed her hands through her hair. Sally hadn't noticed before but Mary had long curly red hair that made her green eyes look even greener. They were the colour of the sea.

"How old are you girl?"

"Ten," said Sally.

"I started my sea life at about the same age. I didn't choose to. Some say that no one chooses the sea life, the sea chooses them."

"I know," said Sally.

"Have you heard of me before this trip?" asked Mary.

"I've heard stories," she said.

"You've heard stories? What have you heard?"

Sally was scared to say any more. She looked down at her feet which suddenly seemed very small.

"It's okay, girl. I won't blame you for any stories you heard, true or not."

"I heard you were captured by pirates when you were a little girl. You and Jacky and that you both...killed the pirate captain and took over his ship."

Mary sat back, her eyes wide and fierce.

"That's just what I heard," said Sally quickly.

Mary chuckled.

"You heard right, girl."

To Sally's surprise Mary seemed pleased.

"Go on," Mary said, "tell me what else you've heard."

"Well, I heard you bought The Black Night and painted it black so that you could ambush any ship in the dead of night. Some people say you stole so much gold from the King of England that he has to borrow money from the Queen of Spain to buy his sausages."

Mary let out an enormous, roaring laugh. She banged her hand down on the table.

"Well, some of that may be colouring the truth a little but most of it is true! Where did you hear this? In the papers they print lies about us, claiming us to be men."

Mary seemed to be getting angry again. She had tightened her hands into fists.

"The women folk around the port talk about it. They all know but don't mention it when there's men around, Captain. Every girl knows about it at school but dare not say or they'll get caned."

"Caned for what?"

"Lying. Except, it's not lying is it?" said Sally.

"No. No, it's not, girl."

Mary walked over to the window and looked out at the sea.

"You know what I would have been if I hadn't been captured by Blackheart Bob, Sally? I'd have been one of those timid women whispering gossip, afraid to speak out amongst the men. I'd be dreaming of a life rather than living one."

Mary took an apple out of her pocket and began peeling it with a knife.

"There have been women like me - women not afraid to get what they want - throughout history. Women equal to men. Better. How many of those women do they teach you about in your history lessons?"

"None," said Sally.

"None," agreed Mary.

She cut a slice of apple and handed it to Sally. It was the first proper fruit Sally had tasted in a long time. It tasted sweet and good.

"Well I reckon it's about time something was done about it," said Mary quietly, "from now on until we dock, you stick with me. This ship is not safe for you and you don't have the eyes to notice danger. Not yet. I'm going to teach you."

In the days that followed Sally spent from daybreak to sunset with Mary as Jacky got more drunk and more dangerous. Mary told Jacky that she was keeping Sally close to see if she remembered the route to the island. It was a lie that helped keep her Sister a little less crazy. She also made sure the other crew members kept Sally's grandfather, Thomas, busy and out of Jacky's sight. One day in the cabin Mary told Sally her plans.

Sally looked at the pictures in the encyclopaedia that Mary showed her - great statues of female empresses, chariots of female warriors, the golden crowns lined with jewels that were crafted in their honour.

"That's real treasure," said Mary.

Sally turned the pages slowly. She had never seen anything like it. There were pages and pages of it - all of great women throughout history - people she had never been taught about at school.

"So what are you going to do, Captain?" asked Sally.

"I'm going to steal them. All of them. I'm going to take them back from the private palaces and museums of the countries that stole them and put them somewhere where girls like you can go and see so you realise you don't have to spend your lives hiding in the shadows of your husbands."

"But how will you steal them?"

"Same way I've always stolen - by letting people underestimate me for being a mere woman."

"But there's so many of them. It will take a lifetime!"

Mary laughed.

"It'll take much longer than that!"

Mary sat back in her chair. She cocked her head to one side and looked at Sally carefully.

"So I'm going to need girls I can trust to carry on long after I'm gone," she said.

Mary looked sad.

"Sally, I've stolen more silver than I could spend in a thousand lifetimes. I have enough to buy palaces, coaches made of gold and the most beautiful islands in the world but the more I've taken, the more I've realised how little it means. Gold does not buy happiness. It will not make your life meaningful. That's something people like Jacky will never understand, unfortunately, but I think you do."

Mary pulled out a purse and emptied it onto the table. A pile of silver coins fell out, spinning across the wood.

"Do you know what these are, Sally?"

Sally picked up one of the coins. It was heavy and nearly as big as the palm of her hand.

"It's a Spanish dollar," said Sally, holding it up to the light.

"That's right, girl. Or as we pirates call it, a Piece of Eight. Do you know how much blood has been spilt over these useless bits of metal? Countless…Countless."

Sally put the coin down. It didn't look quite so shiny anymore.

"Always remember that when anyone tempts you with money, girl. If it helps, try to think of eight good qualities - good virtues if you like - that are more valuable than a piece of metal."

"Which virtues?" asked Sally.

"Now the answer to that question," said Mary with a wry smile, "you will have to work out for yourself."

The Black Night was three days from the Spanish coast when tragedy happened. It started with a blood curdling scream. Mary grabbed her cutlass and ran onto the deck to see Jacky stood at port side looking down into the water.

"He fell overboard," Jacky said.

Jacky's voice was slurry and Mary could smell the rum on her from a good ten feet. Mary looked down into the water to see the body of Thomas sinking beneath the waves.

"What's happening?"

Mary turned to see Sally walking towards them rubbing sleep out of her eyes. She ran over and grabbed her.

"Nothing for you to be seeing, child."

Mary glanced over at Jacky. There was blood drip…drip…dripping from the dagger in her belt.

"Grandpa?" asked Sally.

"He slipped and fell," said Jacky.

"GRANDPA!"

Sally ran to the side and tried to look over but Mary pulled her back.

"GET OFF ME! GET YOUR HANDS OFF ME YOU ROTTEN PIRATE!"

Mary said nothing and held Sally in her arms. Sally beat her fists against Mary, still screaming, until finally she collapsed to her knees sobbing.

"Maybe she wants to jump in and rescue him," said Jacky.

"She'll do no such thing. From now on the child sleeps in my cabin," replied Mary.

For the last few days of the journey Mary did not let Sally out of her sight and tried her best to console her. She didn't speak to Jacky. On the last evening the bowson told her that Jacky had been talking to the crew about forming a mutiny. Her intentions were to steal the map and take the treasure for herself. The crew were not interested. Mary had made sure they had enough silver to retire on if they wanted to. As the ship pulled into the port at Bologna Mary called Jacky to the cabin.

"It seems, Sister, that we should go our separate ways," said Mary.

"Without my treasure, I'm going nowhere," said Jacky.

"The treasure stays where it is for now. If we sailed for it we'd be caught by Pirate Hunter Captain William Aiken and his fleet. We both know it. Best we lay low for a while."

"So you can take the treasure for yourself, Sister? What kind of fool do you take me for?" slurred Jacky.

"I know better than to make a fool of you. I also know that I can't trust you and you can't trust me so I have a proposal."

Mary knocked on the old oak door three times. Sally looked around nervously. She was standing with Mary and Jacky in a dark alley down one of the back streets of the port. It was the dead of night. Drunken sailors playing squeeze boxes and singing shanties staggered past them as they hunched in the doorway. Mary knocked again. Eventually they heard footsteps and moaning on the other side followed by the sound of locks being turned. A lot of locks. The door pulled back and a short man with an oily beard stuck his head out.

"Who are you?"

Mary jangled a purse full of coins in front of his face.

"Late customers," she said.

The room was small, cramped and very, very hot. At the back of the room behind large metal tools and an anvil was a blazing furnace with a couple of red hot tongs nestling in the coals. The silversmith (for that's what he was) wiped the sweat from his brow and stared at the map again.

"So if I understand what you're asking, you want me to make two silver pendants and put half of this map on each?"

"That's right," said Mary.

"Half the map? On each?"

"He's a bit slow, this one," said Mary to Sally.

Jacky sat on some sacks in the corner and opened a bottle of rum.

"Yes," said Mary to the silversmith, "But not a left half and a right half. I want half the details on each so that individually they are useless but when seen together can make up the whole map."

The silversmith scratched his beard. It looked like the kind of beard mice could live in.

"S'tricky," he said, "very fine work that. It'll take a couple of days."

"It gets done tonight. Before dawn," said Mary.

"But where will I get the silver from at this time?"

Mary emptied a purse full of Pieces of Eight onto the worktable. The silversmith's eyes grew wide with greed.

"That should be more than enough and when you are done I'll pay you twice as much again for your services."

The silversmith nodded eagerly and picked up his tools.

Sally could feel someone shaking her shoulder. She opened her eyes and saw Mary standing over her. Mary was holding her finger to her lips, telling Sally to be quiet. Sally looked over to the corner of the workshop where Jacky was snoring on some sacks, clutching her empty rum bottle. Mary knelt down and leant in close.

"Here," she said.

Mary fastened a chain around Sally's neck. On the end of the chain was a piece of eight.

"Don't let anyone see it. Ever. Remember what I told you about greed? These things drive people mad. This is to help you remember the virtues."

"Eight virtues," said Sally.

Mary nodded.

"Have you thought of them yet?"

Sally shook her head.

"You will, Sally, they'll come to you when you are ready."

Mary tucked the necklace inside Sally's shirt and crossed the room where she gave Jacky's boot a hefty kick. Jacky snapped bolt upright and let out a snort.

"We're done," said Mary.

She held out the two pendants the silversmith had made. They spun in the light of the furnace, showing the details of the map on one side and an eye with the words 'Devil's Eye' on the other. She handed one to Jacky and fixed the other around her neck.

"So now, neither of us knows the location without the other," she said.

"What about the map?" said Jacky, getting up unsteadily.

Mary pulled the map off the table and handed it to Sally.

"Your grandpa made it, seems only right you should send it back to him," said Mary.

Sally took it and threw it into the furnace where it crumbled into ash and disappeared up the chimney.

After the night the pendants were made Mary and Sally went back to her grandfather's shop. Jacky had staggered off to an Inn somewhere and they both secretly hoped they'd never see her again. The shop felt empty and strange to Sally, like it belonged to another lifetime.

"We'd better get you to your parents," said Mary.

Sally wandered over to her grandfather's old desk and looked at the documents laid out on its surface. She looked at the neat hand writing of his notes in the margins of his drawings.

"My parents died long ago during the flu epidemic," said Sally, "my grandfather sailed back to England to fetch me and brought me out to live with him here."

Mary looked at the small child with pity. It was an unfamiliar emotion for her. The noise of the port floated in through the windows.

"I can leave you enough money so that you will never have to worry for it. If that's what you want," she said.

Sally circled a finger around the coastline of countries on a map.

"Or you can take me with you," she said.

Mary looked at Sally for a very long time. Finally she spoke, her voice quiet yet more serious than she had ever sounded.

"If you come with me, you'll be a pirate, Sally. You know what I plan to do. It will be dangerous."

"No more dangerous than waiting here for Jacky to come and find me," said Sally.

The girl was right. Like it or not, she was Mary's responsibility now.

"Pack your things," said Mary.

There were dresses, schoolbooks and a few family mementoes including a small family portrait and a stuffed bear given to Sally by her mother. Mary watched as Sally packed them into a chest and then helped her fill another with her grandfather's mapmaking tools and charts. Once packed, they closed up the shutters on the shop for the last time and returned to The Black Night.

CHAPTER TWENTY TWO - A SURPRISE VISIT

"Daisy, get up! You're late for school!"

Daisy sat up hurriedly. Mary's journal lay in her lap. She'd fallen asleep reading it. She was only half way through and wanted to read the rest but school - even Degham's - meant it had to wait. Not having time to change out of the clothes she'd slept in, she slipped on her trainers and ran out the door.

Every head turned to look at Daisy as she burst into the classroom out of breath. Mr Barlow was sat on his desk with arms folded, staring at her.

"It's 9:15 Cooper, where have you been? China? " he said.

Kind of, thought Daisy, remembering the adventures she'd been reading about the night before.

"The Headmaster wants to see you urgently," said Mr Barlow.

Here we go again.

Daisy turned round and marched back out into the corridor.

When she stepped through the door of Mr Thomas' office she got a shock.

"Hello Daisy."

It was Miss Weaver.

"Er, Hello," said Daisy, not quite sure if she was still dreaming.

"I'll leave you alone," said Mr Thomas with a quick disapproving look at Daisy.

Daisy Cooper and the Sisters of the Black Night

When he had gone Miss Weaver wandered over to his desk and picked up the mug that said 'World's Best Teacher', studying it with a frown.

"How are you doing, Daisy?"

Daisy shrugged. She was now feeling slightly nervous. Perhaps something had happened to one of the 88ers.

"I'm okay, Miss," she said, "is everything okay with my old dorm-mates?"

"They're fine. I'm here for another reason, Daisy. Do you know about the International Schoolgirl Competition?"

Daisy nodded.

"Well," said Miss Weaver, "I'm sure you don't need me to remind you but every year we look for replacement International Schoolgirls to fill the shoes of those who are leaving. There are several schools involved and each one puts forward eight pupils. At Darlington it's traditional that one girl is chosen from each house. Out of the sixty four girls who compete, eight are chosen to be International Schoolgirls."

Daisy nodded. She wondered why Miss Weaver was telling her this.

"I want to put you forward for Honour House, Daisy," said Miss Weaver.

Daisy's heart leapt and then crashed almost instantly.

"But I don't go to Darlington anymore," she said.

Miss Weaver smiled at her.

"Since you left I've been speaking to Mistress Aiken about your situation and she's finally had a change of heart. She has agreed to let you enter the competition. She is quite clear, though, that if you don't succeed in being chosen as an International Schoolgirl you will not be allowed back at all."

Daisy found it hard to believe that Mistress Aiken would agree to such a thing. Even so, it felt like a door of opportunity had been opened.

"Daisy, the moment I met you I knew you were a perfect candidate," said Miss Weaver, "but there's nothing more I can do for you now. From here on, it's up to you."

Dad hugged Daisy tight as they stepped out of the car at Darlington. It felt great to be back. There was a loud shout and Daisy turned to see the 88ers running across the courtyard to greet her. They put their arms around her and jumped up and down.

"Look out Darlington, Daisy's back!" said Marsha.

Daisy was back. At least, for the competition. If she failed…well, that wasn't worth thinking about. Millie and Brodie grabbed her bags as she kissed goodbye to her Dad.

"I'll make you proud. I promise!" she shouted as the 88ers pushed her towards Honour House.

"You already do!" he hollered back.

It was good to see her dorm bed waiting for her. What made it even better was seeing a gift in moon and stars wrapping paper on the pillow.

"We got you a welcome home present, D.C.," said Brodie.

Daisy dropped her bags, sat on the bed and picked up the present. Carefully she untied the ribbon and pulled off the wrapping. The gift was a beautiful hand-bound journal and a set of pens.

"Thank you, it's lovely!" said Daisy, opening the journal.

On the inside cover was an inscription:

THIS JOURNAL BELONGS TO DAISY COOPER, OPEN IT AT YOUR PERIL!

Underneath each of the 88ers had signed it. All of them. Even Layla and Tracy.

"How did you get Layla and Tracy's signatures?" asked Daisy.

"We have our ways," said Marsha with a wink.

The school was bustling with energy. Every wall was decorated with posters about the competition. There were pupils dressed in overalls standing on ladders painting the walls, hanging upside down from window frames cleaning the glass and wandering the halls to polish every statue, trophy and painting.

"Wow, I've never seen it so manic!" said Daisy as the 88ers walked to the dining hall for dinner.

"This competition is a BIG deal," said Brodie, "and you HAVE to win a place."

Daisy felt butterflies in her stomach. She did have to win it.

As they entered the dining room Daisy felt all the eyes turning to look at her.

"Why are they all staring me?" she whispered.

"You're big news, Daisycakes," said Marsha, "you're the outsider in the competition. Plus the whole falling off a lighthouse thing, of course."

After dinner Daisy fixed her glow stars back on the ceiling above her bed and chatted with the others.

"I found out a lot of very interesting things from Rotten Mary's journal…" she said.

"Hey, come and look!" interrupted Millie.

She was looking out of the dorm window. The 88ers ran over to join her. The courtyard was filling with busses.

"It must be the competitors from the other schools!" said Millie.

"Let's go down and check it out," said Brodie, grabbing Daisy's hand.

The courtyard was full of activity. Some Prefects waved vehicles into parking spaces whilst others checked names of the visiting girls off clipboards. Daisy and Brodie weaved their way between the groups of schoolgirls and read the names of the coaches out. Three other British Schools were competing. Chancey-Langworth from Oxfordshire who's bus was very similar to Darlington's except it was painted royal blue. Then there was Doveshaw School - a purple bus with a bold green thistle painted on the side. The girls clambering down from it spoke with a charming Edinburgh brogue and wore tartan skirts. Behind Doveshaw was the final British bus representing Angelsworth, a school from Wales. The Angelsworth bus was deep red and matched the uniform of the girls peeking through its window as it backed into its parking space. The rest of the buses were from overseas. There was a jet black coach with the word 'Odessa' written on the side in thick red letters. Daisy knew that Odessa was a place in Russia. It was the newest bus and looked very expensive with its polished metal surfaces and tinted windows. It looked like the kind of bus a rockstar would travel around in.

"This one looks like a school bus from back home!" said Brodie running up to an orange coloured bus.

It did look like the kind of school bus Daisy had seen in American films except this one had a Spanish flag painted on the front of it. The sign across the top of the windscreen showed the school's name, Salazar. Next to this was a shiny turquoise coach from a Swedish school called Olander and behind that the final bus which was from a French school. The French bus was cream coloured and the name of the school, L'ecole des Femme, was written along the side in pretty joined up writing. The girls from this school wore straw boaters and old leather satchels with double straps over their shoulders.

"There's a LOT of girls," said Daisy.

There was a painfully loud shriek a few feet away that made everyone jump. A Prefect had put a bullhorn to her lips and started shouting orders at the excited arrivals.

"COMPETING GIRLS PLEASE REMAIN IN THE
COURTYARD TO FIND THE NAME OF YOUR RELEVANT
DORM HOUSE! TEACHERS AND SUPPORT PUPILS MAKE
YOUR WAY THROUGH TO THE GREAT HALL FOR YOUR
ACCOMMODATION DETAILS!"

The crowd broke up into groups. After a bit of hustle and bustle everyone except the competitors left the courtyard.

"Well I guess that makes things a bit more manageable," said Daisy looking around at who was left.

The other competitors were all roughly Daisy's age and looked fiercely intelligent and determined. The Prefect with the bullhorn spotted Daisy and Brodie and started coughing loudly through the bullhorn.

"AHEM!"

It was obviously time for them to leave.

"Come on, D.C.," said Brodie, "I've got something to show you!"

"WOW," said Daisy as they stepped inside the International Schoolgirl print room.

Brodie and Tina had been busy. Bertha was still sat in the middle of the room but the noisy clank-clanking of the letterpresses had gone. A stream of wires ran from a bank of computers and hooked up to a row of robotic print jets that looked like giant multicoloured pens. They jerked across the surface of the paper as it ran through Bertha's rollers.

"We bought Bertha into the 21st century," said Brodie, "well, we bought her into the 20th century, but that's a start."

Brodie took Daisy over to the computers and opened up a document on one of the screens. It was the cover of the latest issue.

"Darlington hosts the annual International Schoolgirl Competition," Daisy read on the screen.

"It took us ages and a world of hurt but we did it," said Brodie.

She took Daisy over to the run of magazines as they rolled off the press. She picked up a copy and handed it to Daisy. The headline was clearer than she'd ever seen it. The ink didn't even smudge under her fingers.

"You can't believe how difficult it was getting Anita to agree to it," said Brodie, "but to be honest, without you around to help set the letters and change the ink is was impossible so she had to give in."

"I'm impressed!" said Daisy.

"It gets better," said Brodie, "because it's all computerised now. Reporters anywhere in the world can send their story straight through to us via email and - bam - it can be printed straight away."

Daisy looked up at the editorial office. Anita was sat at her desk looking through the latest copy of the magazine. She spotted Daisy and gave her a little wave. She looked more relaxed than Daisy had ever seen her.

Daisy felt like she'd never been away as she walked back to the dorm, arm in arm with Brodie. She'd forgotten how much of a home it had become and how much of a family the 88ers were. In the excitement of the competition she'd also forgotten about The Sisters of the Black Night. It all came back to her, though, the moment she saw Eleanore standing in the doorway of Honour House waiting for them.

"What do you want?" said Brodie, stepping in front of Daisy protectively.

"Calm down, Yankee Doodle, I'm just here to pass on a message," said Eleanore, "Mistress Aiken wants to see Daisy."

"She's done nothing wrong," said Brodie.

"She's done nothing wrong...yet," said Eleanore, "anyway, I think Mistress Aiken just wants to wish her luck in the competition. Believe me, if I had my way, the little oik wouldn't even be here now."

Eleanore looked genuinely upset. Maybe Mistress Aiken had changed her mind about things.

"Don't worry, Brodie. I'm sure I'll be fine," said Daisy.

"Come in, Daisy, dear girl."

Mistress Aiken was smiling. It looked odd, fake, like the kind of smile Daisy had seen on creepy dolls. Not quite sure what to make of it, Daisy stepped inside. Mistress Aiken shut the door behind her, locking it. They were alone.

"Take a seat, dear girl," said Mistress Aiken.

Daisy took a seat. There was a pot of tea with a couple of posh china cups on the big desk. Mistress Aiken filled one and handed it over.

"I'm sure this is all a bit strange to you, dear girl."

Very, thought Daisy.

"The last time we met it got quite heated and a lot of things were said. The truth is, whilst you did commit an act that brought the school into disrepute - something that would warrant expulsion in ordinary circumstances - you did lead us to a discovery that is an invaluable addition to the school museum."

It took Daisy a few moments to work out what the Deputy Head was talking about and then it clicked.

"You found Rotten Mary," said Daisy.

Mistress Aiken nearly dropped her cup and saucer.

"Goodness! You DO know a lot! What else do you know?" said Mistress Aiken.

The smile was starting to slip.

"It doesn't matter. I'm here to do the competition," said Daisy truthfully.

"Yes, dear girl. That's why I graciously invited you back. You do understand that if you DON'T get through, though, that you will have to leave for good."

So this is all just some stupid game, thought Daisy.

"Mistress Aiken, if you're going to force me to lose why did you ask me back?"

"I never said I was going to force you to lose, dear girl! Quite the opposite, in fact."

That surprised Daisy. Mistress Aiken could see it. She put down her cup with a thin, sour grin and leant forward across the desk.

"I was thinking that we could do a deal, Daisy Cooper," she said.

"What kind of deal?"

"When we found Rotten Mary she was holding a chain in her hands. A chain from which something had been taken. Something important to me. I think you know what I'm talking about."

Daisy said nothing but she could feel her cheeks burning red. Mistress Aiken noticed it.

"...A certain pendant," said the Head Mistress.

Daisy put her hand in her pocket and tightened her fingers around the Devil's Eye pendant. She'd been carrying it with her to keep it safe since getting back.

"I don't know what you're talking about," she said.

Mistress Aiken laughed.

"Oh, come now, Daisy. You're annoyingly gifted at finding the truth but you're awful at telling lies. Here's the deal I'm willing to make. You give me my pendant and I give you what you want - a position as an

International Schoolgirl."

So that's why she invited me back. She wants her stupid pendant, thought Daisy.
"And what if I say no?" she asked.

"If you say no, not only will you lose the competition and get thrown out of this school…"

Mistress Aiken stood up slowly, glowering at Daisy with big, wild eyes.

"…but we will come and take the damn thing from you in your sleep and we won't care who we hurt in the process - you, your friends, your family, no one. NOW GIVE ME MY PENDANT."

Daisy realised she didn't have a choice. She pulled out the pendant. Mistress Aiken stepped back, gasping with awe. As Daisy put it on the desk the Deputy Head's hands fell on it greedily. She held it up to the light and looked at it.

"This is it…this is it…" she said, her eyes gleaming .

Mistress Aiken pulled a chain from her pocket, attached the pendant to it and hung it round her neck. It clinked against the silver of the original pendant. It had been nearly two hundred years since they had last been that close together.

"You did well, girl. You did well," said the Deputy Head, "Good luck with the competition. Not that you'll need it with our little deal, of course."

Daisy got up to leave.

"Daisy…"

Daisy turned.

"Yes, miss?"

"If you speak to anyone about this or I hear you've been snooping around the school again, the deal is off. Understand?"

Daisy nodded and left the room.

CHAPTER TWENTY THREE - THE COMPETITION BEGINS

"Come on, champion!"
Daisy was woken by Millie and Brodie jumping on her bed.
"Show me your lion face! Rarrr!" said Brodie.
Millie jumped off the bed and danced around the room, punching the air like a boxer.
"Who's your Daisy?! Who's your Daisy?!" she said between exaggerated puffs.
"Ignore those two," said Penny, "get dressed."
She laid out a freshly cleaned uniform for Daisy.
In the dining hall over breakfast one of the Prefect's voices came over the loudspeakers.
"THE SPECIAL ASSEMBLY TO MARK THE START OF THE INTERNATIONAL SCHOOLGIRL COMPETITION WILL BE STARTING IN TEN MINUTES."
"Ten minutes!" said Brodie, wolfing down her poached eggs.
Daisy smiled at her. She hadn't mentioned anything about her meeting with Mistress Aiken and hadn't slept well at all. When she did manage to get to sleep there had been bad dreams about sharks chasing her through the school sewers. Someone squeezed Daisy's shoulder. She looked up to see Miss Weaver smiling down at her.
"Morning, Daisy. We won't be able to talk once the competition starts

so I just wanted to wish you luck. How are you feeling?"

"A bit nervous, Miss."

Whilst that was true she was actually feeling more guilty than nervous.

"Let me give you a bit of advice. If you feel your nerves starting to get the better of you, take a few deep breaths and count slowly to three as you exhale. It will help you calm yourself."

Miss Weaver breathed in and out a few times to show Daisy what she meant. It was oddly calming just watching her do it. Miss Weaver gave Daisy wink and walked away through the busy restaurant.

"She's seriously crazy, that one," said Penny.

Daisy wasn't so sure. It seemed like very good advice.

The assembly hall was jammed by the time the 88ers got there. Daisy and the others squeezed down a line to a few vacant chairs as Mistress Aiken and the other teachers filed onto the stage to the sound of the school anthem.

"Please be seated," said Mistress Aiken.

There was the sound of a hundred chairs scraping as everyone took their seats.

"I'd like to formally declare this year's International Schoolgirl Competition open. In a moment we will read through the names of the competing girls. When you hear your name please come onto the stage where you will be presented with your competition sash. Sashes must be worn at all times until the end of the competition. Any girl seen not wearing her sash will be automatically disqualified."

"That's a bit harsh!" whispered Millie.

"I will now explain the rules," continued Mistress Aiken, "girls will be assessed on their demonstration of the eight virtues of an International Schoolgirl: Charity, Bravery, Reason, Culture, Grace, Agility, Fellowship and Honour. The nature of the demonstration will be left to individual girls and their support team to determine. There are three days for rehearsal and preparation followed by the actual competition on Thursday which will start at 8am and continue until the closing awards ceremony at 4pm. Marks will be appointed by members of the school staff and the governing board. As I'm sure you are aware the winning girls will join the staff of International Schoolgirl magazine to take over the roles of outgoing girls. I'd like to take the opportunity to invite the leaving girls to the stage so that we can thank them for their tireless work."

The room applauded as the leaving International Schoolgirls made their way up onto the stage. Daisy was shocked to see that Roni was amongst them. She hadn't realised but, of course, Roni was in her last year at Darlington. Once the International Schoolgirls had taken their seats at the side of the stage Mistress Aiken stepped back up to the lectern.

"Normal lessons will be suspended throughout the competition but it must be stressed that all girls will be watched closely and any misbehaviour will be dealt with very harshly indeed."

Mistress Aiken paused for affect.

"So now, let's welcome this year's competitors."

Madame Didier stepped up to the podium and began reading out names. The competing girls walked up, took one of the competition sashes and sat at the back of the stage. Daisy wished she had sat nearer the front. Finally, Madame Didier moved onto the names for the Darlington girls.

"Darlington School for Girls has the following girls competing: Lindsay Lyons…"

Lyndsay, a girl with blonde bobbed hair stood up to cheers and made her way onstage. Daisy didn't know her that well.

"She's a bit of a math's demon so watch her on the science stuff," whispered Marsha.

Lindsay bowed her head as Mistress Aiken put the sash around her neck.

"Margo Tate…" said Madame Didier.

"Uh-oh," said Penny.

Everyone knew who Margo Tate was. She was the tallest girl in the year and was one of the best sports girls in the school - at least, since Tracy had left.

"Annabel Speck…"

"What?" exclaimed Brodie, a little loudly.

The noise of the cheering from the Brat Pack drowned her out. Annabel got to her feet and walked to the stage confidently.

"Well, I guess we knew that this was going to be a fix," muttered Brodie.

Daisy felt her cheeks burn with embarrassment. If only Brodie knew. Annabel took her sash from Mistress Aiken who gave her a toothy smile.

"I hope your teeth fall out, you old bat!" hissed Tina.

"...And Daisy Cooper," said Madame Didier.

Shaking, Daisy got to her feet and walked down the aisle towards the stage, trying to ignore the rows and rows of girls applauding her on either side.

"Go Daisy! Go Daisy!" chanted the 88ers.

Daisy climbed the steps to the stage. The Deputy Head glared at Daisy with fat, bloodshot eyes as she approached the lectern and bowed her head.

"I'm glad to see you accepting how things really work, Daisy," whispered Mistress Aiken lowering the sash over her head, "soon you'll have what you want. Give them a good show. "

Daisy turned and looked out at all the smiling faces clapping and cheering her, feeling terrible. She walked over to the competitor seats and sat down.

"And that completes the opening ceremony," said Mistress Aiken.

Daisy played with the bright gold sash between her fingers. She didn't feel like she deserved it.

Afterwards, Daisy went back to the dorm and pulled out a form she had been given.

"I need to pick people to help me prepare for each of the Virtue tests," she said as the 88ers climbed on the bed next to her.

"First one, Charity."

The girls screwed their faces up, deep in thought.

"You could help a blind person across the road. Or an old lady. Or a blind old lady," said Millie.

"I think I need to do a bit more than that. What about the zoo?"

Millie rolled her eyes.

"Goodness, don't even ask. We've got chimpanzees who keep throwing their business at the gazelles, polar bears who keep eating the penguins and Sankofa, the lion, is so depressed in his cage we can barely get him to move."

"That's such a shame. Maybe I could help out there. That would be charitable, wouldn't it?"

"Oh, yes! Yes it would!" said Millie.

Daisy wrote Millie's name down next to Charity and moved onto Bravery.

"I got that!" said Tina, "You do a motorcycle jump!"

"You want me to jump something on a motorcycle?" asked Daisy, not quite sure she had heard her correctly.

Tina nodded.

"But, I've never even ridden a motorcycle."

"It's easy, I used to do it all the time with my brothers. All you have to do is point it in the right direction and not let go."

"It sounds awfully dangerous," said Millie.

"Not to mention those horrible grease stains," added Penny.

The 88ers got into an excited argument about it. Daisy waved her hands for them to be quiet.

"It does sound crazy and scary, but I wouldn't be showing bravery if it wasn't, so it's perfect."

The others apart from Tina were still not convinced. Daisy wrote Tina's name down next to Bravery anyway.

"Okay, next one is Reason," she said and looked at Marsha.

"Well, you're the smartest. Maybe you can teach me some science skills to show off."

"Aaah…my famous deductive skills!" joked Marsha, "I could get the teachers to arrange a crime scene for you and you could investigate it to find out what happened. Tina and I have been building some great spy equipment in engineering."

Daisy nodded. She wrote down Marsha's name. The next virtue was Grace. Penny offered to help, saying she could teach Daisy to "walk like a lady". She pulled out a large collection of fashion magazines from under her bed which scared Daisy more than the motorcycle jump. The next virtue was Agility.

"That should be Tracy," said Daisy, looking over Tracy's empty bed.

"I have her email address," said Brodie, "is she allowed to help you?"

"I don't know," said Daisy, "the rules don't say anything about it having to be a pupil. She has been expelled though, so probably not."

She moved onto the next virtue on the list.

"Culture. That should be Layla - she's spent her life travelling around the world. Again, I doubt they'll let her back on school grounds," said Marsha.

It was turning out to be very difficult. The final virtue on the list was Fellowship.

"Brodie, that has to be you," said Daisy.

"No problemo. What do I have to do?" asked Brodie.

"I haven't a clue," said Daisy.

The 88ers started talking about what Daisy should do for the different trials. Daisy was hardly paying attention. It all felt like a big lie. It was horrible seeing the 88ers so enthusiastic and willing to help when none of it made any difference. If Mistress Aiken kept her word Daisy was going to be an International Schoolgirl whatever she did.

"What are you thinking, D.C.?"

Daisy looked up to see Brodie staring at her.

"Nothing," she said, "Come on, Millie, lets go and have a look at the zoo."

Sankofa looked very depressed. There was a large chunk of meat in his feed bowl, untouched. The great mane that hung around his head was knotted and dusty and his rib cage poked through his fur.

"He was rescued from a circus where they'd kept him in a cage for twenty two hours a day," said Millie, " the cage was so small he couldn't even turn around in it. We're hoping to build up his strength so he can learn to hunt again and we can return him to Africa but he just refuses to do anything. The only time he moves is when someone opens his cage and then he runs at the door like a mad thing. I think he's just tired of being kept locked up. It's very sad."

"It's a shame you can't take him out for walks," said Daisy.

Daisy looked into Sankofa's huge, sorrowful eyes and wondered what on earth she could do to help. To take her mind off it she assisted Millie around the rest of the zoo by cleaning cages, feeding the bats and piglets and occasionally running away from charging hippos. By lunchtime Daisy was feeling exhausted and in need of a good shower.

"Pee-yew!" said Penny, holding her nose as Daisy sat down to eat.

"How'd it go?" asked Brodie, "Feeling charitable?"

"I can't believe how much help they need," said Daisy.

"She did wonderfully," said Millie, "she's not afraid to get her hands dirty."

"I can see!" said Penny.

"So, what are you going to show for the competition?" asked Marsha.

"I've almost got something," said Daisy.

The truth was, she didn't have a clue.

"Well, eat up," said Tina, "you'll need all your strength. We're jumping motorcycles this afternoon."

* * *

The rusty warehouse that was the school garage sat on a wide stretch of tarmac behind the engineering block. It was where the school bus was kept in working order and also where the sixth form girls came to pass their driving exams. Off to one side of the garage was a huge junkyard. A long, dusty path cut through mountains of car parts, broken televisions and metal drums. In the middle of the path lay the jagged top half of one of the school's old buses. Daisy, sat cross legged on a broken washing machine, watched as Tina jumped it on her motorbike. Tina skidded the bike to a halt and pulled off her helmet.

"There's no way on earth I can do that," said Daisy.

"It's easy," said Tina.

"I can't jump a bus. Not even half a bus. I can't ride a motorcycle."

Tina laughed.

"Can you ride a normal bike?"

"Of course."

"Same thing. Except you don't have to pedal and it's a lot faster."

"There's a BIG difference between cycling to the shops and jumping a bus on a motorbike!"

"We'll start with something smaller," said Tina.

She reached into her pocket and pulled out a tiny toy bus.

"Well, I might be able to jump THAT one," said Daisy.

The bike felt like an angry bull between Daisy's legs, ready to charge. They had moved out onto the tarmac to practice. The breath from her nostrils steamed up the visor of the helmet which made it difficult to see. Tina was standing several meters away waving her arms at Daisy, beckoning her. The jump itself was tiny. Laughable, really. Two ramps rose barely six inches above the ground and faced each other with the toy bus between them. Daisy looked down at the bike handles. They did seem pretty simple. It wasn't that different from the video games she had played with David and Daniel.

"COME ON!" shouted Tina, jumping up and down impatiently.

"Perilous," muttered Daisy.

She tugged the accelerator and felt a jolt as the bike leapt forwards. She raced towards the ramp, her mind focused on keeping the vehicle straight. A few feet from the jump the front wheel hit a bump and the bike shook from side to side. Heart thumping, Daisy adjusted the handlebars but it was too much and the bike was still wobbling wildly as it hit the ramp. The front wheel twisted sideways causing the bike to jerk like a bucking horse and throw Daisy across the tarmac where she skid to a stop on her back. She lay there, out of breath, staring up at the sky through her misty visor.

"You okay?"

Daisy thought about it. She wiggled her fingers and toes. They all worked which was good. She nodded her head. Tina grinned and clapped her hand hard on Daisy's shoulder.

"Good for you, champ! Lets get you back in the saddle!"

"If it's all the same I think I'll stay on the ground a little longer," said Daisy but it was too late.

Tina dragged her to her feet.

Daisy was exhausted as she showered for dinner. She washed the dust from her hair, cleaned the dirt from between her fingernails and checked her legs for bruises. Fortunately, the padding had prevented her from serious injury. It had been a tiring day. By the time she moved back into the dorm to get ready for dinner she was ready to crawl into bed.

Winter was coming. The sky was dark as Daisy trudged across the courtyard with the others to the dining hall. She was half day dreaming and didn't notice the large truck driving across the tarmac until it blared its horn angrily at her.

"WATCH WHERE YOU'RE GOING!"

A muscly looking woman scowled down at her from the driver's seat. Daisy spotted Olga sitting in the passenger seat next to the driver as it drove by. On the back of the truck there was a large pile of empty packing crates and ropes. Written along the side, half hidden by tarpaulin were some words: PRECIOUS GOODS REMOVAL MATERIALS.

The dining hall was full of chatter. Competitors were surrounded by supporters at their tables, all talking tactics. It was only the first day of rehearsals and already Daisy's sash was looking pretty tattered. She wondered what would happen if she tore it off herself right there in the dining room where everyone could see. Would Mistress Aiken still help her win or would she be disqualified?

"So you jumped a bus?" said Marsha, breaking Daisy's concentration.

"I jumped a toy bus. Well, actually, I kind of crushed it," replied Daisy.

"It's just the start," said Tina, "another few hours and she'll be jumping a full size one."

"Do you really think that's possible?" asked Penny, looking doubtful.

Daisy shrugged. Tina started to tell them stories of how she jump cars in the car park of her father's garage. Daisy's thoughts drifted. She started thinking about the removal truck with the packing cases that had nearly run her over in the courtyard. Something about it wasn't quite right. As if on cue, Olga walked into the dining room. She had a suspicious smile on her face as she sat down with the rest of the Brat Pack at the back of the restaurant. They grouped together in a huddle and started talking excitedly.

"Does anyone want any water?" said Daisy.

The 88ers shook their heads. Daisy got up and slowly walked over to the water fountain at the back of the restaurant, directly behind the Brat Pack. They were too busy chatting to notice her. Daisy poured herself a cup and sipped, carefully listening to their conversation.

"….packing up all the museum pieces tomorrow night for the buses to take."

"What about Great Sister?"

"She's going to wait here and oversee the competition to make sure everyone's distracted and no one notices till everything's gone."

"SHHH!"

Daisy turned to see the Brat Pack glaring at her. She smiled at them as innocently as she could, trying not to look shocked at what she'd just heard.

"Don't worry about her," muttered Eleanore, "Mistress Aiken says she's finally learnt to mind her own business."

The Brat Pack laughed at her. Daisy crushed the empty water cup in her hand, threw it in the bin, and wandered back over to the 88ers.

CHAPTER TWENTY FOUR - A GIFT IN A ROSE BUSH

"Rise and shine, Daisy Cooper!"

Daisy was being shaken awake. Her feet felt very cold. She opened her eyes blearily and shivered. There were clouds above her head. She'd managed to fall asleep on the balcony. No wonder she was cold. When they'd returned from dinner the night before Daisy couldn't stop thinking about the Brat Pack's conversation and had sat out on the balcony alone to try and make sense of it. No matter how many times she turned it around in her head, there was only one thing it could mean. The Sisters of the Black Night weren't happy with just the Devil's Eye treasure map. They were going to steal the school museum pieces as well. Just like greedy, rotten pirates.

Penny looked down at her with a frown.

"Appalling start, Cooper. There's no grace in sleeping rough outdoors. Unless you are under a canopy of coconut leaves in the Maldives Islands. Chop, chop!"

Penny marched her to the dorm.

"Time to teach you about Grace," said Penny, "so let's give you a makeover."

Daisy yawned and took her wash bag out of her bedside cupboard.

"Oh, no you don't!" said Penny grabbing the bag out of her hand.

She pulled out the hard block of soap Daisy used, looked at it with disgust and threw it in the bin.

"That's my soap!" said Daisy.

Penny rolled her eyes.

"Look, Daisy, I know I come across as a world class bitch at times but I'm not at all. People think I don't hear what they say about me - that I'm shallow and fashion obsessed - but there's more to me than that. Don't get me wrong, I love fashion and designer clothes but it's not just about looking fabulous. It's for a reason. You met my parents at the Open Day, didn't you?"

Daisy nodded. She remembered being shocked at how different they were to Penny.

"They seemed nice."

"Well, they are nice but they're also slobs. Their idea of dressing up is putting on a clean tracksuit."

Penny reached into her cabinet and took out a large bag containing expensive looking bottles and lotions.

"Are you ashamed of your parents?" asked Daisy.

"I guess so. Sometimes. I wish I wasn't but I also wish they'd make an effort. People judge you on how you look a lot of the time. You can say that's wrong and terrible but it means you can use it to your advantage. It's like wearing disguises."

Wearing disguises sounds useful, thought Daisy.

Penny pulled four bottles out of her bag and pushed them into Daisy's hands.

An hour later Daisy barely recognised herself in the mirror. Her hair was up in rollers that had been wound so tight they were stretching her skin. Penny had also put make up on Daisy's face - bright red lipstick and blue eye shadow. The last time Daisy had worn make-up it was when she went to a fancy dress party in junior school as a clown. It didn't look a lot different to how she looked now.

"I'm not totally sure I'm getting this," she said.

"Shh!" said Penny tickling Daisy's cheeks with a big powdered brush.

Daisy sneezed, blowing powder over the mirror. It was nice of Penny to help but the whole thing felt odd. Not exactly what Daisy imagined when she thought of Grace. When she was done with her makeover Penny instructed Daisy to walk up and down the dorm in a swanky satin dress with a pile of chemistry books on her head to keep her posture.

"You've got to move like a swan, not waddle like a duck!" said Penny as the books fell off for the countless time.

"I appreciate your help, Penny, but I really don't see how this shows Grace," said Daisy picking the books off the floor, "I feel like a box of chocolates on a conveyor belt."

Penny laughed.

"You don't feel different?" she said.

Daisy shrugged.

"I *do* feel different. That's the problem. I don't feel like me," she said.

"So, if you're accepted as an International Schoolgirl and get invited to a posh dinner with presidents and movie stars, you're just going to show up in your grotty plimsolls?"

"Hey, I like my plimsolls!"

Penny stood up and put her hands on Daisy's shoulders which were hunched up by her ears and gently lowered them.

"Think of it as a game, Daisy. It's like dressing up or role playing. That's all it is. You never know when you might have to pretend to be someone else."

Thinking of it as a game helped and after a while Daisy started to relax. Soon she was gliding up and down the dorm without the books falling and even managed a few quick spins until Penny scolded her, telling her it wasn't THAT much of a game.

After her strange morning with Penny, Daisy arrived at the cottage with lunch for Hattie to find the front door locked. On the door, tucked under the old handle, was an envelope with Daisy's name on it. She found a note inside.

DEAR DAISY,

SORRY I'M NOT AT HOME. PLEASE LEAVE MY LUNCH ON THE STEP. I'VE LEFT A GIFT FOR YOU IN THE ROSE BUSH. BRING IT TO THE ISLAND ON THE DUCK LAKE.

HATTIE.

Daisy looked in the rose bush. Buried between the sticky buds and gnarly thorns was an unusual looking object. It was a short pole, a bit like a compact umbrella, made of polished green metal. There were grooves at the bottom that fitted Daisy's fingers perfectly and above them a small round red stone. Below the gemstone was the word 'Narwhal' engraved in silver.

"Narwhal? Is that what you're called?" said Daisy.

She pressed the stone. A guard flipped out above her fingers and a long blade shot out of the end. It was a fencing sword but not like one Daisy had seen before. She held it up to the light and looked at the blade. There were tiny scratches along it, evidence of its use in many battles. Daisy took an *en garde* stance and swished the sword in her hand a few times. It felt perfectly balanced, miles better than the practice swords. Daisy pushed the tip against the wall where it dug into the brick work. It was very strong as well. She pushed the red button again and the blade shot back into its handle.

"Cool," said Daisy, "nice to meet you, Narwhal."

Tucking Narwhal into her belt, Daisy looked across the duck lake. The island in the middle sat in a cloud of mist. Thick trees covered it. It was an odd place to meet. Daisy walked down to the edge of the water where a small rowing boat was tethered to the shore and carefully climbed in.

After rowing across the water Daisy lay the oars in the bottom of the boat and tied it to an old tree stump. The ground was covered in leaf mulch and her plimsolls slipped a couple of times as she stepped onto the bank. Daisy looked up. The trees were incredibly tall and their tops formed a canopy that blocked out the light from the sun. With no sound but the haunting cries of birds and the gentle lapping water the island seemed eerie and dreamlike.

"Hello?"

There was no answer. Daisy looked around and spotted what looked like a narrow path. After taking a couple of deep breaths as Miss Weaver had taught her she made her way through the undergrowth. After a few minutes the lake was no longer visible. It was just trees, trees, trees. Daisy heard the crack of a branch somewhere off to the left. She stopped and looked in the direction of the sound, trying to see what had caused it. Whether it was the murky light or the cold wet air, it suddenly dawned on Daisy that it was very unlikely Hattie could have made it across to the island in her wheelchair. It was most likely a trap. The Brat Pack must have decided not to trust her after she'd overheard their conversation about stealing the museum pieces. Daisy pulled Narwhal from her belt, rested her finger on the red button and held it out in front of her.

"Who's there?" she called.

Quick as lightning, a figure in black zipped past her. There was the silver flash of a blade. Daisy pressed the button and Narwhal snapped into place. She looked down to see if she was injured and noticed that her competition sash was gone.

"Perilous," muttered Daisy.

Gritting her teeth she walked through the trees, looking left and right. There was another flash as the black clad figure whipped past again. This time Daisy saw the blade coming and jumped backwards, parrying. She felt their swords clash and then the figure was gone. Turning carefully, Daisy pulled off her cardigan and tied it round her waist. She kept low, peering through branches and leaves, looking for her would-be foe. There was nothing. She heard another cracking branch, this time further off. Moving towards the sound she pulled the torch from her satchel and swept its beam through the undergrowth.

There was a sudden noise. Daisy ducked as a wood pigeon fluttered past her head and up into the canopy of leaves. It was quickly followed by the sound of running footsteps. Daisy spun round to see the masked black figure charging at her out of the gloom, a blade extended in her hand. On instinct Daisy blocked the attack with Narwhal. The figure crashed into her. Daisy rolled back, grabbing hold of her foe and throwing her over her head into a small clearing. As Daisy got to her feet, the masked figure was waiting for her, waving Daisy's sash in her free hand.

"Give. That. Back." growled Daisy.

The figure tipped her head to one side and beckoned Daisy forward, playing with her. That was enough for Daisy. She ran forward swinging the sword, channeling her anger through her fingers and down the blade like it was electricity. She moved fast and accurately. The figure stumbled backwards under the flurry of blows, desperately trying to protect herself. Daisy felt like everything was moving in slow motion, anticipating every move her opponent made with ease. She leapt aside as the blade swished past where her shins were and retaliated with quick thrusts and parries.

"GIVE. THAT. BACK."

Daisy emphasised each word with another blow. With one last lunge the masked figure thrust forward. Daisy knocked the blade aside and with one, two, three twists of her wrist tugged the sword free from her opponent's hand and sent it spinning off into the bushes. The masked figure fell to the floor, holding her arms up to protect herself. Daisy grabbed the competition sash out of her hand and pointed the tip of Narwhal's blade at her neck.

"Who are you!" Daisy demanded.

The figure laughed.

Irritated, Daisy hooked Narwhal's tip on the bottom of her foe's mask and flicked it off her head.

"Alright, Daisy! Nice work!"

Daisy looked down to see Tracy smiling back at her.

"Tracy?"

"That's me. I was told you needed a bit of Agility practice!"

Hattie was waiting in her wheelchair on the edge of the lake as they rowed back across the water. Tracy told Daisy that Hattie had asked Roni to find her and bring her back to the school to help Daisy with her competition training. Because Tracy had been expelled, though, they'd keep it secret.

"You passed with flying colours," said Tracy.

"I could have taken your head off!" said Daisy.

Tracy laughed.

Daisy, Hattie and Tracy chatted for more than an hour over tea. Tracy was going to a comprehensive that had a very good sports facility. Daisy told Tracy about the motorcycle jump and the makeover from Penny. As the sun was setting, Roni arrived.

"Hi Sweetie."

"Hi Roni!"

"Sorry to break up your party but we need to get Tracy back on a train to London."

Daisy wasn't ready for Tracy to go. It felt too soon.

"Can't you stay?" she asked.

Tracy shook her head.

"You'll be too busy anyway, Cooper. Give 'em what for."

Tracy winked at Daisy, did a backflip and walked off after Roni on her hands.

After they had left Hattie turned to Daisy looking serious.

"How's the little reporter coming along?" she asked.

The truth was that Daisy was confused. She wanted to stop the Sisters of the Black Night. On the other hand if she kept quiet she'd be an International Schoolgirl in less than two days, travelling the world like the reporter she'd always wanted to be. She had to decide. The problem was, she couldn't.

"Your face looks like a squeezed lemon" said Hattie, "I've never seen someone looking so troubled."

"If you had a choice between doing the right thing and getting what you always wanted," asked Daisy, "what would you do?"

Hattie went quiet. She dipped her biscuit in her tea and sucked on it noisily.

"I guess, Daisy, it isn't about what I would do. It's about what you would do and only you can answer to that. I will say this, though. The right decision is very rarely the easy one. You have to ask yourself if you could live with the choice you make."

Daisy got back late to Honour House. The rest of the 88ers were asleep in the dorm. She sat out in one of the balcony chairs, wrapped her duvet round her shoulders and looked out across the school. One by one the lights in the main building went out. The moon was a white crescent in a sky full of stars. One day left before the competition. Daisy took her penlight torch and Mary's journal out of her satchel. She turned the torch on and tucked it behind her ear, opening the journal to the last page she'd read. Maybe Mary could help her make up her mind.

CHAPTER TWENTY FIVE - THE JOURNAL OF ROTTEN MARY

PART TWO

With Jacky gone Mary let Sally have the run of the Black Night. A couple of the crew members built a smaller cabin next to the Captain's and Sally dressed it with her personal things to make it feel like home. Mary had decided not to waste any time with her plan to steal the items in her encyclopaedia and The Black Night set sail for Africa. She knew that the Pirate Hunter Captain William Aiken only had interest in protecting British ships so as long as they steered clear of them they could stay out of his way. The first item Mary planned on stealing was Cleopatra's Egg which was currently held in the palace of a Sultan. To disguise what they were up to they had arranged to buy some spices from the palace to take back to England.

Sally missed her Grandfather but Mary, as gruff as she was, soon become both a teacher and, if not quite a mother figure, a caring aunt. Sally quickly learnt the names of the parts of the ship, how to tie a dozen different knots, how to check for wind and sea currents and, probably most importantly, how to protect herself with a sword.

A few weeks later they were sailing up the Nile under the sweltering Egyptian sun and Sally was starting to feel at home. It was her eleventh birthday but she didn't mention it to anyone. Birthdays seemed a bit of a silly thing to bother pirates about. She was sat on the port side of the deck with her feet in a bucket of water to keep cool and sewing up a hole in one of the sails when Mary called her into the Captain's cabin.

"The crew tells me you've been practicing your sword skills day and night. They say you're a natural. Lets see what you can do," said Mary.

She pulled her sword from her belt and handed it over to Sally. Sally took it carefully. It was heavy. All the swords on the boat were heavy but they were all she'd had to practice with so she was used to it. Sally lifted the blade, jumped into a sideways stance and showed off a few of the moves she had picked up from the crew. Mary laughed.

"Well, you are a natural sea dog! I pity any man who'd be fool enough to pick a fight with you. The question is, where would you keep such a thing about your person?"

Sally balanced the sword on its tip. It was as tall as she was. She may be able to fight with one but she'd never be able to carry it properly. Mary took it out of her hands and put it back in its scabbard. She walked over to a big chest by the window.

"I'm sure I've got something in here that will be of use to you," said Mary rummaging around in the box, "Aah. Here it is."

The Pirate Captain turned round to show Sally a dark green rod about a foot long with a single ruby button towards one end.

"I won this off a pygmy assassin in South America playing cards. He says he found it in an Aztec temple. Here."

Mary handed it over.

"Be careful of that button, especially when it's pointed at me."

There were grooves on the end of the rod that fitted Sally's fingers perfectly so that the ruby button was just above her thumb. Sally pointed the rod away from Mary and pressed the button. With a satisfying click a steel guard sprang up around her hand and a series of spring loaded rods whipped out of the end until they formed a long, sharp blade.

"Heavens!" muttered Sally.

She did a couple of quick sword moves. The metal made a satisfying whooshing sound like it was slicing the air itself.

"How does it feel?" said Mary.

"It feels like it was made for me," said Sally.

She pressed the button and the blade snapped back into the handle.

"And easier to carry I'd warrant," said Mary, "It's yours."

"No, I can't…" said Sally but Mary hushed her with a wave of her hands.

"It's no use to anyone else."

"Thank you," said Sally.

"You'll have to name it, though. All swords need a name."

Sally looked at the rod in her hands.

"I'll call it Narwhal."

Mary nodded. It was a good name.

"Now go practice with it. You'll be needing it sooner than you think."

Sally tucked the rod into her belt and opened the door to the deck.

"And Sally…" said Mary.

Sally turned.

"Happy Birthday," said Mary with a wink.

At the Sultan's palace The Black Night sailed up alongside a long wooden jetty that stretched out from an ornate garden into the river Nile. After checking them for weapons guards escorted Mary and a handful of her crew past trees filled with tropical birds, through high hallways covered in intricate mosaics and finally into the court room. They placed the heavy trunks they had been carrying at the feet of the Sultan with an elaborate bow.

To say the Sultan was surprised when the trunks were opened to reveal not money and jewels but sword wielding pirates would be an understatement. The guards fought valiantly as the Sultan cowered against his throne. The smallest trunk popped open and Sally, wielding Narwhal in her hand, jumped out and snatched Cleopatra's Egg from its pedestal beside the throne. The Sultan cried out after her as she ran from the throne room but the guards were too busy defending themselves. Lungs bursting, Sally didn't look back until she had ran all the way through the halls and gardens and up the gangplank of The Black Night.

"FIRE CANNONS!" she shouted running into the Captain's cabin.

The deck shook as the cannons thundered below. Sally placed Cleopatra's Egg safely in one of the chests and ran over to look through the port side window just in time to see the mighty cannonballs thudding into the walls of the palace. The first mate cast off and the ship started to move away. Mary and the other pirates ran out of the ornamental garden and leapt from the jetty, grabbing at the netting on the side of the ship as a rain of arrows fired from the Sultan's archers crashed around them. The Sultan appeared out of breath to see The Black Night sailing away and his own ships sinking below the water.

After the raid on the Sultan's palace The Black Night shored on a small trade island off the Cape of Good Hope where the crew laid low and Mary plotted her next attack. She had picked up an English news pamphlet from one of the traders to read. It seemed Jacky had purchased a new ship and was up to her old tricks stealing gold from the British Navy. Of course, it didn't mention a female pirate but Mary knew it from the name - The Salty Dog - the name of Blackheart Bob's old ship. Jacky wasn't one for being imaginative. The article said Pirate Hunter Captain William Aiken was in hot pursuit of The Salty Dog and was getting closer by the day.

"Well, at least she will keep the navy off our backs," Mary said to Sally over a lunch of buttered snails.

"Do you miss her?"

Mary scowled, picking snail shell out of her teeth.

"I miss her in the same way you would miss a pet dog with rabies. It'd bite you the first chance it gets but it would still be your dog. We can't let go of memories that easily."

Over the next year the crew of The Black Night managed to steal a number of the items in Mary's encyclopaedia including Bodicea's chariot from a tomb on the outskirts of Rome, a painting of an Empress of Russia, and the armour of Joan d'Arc, the famous French warrioress. In their biggest haul they'd looted eight great statues of goddesses from an abandoned temple in Greece. Soon the ship was overburdened with cargo and the crew were getting a little weary of risking their lives for what they saw as worthless museum pieces. Mary decided that it was time to return to the South Coast of England to unload their bounty and store it in a safe place.

"What are you going to do with it all?" asked Sally.

"When the time is right, I'm going to buy a place to keep it all, somewhere that girls like yourself can see them."

The last stop before returning to England was the port of Amsterdam in Holland. They stopped for a meal in an Inn where they sat at a table by the window and watched the boats coming in and out of the harbour.

"I know who you are," said a voice next to them in a low whisper.

Mary ignored it but Sally looked round to see a ragged old woman with hair that sprang from her head like a wild grey shrub.

"I know who you are..." repeated the hag getting closer, "...Rotten

Mary."

Without looking round, Mary grabbed the woman's arm and twisted it, pulling her down against the table.

"If that were true," she said quietly, "then you'd know that Rotten Mary doesn't like strangers tossing her name about. Those who do often find themselves without a tongue."

"I meant no bother!" whimpered the hag, "I just been told to give you a message if I saw you, is all!"

"What message?"

"Cutthroat Jacky wishes to meet with you. She says all is forgiven. She says sisters is sisters."

"Why should I believe a mad old bag like you?"

The old woman reached into her grubby tunic and pulled out an envelope which she handed to Mary. It was Jacky's handwriting.

"She's been leaving letters for you in all the ports of Europe but I was lucky enough to find you first."

"No one who found me was ever lucky," said Mary opening the letter with a knife.

"What does it say?" asked Sally.

"It says she's ready to retire and wants to meet to reclaim what we buried."

"The treasure!" said Sally, forgetting herself.

The old hag's eyes lit up at the mention of the word.

"And how are we supposed to meet her?" Mary asked the old woman.

"If I was to be let go, I have the very thing you need."

"How do I know you won't call the guards on us?"

The old woman frowned, looking suddenly sad. She pulled back the collar on her tunic to show a nasty scar burnt in the shape of an 'X' on her neck.

"Because I'm already marked as a thief myself," she said.

Mary nodded. She'd dealt with thieves before and knew that whilst they were not trustworthy, they also didn't call the attention of the guards. Mary let her go and she snuck off into a dark corner of the inn.

"You're not serious about meeting Jacky, are you?" asked Sally.

"Of course," said Mary.

"But why?"

"Because as long as that treasure stays buried she will get crazier and crazier and I need less crazy people hunting for my blood on this planet.

Besides which, I could do with the silver myself if I'm to pay for a building to put all our real treasure in."

A box thudded down on the table between them. It was a wooden cage with a pigeon in it.

"Jacky is waiting off the coast of Devon," said the old hag, "She says there's an old smugglers cove there you know of. Let this pigeon go a day before you expect to arrive and she will be waiting for you."

The next morning The Black Night headed out of Amsterdam across the North Sea towards England. Mary and Sally were stood at the jib looking out across the waves. Mary held the homing pigeon in her hands.

"Are you sure you want to do this?" asked Sally.

"Don't ask me what I'm sure of, girl. I'm still Captain of this ship," muttered Mary.

Sally frowned. Mary took a long intake of breath.

"Sea air, girl. You never feel more alive than when there's salt in your lungs. Here, you do it."

Mary handed the pigeon over to Sally. She could feel its tiny heart beating in her fingers. Extending her hands out over the jib she let go. In an explosion of feathers the bird fluttered up into the clouds.

On the way back to England Mary told Sally about the cove. In the cove there was a network of caves built into the rock where they hid firearms and barrels of whiskey and gunpowder when they used to smuggle. The cove was the closest Mary and Jacky had ever got to their home towns so they had sworn that if they were ever lost that's where they would meet.

"Land ahoy!"

Mary pulled a telescope from her coat and opened it up. The white chalky coastline of England stood out from the mist like a mirage. Mary could see the entrance to the cove and the bow of a single ship sticking out from it. She adjusted the telescope until she could read the words 'Salty Dog' written on the bow.

"Crow's nest!" cried Mary, "Any sign of other ships?"

The sailor in the crow's nest put her hand to her forehead and looked in all directions.

"No, Captain! Clear water, Captain!"

Mary tucked the telescope away.

"Sally, you stay close to me," she said, "and don't let your hand stray far from Narwhal."

There was barely room in the cove for two large vessels. The bows rubbed against each other as the first mate steered The Black Night between the rocks. The deck of the Salty Dog was so close Sally could have stepped between the two ships if she had wanted. It was deserted. Like a ghost ship. Mary and Sally climbed into a rowing boat with a couple of crew and sailed towards the mouth of the cave. With sharp shards of granite rock protruding from it, it looked like the mouth of a dragon. Mary turned around and waved a signal to the first mate back on The Black Night.

"What was that for?" whispered Sally.

"That's a precaution," said Mary.

Mary lit a torch as the rowing boat beached against the cave. She stepped inside with Sally close behind her. It took a while for Sally's eyes to become accustomed to the darkness. Mary led her and the crew up a rickety wooden ladder to a smaller tunnel halfway up the cave wall. They crawled down it for what seemed like forever until they reached a wide cliff that overlooked a large indoor pool. There was algae in the pool that gave off a strange green glow. In the middle of the pool there was a small island of rubble piled high with barrels of gunpowder. Stood next to them, was Jacky.

"It's been a long time, Sister," said Jacky, her voice echoing across the cavern.

"Some might say not long enough,'" replied Mary stepping down from the ledge into the pool.

The two crew members stayed back at the mouth of the cavern standing guard. Sally slid down the ledge behind Mary. The pool water was icy cold and made Sally shiver as they waded over to the island.

"Have you got the pendant?" asked Jacky.

Mary lifted the pendant out of her shirt and held it up.

"And you?" she asked.

Jacky nodded and held up her hand to show her own pendant. There was a sound of tumbling rocks off to one side of the cavern. Sally tugged on Mary's coat.

"So where's your crew? I take it you haven't gotten so greedy as to sail a ship yourself?" said Mary to Jacky.

"We're here."

It was a man's voice. A posh English voice. Mary and Sally turned to see Pirate Hunter Captain William Aiken. Sally looked around in panic. At least twenty soldiers in British navy uniform stepped out of the shadows, all pointing swords and muskets at Mary.

"You foul dog!" snarled Mary, turning towards Jacky.

"Now Sister, name calling won't help you."

"But to side with the navy scum!" snapped Mary, "They'll kill us all!"

"Not all of us," said Jacky, "you see, Captain Aiken caught me some time ago and planned to hand me over to the King to give me a right good hanging. Until I told him about a wonderful island called The Devil's Eye, that is. An island with so much treasure buried on it that it would make him and all his men rich enough for several lifetimes. All we needed was the other half of the map."

"IT WILL BE A COLD DAY IN HELL BEFORE YOU GET YOUR TREACHEROUS CLAWS ON IT!" shouted Mary.

She pulled a pistol from her jacket and fired at Jacky. The sound was incredibly loud in the echoing cavern and made Sally's ears ring. The shot knocked Jacky sprawling into the barrels. As she fell, Pirate Captain William Aiken and his men charged into the pool. Mary grabbed hold of Sally and pulled her down under the water just as a ball of fire erupted through the mouth of the cave, knocking the naval officers off their feet.

"What was that?" cried Sally, spluttering for air as they resurfaced.

"That was my precaution, girl. Gunpowder. The crew's been filling the entrance with the stuff - all they needed was my gunshot signal."

Mary pulled the Piece of Eight on the necklace out of Sally's shirt and held it up.

"Remember what I said, girl! Remember what we planned to do. It's all here in this! Find your virtues! Now RUN! Don't turn back!"

Mary shoved Sally in the direction of a small tunnel to one side of the cavern. There was another huge explosion. Pirate Captain William Aiken stepped in front of Sally, holding out his sword.

"Don't move, lass, you're coming with us!" he growled, an evil glint in his eye.

Sally pulled Narwhal out of her belt and pressed the ruby button. The sword sprang open. She ran straight at the Pirate Hunter, knocking his sword back with her blade, catching him off guard. His boots slipped on the algae and he fell into the pool. The cavern exit was only a few feet away. Sally heard a scream of rage and turned to see Jacky staggering to her feet on the island. Jacky lunged towards Mary, grabbing for the pendant but Mary was too fast. She pulled her cutlass from her belt and sliced Jacky's hand clean from her wrist. Jacky screamed in pain.

"YOU ROTTEN LITTLE SWARTHY DOG!"

Sally turned back to see the Pirate Hunter on his feet and charging towards her. She ducked down and slipped between his legs. As he tumbled over the top of her, she made a dash for the tunnel entrance. Another explosion shook through the cavern causing rocks to crash down from the ceiling.

"Jacky! Come on! It's too dangerous!" shouted the Pirate Hunter.

He grabbed Jacky and pulled her towards the tunnel leading back to the cove just as a huge chunk of granite landed in the pool. The force of the rock knocked Mary back against the barrels. Dazed, she looked around and spotted Sally staring at her from the mouth of the tunnel.

"There's no point both of us dying here, girl! Run while you can! Go!" Mary commanded.

Sally turned and ran towards the open sea.

I'm not sure how long I have been stuck in this cavern since the ambush but I am sure it has been days now. My leg was damaged in the explosions - broken, I suspect - so I cannot even stand. I am thankful of the eerie light of the pool which enables me to write this. My only hope is that Sally got away safely and remembered what I told her. Whoever finds this journal - whether it be in ten or a hundred years time - please do me the courtesy of letting people know what really happened between Mary Sweeney, Cutthroat Jacky and the daughter I never had, Sally Darlington.

Rotten Mary Sweeney, Captain of The Black Night.

Daisy put down Mary's journal. Sally had achieved what Mary had wanted and set up Darlington, basing it on the eight virtues. She had done the right thing and the lives of countless girls who had gone to the school since had been changed for the better as a result. Daisy felt like a cloud had been lifted. As much as she wanted it, it didn't matter if she became an International Schoolgirl. She had to do the right thing like Sally. Standing slowly, Daisy took Narwhal out of her satchel and pointed it up to the sky.

"*En Garde,*" she said and pressed the ruby button.

Narwhal's blade shot out at the moon.

CHAPTER TWENTY SIX - THE GREAT MUSEUM THEFT

Daisy told the 88ers everything the next morning. She told them about the deal she had made with Mistress Aiken for the pendant, how having a map to the treasure wasn't enough for the Sisters and how they planned to steal the all museum pieces. At first the 88ers were a little mad at Daisy for not telling them earlier but then their anger turned on Mistress Aiken. They were ready to march straight to the Deputy Head's office. Daisy managed to calm them down, telling them she had a plan. It would be difficult and they only had the last day of rehearsals to prepare but it would be worth it. If it worked out, however, everyone would know what had been going on.

After dinner and a long day of getting things ready Daisy looked out from the balcony at the tell tale glow of the torches flickering in the maze.

"It's time," she said, "let's test the camera."

Marsha and Tina had fixed the camera from the Serpent's Tooth trip and this time made it waterproof. Not only that but they had made it wireless, sending video straight to Brodie's laptop. There was also an ear piece attached so Daisy could communicate with the others. Marsha helped Daisy put the earpiece in and hooked the camera behind her ear.

"Images are coming in nice and clear. Give us some sound," said Brodie looking at the video image on her laptop.

"What sort of sound?" asked Daisy.

"Anything," said Brodie, "I just want to check the levels."

"Daisy, Daisy, give me your answer do….I'm half crazy…"

"You certainly are," said a voice behind them.

Daisy and Brodie turned. Layla was standing in the doorway dressed head to toe in black.

"Hello, Cooper, going off on a little mission?" she said.

"Layla!"

Daisy ran over and gave her a big hug.

"What are you doing here?" she asked.

"I was planning on sneaking back and watching you in the competition but Brodie told me you're up to something way more interesting. What's the plan?"

"The Sisters of the Black Night are using the competition as a cover to steal all the museum pieces. We're going to record what they're up to and show it to everyone on the big screen tomorrow afternoon at the awards ceremony. It might be dangerous. Do you want to help?"

Layla raised a thickly mascara'd eyebrow. She smiled and brushed her hair to one side. There was a camera identical to the one Daisy was wearing behind her ear.

"I'm way ahead of you. Let's go catch some pirates," she said.

The clock in the courtyard struck ten as Daisy and Layla ran through the shadows towards the main building entrance. They crouched down, catching their breath, and took a look around. There were a few girls standing around at the doors to Grace House laughing. A teacher was marching across towards them with a flashlight. No one else was around.

"Can you hear me?" whispered Daisy.

"Hearing you loud and clear, D.C.," replied Brodie, the voice coming over the earpiece.

Daisy looked at Layla who nodded to show she had heard it too.

"Right," said Daisy, "Layla, make your way to the school museum. I'll go through the school maze and we'll meet up in the underground hall in half an hour."

Layla raised her hand to give Daisy a high five but then, after second thoughts, gave her a quick hug instead.

"Great to see you again, Cooper."

Then, silent as a cat, she turned and ran off into the darkness.

* * *

It had been a while since Daisy had been in the maze. She made a couple of wrong turns but eventually reached the statue of the sea captain with the telescope and crept behind it. She peered through the bushes and, sure enough, the centre of the maze was filled with the Sisters.

"Are you getting this, Brodie?"

"Clear as day," replied Brodie.

"How's Layla doing?"

"Hi!" said Layla over the earpiece, "I'm doing good. I'm in the teacher's quarters and on my way to the museum now. It's dreadfully quiet here."

"It's not so quiet here," said Daisy.

The Sisters of the Black Night were chanting. The chanting slowly rose in volume and pitch as Mistress Aiken - dressed as the Great Sister - stepped up to the stone altar. The hooded Sisters all knelt down in front of her.

"WELCOME, SISTERS! TONIGHT WE REACH THE END OF A LONG JOURNEY WHICH BEGAN NEARLY TWO HUNDRED YEARS AGO."

Mistress Aiken raised both hands to show the two Devil's Eye pendants. There was a low rumble of thunder and a large black cloud crept over the surface of the moon. There was a buzzing crackle in Daisy's earpiece.

"What was that?" she whispered.

"Probably interference from the weather. Shouldn't be too much of a problem," said Layla's over the earpiece.

At least, that's what it should have been. What Daisy actually heard was "should...b...t...ch....blem"

Daisy tapped the earpiece.

"How's the video, Brodie?"

"Erm. Okaaaay.....ish," said Brodie.

There was a bright flash of lightning that lit up the whole maze. Daisy ducked back under the statue as drops of rain, heavy as bullets started falling from the sky. In the centre the Sisters had opened up the secret passageway in the fountain and were starting to move underground.

"Right," said Daisy getting to her feet, "I'm not sure if you girls can still hear me but they're moving so I'm going to follow them."

There was no reply.

Daisy ducked out from behind the statue and crept along the bushes until she reached the entrance to the centre of the maze. She peeked round the corner just as the curved stones of the fountain rolled back into place. Unfortunately not all of the Sisters had gone underground. Two hooded figures were keeping watch, walking round the perimeter with sharp looking swords in their hands. Shivering in the rain Daisy watched the guards hoping to spot a gap in their movements where she could slip past. That wasn't going to work. The minute one turned her back to walk away, the other turned towards her on the opposite side.

There was another flash of lightning followed almost immediately by a crack of thunder which meant the eye of the storm was very close. Daisy wondered if she should just wait for the lightning to strike the swords the girls were carrying but then remembered she had Narwhal clipped to her belt so wasn't exactly safe herself. Over the sound of the rain she heard a loud roar from the school zoo. It gave her an idea. A dangerous idea.

"Are you mad enough to do it, Daisy?" she asked herself.

"Mad enough to do what?" asked Brodie, suddenly back in her earpiece.

"I've got an idea," said Daisy.

"MAD ENOUGH TO DO WHAT??"

"Tell Layla to hold up for five minutes," said Daisy.

Shaking the droplets of rain out of her hair she turned and sprinted off towards the maze entrance.

The inside of the zoo auditorium was scary in the darkness. Shadows of the caged animals bounced across the huge dome as squawks and growls filled the air

"D.C., I think you need to carefully rethink what you are about to do," said Brodie.

Daisy ignored her. She pressed Narwhal's ruby button and the blade shot into place. Balancing the raw steak she had found in the supplies cupboard on the end of the blade Daisy picked up a wooden chair and dragged it towards Sankofa's cage.

"VERY. BAD. IDEA!" said Brodie loudly over the earpiece.

Sankofa was awake and not very happy. Disturbed by the thunder and lightning he was prowling back and forth in his cage growling.

"What's that noise?" asked Layla.

"Daisy's trying to turn herself into lion lunch," said Brodie.

"Shh!" said Daisy.

Honestly, it's hard enough without your commentary, thought Daisy.

Before Brodie or Layla could say another word Daisy flicked the lock open on Sankofa's cage.

"Oh boy," whispered Brodie.

Daisy walked away from the cage dragging the chair in front of her for protection as the door creaked open. She waved the meat on the end of the foil. It felt rather oddly like fishing, which in a way she was. Except for lions.

"Come on, boy...come on, boy..."

Sankofa had stopped pacing. He stood in the doorway staring at Daisy, his huge eyes unblinking. He sniffed the air a few times and licked his nose, revealing rows of sharp powerful teeth. There was another crash of thunder and he jumped at the sound, scared. It was just like how Gibbon reacted to storms and it made Daisy feel sympathy for him.

"Come on, Sankofa...Come on, big feller..."

With a gruff snort Sankofa put his front paws through the doorway. Daisy took a step backwards, wafting the meat in the air. Sankofa stepped towards her with growing confidence, his eyes on the steak. Daisy kept going, moving away towards the exit with the lion slowly following her. After a few feet her elbow touched the door to the auditorium. She reached behind and opened it slowly. Making sure not to fall, not taking her eyes off the lion, Daisy backed through it into the rain.

Once he'd got over his initial reluctance to move outside into the storm Sankofa became bolder with each step and started moving faster. Daisy walked backwards quickly through the zoo, across the grounds and towards the school maze. She could hear Brodie's nervous breathing in her ear piece.

"What's happening?" whispered Layla.

"I'm not quite sure. All I can see is a hungry lion," said Brodie.

"Shh!" whispered Daisy.

As she walked towards the maze entrance Daisy hoped that no one in the school was looking out of their window. Releasing lions would DEFINITELY be grounds for expulsion. At least the thunderstorm was keeping nosy people away. Once inside the maze Sankofa started getting impatient and waved a mighty paw at the chair with each step. Sensing she was coming to a corner and not wanting to back herself into a dead end, Daisy glanced over her shoulder. At that moment Sankofa leapt for the meat. Daisy jumped back just in time but the lion crashed into the chair, snapping it in two. Daisy's heart stopped. She froze. Sankofa roared at her and pulled back onto his haunches ready to jump. As he leapt through the air Daisy rolled to one side and flicked the steak from her foil. Sankofa caught it and landed inches from her feet.

"Perilous!" muttered Daisy.

She watched, hypnotised, as the lion tore into the meat hungrily.

"Well, don't just sit there, Daisy! Run! Run!'

Brodie's voice snapped Daisy back to her senses. She jumped to her feet and dashed through the maze as fast as she could. By the second corner she could hear Sankofa's roars close behind her and the wet splashes of his paws as they crashed through the puddles. Daisy ran faster than she'd ever ran, her lungs burning as she gasped for air. She didn't dare look round. All she knew was that she could feel his hot breath on the back of her calves.

Almost there...almost there... she told herself.

Daisy skidded round another corner and spotted the entrance to the maze centre ahead. Without stopping she charged through it. The hooded guards turned and raised their swords at her.

"WHO THE HELL ARE YOU!" they shouted in unison.

Daisy ran past them and ducked behind the fountain.

"WHAT THE HELL IS THAT!" they shouted as Sankofa charged in after her.

The lion pounced into the centre and let off a roar as thunderous as the black clouds above. Even though it was one of the scariest things Daisy had ever seen it was magnificent to see Sankofa finally acting like a proper lion. The guards screamed, dropped their swords and ran past him through the maze. Sankofa followed them. Daisy waited for a moment, listening to the screams and roaring become more and more distant, before sticking her head out above the fountain wall. The centre of the maze was empty.

"Brodie, can you ask Millie to take care of that? Say sorry for me. If it's any consolation he seems happy," said Daisy into her mic.

"Sure thing, psycho," said Brodie.

Daisy laughed. She climbed the fountain wall, threw a rope over the orb and gave it a turn. The water poured away and the steps to the school tunnels opened up at her feet.

"Okay, Layla," she said, "let's rock 'n'roll."

* * *

Daisy made her way through the tunnels, carefully checking every now and again to make sure she wasn't being followed. Finally she reached the wooden door to the underground hall.

"I'm in place," she whispered, "How are you doing, Layla?"

"I'm inside the museum. There's lots of those hooded creeps moving stuff out."

Before Daisy could ask for more information the wooden door started opening. Quickly she ducked into an alcove. One of the Sisters stepped into the tunnel and walked past her towards the sewers. Daisy knew if the Sister made her way out to the maze she would notice the guards were missing and alert the others. She had to act fast. Stepping out of the alcove, Daisy coughed loudly.

"Hey!"

The hooded figure pulled out a dagger and ran towards Daisy. Thinking fast, Daisy stepped sideways and grabbed the hood, pulling it down over the girl's face. The girl kept going, ran headfirst into the wall and collapsed to the floor. Daisy pulled the hood back and recognised one of the visiting Russian girls. She was knocked out cold.

"Sorry," whispered Daisy, " but I think there's a design flaw in your costume."

Grabbing the girl's legs Daisy pulled her into the alcove and removed her cloak. She took the girls' tie off, gagged her with it and then bound her hands and feet with twine from her emergency bag. When she was satisfied the girl wouldn't be able to escape Daisy put her ear to the door. She could hear a lot of heavy objects being moved and many voices. If she was going to go any further she had to disguise herself. Daisy slipped on the Russian girl's cloak, pulling it down over her satchel. Would they recognise her? Daisy took a couple of deep breaths. She remembered what Penny had told her about dress just being a form of disguise. If she acted like she belonged there no one would notice. Daisy straightened her back. She walked up and down a couple of times, practising looking mysterious. When she was ready she lifted the heavy wooden latch.

"I'm going in, girls," she said and stepped through the door.

The hood was itchy and the cloak too long. Daisy had to lift it over her feet to keep from tripping. As she stepped onto the balcony she could see The Sisters of the Black Night were very busy. The central section of the ceiling where the chandelier had once been had gone leaving a large hole that lead directly into the museum above. Hooded figures stood on a tower of scaffolding carefully guiding the hull of The Black Night ship through it. Everyone was occupied with what they were doing and Daisy moved between them easily, turning her head left and right so that the camera above her ear could capture what was happening and send it back to Brodie's laptop. Most of the museum pieces were already in the hall. There was Bodicea's chariot, the World War Two courier motorcycle and the engine from Amelia Earhart's plane.

"You getting all this, Brodie?" whispered Daisy.

"Every bit of it."

"Where are you, Layla?"

"I'm above you in the museum. They've nearly emptied the place out."

"HEY!"

Daisy froze. One of the Sisters was looking over at her. She was holding the ends of two ropes wrapped around the statue of Hera as a couple of other girls struggled to push it up onto a cart. The Sister threw one of the ropes to Daisy.

"Don't just stand there watching, help out!"

Daisy caught the rope, cautiously climbed onto the cart and helped pull the statue into place. Just as they finished there was a loud rapping sound and the room went quiet. Daisy turned to see Mistress Aiken dressed as the Great Sister standing on a podium and banging on the stone with the ceremonial sword.

"SISTERS! We are almost finished. Soon, some of you will transport the artefacts to a boat that is waiting for the next stage of our journey. It's been a long time for us - the descendants of Jacqueline Lyle, William Aiken and their crew - but finally we have everything we've been looking for!"

Mistress Aiken pulled back the hood on her cowl. Her hair, fixed as always in a stiff bun, wobbled.

"Now we got her!" said Brodie over the earpiece.

"Sisters!" said Mistress Aiken, "There is no need for secrecy between us now. To avoid suspicion outside we should discard our robes before we leave."

All of the Sisters started taking off their robes.

"Perilous," muttered Daisy.

"Get out of there, Daisy. We've got what we need!" said Brodie.

Daisy stepped down from the cart. A staircase to the balcony was only a few feet away, unguarded. She tiptoed over to it and ran up the stairs. As she reached the top someone shoved her hard in the chest.

"Hello, Oik."

It was Eleanore.

Eleanore had been waiting at the top of the stairs.

"I'd recognise those stupid plimsolls of yours anywhere," she said.

Daisy turned, hoping to run back down the steps only to see Dorothy and Olga coming up behind her. She reached into the robe and tried to grab Narwhal but Eleanore was too quick. She yanked Daisy's hands away and pulled back her hood.

"SPY! SPY!"

Daisy kicked Eleanore's shins, knocking her to the floor. She tried to jump over her but the long robe caught in her feet and she fell face first onto the balcony.

"SPY ON THE BALCONY!" cried Eleanore, grabbing Daisy's ankle.

Daisy tried to struggle free but it was too late. Olga and Dorothy pulled her up, twisted her arms behind her back painfully.

"BRING HER HERE!" shouted Mistress Aiken.

The Brat Pack marched Daisy down the stairs into the centre of the hall where Madame Didier and the Deputy Head were waiting.

"And I thought we had a deal," said Mistress Aiken.

She tore the robe off of Daisy.

"You don't deserve to wear that. Take the other stuff off her too. I want to make sure she has nothing to distract her whilst she thinks about the bad choices she's made. Not that she'll have long to think."

Eleanore pulled off Daisy's Satchel and Narwhal and tossed them to one side.

"Open the well."

Daisy watched, horrified, as a couple of the Sisters unlocked the heavy chains on the large semicircular grates in the middle of the floor. They pulled the grates aside to reveal the black mouth of a deep well. Mistress Aiken grabbed hold of Daisy's hair and marched her over to the edge. She dangled Daisy out over the darkness.

"Daisy! Daisy!"

It was Brodie's voice in the earpiece.

"Layla, quick, Daisy needs help!"

It was too late.

"Time to throw out the garbage," said Mistress Aiken. With an evil cackle she tossed Daisy into the well.

CHAPTER TWENTY SEVEN - THE WELL

"Daisy...Daisy..."

Daisy opened her eyes slowly. Her head was throbbing. She looked around but couldn't see very much.

Not again, thought Daisy, *If I ever get out of here I must learn to stop people throwing me off of things.*

"Daisy...Daisy..."

"Brodie?" asked Daisy.

There was no reply. The voice was coming from above. Daisy looked up and saw a small circle of light. A figure was looking down at her from it. A figure with hair shaped in a ridiculous bun. Daisy stood slowly, her legs wobbling. She was at the bottom of the well. The walls were made of sharp rocks, sticky with algae.

If this is a well, how come I'm not drowning? she thought.

Daisy looked down. Beneath her feet were wooden boards that met in the middle, like a couple of doors laid on their back. Daisy stomped her foot. It sounded hollow underneath. So she wasn't quite at the bottom of the well. Maybe it was a way out. Daisy knelt down and put her ear to the wood. She could hear sloshing water and something else, something big and old.

"Oh don't worry, Daisy, dear girl," said Mistress Aiken, her voice echoing down the well, "you'll find out what's on the other side of that soon enough. Maybe your friends can watch you die now."

Daisy put her hand up to the video camera behind her ear.

"We've been working for decades to take back what is ours from Sally Darlington and this stupid school and we've always dealt with troublemaking oiks like you," growled Mistress Aiken, "so you should feel privileged that you and your friends, when we get them, will be the last. My Sisters are on their way to pick up that vulgar American friend of yours right now."

Daisy tapped at the earpiece.

"Brodie? Brodie??"

There was no reply. She heard the sound of metal grinding against stone and looked up to see the covers of the well being dragged back over.

They locked into place leaving Daisy alone in the darkness.

"It's okay, Daisy," she told herself, not quite convinced by her own words.

The earpiece was making a clicking noise. Daisy hoped it wasn't too damaged from the fall. She checked her body for bruises. Her knees felt grazed but nothing too bad. Amazingly, she was still wearing the International Schoolgirl sash. Maybe it was Mistress Aiken's idea of a cruel joke.

There was a low rumbling sound and a rush of cold air blew up over Daisy's plimsolls. The floor was moving. Daisy searched her pockets for anything that would help. A ball of elastic bands, a couple of mints covered in fluff and a box of matches.

Matches!

Daisy struck one and looked down. The two halves of the floor were sliding apart. Beneath them Daisy could see a large pool of oily water and in it, big shapes moving around. The match burnt Daisy's fingers and she dropped it. It fell through the widening gap and lit up the faces of two sharks waiting a few feet below.

"Perilous!" muttered Daisy.

So Dr Penrose hadn't been exaggerating when she said there were sharks loose in the school.

Think, Daisy. Think, think, think.

She remembered what Miss Weaver told her and took three deep breaths to calm her nerves. The half of the floor Daisy was standing on was disappearing quickly and had almost reached the end of her plimsols. She put her back against the wall and lit another match. The sharks had spotted her and were turning over one another, churning up the water. Looking up she could just about see a tiny chink of light between the metal cover and the floor above. If she could climb up there somehow.

The match burnt out in her fingers and Daisy struck another. The floor was almost gone. She was clinging on to what was left of it with her heels. Daisy looked around. Though the well opened up into a large pool, the neck of the well was narrow - no wider than Daisy was tall.

"Right."

Daisy let the final match drop down into the faces of the sharks. She raised her arms up as high as she could.

"Here goes nothing."

Daisy took a deep breath and toppled forwards towards the sharks.

As soon as Daisy had been thrown in the well Brodie's instinct had been to run to the hall and rescue her. Daisy had been absolutely clear beforehand, though, that they should stick to the plan and show the footage to the parents and children at the International Schoolgirl ceremony no matter what happened. Leaping from her bed Brodie stuck the laptop in her satchel and darted out of the dorm.

"Layla, what's happened to Daisy?" she said, running down the stairs and dodging between sleepy girls in pyjamas.

"I'm not sure but everyone's cleared out of the museum. I'm going down into the hall now. Are you okay?"

Brodie stopped short. As she reached the bottom of the stairs Eleanore, Olga and Dorothy ran in through the doors of Honour House.

"There she is!" shouted Eleanore.

"Drat!"

Brodie turned and ran back up the stairs.

"Can't talk now, Layla. Find Daisy!" she said, barging past a confused group of girls with toothbrushes in their mouths.

Layla peeked around a display cabinet. Quietly as she could, she slipped through the shadows and peered through the hole in the museum floor to the hall below. The hall was almost as empty as the museum though she could hear voices drifting in from the adjacent tunnels. Layla dropped down onto the scaffold platform and jumped across to the balcony.

Daisy took a deep breath and opened her eyes. It was still dark and she could barely see. What she did know, however, was that she hadn't become shark lunch. Her idea had worked. By holding up her hands and falling forward she had managed to wedge herself across the well. The floor had completely disappeared and the sharks were lunging up at her, jaws snapping. Though Daisy was out of their reach she could smell their rotten breath. It was probably a good thing that she couldn't see them properly.

Okay, Daisy. What next? she thought.

Obviously, she couldn't stay this way forever. The floor didn't look like it was coming back any time soon. There was only one direction to go. Daisy lifted her right hand up and grabbed one of the bricks slightly higher in the wall of the well. Next, she did the same with her left foot and carefully - very carefully - raised her whole body a few inches higher. A memory popped into her head from home. When playing Hide & Seek with her brothers she always managed to hide from them in the downstairs loo by crawling up the walls in the same way. As she climbed slowly, Daisy thanked David and Daniel for the practice.

At the same time back in Honour House, Brodie ran out onto the balcony where the 88ers were sat watching stage props being moved into the main building ready for the morning's competition.

"Help!" said Brodie, "No time to explain! Daisy...trouble! Brat Pack coming! Evidence on laptop!"

Marsha, Tina, Penny and Millie looked at each other. Brodie climbed up onto the balcony ledge.

"You won't get away on the roof!" said Millie.

"I have an idea," said Marsha.

Layla ducked behind a cart. Off to the side of the hall a curtain had been pulled aside revealing the entrance of a large tunnel. The museum pieces were being wheeled down it into the darkness. Looking around for signs of Daisy, Layla spotted the satchel and Narwhal lying next to a statue. Carefully, she crept over and ducked behind it.

"I don't want to hear it! If you aren't grown up enough to face the real world and do what you're told, you're going to find yourself in a very uncomfortable situation, young girl."

The voice was coming from the other side of the statue. Layla peered round it to see Mrs Lyle, the head of the school board, standing there talking to Annabel.

"But it doesn't seem the right thing to do. None of this does!" said Annabel.

"Right thing to do!" hissed Mrs Lyle, "What do you think this is? One of your playground games? If you weren't my sister's daughter I'd throw you down that well after Daisy myself! Now go and get ready for the competition. We still need girls on the magazine when we're done here!"

Layla ducked out of sight as Annabel, looking terribly confused, walked over to the group of girls by the tunnel entrance.

"Where is she?"

Millie and Tina looked up as Eleanore burst out onto the balcony, hockey stick in hand. Penny shrugged, blowing onto her nail varnish. Marsha, tapping away on her laptop, ignored her.

"I SAID WHERE IS SHE?" growled Eleanore.

"Where's who?" said Millie.

"Don't be smart, drippo," said Eleanore.

'Drippo?' repeated Millie, quite shocked.

Eleanore marched over and snapped Marsha's laptop shut on her fingers.

"Where's BRODIE?" she hissed in her ear.

"WE'VE GOT HER!"

Everyone on the balcony turned to see Dorothy and Olga marching Brodie out of the dorm.

"She was hiding under the bed."

"Let go of her!" shouted Tina, standing and rolling up her sleeves.

Eleanore jammed the butt of her hockey stick into Tina's stomach, knocking her to the ground.

"ANYONE ELSE?" she shouted.

Millie and Marsha gritted their teeth but said nothing.

"Where's the laptop?" said Eleanore.

Olga lifted up Brodie's satchel.

"It's in here. She was trying to hide it under her mattress."

Eleanore walked over and pulled the laptop out of the satchel. She turned it on. A password screen came up.

"What's the password?" asked Eleanore.

Brodie bit her lip. Dorothy and Olga lifted her up by her armpits until her feet weren't touching the floor.

"OW! I'll never tell!" cried Brodie.

Eleanore smiled. She grabbed Millie and dragged her over to the balcony railings.

"Maybe if I start throwing your stupid friends down into the courtyard you might change your mind."

She pushed Millie against the wall and there was a large, collective gasp behind her. Eleanore turned round. Every girl from Honour House had heard the commotion and was standing huddled in the doorway watching. For a moment there was a flicker of fear in Eleanore's eyes. She stepped away from Millie.

"No problem. Bring Yankee Doodle and her laptop with us. We'll do this in private," she said.

Daisy's arms and legs were trembling but somehow she'd made it to the top of the well. Extending shaking fingers she put her hand out to the metal grate and gave it a push. It didn't budge. She tried again, pushing until her feet were slipping on the wet bricks but it didn't move a millimetre. It wasn't fair. She had climbed all this way for nothing. She could feel tears of real fear starting to well up in her eyes and fought them back knowing that if she started sobbing she would fall and it would all be over. Not just Darlington, but everything. Angry and scared she lifted her hand from the rock and pounded it again and again on the metal.

Mrs Lyle froze. So did the remaining girls in the hall. Slowly they all turned to look at the rusty metal grate in the centre of the room. Layla heard it too and decided she had spent enough time hiding in the shadows.

With a loud scraping sound the grate slid back and Daisy stared up into the light.

"Daisy!"

It was Layla's voice. Still squinting, Daisy reached up a hand. Layla grabbed hold of her wrist and pulled. Rolling over onto the checkered tiles Daisy lay there for a moment, arms outstretched, enjoying the safety of the solid ground. She wasn't allowed to enjoy it for long.

"WHAT THE HELL ARE YOU DOING?"

It was Mrs Lyle. Layla stood over Daisy protectively.

"What the hell are we doing? What the hell are YOU DOING?" she shouted back.

Mrs Lyle stormed over with six girls.

"YOU HAVE NO IDEA WHO YOU ARE DEALING WITH!" snapped Mrs Lyle.

She grabbed Layla by the hair and held her over the mouth of the well.

"It's about time we got rid of all you troublemakers!" she hissed.

"NO. IT'S ABOUT TIME WE GOT RID OF TROUBLEMAKERS LIKE YOU!"

It was Annabel. She leapt from the group of girls and gave her aunt a colossal shove in the back.

Everything went into slow motion. Daisy saw Mrs Lyle's face turn from a look of evil hatred to one of surprise. She let go of Layla and toppled forward, fingers clutching at the air. It was no use. There was nothing to stop her fall. Mrs Lyle was so shocked she didn't make a sound as she fell all the way down the well into the snapping jaws of the hungry sharks.

Daisy got to her feet. Everyone was staring at Annabel.

"You pushed your aunt down the well," said Layla, not quite believing it.

"WHO'S IN CHARGE NOW! HUH?" Annabel shouted down at her aunt who was, to be frank, too busy being eaten to hear, "ALL I WANTED TO DO WAS RIDE HORSES BUT, NO, I HAD TO COME TO YOUR STUPID SCHOOL AND JOIN IN ALL YOUR PIRATE RUBBISH! WELL I DON'T HAVE TO DO WHAT YOU TELL ME ANYMORE YOU EVIL OLD BAG!"

"I think Annabel's broken," whispered Daisy.

She tugged Layla's sleeve and they stepped away from the shocked group of girls quietly.

"Here," said Layla handing Daisy her satchel and Narwhal, "They've moved everything down the tunnel. I think they're getting ready to leave."

"We have to stop them," said Daisy, "but I think Brodie's in trouble."

"Leave her to me," said Layla.

"Thanks for saving my life, Layla."

Layla gave Daisy a quick wink.

"I'm sure it won't be the last time," she said.

Daisy nodded. Throwing her satchel over her shoulder and tucking Narwhal into her belt, she run off down the large tunnel.

The brickwork tunnel opened into a carved rock passageway and as Daisy reached the end of it she could see figures standing in a field lit by moonlight. She put her back against the rock and edged forward slowly until she was in hearing range.

"Careful with that!"

The high tech Russian coach was parked at the mouth of the passageway with its back opened wide like a metal jaw, the seats laid flat. It was full of museum pieces. Madame Didier, sword hanging from her hip, was climbing up into the passenger seat at the front. The earpiece in Daisy's ear crackled.

"Brodie?" said Daisy, tapping it with a finger.

There was no reply.

The big heavy drums of the printing press were turning so fast they looked a blur. Brodie was trying not to look at them, however.

"I'll ask you one more time," hissed Eleanore, "and if you don't give me the password, you'll be tomorrow's news."

They were in the print room. Brodie was tied to a chair that was dangling over Bertha's dangerous spinning machinery. The chair was held in place by Dorothy and Olga as Eleanore stood leaning against the guard rail with the laptop open in her hands.

"LET ME UP AND I'LL TELL YOU ANYTHING YOU WANT! DON'T KILL ME!" shouted Brodie, hoping that a passing teacher or girl might hear her.

Olga and Dorothy tilted the chair forward. Brodie wriggled her arms desperately but they were fixed tight.

"What's…The…Password," said Eleanore.

Brodie looked up into Eleanore's eyes. There was a madness deep inside them. An evil madness.

"How do I know you won't drop me anyway?" said Brodie.

Eleanore shrugged. There was nothing Brodie could do.

Now fully loaded, the back of the coach was slowly lowering into place. There was still no sound from the earpiece except the occasional crackle. Daisy hoped that somehow Brodie was filming what she was seeing. The red lights on the back of the coach lit up and the engine gave a low rumble. They were getting ready to move. Daisy edged her way to the mouth of the tunnel. Several pieces from the museum were still left over and the Spanish coach was being prepared to transport them. Mistress Aiken was standing between the two vehicles coordinating everything. The Russian coach lurched forward and began moving along a dirt path that led through trees onto the main road. Daisy looked around desperately. She couldn't let them get away. Her eyes fell on the old World War Two courier motorcycle standing with the remaining museum pieces.

"BUTTERFLY!" cried Brodie, "THE PASSWORD IS BUTTERFLY!"

The spinning drums were barely inches from her head.

"Pull her up," said Eleanore, "and let's see if she's lying."

Olga and Dorothy tipped the chair back onto the platform. Eleanore tapped the password into the computer and hit enter. The computer gave a happy chime.

"So you're not lying. Well, let's see what you've been recording."

Eleanore opened up the video player.

"What on earth is this?" she said, frowning at the screen.

The video player showed footage of Marsha and Tina performing rocket tests. Eleanore looked confused for a moment and then it dawned on her.

"They switched the laptops!"

Eleanore threw Marsha's laptop on the floor and stomped towards Brodie.

"YOU. ARE. DEAD."

Brodie turned her head away, waiting for the worst. There was a sudden loud whooshing sound and a jet of water came out of nowhere, blasting Eleanore clean off the platform. Olga and Dorothy had just enough time to exchange looks before another two jets knocked them flying to the ground too. Brodie stretched her neck to peer over Bertha's platform and saw Layla, Tina, Marsha, Millie and Penny holding the printer cleaning hoses in their hands.

"NO ONE MESSES WITH THE 88ERS!" shouted Layla.

* * *

The keys to the courier motorcycle were in the ignition. Daisy jumped onto the saddle, turned them and kicked the kick-starter. The engine gave a hollow cough and a belch of black smoke puffed out behind her.

"HEY!"

A couple of the Sisters had spotted Daisy and were running towards her. There was no time to worry about them - the coach was turning into the traffic on the main road. Daisy jumped on the kick-starter again and the engine gave a loud roar. Daisy spun the throttle and the bike leapt forward, charging across the field.

"What are we going to do with them?" asked Millie.

The Brat Pack looked like half drowned rats. Every time they had tried to fight back a quick blast from a hose had knocked them down again.

"You might think you've got the better of us but whilst you're wasting your time, everything this stupid school owns is being stolen," said Eleanore.

"Yeah?" said Brodie.

She took her laptop from Marsha and put on her headpiece.

"Well, you didn't count on Daisy Cooper."

Brodie turned the laptop round to show live video footage of Daisy hurtling through the traffic on the motorbike in pursuit of the Russian bus.

The rain stung Daisy's cheeks as the bike whizzed between cars. The coach was some way ahead and the old wartime motorcycle could only just keep up with it. The scary thing was that Daisy wasn't wearing a helmet. The even scarier thing was that she was being chased by the two Sisters who had spotted her. They were on much newer and much faster motorcycles.

Daisy zipped between an estate car towing a caravan and a white van. The two Sisters were closing in on her.

"DAISY!"

It was Brodie's voice. It was great to hear her again.

"Brodie, are you okay?"

"Cool beans, D.C. How's you?"

"I'm a little busy," said Daisy.

Car horns beeped as she snuck along the dotted line between the middle and fast lanes.

"I can see. Just so you know, we're still recording."

"Great, Brodie. I'll speak later when I'm not so..."

Daisy swerved between a couple of lorries.

"...distracted."

One of the lorries gave of a loud, low honk. Daisy kicked the brake and snapped back behind a couple of cars. She could see the Sisters level with her on either side. Both of them had hockey sticks raised menacingly in the air.

"Doesn't anyone at Darlington know how to play hockey properly?" muttered Daisy.

She spun the throttle and the bike jolted forward back between the two lorries. They were both now sounding their horns. Between them it was very narrow. Daisy's elbows were almost touching the flapping tarpaulin on their cargo trailers. At least it kept the Sisters out of the way. Unfortunately the lorry drivers had other plans. The road came up to a junction and they slowly peeled away either side of her. The hockey stick wielding girls were quick to fill their place. The one on Daisy's left swung out at her and she had to duck low to avoid the stick. The bike wobbled beneath her, slipping on the wet tarmac.

"YOU'RE ROAD KILL, COOPER!" shouted the Sister on the right, swinging at her.

The toe of the stick caught Daisy painfully in the ribs. The bike swerved over into the left hand rider who grabbed at Daisy's satchel. Daisy kicked out at her, knocking her away. It bought a few precious seconds.

Think, Daisy, Think. Think. Think.

Up ahead there was a car transporter lorry, its back empty of cars and laid low like a ramp. Ahead of it was the Russian coach. Daisy glanced quickly at the Sisters. Both girls were level again and spinning their sticks like clubs above their heads. Daisy waited until they were both close enough and then pulled the accelerator as hard as she could, jumping the motorcycle onto the back of the transport lorry's ramp. The Sister's sticks swung through the empty space where Daisy had been, and they knocked each other clean from their bikes. Daisy shot up the ramp of the transporter and flew into the air. There was a brief, giddying moment in which Daisy could feel the wheels of the motorcycle spinning freely before it hit the top of the Russian bus. The bike buckled as it landed, throwing Daisy off. She rolled across the metal roof and grabbed hold of a sun roof, ducking just in time as the motorcycle bounced over her head and into the traffic.

"Nice bus jumping, D.C.!" said Brodie in her ear.

Daisy lay flat for a long while, catching her breath. She peeked down through the skylight to see if anyone onboard had noticed. Fortunately the Sisters in the back of the bus with the museum pieces were too busy listening to music on their phones to notice. Checking she still had her satchel and Narwhal, Daisy straightened herself up to face the front of the bus. The rain stung at her exposed skin. It was going to be a long ride.

CHAPTER TWENTY EIGHT - ESCAPE BY SEA

It was at least an hour before the Russian bus pulled into the docks of a port. Fresh sea mist replaced the grey drizzle of the rain. The sea was noisy, its waves crashing against the stone walls of the harbour. Small beacon lights ran the length of the old walls, winking in the darkness. A couple of forklift trucks moved back and forth unloading cargo from enormous freight ships. Apart from that it was deserted. The bus stopped and Daisy wriggled along the roof to the front to see what was happening. Peering over the top she watched Madam Didier pass a brown bag to a couple of guards standing at a barrier. One of them pulled a handful of fifty pound notes from it and stared at them greedily. Madame Didier snatched them back and stuffed them in the bag, looking around nervously.

"Are you getting this, Brodie?"

"Sure am. Lets add bribery to the long list of crimes. What do you think they are up to, Daisy?"

"Looks like they're going to load the museum pieces onto a boat."

The bus started up again as the guards lifted the barrier. It drove across the port and took a left turn down a narrow concrete ledge that was dangerously close to the water. The ledge snaked around the big ships towards the large mouth of the harbour that lead out to sea. Finally, the bus slowed and reversed into a small concrete loading dock that was hidden from the main area. Off to one side, being rocked back and forth by the waves, was a boat.

The back of the boat was open and a ramp led down from the dock into the hold. The name of the boat, The Shellback, was written on the raised stern. The bus engine switched off and the Sisters jumped out. They unloaded the museum pieces onto trolleys and began pushing them down the ramp. Daisy watched Madam Didier run down a narrow wooden jetty beside The Shellback where she ducked a couple of massive waves and climbed the gangplank to the boat. There was a commotion from below. Daisy looked down to see two of the Sisters had dropped the portrait of the Empress of Russia and were arguing over who's fault it was. She took the opportunity, slid down the side of the bus and snuck through the shadows to the boat.

There were too many girls on the ramp to the hold. Daisy looked across to the jetty. It was deserted but the waves were crashing into it hard. If she was caught on it when one of them hit, it was very likely she'd be swept into the water. Daisy counted under her breath, timing the gaps between each wave. It was no more than six seconds. Not much time, but enough. Hearing a shout, Daisy turned. The Spanish bus had arrived on the dock. That meant more girls arriving. More people who might spot her. Daisy looked back at the jetty as another big wave crashed against it and, counting out loud, ran across it.

"One...two..."

Halfway across the jetty the water looked even more angry. Daisy's plimsolls slipped on the seaweed covered planks and she reached out to stop herself falling, catching one of the thin guide ropes for support. The rope was held in place by rusty iron poles that ran the length of the jetty to the gangplank.

"Three...four..."

Daisy pulled herself along the rope until she was level with the gangplank. High above, an old lantern hung in the centre of the Shellback's cabin making silhouettes of Madame Didier and a couple of mysterious strangers. The sea was lurching back, ready to throw another wave at the jetty. It was moving very fast. Daisy realised she'd never make it up the gangplank in time. She crouched down, grabbed hold of one of the iron poles and held her breath as the wave hit.

Footsteps were coming down the stairs to the International Schoolgirl print room. Lots of them. Brodie snapped her laptop shut and slid it into her satchel.

"We're down here!" shouted Eleanore, "Help! We're being held hostage!"

Brodie and the other 88ers ran past Bertha and ducked under the stairs. Mistress Aiken burst in with at least ten girls.

"Good heavens!" exclaimed the Deputy Head when she saw the drenched Brat Pack, "Can't I trust you fools to take care of anything!"

The 88ers snuck out and crept up the stairs to the courtyard. It was too late. Eleanore spotted them.

"They're getting away!"

"Stop those girls!" barked Mistress Aiken.

"Quick! Let's hide in the maze!"

The wave lifted Daisy clear off her feet, pulling her first one way and then the other, but she managed to hang on. As the sea receded she ran for the gangplank and jumped up it to the deck of The Shellback. It felt much calmer on board. Daisy stepped through a pile of ropes and sheltered beneath an iron platform above the engine block. A fixed metal ladder at the back led upwards to the cabin. Daisy squeezed the sea water out of her jumper. Her plimsolls were squelchy but there wasn't much she could do about that. The competition sash - now looking a muddy green rather than gold- was still in place.

Well, I suppose I should get a medal just for that, thought Daisy.

It was then that she noticed the camera and earpiece were missing. She looked around in the ropes at her feet but it was nowhere to be seen. As another wave hit the gangplank Daisy realised what had happened. The camera and earpiece had been washed away when she'd been hit by the wave.

OK, Daisy, from now on you're on her own.

She looked around. Apart from the rope and a few piles of fishing nets, there wasn't much on deck. At the bow there was a long platform - a thin railed plank - that pointed out to sea. On the end of the platform was a harpoon gun mounted on an iron pole. On the port side a dingy with an outboard motor hung from two metal winches. Daisy felt a vibration rumble through her feet. The engine was running. The Shellback was about to set sail.

* * *

As they entered the maze the 88ers split into two groups. Millie, Tina and Marsha ran to the centre, creating enough noise to make sure that Mistress Aiken and the other Sisters followed them whilst Brodie, Layla and Penny hid behind a statue in one of the dead ends.

"I heard them go down here!"

It was a tall girl from the Swedish school.

"It's a dead end," said another girl who Brodie recognised as a third year from Darlington.

"We should check anyway."

Layla reached into her rucksack and pulled out an odd looking device about the size of a large matchbox. There were two nasty looking prongs sticking out of one end. Brodie recognised it. One of her uncles, a police chief in New York, had shown her one on a visit.

"You bought a Taser with you? Where did you get that?" she asked.

As the two Sisters got closer Layla turned a dial and the box made a high pitched whine that sounded dangerous.

"You'll be surprised what I've been up to since I've been away," whispered Layla.

"What's a Taser?" asked Penny.

"It's a box of electricity that makes people fall over when you touch them with it. It hurts, apparently," said Layla.

She stood up behind the statue, getting ready to stun the first girl to find them.

With a loud bang the back of The Shellback lowered into place. Hearing a loud scraping Daisy turned to see a great metal chain chug out of the water, pulling a seaweed covered anchor up onto the deck. The ship began to lurch across the choppy water towards the mouth of the harbour. Daisy searched the engine block hoping to find a way in so she could stop the ship but there was no door, only metal panels fixed with heavy bolts. Within minutes they were already at the mouth of the harbour. The waves of the open sea looked even more angry on the other side. A large wave washed up over the side dropping a few snapping crabs on the deck.

Daisy pulled Narwhal from her belt. She didn't fancy her chances against Madame Didier but what else could she do? Maybe she could stab her in the foot and hope for the best. She took hold of the ladder that led up to the cabin and began to climb slowly. Stepping onto the iron platform she could hear voices coming from inside the cabin. Daisy peered through the porthole. The cabin was split in two sections. The nearest section was a small living space with a bare foam seat and a gas cooker. Mounted on the wall was a glass cabinet containing a lifejacket and an emergency flare gun. Next to it was a sliding door with a glass window that lead to the control deck. Inside that Daisy could see three figures with their backs to her. Madame Didier was in the middle. To her left was a broad shouldered man in a chunky woollen sweater who was steering the boat. That had to be the Captain. Next to him, sat in a small seat fixed to the wall was a very scary looking man. He was dressed in a long black waterproof jacket, a wide brimmed black hat and small black round glasses. In his hands he held a walking stick topped with a silver skull that had the number '13' carved into its forehead. As they were talking, the scary looking man turned towards Daisy. She ducked down quickly, heart pounding, waiting for them to come and grab her. After a moment though, the mumbled talk started up again. Daisy breathed a sigh of relief.

What now, Daisy? she thought.

The mouth of the harbour, its tiny lights winking in the darkness, was behind them and disappearing quickly. Daisy could just make out a hut perched on the end of one of its high walls. There was a light on inside and there were figures moving around. It had to be the Coast Guard office. The Police of the sea. If Daisy could get their attention, they would stop the boat.

There was a shout from deep inside the maze. It was Marsha's voice. The two Sisters approaching the statue turned and ran off in its direction. Brodie, Layla and Penny stepped out with a sigh of relief. Layla tucked her Taser away. Brodie pulled out her laptop and opened it up.

"Daisy?" she said into her earpiece, "Daisy, can you hear me?"

There was no answer. The picture looked a murky green.

"Daisy, are you okay?"

A fish swam past on the screen. Brodie and Layla exchanged looks.

"She could have dropped it," said Layla.

"Let's hope so," said Penny.

"We should head to the Assembly Hall so we can see how they're setting things up for tomorrow."

Keeping an eye out for Mistress Aiken and the Sisters, they ran back through the maze towards the school.

Daisy had an idea. She peeked through the cabin porthole at the emergency cabinet. She could reach it if she was careful. As The Shellback rocked to one side Daisy turned the handle on the cabin door as quietly as she could and ducked inside. She tip-toed quickly across the room, ducked beneath the cabinet and peered through the sliding glass door. The man in black was holding up the Devil's Eye pendants in a gloved fist and staring at them through his dark glasses.

"So that's some kind of map?" asked the Captain.

The man in black ignored the question.

"What are they a map to?" asked the Captain.

"You aren't being paid a year's wages to ask questions. You're hear to sail us across to Amsterdam," said the man in black.

He had an accent that Daisy couldn't quite place.

"No offence, governor. I'm just curious."

"Curiosity killed the cat," said the man in black.

The man in black looked like he'd have no trouble killing cats. Or anything else for that matter.

"Let's just get across the sea, gentlemen," said Madame Didier.

Daisy reached up and tipped open the door of the emergency cabinet with her fingers. Carefully she lifted the flare gun out. It was heavy in her hands. Slowly, keeping her back against the wall, she made her way back out of the cabin.

The walls of the harbour were far away now, almost impossible to see in the mist. Daisy looked down at the main deck. It seemed awfully low in the water. There was no doubt that The Shellback was struggling with its heavy cargo. Waves crashed into the stern and cascaded over the deck. There was no choice. Daisy was going to have to fire the flare gun from up on the gangway. If she aimed right, if she was lucky, it would alert the Coast Guard and they would send out patrol boats. Daisy raised the gun in both hands. She closed an eye for aim and held it high in the direction of the blinking lights in the mist.

"Perilous," muttered Daisy.

She pulled the trigger.

Amanda Kepper poured herself a cup of steaming coffee and let out a huge yawn. She was used to early mornings but not ones that started at 3AM. Not only that but the stiff starchy collar of her Coast Guard uniform was making her neck itch like mad. She walked out of the kitchen into the office where her new work mates, Ray and Phil, were sat reading newspapers. The weather was choppy outside and the air thick with mist. The wind shook the windows. She was glad to be inside.

"What's on the schedule?" she asked.

"We've got a couple of container ships due to leave at six but nothing else," shrugged Phil, "you'd have to be out of your mind to sail anything smaller than that out in this tonight."

Good, thought Amanda, *a quiet night*.

She stepped up to the glass and peered out into the murky sea, taking a large slurp of coffee. Somewhere off in the darkness there was a sudden flash followed by an orange streaking glow that got larger and larger in a matter of seconds. It was headed straight for the Coast Guard office. Amanda dropped her mug, eyes wide, and jumped back as the flare hit the middle of the window and exploded, filling the room with light.

"HOLY COW!" she cried.

The glass stayed intact but the afterglow left her with bright stars dancing in her eyes.

"WE'VE GOT AN EMERGENCY!"

Amanda picked up the radio and shouted into it.

"EMERGENCY! EMERGENCY! We have a flare fired from a vessel half a mile south of harbour!"

Ray ran across the room and hit a large red button. The enormous emergency sirens on the harbour wall started shrieking.

It wasn't going to be a quiet day for Amanda Kepper after all.

The force of the flare gun knocked Daisy off her feet and sent her sprawling backwards through the door into the cabin. All three figures in the control room jumped up and turned. Madam Didier's mouth opened wide with surprise and then turned into a vicious snarl.

"Get her!!"

Daisy didn't need to hear any more. Tossing the empty flare gun aside she jumped to her feet and slid down the ladder onto the deck where she slipped and rolled awkwardly towards the bow. Somewhere far off she heard the explosion of the flare and then, to her delight, the sound of the harbour sirens. The delight didn't last for long. Madame Didier was halfway down the ladder. She had her fencing sword in one hand and a large fishing knife in the other. Behind her the man in black was standing in the doorway and pointing something at Daisy. There was a loud cracking sound and a bullet ricocheted off the deck next to her.

"He's shooting at me!" said Daisy in disbelief.

As Madame Didier lunged towards her Daisy took advantage of a large wave crashing into the boat and rolled with it across the deck. The fencing teacher staggered past her and Daisy got to her feet, running around the engine block to the front of the ship.

"COAST GUARD!" shouted the Captain through the window above.

He slammed hard on the engines and the ship plunged forward, throwing Daisy against the exhaust funnel. The Shellback tossed wildly from side to side as the Captain pushed it into the waves to try and outrun the Coast Guard boats. Great walls of water crashed over the bow. There was another cracking sound and a bullet tore a hole through the funnel next to Daisy's hands. She turned to see the man in black above her on the gangway getting ready for another shot. Daisy looked across at the dingy. Maybe she could use it to get away. Another bullet flew past her ear. Daisy leapt across towards the dingy. As she did so, Madame Didier stepped out from behind the engine block and grabbed her.

"I'm going to gut you like a fish!" she snarled.

Madame Didier raised the fishing knife up. A wave hit the starboard side of the boat sending them both stumbling across the deck. Above, the man in black fell against the gangway railings. The gun slipped from his grip and hit the deck. As it bounced over the side of the boat it fired a bullet that knocked the knife out of the fencing teacher's hand. Daisy seized the moment. She grabbed a pile of orange fishing nets and hurled it over Madame Didier.

"THIS IS THE COAST GUARD! STOP YOUR VESSEL AND PREPARE TO BE BOARDED!"

The Coast Guard boats, four of them, were charging through the water about a hundred meters behind The Shellback. Daisy ran around Madame Didier and threw the winch to release the dingy. It swung out over the side of the boat. The Shellback tipped to one side dangerously. Daisy could feel the museum pieces sliding across the hold beneath her feet, tipping the boat even more onto its side. Daisy jumped and grabbed the side of the dingy. Something black flew past her head. She looked up to see the man in black smiling down at her. He cracked the skull head of his cane against Daisy's fingers, knocking her back onto the deck.

"THANK YOU, LITTLE GIRL!" he shouted through sharp, evil teeth, throwing the second winch.

The dingy dropped out of sight into the water.

There was a loud angry scream. Daisy turned to see Madame Didier had freed herself from the netting. She was coming towards Daisy with her fencing sword extended. The boat was so lopsided now it looked like she was running up a hill.

"YOU RUINED IT! YOU RUINED EVERYTHING!" shouted Madame Didier.

The blade flashed towards Daisy and she ducked out of the way just in time. She pulled Narwhal from her belt and pressed the ruby button. The blade shot out of the end.

"EN GARDE!" cried Daisy.

Madame Didier jumped towards her. Daisy managed to knock the first attack aside. She kept herself calm, breathing evenly. Even though she was mad with anger Madame Didier was good. Very good. As soon as Daisy parried a shot the fencing teacher was coming back with another. It was a flurry of blows from a master, forcing Daisy towards the front of the boat.

"STOP YOUR VESSEL!"

The Coast Guard boats were only minutes away from boarding but Daisy had to fight for her life through every second. Lunging, parrying, swinging low, she managed to catch Madame Didier across the thighs, causing her to howl in rage. The teacher swung the blade at Daisy's chest forcing her to jump backwards. Her plimsolls landed on something slippery and narrow. It was the wooden torpedo platform on the front of the bow. Beneath it and on either side was nothing but black water. She was trapped. Madame Didier laughed and raised her sword high in both hands, beating it down against Daisy. Daisy fell to her knees, holding Narwhal above her head to protect herself against the blows which just kept coming. She pushed herself as far away as she could until her back thudded against the turret of the harpoon mount. Madame Didier jumped up onto the platform and pointed the tip of her sword at Daisy's throat.

"WHAT'S THE MATTER STUPID LITTLE GIRL? NOWHERE

ELSE TO GO?" snarled the fencing teacher.

Daisy looked about desperately for something, anything, to protect herself with. Then she spotted the coiled rope of the harpoon. She started laughing. She looked up at Madame Didier with a smile.

"I'VE GOT NOWHERE ELSE TO GO," Daisy shouted, "BUT YOU HAVE!"

She reached up and slammed her hand against the firing trigger on the harpoon gun. The harpoon shot out with a huge force. Madame Didier, feeling something wasn't right, looked down. To her horror she saw that one of her fancy Paris boots was tangled in the rapidly disappearing coil of torpedo rope. She looked up at Daisy and dropped her sword.

"Sacré Bleu!"

The harpoon rope snapped around Madame Didier's ankle and whipped her body off the platform, out into the sea.

Daisy climbed back onto the deck. The Captain was still trying to push the boat at full speed but it was too late. The coast guard boats were alongside The Shellback. Daisy staggered to the back of the boat and collapsed against the metal ladder leading up to the cabin. She was still gripping Narwhal in her hands, planning to hold the Captain prisoner if he tried to escape. She was exhausted. There was a flash of lights as the Guards in their bright orange lifejackets clambered aboard.

"How are you doing, little girl?"

Daisy looked up to see a kind female face staring down at her. The name on her lifejacket read 'Amanda'.

"I'm quite wet, Amanda," she said, "and cold. And tired."

Amanda pulled out a blanket and put it round Daisy's shoulders, lifting her up from the wet deck. The blanket felt warm and cosy.

Daisy was asleep even before they got her off the boat.

CHAPTER TWENTY NINE - INTERNATIONAL SCHOOLGIRL

The competition was in full swing. There were girls showing off their skills in athletics and gymnastics in the sports block, language recitals in the geography and language building and musical recitals in the concert hall. Teachers, pupils and visiting families sat and watched, applauding. Brodie, Layla and Penny made their way through the crowds around the sports block trying not to get noticed.

"Brodie!"

It was Millie, Tina and Marsha. The 88ers hugged each other and ducked under one of the seating stands at the edge of the race track.

"How are you girls?" asked Brodie.

"We're fine," said Marsha, "when we got into the centre of the maze we hid behind the fountain."

"And they didn't catch you?"

"Well," said Millie, "Sankofa kind of scared them away."

"Sankofa?"

"He's been trapped in the maze all night."

"And he didn't eat you?"

"Oh no," said Millie, quite matter of factly, "you just have to treat him like a big cat - which he is, I suppose. The trick is to remember that he's going to be treating you like a big mouse."

"Where is he now?" asked Brodie.

"We spent all night trying to get him back to the zoo but there were too many people around there and we didn't want to create a panic so we put him somewhere safe. How's Daisy?"

Brodie shrugged.

"I haven't heard from her in hours. I hope she's okay."

"Wherever Daisy is, we can't do anything about it now," said Layla, "we need to get the video ready. She'd want us to go ahead with the plan."

"That's cool," said Brodie, "I need to edit the video we filmed but I'll need somewhere to plug in my laptop. It's nearly out of power."

The 88ers stepped out into the crowd.

"Brodie!"

Brodie froze. There was a short middle aged man smiling at her with two troublesome looking boys stood next to him. They looked vaguely familiar.

"It is Brodie, isn't it?" asked the man.

"Erm, who's asking?"

"Mr Cooper, Daisy's dad!"

Of course, thought Brodie. The two boys were Daisy's brothers.

"Oh, hi!" said Brodie.

She wasn't sure what to tell them about Daisy.

"Have you got any idea where Daisy's doing her competition? This is very confusing. We've been everywhere. STOP THAT, DANIEL!"

Daniel was tossing stones up onto the seats above trying to knock a woman's hat off.

"Daisy's not competing yet. She's getting ready to do her stuff at the end," said Brodie, "we've got to go and help her. Get to the main hall at four o'clock."

Brodie and the other 88ers smiled apologetically and quickly ran off through the crowds.

It looked like there was a carnival going on in the courtyard. There were exotic food stalls dotted all over the place and people in fancy dress entertaining the visitors. The 88ers stopped between a girl on stilts and a juggler.

"Where are we going?" asked Penny.

"Back to the dorm unless anyone can think of somewhere better?" said Brodie.

She stepped around a cake stand and came face to face with the Brat

Pack.

"Well, what have we here?" said Eleanore.

She grabbed the satchel off Brodie's back and pulled out her laptop.

"And I suppose this is the REAL one, then," she hissed.

"Give that back!" said Brodie.

She grabbed Eleanore's tie and pulled. Eleanore's face landed on the top of Brodie's head.

"OW! She head-butted me," cried Eleanore, holding her nose, "I can't believe she head-butted me!"

"What are you girls arguing about?"

Everyone turned to see Roni standing with her hands on her hips. The International Schoolgirl badge, freshly polished for the competition, shone on her tie.

"They're stealing my laptop!" said Brodie.

"She's lying!" said Eleanore, "she stole it from me!"

Roni shook her head with a frown.

"Dear, oh dear, girls. It's really not the best day to have an argument in public. Grace is one of our school virtues and this is not particularly graceful, is it?"

Roni took the laptop out of Eleanore's hands.

"So, I guess I'LL keep hold of this until the competition is over. We can all have a lovely chat about it then."

Eleanore opened her mouth to speak, clenching her fists. She looked ready to go crazy.

"I don't think you'll want to see what's on it, anyway, Eleanore," said Layla, "not unless you want to see what happened to your mother."

"What do you mean? What happened to my mother?"

"Well, I couldn't actually say because I was too grossed out to look," replied Layla, "but it involved sharks."

"That's a lie!"

"Is it? Everyone else's parents seem to be around here? Where's yours? I think you KNOW where you'll find her."

Slowly the colour drained out of Eleanore's face. She looked very afraid.

"Come on," she said, starting to walk away.

"What about the laptop?" asked Olga.

"COME ON," said Eleanore grabbing Olga and Dorothy and pulling them through the crowd.

"I'm not entirely sure what's going on, girls, but I've got a feeling that what's on this laptop is pretty important," said Roni.

"We could show you," said Brodie, "but we need somewhere safe until the ceremony starts."

Roni thought for a moment before snapping her fingers.

"Come with me."

"They can't come in here!"

The girl at the desk stood up when Roni and the 88ers entered the International Schoolgirl dorm.

"Sweetie, trust me. We all know there have been some bad eggs around here up to frightful nonsense and I think these clever girls might have some answers," said Roni, leading the 88ers past the desk.

"Well, they're your responsibility!"

"As always!" said Roni.

She led them through the technology room where International Schoolgirls were pushing buttons and talking different languages into their headsets.

"Cooool," said Marsha, looking across the banks of computer screens.

"Try not to stare, Sweetie," said Roni pushing the button for the lift.

There were more 'oohs' and 'aahs' as Roni took them into her dorm room and set them up on the desk in front of the big round window.

"Now, if you girls need time to do what you have to do, I'll fix us all a lovely pot of tea. You can explain it all to me as we go along."

A phone was ringing somewhere but, to Daisy's annoyance, no one seemed to be answering it. Slowly, she opened an eye and looked around. She had no idea where she was. Lots of people and lots of noise. At least it was warm. She shut her eye again and tried to go back to sleep. Then she remembered what had happened and sat bolt upright.

"You're awake, I see."

It was Amanda, the kindly coast guard. Daisy realised she was in the coast guard office on top of the harbour wall. It was daylight outside. Bright. In the harbour, The Shellback was moored to a jetty surrounded by coast guard boats. The museum pieces were standing on the dock next to the two coaches and several police cars.

"Where are the girls?" asked Daisy.

"What girls?" asked Amanda.

"The ones from the coaches."

"They tried to escape when we alerted the police. They're all down at the local police station where they've been questioned. There were quite a few of them and none of their stories matched. It's taken several hours," said Amanda.

"Several hours?" said Daisy.

She looked across the office at the big clock on the wall. It was three o'clock in the afternoon. She had slept most of the day.

"I have to get back to Darlington!" said Daisy, slipping on her plimsolls.

" I don't think you'll be going anywhere, dear," laughed Amanda, "I'm afraid you've got a few questions to answer yourself."

"I can explain everything! Better still, I can show you but I HAVE to get back to the school. The person behind all this is still there and if she finds out what's happened, you'll never see her again!"

"We really can't do anything until the police have done their work. There were shots fired on that ship," said Amanda.

"I know, I was the one being shot at! Please, Amanda, you have to trust me. Bring the police. Bring EVERYONE."

Amanda thought for a moment.

"Wait here," she said.

Amanda crossed the room to where a tall policeman with lots of stripes on his uniform was standing. He looked at Daisy with a frown as Amanda spoke to him. After a couple of minutes they both walked over.

"Hello, Daisy. My name is Sergeant Kirkland. You say you know who's behind this?"

"Yes!" said Daisy, "but we need to get there fast before she does a runner!"

"Get where exactly?"

"Darlington School for Girls. It's near Hamley village."

"Hamley village? That's about two or three hour's drive from here with traffic," said Amanda.

"That'll be too late!"

Daisy buried her head in her hands. She was heartbroken. Sergeant Kirkland sighed. He took off his cap and crouched down.

"You know, if you send us on a wild goose chase you'll be in big trouble, don't you?" he said.

"I know," said Daisy, "and quite frankly, I've had enough goose chases for one day."

The policeman laughed. He stood up and switched on the radio mounted on his jacket.

"This is Sergeant Kirkland at Aylsebury port. Fire up the bird and clear it with air traffic. We need to get to Hamley ASAP. Over."

He turned to Daisy and gave her a wink.

"You ever flown in a helicopter before, Daisy?" he said.

"Oh, my word," said Roni.

She had just finished watching Brodie's edited video.

"I knew things weren't right but I had no idea this was going on," she said, "We're supposed to be the investigative reporters. It's quite shameful."

"To be fair," said Layla, "you've been busy reporting in other countries."

"Well, it's a good thing we've got some brave girls who aren't afraid to do a bit of snooping at home," said Roni.

The clock on the wall chimed. It was quarter to four.

"The ceremony's about to start. They're going to announce the winners. I assume the idea is to show this to everyone there?"

"That's the idea," said Brodie.

"It's not going to go down awfully well but I think it's best to get it all out in the open. I'd better get you some seats near the projector. Jo-Lacy is running it and she's a good egg so I'll have a word."

While Roni made her phone call Brodie gave Layla copies of the film on DVD for safekeeping.

"Are you sure you're not staying?" Brodie asked.

Layla shook her head.

"But why?" asked Millie.

"You remember the Tazer I took out in the maze? It's for protection. I've been involved in some pretty exciting but dangerous things since I left. I guess with my parents being spies, the whole cloak and dagger thing runs in my blood. Have you heard of The Thirteen?"

Brodie shook her head.

"The thirteen what?"

"Well, it's probably best that you don't know. There are some dangerous people looking for me at the moment and I don't want to be anywhere too public."

"But will we see you again?" asked Penny.

"Of course!" said Layla.

She left the room. After a couple of seconds the 88ers heard a loud wolf howl coming from the hall. Laughing, they howled back at her. Roni gave them all a funny look as she put her phone back in her pocket.

"Jo-Lacy is ready," she said, "let's go and cause some trouble."

The helicopter ride was amazing. The clouds were full of hot air balloons as part of the competition festival and the pilot had to weave between them as they approached the school building. Darlington was even more impressive from the air. Daisy could see the sports block, the maze, the zoo and the eight tall dorm buildings surrounding the courtyard. The whole grounds were deserted. Daisy looked at the clock on the helicopter dashboard. It was twenty minutes past four o'clock. Everyone would be in the assembly hall for the ceremony.

"So if this Mistress Aiken is behind it all why would she still be at the school?" asked Sergeant Kirkland.

"If she disappeared, everyone would be suspicious. They'd probably look for her in the museum and find out everything had gone," said Daisy.

"But why take all the museum pieces if they have this treasure map?"

"They're pirates!" said Daisy, "Pirates are greedy!"

She was tired of the questions.

The helicopter landed in the empty courtyard and Daisy jumped out.

"They're in the assembly hall!" she said running ahead.

The policemen started to run after her. Sergeant Kirkland held them back.

"Let's wait a few minutes," he said, "this girl's been through a lot. It would be a shame not to let her have her moment. Call for back up, I don't want anyone getting in or out of this place."

Daisy walked into the foyer slowly. She looked up at the great map. This was it. Taking a deep breath, she put her ear against the assembly hall doors. She could hear Mistress Aiken's voice on the other side followed by the sound of people clapping and cheering. At least the old bat was still here.

But what if Brodie hasn't managed to capture the video? thought Daisy, *What if I've dragged the police here and we have nothing to show them?*

"Oh, there you are dear."

Daisy turned around. Hattie was sat in her wheelchair smiling up at her.

"I've been wondering what you've been up to. It took me ages to wheel myself over here."

There was a loud round of applause on the other side of the doors.

"Well, come on, come on," said Hattie, "wheel me in, I'm not getting any younger."

Hands shaking, Daisy took hold of Hattie's wheelchair.

"I wouldn't miss this for the world," Hattie chuckled as Daisy pushed her through the doors of the assembly hall.

"...AND WE'RE HERE ONCE AGAIN TO SELECT THOSE GIRLS WHO HAVE SHOWN THAT THEY HAVE THE RIGHT QUALITIES TO BE INTERNATIONAL SCHOOLGIRLS!"

The Deputy Head's voice boomed over the loudspeaker system. She was standing at the podium in the middle of the stage. Daisy pushed Hattie over towards the seats at the back, delighted to see Brodie and the other 88ers sat next to the projector. Brodie gave Daisy the thumbs up.

"THOSE QUALITIES WE ALL VALUE SO HIGHLY," continued Mistress Aiken, "CHARITY!"

There was an explosion of applause. A few heads looked round to see who had entered late.

"Well, go on, girl, get up there!" said Hattie giving Daisy a nudge, "Are you wearing a competition sash or aren't you?"

Daisy looked down. Tattered and worn but still firmly there, the competitions sash hung over her blazer. Daisy swallowed hard and started to walk down the long aisle towards the stage. There were hundreds of pupils, staff and families either side of her. She didn't dare turn her head to look at them.

"BRAVERY!"

Daisy kept walking. She could hear gasps and mutters as she passed each aisle.

"REASON!"

Daisy saw Roni sat on stage with the other senior International Schoolgirls and kept her eyes fixed on her.

Keep walking, Daisy, keep walking, she told herself.

"CULTURE!"

The gasps were getting louder like a wave that followed her as she got closer to the stage.

"GRACE."

Now Mistress Aiken had noticed something wasn't right. Her voice sounded less certain. She peered through her glasses, not quite wanting to believe what she was seeing.

"ER, AGILITY!" she said, clapping hard herself, hoping to encourage the rest of the hall to join in but everyone's attention was now on the small, slightly wet and very disheveled looking girl walking down the aisle towards her.

"FELLOWSHIP."

Apart from Mistress Aiken, no one else was applauding. There were lots of excited mutterings as Daisy climbed the steps of the stage and walked slowly towards the podium. Mistress Aiken glared at her like she had seen a ghost. Daisy stopped in front her. There was a long pause. The whispers in the hall fell silent. Daisy looked up at the Deputy Head and all the memories of what had happened filled her head in an instant. Tracy and Layla getting expelled. Getting pushed off the lighthouse. Being pushed in the well. The museum theft. Worst of all was the fact that Mistress Aiken was standing in front of everyone pretending to represent all the great virtues of this brilliant school. The fear Daisy had felt walking up to the stage turned into something else, something strong. She grabbed the microphone from the lectern.

"WHAT'S THE MATTER, GERTIE?" she said, "DID YOU FORGET THE LAST VIRTUE? I'LL HELP YOU OUT. IT'S HONOUR!"

The lights in the hall went black. Brodie hit play on the video projector.

"Daisy...Daisy..."

The voice was the Deputy Head's. Not the voice of the woman stood at the podium next to Daisy but the one on the large screen hung above their heads. Mistress Aiken turned and looked up at the video footage in horror. It showed what Daisy had recorded from the bottom of the well in the underground hall.

"Maybe your friends can watch you die now," growled Mistress Aiken's image on the large screen, "We've been working for decades to take back what is ours from Sally Darlington and this stupid school and we've always dealt with troublemaking oiks like you. You should feel privileged that you and your friends, when we get them, will be the last."

The crowd let out an enraged gasp. The video cut to different footage showing The Sisters of the Black Night lowering the museum pieces down into the hall and loading it onto the carts.

"They're stealing the school museum!" cried Miss Gaynor getting to her feet.

The footage cut again, showing the Sisters taking off their robes and revealing who they were. Some of the pupils recognising themselves on the screen got up and ran for the doors only to find Sergeant Kirkland and his officers blocking the way. A couple of members of the school board on the stage jumped up to run but Roni and the other International Schoolgirls grabbed hold of them. The crowd went into an uproar. There seemed to be bodies and noise everywhere. Suddenly the projector got knocked to the floor and the room plunged into darkness.

There was the sound of police whistles and the lights came back on.

"EVERYBODY SETTLE DOWN!" bellowed Sergeant Kirkland.

The room looked a mess. Chairs were scattered and some pupils were still fighting to get away.

"Where's Mistress Aiken?" said Roni.

The Deputy Head had gone. Daisy looked round quickly and spotted the a fire door behind the curtain at the edge of the stage swinging shut. She ran across the stage and through it out into the courtyard.

There was no one around outside. Daisy dashed between the cars looking for the headmistress and then spotted her pulling open the doors on the vacant French bus.

"YOU'RE NOT GETTING AWAY!" shouted Daisy running towards the bus as the Deputy Head shut the doors and fired up the engine.

Then Daisy stopped dead in her tracks.

A sign written in big red pen in Millie's handwriting was stuck to the door of the bus. The message was underlined and had several exclamation marks after it. Mistress Aiken had been in such a hurry she hadn't noticed. It read:

DO NOT ENTER! DEADLY LION ON BOARD!

"Perilous," muttered Daisy.

* * *

Mistress Aiken put the accelerator to the floor and steered the bus out of the courtyard, knocking aside a couple of police cars to make way. The bus sped down the winding drive across the school grounds. She let out a low laugh to herself.

"It's going to take more than a stupid school full of brats to stop me," she said to herself.

The school gates were up ahead and behind them the main road. A strand of hair came loose from Mistress Aiken's bun and tickled her face. She tried to stick it back in place but it kept falling loose. Tutting to herself, Mistress Aiken adjusted the rear view mirror to get a better look at it. Then she saw what Millie had been so careful to warn people about on the sign.

"Oh dear…" she said.

Sankofa, opening his jaws wide and letting out a loud roar, leapt towards her from the back of the bus.

CHAPTER THIRTY - THE CEREMONY

"So you thought a safe place to put a lion was on a school bus!" said Daisy.

"You try finding somewhere to trap a lion!" said Millie, "It's not easy. Everyone was inside. I put a sign up and everything."

"I guess she was in too much of a hurry to notice," said Penny, pouting at herself in a hand mirror.

They were sitting on the balcony of Honour house looking out across the school. Tracy had been invited back and there were two new members of the 88ers - Karen and Sandy - who had been reinstated at the school as well. It felt odd not to have Layla there, but she was off on her own adventures.

After the uproar of the ceremony the 88ers handed the footage over to the police. The board members involved were arrested and the girls who had been Sisters were expelled. Daisy and the others showed the police and teachers how to get to the underground hall where they'd found Eleanore, Olga and Dorothy trying to fish what was left of Mrs Lyle out of the well. They were taken into custody and sent to a juvenile prison where they couldn't cause any more trouble. Dr Penrose, Millie and a couple of other zoo assistants recaptured the sharks as well as Sankofa from the bus and returned them to the school zoo.. Sankofa seemed a lot happier after his little spell of freedom. He also looked very well fed after his dinner of Pirate Deputy Head Mistress. The museum pieces were brought back and put back in place. Things slowly settled back to normal. Well, better than normal. With Mistress Aiken gone, Miss Weaver was quickly promoted as the new Deputy Head. Her first plan was to ensure that they opened up school admissions to every junior school in the country so that any girl could apply, regardless of background or money.

"What happened to Madam Didier?" asked Marsha.

"Last I saw of her, she was flying out to sea," said Daisy with a shrug.

"Do you think she drowned?" asked Millie, concerned.

"Maybe she managed to swim to Amsterdam," said Tracy.

"And what about that weird dude in black, the one who was shooting at you?" said Brodie.

"They never caught him. I guess we'll never know. He was scary, though. He had a cane with a skull on the top with a number thirteen carved into it."

"Thirteen?" asked Brodie, "Layla talked about something called The Thirteen before she left. Do you think he could be involved in that?"

"I don't know," said Daisy, "next time I see her I'll ask."

The bells in the towers began tolling.

"Uh-oh!" said Daisy, "I'm late to meet my family!"

Daisy slid the latest copy of International Schoolgirl across the restaurant table to her father. He picked it up and read the cover.

"The Sisters of The Black Night by Daisy Cooper. So you finally got something published?"

"Yes!" said Daisy beaming proudly, "but you're not really supposed to have a copy, what with being a boy and everything."

Daniel and David groaned.

"So it's all boring girl stuff," said David.

"I suppose so," said Daisy, "if you think pirates, sword fighting, motorcycle chases, lions and sharks are boring."

"Cool!" said Daniel.

He tried to grab the magazine out of Mr Cooper's hand.

"Get off, oik!" said Mr Cooper slapping Daniel's fingers with a spoon.

"We'd better go," said Daisy, "the ceremony's starting."

The hall was full of people. This time things were going to be right.

Daisy sat on the stage with the other International Schoolgirl candidates and smiled at her family in the crowd. One by one, the girls were called up to accept their International Schoolgirl pins from the reporters who were leaving. Daisy didn't really know any of the other girls that well but she supposed she would soon. Some of them might even save her life someday. She looked down at the tattered competition sash she was wearing and stroked it fondly. The teachers had offered to give her a new one but she insisted on keeping it. It had much more value.

"AND THE FINAL GIRL TO BE ACCEPTED TO REPRESENT US AS AN INTERNATIONAL SCHOOLGIRL IS DAISY COOPER!" said Miss Weaver into the microphone.

Everyone in the hall applauded wildly as Daisy walked to the podium.

"Well done, Daisy," said Miss Weaver.

She shook her hand firmly with fingers that were, of course, covered in spots of paint. Roni stepped up and removed the gold and green International Schoolgirl pin from her tie.

"I can't think of anyone more deserving of this, Sweetie," she said, pinning it to Daisy's blazer.

Daisy turned to the hall and smiled. Everyone jumped to their feet, clapping and cheering loudly. Brodie and the other 88ers let out a howl and Daisy howled back. It was the best moment of Daisy's life.

So far.

After the ceremony everyone went outside. Daisy stood with her brothers and the 88ers taking it all in. They were on the green next to the school restaurant where a huge marquee had been erected. Live music was being played by girls from the music department and there were rows and rows of tables filled with food and drink. Daisy spotted Hattie sitting in her wheelchair by the side of the food stalls smiling at her.

"How are you doing, Hattie?" said Daisy, walking over.

"Lovely," said Hattie, "though I'm looking forward to getting back to the cottage. There's a big wrestling match on tonight and I've bet a few pounds on The Brighton Masher. I read your article. Very well written. For a beginner, that is."

She nudged Daisy in the ribs playfully.

"It's so bizarre that they would work for years and year in secret just to get their hands on some treasure," said Daisy.

"Well some people like to carry grudges with them and pass them onto their children. That's how wars go on and on. They wouldn't have had any luck, anyway," said Hattie.

"Luck at what?" asked Daisy.

Hattie laughed.

"They wouldn't have had any luck finding the treasure."

There was a twinkle in Hattie's eye.

"You wrote about Sally Darlington, you should be able to work it out," she said.

"I assume when she escaped from the Serpent's Tooth caves, she set up Darlington school like Mary had asked her to."

"Where do you think she got the money to do that?!" replied Hattie, laughing, "I mean, look at the place!"

Daisy look across the courtyard at the eight tall dorm buildings, one for each of the virtues. She noticed the flags flying at the top of every bell tower like the flags on top of a ship's masts.

"Are you saying she found the treasure? How could she without the map?"

Hattie reached into her blouse and pulled out an old, weathered medallion on a long silver chain.

"This is the Piece of Eight that Mary gave to her when the maps were made."

She placed it in Daisy's hands.

"Turn it over."

Daisy turned over the coin. On the back, barely visible, was a copy of the map. There was a clear path along the coast of Asia to a series of small islands, one of which was labelled with the words 'Devil's Eye'.

"This is Sally's Piece of Eight?" said Daisy.

Hattie nodded and tucked it back into her dress.

"She found the treasure long ago. You're standing in it. It built this school."

"So how did you get…"

Daisy stopped. There was a knowing twinkle in Hattie's eye.

"I'm Hattie Darlington, Great Great Granddaughter of Sally Darlington", whispered the old lady.

"But why don't you run the school?" asked Daisy.

"No, thank you! I've lived a life much more exciting than being the head of a school could have given me. Well, I used to. You've seen the pictures in my cottage. That's me, not my sister. Now I like to stay in the background and keep an eye on things. Promise to be a good pirate and keep that secret to yourself."

Daisy wasn't sure if she could keep it to herself. She was dying to run over and tell the other 88ers right there and then. Fortunately, Anita Walker came over and put her arm over her shoulder.

"Hi Daisy, welcome aboard," she said.

"Thanks!" said Daisy.

"Are you ready?"

"Ready for what?"

Anita smiled at her.

"Ready for your first assignment, of course. Do you know the painter Rembrandt?"

"I think so" said Daisy, "Isn't he Dutch?"

"That's the one. His most famous painting, The Nightwatch has been restored. We want you to go and write a report on the unveiling at the Rijksmuseum."

"Rike's Museum?" said Daisy, "Where's that?"

"Amsterdam."

"AMSTERDAM?"

Anita laughed.

"Well, you are an INTERNATIONAL schoolgirl, are you not? Don't worry, your flights aren't until tomorrow so you can enjoy the rest of the day with your family and friends. Come to the magazine office at eight in the morning and we'll go through the travel details."

"But I don't have a passport!" said Daisy.

"YOU DO NOW!" said Anita, walking away into the crowds.

Daisy looked over at the 88ers who were laughing and joking with her family. Brodie spotted her and gave her a wave. Daisy waved back, stunned. She looked down at the the gold and green pin on her lapel and rubbed it between her fingers.

"Perilous," muttered Daisy.

THE END.

COMING NEXT

Daisy Cooper and the Devil's Masquerade.

The second book in the Daisy Cooper: International Schoolgirl series.

Printed in Great Britain
by Amazon